ALIEN™

INTO CHARYBDIS

ALIEN™

INTO CHARYBDIS

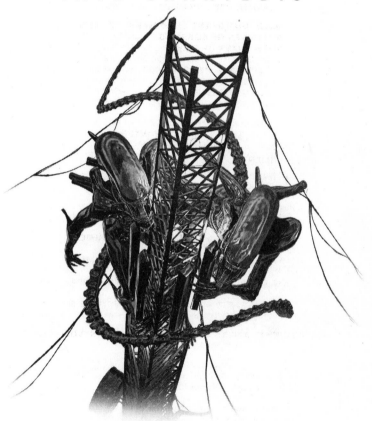

A NOVEL BY

ALEX WHITE

TITAN BOOKS

A L I E N ™ **: I N T O   C H A R Y B D I S**

Hardback edition ISBN: 9781789095531
Signed hardback edition ISBN: 9781789097214
E-book edition ISBN: 9781789095289

Published by Titan Books
A division of Titan Publishing Group Ltd
144 Southwark Street, London SE1 0UP

First edition: February 2021
10 9 8 7 6 5 4 3 2 1

A CIP catalogue record for this title is available from
the British Library.

Printed and bound in the USA.

Did you enjoy this book?
We love to hear from our readers. Please email us at readerfeedback@
titanemail.com or write to us at Reader Feedback at the above address.
www.titanbooks.com

For peace

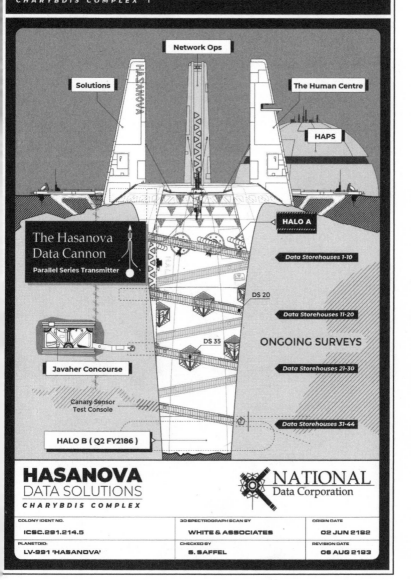

HASANOVA
DATA SOLUTIONS
CHARYBDIS COMPLEX

ICSC ENTACOMM
PRIMARY NODE
HIGH THROUGHPUT DATA CANNON

Network Ops

Solutions

The Human Centre

HAPS

HALO A

The Hasanova
Data Cannon

Parallel Series Transmitter

Data Storehouses 1-10

DS 20

Data Storehouses 11-20

DS 35

ONGOING SURVEYS

Javaher Concourse

Data Storehouses 21-30

Canary Sensor
Test Console

HALO B (Q2 FY2186)

Data Storehouses 31-44

HASANOVA
DATA SOLUTIONS
CHARYBDIS COMPLEX

NATIONAL
Data Corporation

COLONY IDENT NO.	3D SPECTROGRAPH SCAN BY	ORIGIN DATE
ICSC.291.214.5	WHITE & ASSOCIATES	02 JUN 2182
PLANETOID:	CHECKED BY	REVISION DATE
LV-991 'HASANOVA'	S. SAFFEL	06 AUG 2183

PART I

FIRST IN, FIRST OUT

EIGHT MONTHS AGO:

TOP SECRET//AMEREYES//SPECIAL ACCESS REQUIRED -
CANNERY GRIM
TRANSCRIPT STE 1215.131.51.660-1AA
2183.12.02 23:01:04

(TSAE//SAR-CG)

HOPE:	Hasanova is back on the table.
CITTADINO:	Not gonna happen. The AG said no. What's changed?
HOPE:	Freelance contractors just filed for State Department travel clearance, eight months from now.

[TRANSCRIBER'S NOTE: 15s SILENCE]

HOPE:	Are you still there?
CITTADINO:	Keep me updated.

1

STARTUP

"Good morning. I'm Marcus. What's your name?"

Cheyenne Hunt creaks open her eyes and looks at the figure looming over her—hair perfectly coiffed, skin pristine but for a few blemishes. His smile, however, only extends to one half of his face. The right eye droops along with the corner of his mouth, the results of a catastrophic neural net failure.

Her memories finally thaw, and she recognizes the synthetic. He must've experienced another reset while she was under.

"Same as last time," she croaks, fatigue suffusing her bones. "I'm Cheyenne. You're supposed to call me Shy."

He smiles and offers a hand. "You don't seem shy. Allow me to assist."

"Said that last time too, bud." Shy wraps weak fingers around his forearm and he helps her out of the cryopod.

Every muscle in her body seems to yawn, and if someone gave her a warm blanket, she might pass back out.

Yellow, floral-print curtains surround her on either side, held in place by collapsible privacy screens. Her vision clears and she recognizes the embroidered roses and hand-carved wooden frames from the antique mall in San Antonio. Scents of lavender and honeysuckle stain the air.

There are eight cryogenic hibernation chambers in the bay, laid out with the heads toward the center, like a star anise seed pod. Shy has always hated this style of cooler—waking up in her skivvies beside her colleagues could be unpleasant. During their last week on Earth, Shy and Mary decided to remedy the situation with some help from the install techs. It wasn't easy to anchor the cheap screens to the deck of a starship, and it didn't add a *ton* of privacy, but it helped.

"Look at this." Jerry Fowler's voice comes from the other side of the divider. He sounds rough; his body is on the young side of seventy years old. Given the many stints he's spent in cryo, Shy thinks he must be over a hundred. "Dang, what's with the herbal diffusers? Marcus, did you turn those on?"

"Language, Jerry." Mary Fowler's voice comes from another pod, cutting Marcus off before he can respond.

"I just said dang," Jerry mutters. There's a rustling, as if he's trying to extricate himself.

"Let Marcus help you up, honey," Mary says. "You don't want to fall like last time."

"Duty calls," the synthetic says to Shy, dropping a cloth robe at the foot of her pod. A moment later she hears him two units away. "Good morning. I'm Marcus."

"So I've heard," Jerry says. "As always, I'm Jerry. You going to pry me out of this sardine can?"

"It would be my pleasure."

Shy pulls on the robe Marcus left for her. Noah Brewer—the data links guy—will be up soon. The last time Shy came out of cryo, Noah couldn't stop staring at her breasts. He'd never been great about hiding his leering, and took the lack of a bra as license to gawk. When Shy brought the problem to Jerry, he'd assured her Noah was harmless.

When she brought it to Mary, the older woman helped her install the dividers. Shy wanted utility. Mary wanted the Yellow Rose of Texas.

Shy wishes they'd just fire the guy, but apparently that's too much to ask.

"Fuck me..." Noah groans from the nearest pod on the other side.

Not if you were the last man alive.

"Language," Jerry says.

"Who else is up?" Noah asks. After some rustling, he pokes his head around the corner of Shy's privacy screen.

"Me," she says, arming herself with a smile so thin it could cut him. "Just me... and this comfortable robe."

He blinks slowly and scratches his head, coming into full view, wearing boxers and nothing else. Noah strikes her as inordinately proud of his wiry, pale body as he places his hands on his hips and cracks his back with a hip thrust in her direction. Shy is pale, but Noah is practically translucent.

"You got some coffee for me?" Shy asks.

"That's what synthetics are for."

"Then you're between her and the exit, son." The baritone is Arthur Atwater's voice. Their statuesque crewmate strides over as if to show the younger fellow how underwear is supposed to be worn, and it's Shy's turn to control her gaze. She prays she does a better job at it.

"Y'all know there's food getting cold, right?" Arthur wraps his arm around Noah's neck like they just rolled off the football field. "Why are you wasting time in here?"

"Yes," Marcus says from behind Mary's divider. "I've prepared breakfast per Mother's instructions. I'm sorry I can't show you over, myself, but I'm otherwise occupied. I'm Marcus."

"And I'm Arthur," the big man says, then he grins and heads for the exit. When the bay door slides open, the faint scent of bacon tickles Shy's nose.

"Well, I'd love to stand around jackjawing," she says to Noah, "but breakfast calls."

"Wait for me," Noah says.

Shy doesn't.

She makes her way through the bright halls of the USCSS *Gardenia*, a light commercial towing vessel that's at least sixty years old. It shows its age in dings and scuffs along the support struts, ratty upholstery, and busted intercoms. It's not a huge ship, but there's a decent walk to the galley. By the time Shy arrives, Arthur already has a heaping plate of bacon, eggs, and a pair of pork chops.

"You going to put on some more clothes, champ?" Shy asks.

His grin is incorrigible. "Taking this back to my room. I like to start my day with—"

"Arthur o'clock. You've mentioned it."

"Which means coffee, showering, shaving… and some quality time with this here protein." He regards his meal like a beloved child. "Want to shoot a message home, too, and let them know I got here okay."

"Remember what Mary says: 'Family always eats together.'" Shy parrots the phrase in a singsong voice.

"Then I guess I better get the fuck out of here before she can haul her ass across the ship."

"That's right," she says. "Get all of the bad language out of your system before we land. We don't swear in front of the fucking customers."

"Yeah, we never do that shit," he replies, and they share a fist bump in the spirit of minor rebellion. Then he departs, just as Noah comes rushing past to pick up a couple of biscuits, jam, and coffee. He's headed for the door when Shy stops him short.

"Mary said she wants us to eat together. Remember?"

"Fuck that," he says with a snort. Noah hates the way Mary prays before every meal, as well. Shy would never admit that she agrees, and before she can respond, he's gone with his food.

The scent of old cigarette smoke caramel-coats the galley, triggering a familiar anxiety in her. Her hand itches to hold a lighter after a stint in cryo. Searching the galley cabinets, she finds her carton of Balaji Imperials and tears into it. The familiar rectangular box comes sliding out into her hand, and Shy instantly feels better.

How anyone quit smoking in space, she'd never know.

Joanna Hardy, their itinerant mechanical support tech, shambles into the room, blinking hard. Her orange flattop pokes out at odd angles, and there's an angry welt on the freckled skin just above her eyebrow. She must've forgotten to take out her piercings before going into hibernation.

"Pass me one of them bastards when you're done," she growls. "I just puked." Shy lights two sticks and passes her one. She takes a deep puff, and warm smoke roils into her lungs, and the knot in her stomach unwinds.

"Sick after cryo again?"

"Yeah, Marcus was trying to tell me there was something wrong with my cooter."

"Cryostatic vasovagal syncope syndrome," the synthetic corrects her, breezing into the room. "Humans sometimes experience sharp drops in blood pressure when stretching or urinating after hibernation."

"So it's not a vag thing?" Joanna stares at him with half-lidded eyes.

"Jesus Christ." Shy chokes out a puffy cloud.

Marcus shakes his head.

"So how come you can remember shit like that," Joanna asks, pointing with her cigarette, "but not my name?"

"I remember your name," Marcus says. "It's Joanna. You told me that only five minutes ago."

"Yet we've been on the same ship for two years." Joanna shakes her head, blowing out hard. "I don't know why I bother. We have this conversation every time."

"Be nice." Shy pulls Marcus in for a hug. "He's harmless, and he can't help it."

"All right, but when I come into your room and find him all fucked up and eating your face, I'm just going to shut the door and head for the lifeboat." Joanna tries to smooth her hair into place, but the springy buzzcut pops up the second her fingers are gone.

"Okay, folks, we're fully awake!" Mary announces, entering alongside Jerry and wearing her silk nightie and a housecoat. "So y'all need to control your heathen mouths!" The Fowlers are mismatched, yet somehow perfect for each other. Jerry stands about a foot taller than Shy, while Mary is a foot shorter. Jerry has a ruddy, leathery complexion with a veinous nose like a cartoon drunk, whereas Mary's skin is snowy, wrinkled, and delicate. Jerry is so bald his head shines. Mary has a white perm that looks like cottage cheese.

The *Gardenia* was Shy's first job after college, but she's pretty sure most starship captains and flight officers aren't married, nor are they quite so old.

"Listen, ladies," Jerry says, tugging his robe closed, squishing the tuft of curly white hair on his chest. "We're on the ground in two weeks, so I'm going to be crystal clear: our customers don't want to hear your foul language, they don't want to see your gross eyebrow ring, Jo, and you're not going to be able to smoke, Shy. Not off the ship, you understand."

"'Jo?'" Joanna repeats.

"It's something I'm trying out," Jerry says. "Makes you sound cool, like Shy."

"There are doilies on this ship, *Jer*," Joanna replies, flicking ash into the tray. "Nothing on it can be cool."

"I like the doilies," Mary says, heading for the serving line and fetching some bacon and eggs. "Y'all need to eat this pork before we land, too."

"Oh, yeah?" Shy already knows what's coming.

"You know they don't let you have pork down there." Mary slings food onto plates with practiced hospitality, pushing them into Shy's and Joanna's hands. "It's a Muslim colony."

"We've discussed this, hon," Jerry says. "It's not a Muslim colony any more than this is a 'Christian' ship."

"I guess…" Mary begins, mild vinegar mixing into her sweet voice, "I just hate that we have to drum up business in such hard-to-reach—"

Stopping her, Jerry gives her his big Texas smile and throws an arm around his wife.

"It's good money, and they're friendly people. That's a great day at the office, is all I'm saying."

With a toss, Mary's serving spoon clatters onto the plate of scrambled eggs. She turns and stares down her husband, and Shy realizes they've had this conversation before. Maybe it never got resolved.

"I'm sorry, y'all." Mary chuckles, clearly forcing it with unblinking eye contact to Jerry. "It might just be the Cryoprep in my belly, but I think I'd like a hot shower. I might like to be somewhere I can finish my sentences."

She departs, short-striding from the galley.

"That's the problem with a southern girl," Jerry says, hands falling to his hips. "They say one thing, but you know you're in trouble."

Joanna lowers her coffee cup, barely restraining laughter. "I'm sorry, Jerry, I missed what she said over the way her eyes were screaming fuck you."

Shy elbows him, ever the peacemaker. "Besides, every woman on this boat is a southern girl."

"Aw, don't call her a boat."

"Then don't go maligning our charms."

The remaining trio take their food and scoot into a booth. Marcus begins working on the buffet to keep the serving trays fresh. Joanna leans over the table and grabs the salt before shaking out a disturbing amount onto her ham.

"You're not getting laid tonight, Jerry."

"Joanna—" A bit of coffee dribbles from Shy's mouth as she tries to stifle her snort.

"No, she's right," Jerry says. "This Hasanova job doesn't sit well with the missus, and it's straining the old marriage."

"I was joking, *Jer*," Joanna says. "You don't need to tell me about your sex life." She cuts her salted ham and uses it as a shovel for her grits. "I don't know what Mary's problem is. They're just Iranians, dude."

"They're really nice over email," Shy adds. "I've talked with Mr. Hosseini a couple of times."

"I know. I know…" Jerry takes a fork and cuts into his biscuits and gravy. "It's just, she… well, the work is great, and I'm excited to be doing it, and the money is good…"

"But it sucked having to sign a travel waiver with the State Department," Joanna finishes. "Hey, look. I get it. Our countries might not get along so great, but cash is cash. I didn't take a job in the Outer Rim so I could be safe."

"Please don't listen to Joanna," Shy pleads, biting into the first glorious forkful of hash-brown casserole. Marcus must have studied up on southern cooking while they were under. "I'm all about the safety, but for what it's worth, I think the whole thing is overblown. They're just people."

"Well, that's what I said," Jerry replies, "but you know the wifey. She can't help seeing this as, well, enemy territory. She's all worried about getting kidnapped or something."

"Her dearly departed first husband bankrolled the ship, boss," Joanna says with a wink. "I'd kidnap her myself if it got me y'all's fortune."

"Stop, Joanna." Shy kicks her under the table. "This is just a job, like any other."

"Not so." Jerry laughs, and when he does he shakes all over. "It's way better than most contracts. It's just lights, cameras, and HVAC—that's it."

"Yeah, I don't know what jumped up Mary's butt, but the gig pays good," Joanna says, rubbing her fingers together. "When do we land?"

"Two weeks, six hours, and forty-two minutes," Marcus says, pulling up a chair and sitting down at the end of the booth. "We should land at approximately pointer null."

"Ah, pointer null," Joanna says. "My favorite time of day."

"Don't tease him," Shy says, and she means it. Ever since she joined up with McAllen Integrations, Marcus has made her feel at home.

"That's right," Jerry says. "Our synthetic is family."

"Thank you," Marcus replies with his lopsided smile. "I prefer the term artificial person, myself."

"They all say that," Joanna replies, shoveling the last of her food into her mouth, and scooting out of the booth. "You need to get that thing repaired, Jerry. Gives me the willies."

"I assure you, it's not—" Marcus begins.

"As a being of pure logic, *Marcus*," Joanna cuts him off, "you can appreciate that Jerry is breaking ICC regs just by having you on board."

"Yes." Marcus's politeness breaks Shy's heart. "I have informed him that I am two years, one month, and fifteen days out of inspection, and inappropriate to be on the *Gardenia*."

"Yeah," Joanna says, talking over the synthetic as if he isn't there. "We should be way more worried about our 'artificial person' than the Arabs." She dumps her plate onto the counter for Marcus to clean later.

"They're not Arabs, Joanna," Jerry says. "They speak Farsi. Do *not* mess that up when we get there."

"Don't worry about it," she replies. "After all, who's going to fuck with the air conditioning repair crew?"

"Thank you for your assessment, *Joanna*," Jerry says, making it clear that he'd like to change the subject.

"Okay, okay," she says, again trying to smooth her flattop back into place. "See you at seven bells." With that, she heads for the door.

"I want those VAVs indexed!" Jerry calls after her. "Get Arthur on the load balancing, too!"

"In that case, let's go, Marcus," she calls from down the corridor. "You've got some heavy boxes to lift." The synthetic follows after her with a quick-footed step.

Jerry busies himself poking through his plate for all the best remaining morsels, and Shy figures he's trying to process all the different ways his morning has gone wrong. No one else appears for breakfast, and that doesn't help his mood.

"So why *haven't* we gotten Marcus checked out?" Shy asks. "I mean, he tends us during hibernation."

"Don't let it worry you," he says. "Mother manages the cryo pods. You're perfectly safe."

"That's not what worries me. He seems… sad."

There's pain in Jerry's smile.

"It's not in this year's budget, Shy," he says, then he stands to leave. "See you at muster."

2

BIRDS OF PARADISE

"Charybdis" is a bottomless hole surrounded by a small, rocky island. Brackish water stretches in all directions, as far as the eye can see. The sky above is perpetually cloudy and grim.

Though the hole's exact provenance is unknown, the Weyland Corp scientists who first explored the planet identified Charybdis as a stable lava tube. Water washes over the edges of the atoll and into the starship-sized aperture, plummeting through four hundred meters of roaring pipes and thrumming industrial gear, before disappearing into the swirling maelstrom below.

From his vantage point far below the edge of the tube, Kamran Afghanzadeh squints upward, feeling a familiar awe. Glittering droplets encrust his safety glasses like crystals, and he pulls them off to get a better look at the marvel of human engineering that surrounds him.

Turbines and heat exchangers guzzle limitless liters, blasting them out in a rainforest mist.

When sunlight manages to break through the perpetual cloud cover, rainbows dance in all directions.

Inspired by the poetry of Hafez, their bosses at the Hasanova Colony Corporation have ordered all staff to call this facility *Tagh-e-Behesht*, "The Vault of Heaven," but everyone here knows better. It's a thirsty hole sucking up everything that falls into it.

It's the Maw.

Kamran backs away from the safety rail and under the protection of the rock. This pathway, casually known as the Spiral, is a laser-cut ramp rifled into the sides of Charybdis. The top forty-four stories of the Maw contain glass-windowed data storehouses, each airlocked and climate-controlled.

Below the storehouses, though, the Spiral is unfinished, open to the elements. The company put up barricades, but they only come up to his thighs, and he easily could tumble over them. A thrill ripples through him every time Kamran steps to the edge to look out.

"Salam, Kamran!" Reza Hosseini shouts, waving at him from further ahead. "Come on, and try not to hit your head." The ceiling of the carved path is at least three times Kamran's height, but he's no stranger to the joke. When he first arrived Kamran bonked his head on the man's office doorway every day for a week, and Reza coined the nickname "Tall Kamran."

He jogs down into the mist, puddles on the pathway splashing and scattering reflections of the caged work lights hanging overhead. Luminescent safety lining on Kamran's rain gear casts the rock around him in a sickly green—annoying, yet a necessity when one might be swept into the navel of the world. The slick path is only a twenty-degree grade, but it seems to slope away forever. He thanks God for the nanocleat soles of his Reeboks.

"You didn't have to come with me to check the pilings, you know," Reza says as Kamran catches up. "I told you I'd do it myself."

Kamran smiles at his mentor. "You gave me design leadership of Halo B, boss. That's standards and QC, too."

"Nevertheless, I offered," Reza says. He's handsome, classically so when he worries, like a black-and-white-film star of old. "You're never going to be a decent branch manager if you don't delegate."

"And I'm never going to be decent *at all* if I sign my name to an inspection report I didn't conduct personally," Kamran replies, getting a little annoyed. He knows his old boss is only trying to help, but the constant handholding is driving him crazy. He's been the project manager of Halo B for over a month, and Reza keeps doing things for him. "I know it's only a little thing, but I'd be signing my name to a lie."

Reza regards him for a brief moment, and Kamran fears he may have given offense. Instead, his mentor softens and nods.

"That's what I like about you."

He pats Kamran on the shoulder and continues the trek.

"I haven't been down here in over a year." Kamran glances back up the Spiral toward the data storehouses, the Solutions spire, and the colony proper. "I have to admit, I'm intimidated. Haroun said he was coming to look, too."

"That'll be the day. It's out of his chair, so it's out of range."

"No respect for my new boss?"

"That useless ass needs to earn it." Reza leans in close enough that Kamran can smell his sweet, sea-spray deodorant. "He pushes too hard and doesn't know what he's doing."

"I bet his wife says the same thing." Kamran cuffs his friend on the shoulder. They laugh, and it feels good.

Haroun, the VP of Operations, has had Kamran working eighty-hour weeks for two months straight. He's belligerent and disgusting, and it's clear he doesn't appreciate Reza's pick for Safety Design branch manager. But those worries are muted by the majesty of their surroundings, the thunder of water and the gentle kiss of rainbows every time he looks up. It's nice to take this excursion out to his project—the anchor infrastructure for Halo Unit B—to check the pilings for the anchors. They'll provide moorings for some of the largest fans ever manufactured—another superlative for Charybdis.

Unit B is a partner to Halo A, the venting system already installed in the upper levels at carefully calibrated angles. There's a dense hydrogen sulfide buildup down around the raging maelstrom, where the constant flow of water traps some of the gas and drags it into the planet. Should the air inside the Maw dip below a breathable concentration, Halo A will kick on automatically, blasting atmosphere from the surface down through the Maw, simultaneously displacing toxins into the sky.

While Halo A is critical to their ability to operate inside the Maw, Halo B is more of a precaution. The data storehouses won't be built this far down for a long time.

Reza continues with the sure pace of a construction veteran. That's something Kamran admires about his former boss—he's at home behind a desk or digging a trench. Beneath Reza's transparent rain gear, his jeans are faded, Hasanova-branded polo showing blotches from where it's been aggressively washed a thousand times, and the seams of his steel-toe sneakers are frayed. Like Kamran, he wears a bright yellow construction helmet. He's a magnetic fixture of so many projects.

Kamran wonders if he'll ever be the equal of his mentor.

They stay close to the safety rail, and details emerge from the mist. They're only a quarter of the way into the unfinished part of the Spiral, and already Kamran spots the unrelenting churn below. It might as well be a black hole. They've flushed sensor after sensor down there, and the devices always lose signal.

"I... also had to cancel the exploratory project," Reza says.

"What? Why? I've already hired a geologist!"

"There's nothing to be done about it, dadash," Reza responds. "It was decided at the top, and it's out of my hands."

"We don't want to know *where the water goes*?" Kamran gestures to the vortex and wrinkles his nose. "The company has a substantial capital investment built on top of this shaft, and—"

"—and there's not enough money to spare for a study they consider entirely optional," Reza says. "The United Americas just embargoed us. Hasanova stock took a hit." Reza watches Kamran's reaction and adds, "Don't look so shocked. You knew this would happen when our country joined the Independent Core System Colonies."

"Yes, but I didn't think it would be so quickly!"

"This place has been classified as a threat."

"It's a data center."

"Sponsored by Iran," Reza counters. "That means the Americans hate it. Think, Kamran, if you can get enough oxygen to your brain up there."

"I'm the Safety Design branch manager," Kamran persists. "If we don't know where the water goes—"

"As was I, before you, I'll add." Reza holds up a hand to cut him off. "No significant seismic events have been recorded here in fifty years. Before us, the Weyland Corp claimants didn't find anything. The UPP didn't have problems when they took over and put in the hydro plants. Why should we care where the water goes?"

"You're not worried this will one day close up and flood?" Kamran glances nervously down into the volcanic tube. As he does, Reza shakes his head.

"The surrounding islands are covered in geysers," he says. "There are at least five hundred known black smokers. Personally, I favor the 'reverse artesian well' theory."

"You always have," Kamran replies, "but I think we need proof."

"We did the models," Reza insists. "I know you wanted those answers, but Unit B is more important."

Kamran starts to reply but thinks better of it. He checks his watch.

"We should've brought a Polaris," he says. "We're not going to be back in time for my team's standup."

"You can miss a day."

This deep, the rock has gone from slick gray to jet black, a reaction to the extremophilic bacteria living inside the water. Little natural light makes it down this far, so the HCC compensates with hundreds of floodlights lining the spiral path. The shape of the Maw grows bumpier at this level; tumescent lumps of dark igneous rock protrude from the walls, ranging from the size of a human head to that of a mining hauler.

"There's the gate." Reza points down the slope, where the curve of water takes the path out of sight. A few more steps brings a flashing safety cordon into view, the lowest point in the Spiral thus far, and Kamran sighs with relief. He isn't looking forward to the return climb.

"I'm going to have to borrow one of your team's bikes to get back," Kamran says. "No way am I walking that uphill."

"I offered to inspect the pilings for you, but you declined," Reza says. "Relax, you can take the end of shift bus back."

"That's not for five hours, my friend."

Reza shrugs. "Work on that SiteSys camera you love so much, then."

"They installed it?"

"They have done *everything* you asked."

"What was with that tone?"

"Honestly, Kamran, insist on coming, and then you whine about walking. It's not impressing me right now."

Kamran grimaces.

"Sorry, boss."

They reach the work crews at the bottom of the shaft, who are busy cutting the Spiral deeper into the tube. Four people work the stations of a rover-sized laser lathe while the others run power cables and conduit for the temporary sections.

Kamran follows in Reza's wake as he checks in with everyone he encounters, helps haul supplies, and joins in the tangle of activities. He's easy with the workers, far more familiar than a bookworm like Kamran. Reza inspires him with the ability to remember an ailing child, a sister's wedding, a cousin's pregnancy, and a dozen other trivial details. That's what makes him a leader.

"What brings you two down here?" Fatemeh, the shift leader asks. She's covered in grime, and she folds her leather-gloved hands under her arms.

"Kamran needs to check the pilings," Reza replies. "Make sure our department installed everything right."

"It's just a formality," Kamran adds. "Takes thirty minutes."

"That's not on the schedule, Reza," Fatemeh says. "We can't shut down the lathes right now or we'll crack the floor."

"'Not on the schedule?'" It's hard for Kamran to hide his annoyance, but he tries.

Reza pulls a hand over his silver-stubbled face. "I—I'm sorry. I really didn't think you'd actually come today."

"Look." Fatemeh halts Kamran before he can reply. "Lunch is in an hour, and we shut down the lathes for that. Just wait, and you can check the pilings then."

The crew takes lunch on a clockwork schedule, cramming into a small antechamber that limits the noise of the Maelstrom. Battered lunchboxes come out, and Reza pulls Kamran aside.

"I'm sorry I didn't put your inspection on the schedule," he says. "Do you want help?"

"No, I've got it. Won't take long." Kamran runs his fingers through his curls before reseating his construction helmet.

"Shout if you run into trouble down there."

"Sure. Fine."

Pulling his hood up to keep the water off his neck, he trudges out of the staging alcove and into the drilled-out cave. The rock has been laser cut and cleaned, leaving exposed red iron deposits along flat surfaces. One hundred and forty-four pilings jut from the wall, twelve to a side, threaded heads glinting silver against red. Those will hold a titanium plate responsible for twenty tons of fan.

Unclipping his laser compass from his tool belt, he stamps it onto the wall. After a moment of scanning the bolt heads, it spits out the results—one degree off from the angles in Kamran's blueprints.

"Oh, no…"

If that's truly the case, the blast fan mountings won't sit flush with the rock face and, over time, Halo B might be tugged into the Maelstrom—potentially clogging the chasm and threatening the colony's entire infrastructure.

"They're making me bald," Kamran whispers, backing away from the wall. "Reza!" When there's no response, he heads back to the lunch alcove. Along the way, Kamran catches a fart-whiff of sulfur, as is common at this level, and restrains a curse.

Of course, he muses. His day is ruined. His *month* is ruined. *And now the planet's asshole is farting into my face.*

"Reza," Kamran says, short on breath when he arrives. Six other men stand or sit around the room. "They're wrong."

The room goes quiet.

"What?"

"The pilings. They're at the wrong angle."

That prompts a chorus from the six others who are present. Kamran throws up his arms.

"Listen!" he calls over them. "Listen! I just measured it, okay?"

"Maybe your tool got water in it," one offers.

"Maybe the gravitational field of your giant head messed up the calibration," another says, and everyone laughs. Kamran has never seen a mutiny quite like this. In the past, his word was Reza's word. Now it's Haroun's power behind him, and that carries less authority.

"Come on, now, that's not—"

"It took two weeks to drive those pilings," Bijan says, plopping his fork into the *khoreshteh gheimeh*. "But if your drawings were wrong, we can just drive them again somewhere close by. There's more than one place to hang a picture."

"No, you can't, because that'll weaken the overall rock face, and we have to recalibrate the angles. Those blast fan moorings are aimed at specific parts of the Maw."

"*Vault of Heaven*," Fatemeh the shift leader says with a laugh, and the rest of the crew follows suit. "And for what it's worth, I'm the one that mounted the driver, so I'm the one that double-checked *your team's* blueprints."

"Kamran—" Reza tries to calm him, but he's not about to shrug it off.

"*Fatemeh khanoom…*" A thousand biting insults fill Kamran's mind, all in his father's voice, and he stifles them. He's not like that. "After lunch we'll have to conduct a pulse time-domain survey, before any work can continue."

The collective exasperation hisses through the small space as surely as the waterfall outside.

"I authorized the work orders," Reza says, his tone steady. "We can check them when I get into the ops center tomorrow. Finishing out the shift won't—"

"I don't answer to you, though," Kamran says. He refuses to be charmed out of his anger. "What message shall I convey to Haroun about this?" Reza looks long into his eyes, as though searching, then gives a contrite smile.

"Okay, okay. You can tell him that you came down here and did a pulse time-domain survey to make sure everything was right. This is a misunderstanding. Now sit down with us. Bijan said you could have some of his *khoresht*, right?"

Kamran relents, and Bijan reluctantly hands him some of the *khoreshteh gheimeh*. Kamran spends the rest of lunch ashamed of his outburst. After they pack away their refuse, he issues the work lockout and sends the crew home for the day, exchanging them for several of his on-call personnel.

His teammates are annoyed at having to venture so far down, but the issues with the pilings demand a serious response. It's going to be a long afternoon.

* * *

Kamran and his second in command, a fellow from Tabriz named Babāk, set up the pulse lens further up the path. Because of the Spiral, it's easy to mount the tripod diametrically opposite the pilings, allowing for the best magnification. The rest of his crew set about the arduous task of spraying the wall beside the bolt heads with a thick coat of damper. With the nanoscale absorption, Kamran figures those pilings will ring like bells to his scanners.

"*We're blacked out over here*," Reza's voice comes through Kamran's earpiece, magnified by his construction helmet. "*Here's hoping it's all just a misunderstanding.*"

"Okay, good." He might be embarrassed, but he's still angry. Reza just has to deal with that, because Kamran knows he's right. "Arming the PL scanner in ten seconds. Comms off. I don't want any EM noise." He pulls out his radio and twists the volume to off. Babāk follows suit.

"Okay, firing," Kamran says, pressing a button on his remote.

The little screen on his portable terminal begins to fill with points of light as the PTD scanner paints the far wall through the waterfall. Kamran zeroes in on the pilings and tensions down the tripod.

"Well?" fat Babāk asks.

"We wait thirty minutes, and hope that I'm the one who needs to apologize for wasting everyone's time."

Spirits damp as his trouser legs, Kamran thrusts his hands into his pockets and walks to the safety railing to watch the Maelstrom. There's something hypnotic about its whitewater vortex, and he's put in mind of Nietzsche's cliché about staring into the abyss. The tumult seems worse today, and the mist stinks like boiled eggs. Babãk joins him and, together, they share a bag of pistachios while they wait for the scan to finish.

There's a digital honk from below, and one of the floodlights halfway to the Halo B anchor point goes red. So far away and a few stories down, it's hard to make out the details through all of the rain.

"The HS sensors!" Babãk drops his pistachios, which tumble into the rapids. Each floodlight contains a canary sensor, and they're accustomed to catching occasional false warnings up in the ops center. If they responded to every single alarm, they'd never get anything done. No one even checks the alarm console log anymore—it has thousands of brief entries a week.

"It's fine," Kamran says, chuckling at his subordinate's nerves. Babãk probably hasn't been down this far before. "Notice how bad the smell is today? We don't need to worry until—"

A huge bubble spurts up through the Maelstrom, exploding like a pimple and spraying gouts of water up from its depths. A spiral of crimson light winds up the shaft of the Maw as every canary sensor lets loose with an apocalyptic screech.

"Shit! Kamran!"

"I see it!" The smell of hydrogen sulfide hits him like a hot poker up his nostrils. Tears blot out his vision, and he staggers, breath coming in short gasps before he can hold it.

High above, Halo A blares an alarm and high-output capacitors dump charges into mighty engines. Fans thunder, and a light breeze tickles Kamran's neck as the waterfall shuts off. All waves that had been washing inside the Maw instead will be blasted out into the surrounding lake. Loudspeakers burst forth with a warning.

"Attention: Toxic Environment Detected, Halo A ignition response. All personnel return to colony structures and shelter in place. Repeat…"

"We have to get higher!" Babāk gasps. "Grab your oxygen tank!" He stumbles for the Polaris.

The treaded bike can seat two, and convey them to the safety of the data storehouses. Babāk gets to the bike and rummages through the saddle compartment, grabbing an oxygen tank and hurling another to Kamran. The bird's nest of plastic tubing and mask come undone mid-flight, and with blurry vision, Kamran can't figure out which part of it he's supposed to catch. The cylinder strikes him in the cheek before clattering to the ground and rolling under the roadway safety barrier.

"No!"

Kamran dives for his lifeline—the tangle of plastic tubing unfurling from the bottle. He snatches the assembly by the mask and tugs the tank back up from oblivion, clutching it to his chest and fumbling for the knob. Sweet, cool air flows into his lungs, and he mashes the nozzles to his face. It's not airtight, however—the nose cup is designed to add oxygen, not filter it.

Must call Reza.

Kamran switches on his comm and coughs out a few sputtering hails. No answer. The people down there would be dazed, unable to see, perhaps too poisoned to think. They might not have switched on their radios. Kamran tries to remember the safety briefing he took two years ago—high concentration, five minutes to live.

Sting the eyes.

Hurt the brain.

Dizziness pushes its fingers into his skull.

Floodlights near the surface begin turning from red, to yellow, to blue as Halo A does its job sucking away the gas. The line becomes a fuzzier orange below the Maw, where they stand. The hydrogen sulfide concentration is no longer enough to burn his lungs, but it'll still be a lethal dose if he doesn't get out of there.

Canned oxygen awakens the parts of his mind that know how to survive. He pulls himself up on the guard rail, clutching the mask and trying to ignore his searing lungs. He has a brief vision of coughing up chunks of bloody tissue in the infirmary, and tamps it down. He can't think about dying, or it'll come to pass.

A few more gasps at the O_2 tank and his mind clears further. Reza and the others might still be alive, and there are Polarises near them. Kamran has an oxygen tank and a decent enough lung capacity. It's downhill. If he were to go to them, he could squint through the pain…

"Kamran!" Babāk has already spun the Polaris to face up the ramp.

"Go!" Kamran says, gesturing to his oxygen tank. "Get help! I'll be fine!" He doesn't wait for the other man to respond. Babāk didn't volunteer, and it might be suicide, anyway. Better to go alone.

Screwing his eyes shut, Kamran jogs down the path into deepening red light. He runs his fingers along the cut stone wall to guide himself. When he arrives, he'll have to force himself to open them again, and fight through the agony to search for Reza. This might cost him his sight, but he would gladly trade that for a friend's life.

He slits his eyes open and spots the flashing safety cordon.

"Reza!" he cries, fetid air pouring in around his mask.

Halo A has reached deafening speeds above, drowning out his voice, yet providing no assistance.

"Reza!" He begs his eyelids to stay open, and it's like staring into the sun. A man emerges from the work site with another person, Mitra perhaps, slung over his shoulder in a firefighter's carry. The figure staggers toward a nearby Polaris and shoves her limp body across the carriage.

It's Reza, and he's attempting his rescue without even an oxygen bottle. Kamran calls to him—if he'll wait, Kamran can drive while he holds onto Mitra's body.

Reza swings his leg over the Polaris and revs it.

His head lolls, and he slumps forward, unconscious.

The Polaris, Reza, and Mitra go zipping toward the edge.

"No!"

The bike strikes the cement safety barricade, catapulting its passengers over the handlebars into the abyss. The cruelest part is that there is no extra air to scream.

"Attention. Halo A at maximum capacity. All personnel return to colony structures and shelter in place."

Kamran staggers to the edge and clutches the guard rail, searching for his friend, praying that Reza got caught on a rock. Through tears of grief and agony, he sees nothing but jagged lumps of sooty stone around the mouth of the Maelstrom. Reza's rain gear safety lining would've shone bright yellow even to Kamran's half-blinded eyes. He's dead, gone forever, never to be recovered.

Kamran looks up. The blue line of safety fizzles out three quarters of the way to him—they can't vent the heavy gasses this far down. They could've, if Halo B was online, and Kamran curses. He turns to run, but just the sight of the ramp ahead makes him want to lie down and die.

Your parents didn't drag you across the Hindu Kush to fall here.

He searches out the abandoned Polaris now wedged in between two of the heavy pylons. It's deep in the gas, but so is he, so he might as well go for it. Holding his breath, he shuts his eyes and charges forward, hoping he can make it to the bike. It's also a run directly toward the Maelstrom, and he meters every step as best he can.

He tangles into the handlebars, catching one straight in the kidney. The bike is still idling from Reza's intended escape. Guilt grips Kamran as he mounts it and flips it into reverse. His head swims, and the oxygen isn't enough, so he backs into the stone wall. It knocks the daylights out of him, but he shakes the hit off. He has to climb out of here.

Twisting the handlebars, Kamran takes off up the ramp, wobbling like a child learning to ride. His legs are gelatin. His mind feels mushy. He can't crash—if he does, he dies. He won't have enough energy to recover a second time.

Red becomes orange, becomes yellow as he ascends. Simple shapes begin to take on discernible features. Within a couple of minutes, he's outside the hatch to Data Storehouse Forty-Four.

In a cruel twist, his body refuses to dismount the bike. He slumps off the saddle and falls onto his back, gasping for dear life.

I almost made it.

Strong hands seize him about the shoulders, fingers digging into his muscles as they haul him inside. When it becomes apparent that he won't be allowed to die today, every second of his suppressed pain overtakes him. Voices ask him what happened, but all he can do is weep for his friends.

3

PLANS

Shy sits at her bridge workstation, lit by the green light of her monitor, trying to smooth the tension headache from her brow. Blueprint after blueprint flickers past.

In order to commission a colony, someone has to hook up all the lights, sensors, cameras, HVAC, and locks to a central server. It's an arduous process, from the individual light bulb all the way up to the central chilling plants for each complex. Someone has to connect each device, translate its data into a language the central ops server speaks, and create the external control schema to run them. Hasanova Data Solutions has over a hundred thousand edge devices, using four hundred different manufacturer comm protocols. Many of them are already hooked up. It's like trying to untangle a ball of yarn.

Shy is a front-end developer, which means she makes the interfaces.

"Y'all really like that word," she mutters, tapping her lip. "'Hasanova.' HASS—a-nova. Sounds like Casanova. Ah. There it is again." This customer wants their logo on every screen, and Shy's getting tired of looking at it.

The corridors of the *Gardenia* are quiet, running lights dimmed for a sleep cycle. Shy often takes the night watch on the planetary approach slowdown. It's a good time to pore over her notes and ensure there aren't any gaps. Though Noah is insufferable, they have it down to a science: he plans the connection and writes the acceptance criteria, she designs the UIs, then together they wire everything up onsite as quickly as possible.

Opening the latest set of acceptance criteria, she finds the interface drawings already completed.

"What the hell?"

She leans in close to regard the name on the diagram. "N. Brewer." Flipping to the next screen, there he is again, and again. He's already come in behind her and done her job—poorly.

"Oh, come on." His work is functional, but it's brute force, more engineering than art, and it'll be a menace to the inhabitants. His arrogance is going to cost her—she'll have to spend forever redoing these.

Shy goes to take the file out of storage for modification, and gets an error. *The fuck?* The design has already been approved for production and committed to the commissioning repository. Jerry's name hovers in the info box as the approving authority.

"Marcus?" Shy calls into the darkness. The nice thing about a starship at night is that she could practically shout for him, and she wouldn't wake the others in their soundproof bunks. As it is, his approach is so silent she almost leaps out of her skin.

"Yes?"

"Why are my drawings already done? Have these been compiled?"

"I believe so," Marcus replies. "Noah submitted a drawing package shortly before going under."

"That's not his job. How did it happen?"

"Let me pull up the records." The synthetic might as well be the galaxy's most expensive stenographer, given how Jerry uses him. Marcus sits down at another workstation, his fingers like a drum solo on the mechanical keys. "Ah. Here we are. Meeting from August fourteenth of this year. Jerry approved the drawings, on the condition that Noah got your approval."

"I didn't give it!" Her voice echoes in the silence, and she tamps it down. "I'm not vouching for work I didn't do."

"According to this record, Noah told Jerry he already had your approval. Quote, Jerry: 'What does Shy think?' Quote Noah: 'She's looked them over. No changes.'" Marcus sends the link to her workstation, and she checks the log. Shy leans back in her chair, doing her level best not to be any angrier than she is. If she comes after Noah in front of Jerry, he'll frame her as a temperamental bitch.

"Okay, like what am I supposed to do, though? If he's already done my job… terribly…"

"I'm certain this is a misunderstanding."

"I'm certain it's not." She folds her arms and swings a boot up onto the console. "He thinks he's better than me at, like, everything, because he knows WhiteCap. Like *whoopty-shit*, who cares that you can code?"

"I'm sorry you're agitated." The synthetic looks into her with green eyes, and she wonders what he sees.

The flames of annoyance are best chased by cigarette smoke, but she's trying to cut down. Shy chews her pen instead. "No sense worrying about it now. I'll talk to Jerry in the morning. Have we made contact with the beacon?"

"We established Hasanova Data Solutions approach protocol at eight bells."

"What about planetary control?"

"Ah. Let me clarify. 'Hasanova Data Solutions' is the name of the planet. Iran's National Data Corporation petitioned the IAU that the designation be changed from LV-991 after they acquired the world in a blind-bid UPP auction."

Shy backs out of the drawings and requests a map of their destination. Sure enough, the beacon says "Hasanova Data Solutions." The corporate pricks finally figured out how to jam advertising into the registry of worlds. Not even the International Astronomical Union is safe.

Marcus perks up, hearing something Shy can't—a radio transmission—and his eyes roll back in his head.

Apparently, the wireless link is mostly a Marcus thing. When she first signed up with McAllen Integrations, that phenomenon freaked her out, like he was hearing voices. This Marcus unit wasn't quite right to begin with, and she'd heard some dark tales about synthetics losing their shit in the frontier.

"Mother requests my presence on the lower decks," he says. "Routine maintenance of the landing gear."

"Sure. Of course."

As he leaves Shy alone at her monitor, she dons her headphones and pops a few tunnel pills. The focus is great, and she uses it to slice up every one of Noah's shitty designs, continuing nonstop over the course of five hours. By the time the meds wear off, she's at least twenty percent of the way through the damage he's done. With a combination of exhaustion and time, she's calm, and decides it's probably best if she slogs back to her bunk and passes out. They'll want her help prepping to land at oh-five-hundred, maybe sooner. That's only a few hours at best.

Shutting down her monitor, she takes one last long stretch and rises to her feet. On the way to her bunk she passes the galley and spots Noah. She tells herself not to engage, for fear of anger chasing away her exhaustion. He's making the coffee for his shift, and swearing because there's no powdered creamer left on the vessel.

"Hey, fuckwad," she says, despite herself. A ripple of annoyance wakes up the rest of her body, chased by her outburst. "You need to quit doing my job."

He turns to face her, placidly stirring his drink, and takes a long sip before answering.

"Just trying to speed up the process."

"You didn't—you *fucked* it up. I've been spending all night redoing your work." She wants to slap the coffee out of his hands, but restrains herself. "You need to admit when you're out of your depth."

"Shy, I know I'm not a professional *artist* like you," he says with a tang of sarcasm, "but you don't have an art degree, either. Or a degree of any kind, as I recall."

"Oh, fuck you, Noah."

"You need to accept that your designs are just your opinion, and that other people have opinions, too," he persists. "My stuff looks fine. Better than yours, in a lot of cases."

Oh, no, you did not go there, she thinks. "Yeah, because you left a bunch of user interfaces that make no sense. There are rules to UI design, none of which you appear to understand."

"That's what makes me better. I don't play by the rules that tie you down." He pushes past her, headed for the bridge. "Now excuse me. Jerry is going to be up any second—he and I have to review the backend before we land."

She considers closing the door in front of him to block his path. There are switches on every side of the galley, and she could make him stay and hash it out. Instead, he waves at her with his free hand as he leaves.

Her heart burns off her sleepiness like a sunrise. What if she just let Noah get away with it? She only has one job, and he's trying to do it for her.

"Man, fuck you, dude." She still has a couple of Balaji Imperials in her pack, and one of those will do nicely right now. She'd rather not smoke in the galley, though, since Mary hates it. A couple of ladders and passageways bring Shy to the *Gardenia*'s cargo bay. Joanna and Arthur are there, scanning each crate's barcodes and calling out last-minute inventory. Out in the frontier, there isn't much they can do if anything is missing from the manifest, but it's always better to know before the customer does.

Both of them are eager to take a smoke break, and sit beside Shy on a crate.

"Can I bum one?" Joanna asks.

"It'd be downright weird if you actually had your own," Shy replies, passing out her precious smokes. She can only hope the Hasanova canteens sell cartons of cigarettes, or this'll be a difficult trip.

Arthur turns her down, but enjoys being around people who aren't working. The three of them make small talk, and Shy relates her troubles. She expects Joanna to be her typical shade of indignant.

"I wouldn't go making waves right now."

"I'm not 'making waves.'" Shy recoils. "I'm just trying to do my job."

Joanna shakes her head. "You need to be more strategic, sweetheart."

"Arthur, back me up!"

"She's right, Shy." Their air systems engineer massages the light brown skin of his palms with a calloused thumb. "I wouldn't go playing with Noah. He's a lot harder to replace, so if Jerry feels like he has to choose—"

"He won't," Shy insists, "but if he did, he'd pick me. I've been here for almost five years. We took on Noah like a year ago at most, if you don't count cryo."

Joanna shrugs. "Uh, sure, but like, money is tight. Maybe don't go yelling at people."

Shy opens her mouth to talk, but shuts it to think instead. That fit with what Jerry had said.

"What do you mean?" she asks.

"This ought to be a top-flight run," Joanna says, "given what the Iranians are paying. But look"—she gestures around them—"all Rimco parts and controllers. This whole bay is full of cheap shit. Why would Jerry do that?"

"Rimco is fine," Shy says, and Arthur laughs at her.

"No, he's trying to get a big margin here," Arthur says. "The man is cutting corners."

Shy looks over the dozens of crates all stamped with the Rimco logo in English and Vietnamese. She has to admit that they don't have the best reputation.

"Jerry wouldn't do that."

"Honey," Joanna says, taking a drag and blowing it out, "you never know what a businessman will do until he's actually in trouble. No matter what Mary says, we *ain't* a family. When profits are stressed, the knives come out."

"Just keep your head down, okay?" Arthur stands and brushes off his legs. "For your own good."

Shy draws in one last lungful, then stamps the butt out with a twist of her toes like she's crushing a spider. "Fine," she sighs, "I'm going to catch some shut-eye before approach."

"Okay, but you're back down here at seven bells to help me configure the thruster tests," Arthur says. "We load program down the main engine at fifteen hundred for approach, and I want them to be long done by then."

"I know."

"I'm not sure you do," Arthur says. "That's not enough time to sleep, iron out Noah's fuckups, and help with docking."

"Then I got you for landing gear checks," Joanna says. "The last shift before landing sucks, but all hands means all hands."

"Does, like… everyone know how to do my job better than me, today?" Shy asks. Arthur's big, brown eyes show hurt, withering her anger into guilt. She can't be mad at him. He's only looking out for her.

"Shy…" Now he's smoldering at her on purpose, the jerk.

"Okay," she grumbles. "I'll see you in an hour."

She wanders off to collapse in her bunk, and is asleep the instant her head touches down. It's like she blinks, and Marcus is gently shaking her awake. If he's here, that means it's time to get up, but she can't recall sleeping at all.

"Please allow me to introduce myself. I'm Marcus."

"Goddamn it," she says, sliding past him to her house shoes. She pads down the corridors to the engine room, where Arthur stands ready with a portable terminal in hand. The roar of the *Gardenia*'s power plants ripples through every fiber of her being, rendering any thought of sleep a thing of the past.

Though she would never admit it, Shy has imagined catching Arthur down here and having some fun where the engine drone could wash out any noise. It's less sexy, though, when she's wearing a housecoat, a cold half-cigarette hangs from her lip, and her hair is a mess. Also, she could probably use a shower.

The engine tests are good, so they move to the landing gear actuations. That's Joanna's responsibility, so she goes EVA to check the locks, while Arthur watches readouts and Shy communicates. As they're finishing the final landing strut, Jerry's voice comes over the comm.

"Ready crew come in. This is the bridge."

"Bridge, this is Arthur, what's the story?"

"Ready crew, we've got laser links established with Hasanova guidance sats. Shall we head down and meet our new friends?"

"Copy. We'll reel in Joanna and head that way," Arthur says, sending a "hurry up" motion to Joanna's suit over their video uplink. The astronaut outside flips off the nearest of the many nav cameras, and Mother makes sure everyone sees.

"Joanna, Bridge—stow that and get to your crash couch," Jerry says. "Bridge out."

After retrieving Joanna from the airlock and helping her out of her suit, they head up to the bridge. Every member of the crew pulls double-duty—some more than others. Jerry is both the captain and the president of the company. Mary is the vice-president and flight officer. Noah handles navigation data and information security. Joanna is a hell of an installer, and manages the supplies, as well. Arthur serves as a climate systems engineer and the engine officer. Marcus and Mother handle all the rest.

Shy is a "floater," a title which has always made her feel like a piece of shit.

The silvery surface of Hasanova Data Solutions sparkles through the viewports, covered with platinum clouds. Very few land masses blemish its water-covered sphere, visible only on instrumentation, and the setting sun graces its edge like a welding arc. Shy has seen pictures, but it never impressed her before now.

"Load program down, and bring us into orbit," Jerry says, puffing his chest.

"LPD acknowledged," Mary repeats, and the descending whine signals that the braking approach system has shut off. A couple of thrust nozzles fire, and it sounds to Shy like someone blowing into a microphone.

"Mother is giving me a clean maneuvering test," Mary says, looking up from her console. "We're good for orbit in ten. Noah, do we have a lock on the pilot beacon?"

"Of course not. It looks like amateur hour down there." Noah leans forward to talk into his console mic. "HCC VTS, HCC VTS, this is *Gardenia* channel 1-6, over."

"*HCC VTS back to the station calling.*" It's a man's voice, so heavily accented that Shy can scarcely make out the words through the static. She gets a little thrill at their first voice contact with the customer.

"HCC VTS, *Gardenia*," Noah says, condescension in his voice, "we're not seeing your pilot beacon. Is the weatherman asleep today?"

"Noah," Mary hisses. "Be nice."

A stream of weather and topographical data sprays across the central console screen—wind patterns, humidity, water depth. Shy spots a few alternative landing zones designated on nearby islands. They've never had to divert on landing, and she hopes they never do—once the *Gardenia* is down, it has to be refueled, and the surrounding islands look abandoned.

"Gardenia, *HCC VTS*," the man's voice replies, "*be advised, we have a supply ship departing. Maintain altitude and loiter, over.*"

"VTS, *Gardenia*, are you sure we can't scoot on down there?" Jerry cuts in. "It ain't free to burn maneuvering fuel, over."

"Gardenia, *negative. Maintain and loiter until otherwise instructed.*"

Jerry clicks off the comm and glances around. "Would you look at that? Not even offering to reimburse us." He clicks it back on. "*Gardenia* acknowledged. Loitering at two thousand kilometers."

Through an endless litany of calls and responses, Shy watches a pillar of light rise above the planet's clouds— the Hasanova resupply vessel. At this range, it's only a star on the horizon, but it's good to keep a distance. Ships can come together pretty quickly in orbit.

She hopes they left behind a supply of cigarettes.

"Gardenia, *HCC VTS, you are cleared to approach, over.*"

"VTS, *Gardenia* acknowledged," Jerry says. "Down there in two shakes."

4

TOUCHDOWN

Pierced by the buildings of the colony, the atoll bleeds.

At least, that's how the red streaks in the rock appear to Kamran. The HCC geologists told him it's from sulfites like pyrrhotite encased in millennia of coral buildup. It reacts with Hasanova's acidic water, producing a trail of crimson from any rift in the black rock. In the gloaming of the planet's brief sunset, it's positively sanguine.

His bosses called the phenomenon *gol-e-fars*, the "Flower of Persia," and he's always liked the way it streamed between the gleaming colony facilities. With Reza washed into Charybdis, however, it feels more like blood than ever before.

Kamran waits for his company in the safety of the atmospheric processor control room, which affords him a nice view of the golden hour on the water. The USCSS *Gardenia* breaks through the cloud cover, leaving streamers of vapor in its engines' wake. At first it's a tiny vessel, a speck of fire on the tip of a silver needle. It grows in his view until the station begins to rattle with its approach. The rumbling reaches an uncomfortable pitch, and Babāk looks over to him with an expression that says, *they're not about to crash into us, right?*

It sounds unhealthy.

The ship descends toward a landing pad, and whenever Kamran thinks the roar can't get any louder, it does. The vessel settles with a loud clank, and the engines' fury rises into a thin whine, then disappears. Kamran shuts his eyes and takes a deep breath, steadying himself. Managing these American contractors was supposed to be Reza's job, not his.

"Let's go greet our guests, shall we?"

Babāk nods, and gestures for the docking crew to follow. Silently they make their way through the serpentine labyrinth of the processor. Kamran doesn't like landing ships beside the ailing UPP relic, but the old pads are the only ones rated for the *Gardenia*. Provided the previous Azerbaijani inhabitants built everything to spec, there shouldn't be a problem.

"Haroun should be doing this," Babāk whispers. "We should be overseeing Halo B, not—"

"We're not welcome down there," Kamran says. "Farzad won't even look at me after…"

"I lost three of my friends," Babāk persists. "His work team wasn't even there when it happened."

"Drop it."

Kamran doesn't mean for his words to come out so harshly, but he's been ragged ever since the funeral. How close had he been to Reza when he'd crashed? Maybe fifty feet? Even if Haroun hadn't banned Kamran from the Maw to keep him safe from retaliation, he's not sure he could handle going down there.

At the exit to the docking platform they pause to don rain gear and cinch it tightly. The lake's water isn't acidic enough to burn, but it bleaches clothes and generally frays them if left on there long enough. Kamran mashes the loading dock button. The door slides up and cold, wet air blasts inside, along with the roar of the waves.

The *Gardenia* stands before him, hull stained by the patina of carbon scoring. Steam corkscrews into the buffeting winds, glowing dragons in the colony searchlights. Heat from the hull beams upon Kamran's bare face like the sun's rays, a nice contrast against the cold spit of the lake. Docking crew members fan out across the platform, rushing to supply fresh coolant and speed the process.

Lights on the *Gardenia*'s bridge draw his eyes, and when he looks up, the thin silhouette of a woman waves from the window. He musters a smile and waves back. His radio crackles.

"*Cooling lines secure,*" Babãk says on the walkie. "*Clear to disembark.*"

"Send our guests the all-clear and bring the crawler around," Kamran says.

A few minutes later a ramp descends from the belly of the *Gardenia*, floodlights blinding in the dimming evening. Five silhouettes emerge, their shapes sharpening as they draw closer to him. In the lead is a bald, white fellow, an American with a pot belly identical to Haroun's. He extends a meaty hand, which Kamran takes and has the life wrung from his fingers.

"Jerry Fowler. I'm the owner of McAllen Integrations."

"Dr. Kamran Afghanzadeh," he says, switching to his posh English. He learned as a child, then perfected his accent in graduate school at Eton, which he's found immensely beneficial when dealing with Westerners. "Project management. I thought there would be more of you."

Fowler does a double-take, and Kamran tries not to be insulted. "Oh, Mary and Marcus are going to stay on the ship for now. Help get the transfer coordinated." He then introduces each crew member in turn. "Noah Brewer, networking, Arthur Atwater, climate systems, Joanna Hardy, mechanical installer, and Cheyenne Hunt, our front-end dev." To the last one, he adds, "Just call her 'Shy.' She makes what we do look pretty."

Kamran doesn't know much about Americans, but he can tell "Shy" doesn't appreciate the sentiment.

"I'm here to show you to your quarters," Kamran says. He lifts his rain gear and digs through his satchel for his portable terminal. Speckles of mist settle on the screen and keys when he draws it out, and he thanks

God for weatherproofing. "Before I can let you off the platform, however, I'll need you to sign for the refueling procedure, and each of you will need to sign a waiver."

"Waiver?" Fowler's raised eyebrow leaves a wake of wrinkles across his shiny forehead. "We already signed one with our State Department."

Kamran has been dreading this. Before Reza's accident, he never would've had to undertake such a procedure. However, Haroun insisted that they all sign, *"because Americans are litigious dogs."*

"It is just a formality," Kamran says. "While you are here, your safety is my ultimate priority. You are not to stray into any areas except the ones you've been cleared to service. Any breach of this waiver absolves the Hasanova Colony Corporation of responsibility for whatever befalls you."

The five Americans look to one another.

"It's new," Kamran continues, repeating the excuse Haroun demanded of him. "We're making all of our contractors sign them. Your McAllen Integrations is licensed and bonded, yes? You should still maintain your own insurance."

"Of course." Fowler laughs and takes the pad. He and the others take turns with Kamran's stylus, signing their names in glowing green pixels. Then Kamran switches it to the refueling agreement, and motions for Fowler to read over his shoulder.

"In exchange for a fifteen percent discount on goods and services rendered, we're providing you with sixty tons of fertile thorium two-thirty-two. These materials will be provided to you as a byproduct of atmospheric processing, with no warranties made for speed. However, the full load should take about a month to generate."

"Yup, yup, yup," Fowler says, tapping accept and signing. "We sure do appreciate that arrangement. Keeps it cheap when we don't have to carry a load on landing. Every pound is a profit."

"Of course," Kamran says. "It's our pleasure."

The growl of the crawler signals its arrival, and Kamran turns to see their shiny new Daewoo Decade Personnel Carrier trundling through the atmospheric processor door. It reminds him of a white scarab with big, square eyes where the windshield sits. He's pleased that Haroun has decided to send HCC's best vehicle for their guests, instead of leaving it to rot until the big brass visits.

They climb inside the bus. Five calfskin bench seats line the sides, atop plush navy carpets. Accent lines of gold and mahogany break the monotony of glossy white walls. As rugged as the Decade might be outside, it's fit for a prince on the interior—

—which is good, because they've had one or two royals visit in the past. Kamran looks to the Americans for their reactions.

"Hot damn," the tall black fellow, Atwater, mutters and Fowler slaps him on the stomach before smiling politely at Kamran.

"Where's the minibar in this thing?" the pasty one—Brewer—asks. Again Fowler looks chagrined.

"I'm afraid you won't find any alcohol on the colony," Kamran replies. "Its consumption is strictly forbidden while on premises, but you may indulge aboard your ship. Other common items that are forbidden include recreational drugs and pornography."

"Oh yeah," Brewer says, looking somber.

"It's our way, I'm afraid," Kamran says diplomatically. "If you'd like something to drink, please enjoy the use of our fine tea station in the back." He motions to Babāk in the driver's seat. "This is my companion, Mr. Babāk Rashid." Babāk doesn't speak English, but recognizes his name and gives them a timid wave.

"Lay on, please," Kamran murmurs in Farsi, and they lurch to a start, journeying into the atmospheric processor's winding pathway of mazes and pipes—simultaneously a triumph of human engineering and an absolute nightmare to manage.

"This is the Hasanova Atmospheric Processing Station, or HAPS," Kamran explains as they roll through the heart of the plant. "This facility is the oldest part of the colony, predating the modern installation by almost thirty years. When we're not fueling your starship, the excess fertile material from this breeder reactor is shunted to our power plant for supplemental electricity."

"I thought this was a hydro facility," Fowler says, leaning close to the window to get a better look.

"This is the galaxy's most advanced data center." Kamran knows this speech well. He's heard Reza give it to a dozen tours. "We pride ourselves on redundancies, Mr. Fowler. In the event that our hydroelectric facility is taken offline, HAPS-E will switch on and handle the load indefinitely."

The Decade reaches the far side of the facility, and a shutter rolls open to allow egress. The remains of the day have vanished during their short jaunt through the processor, leaving a dark sky. With the domed facility behind them, the road stretches ahead of them through a corridor of dim sea spray. Tall pylons line either side, with steel cables stretched taut to the bridge.

"We call this the 'Long Walk,' but please do not walk it," Kamran says with a chuckle. "Swells up to three stories high can strike this bridge, along with gusts of thirty knots. Beaufort wind force seven and up—not enough to damage our crawler, but dangerous on foot."

"Cool," Joanna Hardy says. "I take it that's in the waiver?"

"Most definitely," Kamran acknowledges. "While this is island living, it's a far cry from beaches and cabanas. You'll want to refrain from any outdoor strolls." At the other end of the bridge they reach the three spires of the colony proper. Windows twinkle up and down their towering lengths like fires burning in the night.

"These three buildings contain all of our day-to-day operations, and they'll be where you conduct the majority of your business. To the left, you have Solutions. That's our office complex, meeting rooms, and so on. To the right, you have Network Ops. As you can imagine, we will have a significant amount of data routing to do when the facility goes online. Directly ahead of us is the Human Centre, where you'll be staying and enjoying leisure time. All three buildings include canteens, though my favorite meals usually come from the Human Centre."

"I'm a fan of eating," Hardy says.

Kamran nods appreciatively. "I think you'll find that vegetables like eggplant thrive in our hydroponic gardens with a taste far superior to their Earthly counterparts." The woman seems less enthused after the word "eggplant," so he swallows and drops it.

He gestures to the structure ahead, the central hub around which the colony is organized, and points out the low, flat landing pads. "Those are the Lilypads, used for private craft and small shuttles. Only one platform is rated for the *Gardenia*."

As they reach the main vehicle bay, a massive swell hammers the colony shield, raining down onto the Decade's roof like small arms fire. It elicits a gasp from the Americans, and judging from their faces, Kamran has little concern that they'll try to run out into the storm on their own.

"*Daaryacheh-e Tavus* is angry tonight," Babāk says in Farsi, and Joanna gives the others a nervous look.

Already the Americans are on edge, Kamran thinks. *Wonderful.*

"Lake Peacock," he says, reassuring them. "He's saying it's angry."

"Lake?" Atwater speaks up, sounding incredulous. "It's the size of an ocean!"

"Yet that indicates a certain amount of salinity, and our water scientists are quite finicky about nomenclature," Kamran says. "The surface is beautiful by day."

"I saw the pictures Mr. Hosseini sent," Shy says to the others, and Kamran thanks God no one sees his smile falter. "Really pretty. There are pink parts near the islands sometimes, like bubblegum pink." She looks to her friends, as if unsure she should've spoken up. They're all staring at Kamran for his reaction.

So she's the adventurous one. In any group of Westerners, there's at least one person who wants to try all of the food and learn more than just the swear words. He's glad to see that, but hopes she isn't as annoying as some he's met.

"That's right," Kamran says as the Decade pulls into the vehicle bay. "Extremophilic bacteria thrive in these waters, and when they die, their fats dissolve into beautiful pink foam. I'm not a biologist, but I think you'll find a lot to enjoy on Hasanova. If you'd like, I can arrange for our science teams to speak with you."

"Oh, just ignore her," Fowler says. "Shy gets ahead of herself, and I doubt we'll have time. No need to go to any trouble on our part." Kamran recognizes that for what it is, a managerial reprimand, and nods politely. He'll circle back with Shy and offer again when it's more polite.

He stands and opens the side door.

"Right this way, please."

The passengers disembark into the vehicle bay, where the maintenance crews store their Decade and a couple of Citroen MR2 hovercraft for journeying to the surrounding islands. The Citroens are a lot more beaten by the elements, covered with gray dust and corrosion from their many ventures around the lake. Kamran ushers the McAllen staff from the crawler and Shy, the last one out, stops beside him.

"I..." she says quietly so the others won't hear. "I want to be sensitive, and in the onboarding videos I saw a lot of women wearing hijab, so do I..." She gestures around her face. Kamran almost dies of embarrassment on her behalf, but holds it together.

"That's between you and God, Miss Hunt."

"Kamran!" Babâk calls to him from the far end of the motorcade. The others stand around him, while he does his best to look like an informed tour guide. To Kamran, he seems more like a man surrounded by curious wolves. "*Berim!*"

"This way," Kamran says, ushering Shy toward the door with a little bow. It's only meant as a polite flourish, so it's awkward when she blushes and bows back before joining her colleagues.

As Kamran opens the door to the colony interior, an explosion rumbles through the halls. The McAllen people look as if they want to leap into one another's arms, but Kamran has felt it a thousand times.

A trapezoidal corridor stretches to the left and right, curving away from the party. A row of interlocking triangular windows, each as tall as a person, allows full view of the waves that batter the structure. This part of the facility is spotlessly clean, and thin lights at even intervals illuminate gold inlays across the black floor. Kamran beckons them to follow him to the right, and takes them to his favorite spot.

"Quickly, now. Quickly. I think you'll enjoy this."

He stands with his back to *Daaryacheh-e Tavus*, its chop cloaked in nightfall, hands folded. They gather just in time, and he tries to hide how happy that makes him. "We call this place—"

When he pauses for dramatic effect, a surge of water slams the windows behind him, turning bright cyan in the facility searchlights. It's like a bomb going off, and the one called Joanna actually falls onto her rump trying to back away from the swell.

Kamran grins widely, relishing the reaction.

"*Halgheyeh Rād-o-bārgh*, or 'The Thunder Ring.'" He gestures to the windows. "Have a closer look." Seeing their hesitation, he adds, "It's perfectly safe." The contractors gather near the windows, amazement clear in their features, flinching every time a wave smashes into the complex.

"These windows are ALON panels as thick as your arm," Kamran says, "and the wall you see before you extends two stories into the rock of the atoll. The Thunder Ring was designed to improve flow into the mouth of Charybdis, thus the sloping sides. The inlays you see in the ground are a gold alloy, produced inside the water purifiers in the Vault of Heaven."

"This is… gold?" Atwater looks down, lifting up his boot like he's accidentally stepped on a famous painting.

"Raw gold would be too soft," Kamran says, "but yes. We produce nearly one ton every year as a byproduct of the *Cupriavidus metallidurans* living inside the exchangers themselves. They eat toxic metals and excrete gold as a happy accident. It compliments the classical Persian design quite nicely." He gestures to the windows on the other side of the tunnel, behind the contractors. "Though I think you'll find this final part to be our most arresting feature, Mr. Atwater."

The contractors turn and head for the windows across the hall, reverence in their steps. Kamran remembers how they feel and, for a split second, the naive part of him emerges—the part that wants to show them the Maelstrom up close, show them the mechanical marvels lining the Maw, let them feel the fury. The thought of Reza's glowing yellow safety gear, vanishing below the surface of whitewater, dampens his enthusiasm.

He stares out the window into the thirsty hole until the boom of a wave strike slams him back to the present.

The Maelstrom leers from far below.

"This is Charybdis," he says. "It's two hundred meters across. At least fifty stories deep, it consumes enough water to run a hydroelectric plant and heat exchangers for the data centers that are built into its rings."

"That"—he points to a central structure, suspended directly over the Maw by moorings attached to the colony buildings—"is the Hasanova Data Cannon, the latest in entangled communications. The quantum particle array contained therein is keyed to relays placed across the galaxy, with a bandwidth of one hundred exabytes per second. Those particles might be the most expensive part of the installation."

"Entangled comms?" Brewer barks a laugh, and Kamran starts to bristle. Then the man adds, "Incredible. It's hack-proof."

"Correct," Kamran says. "No one has ever intercepted or performed a man-in-the-middle attack on an entangled transmission."

"Well, sure," Brewer says, craning his neck to get a closer look. "You'd have to break physics. Why the bandwidth limitation?"

Kamran shrugs. "It's the fastest anyone can access a hard drive. This installation is nearly future-proof. While we're on the subject of Charybdis, I need to remind you that the waivers you signed release us from liability, should you journey past the data centers below. Please consider those areas forbidden to you."

"Wait." Fowler shakes his head. "That's not right, because I thought... What about hooking the Canary system to the gateway?"

"I understand your confusion, Mr. Fowler," Kamran says. "Circumstances have changed, and we'll be performing those checks ourselves."

The older fellow holds up a finger. "Not if you want the system to be safe. Our contract clearly states—"

"You will be paid in full for the contract," Kamran says. "Just give us your firmware, and the connection instructions, and we'll take it from there."

"I don't think you appreciate how hard it is to do someone else's job," Brewer says. "That's my work, and I want to make sure it's done right."

"I see." Kamran regards him for a moment, trying to ascertain if he's actually offended, or putting on a show for the boss. "I'll confer with my superiors and ask, Mr. Brewer." Then he turns. "Your quarters are this way."

The group moves down the hall toward the Human Centre, but once again Shy remains behind. Kamran braces himself for yet another awkward cultural question.

"Where is Mr. Hosseini?" she says. "I was looking forward to meeting him." He swallows hard. It's only natural she wants to know. Reza took a personal interest in everyone who worked on his projects. They'd spoken in emails. She might care that he died.

Then again, the McAllen Integrations people might want to renegotiate their contracts if they think there are hazards. He'll keep them out of Charybdis, and that'll be that. So, Kamran repeats the line that Haroun gave him, even though it makes him sick to his stomach.

"I'm afraid Reza... He's no longer with the company," he says. "If you'll follow me, I'll show you to your apartments."

5

DIPLOMACY

Shy isn't used to a king bed, much less a luxury suite with a parlor. Unlike the raw utility of a "shake and bake" colony, the walls are stucco, adorned with more of the arabesque ornamentation.

She loves it. On the *Gardenia*, she gets either a bunk room with Joanna or a cryopod, and she's gotten used to both. Even when they moor at the Astropuerta de Juarez, she stays at a capsule hotel, leaving her things on the ship.

With the ascetic life of a starship, however, comes one big benefit. She gets paid in lump sums, and spends years in cryo. By the time she's in her late thirties she'll be ready to retire with the body of a twenty-five-year-old.

She could see giving it up to work somewhere like Hasanova.

The locals aren't nice, but they're not mean, either. Only about half of them speak any English, and all of them seem intimidated to talk to her. She doesn't blame them. Who knows what they think of Americans?

On the morning of the fourth day, it's time to get to work wiring up the conference rooms, and that's when things go south. She's in Three East AB, prying off a panel to get at the switch pod. She pulls it out and discovers spiderwebs all over the case wiring.

"What the fuck?" She's never seen this phenomenon outside of their occasional Earthly gigs. *Maybe it's a cobweb*, she tells herself. If a filter was breached in one of the main habitat areas, it'd suck up all the skin dust and spin it into webs like cotton candy. She waves her hand over the opening, feeling for the telltale airflow.

A set of long, black spider legs emerge at the edge of the hole. Shy gasps and trips backward over one of the chairs, a tangle of fear, mahogany, and leather.

"Nope, nope, nope!"

She grabs her LuxMOS tool and scrambles back a few feet, leaving the rest of her bag under the switch pod. Chest heaving, she watches a creature emerge, with legs the span of her palm. Something tickles the back of her hand, and she looks down to see that, no, those weren't spiderwebs on the back of the switch.

They were egg sacs, she has disturbed them, and her hand is covered in fresh, translucent spider babies, like chips of obsidian.

Screeching, she slaps her hand against the carpet. The tool, her bag, and her sanity go by the wayside as she flees the room, stripping out of her McAllen Integrations jacket and tossing it to one side.

Her appearance in the bustling corridor attracts attention. The incident brings ten people and a chatter of confused Farsi, but no real help. No one wants to touch her. Shy frantically checks her hand for bites, but it's bright red from where she grated off bits of skin on the rough carpet.

"Spiders!" she shouts, gesturing to her back and spinning for inspection. "Please tell me there aren't any more."

They smile, looking for whatever she might be pointing to. A maintenance worker pulls out a radio, calling something in. She makes out the word "Kamran," but she's not willing to wait.

Fuck it. She abandons all dignity and rolls around on the ground for a few seconds, hoping to crush any passengers remaining on her body.

"Miss Hunt!" Kamran comes jogging down the hall. "Shy, are you all right?"

She stares daggers at him. "No, I am fucking not—" She reins herself in. "No. I have been in contact with some of the local animals, and I was under the impression this was a rock! No indigenous life! *That's what Jerry said.*" So much for self-control.

He nods to a nearby woman, an older Iranian. "*Lotfan bolandesh kon. Roosh ankabut hast.*"

She kneels and helps Shy to her feet. Her weathered hands gently travel over Shy's clothes, and Shy can hear soft laughter coming from behind a coy smile.

"Was it a black spider?" Kamran asks.

"Yeah. A big one," Shy replies through clenched teeth. She can't stop shaking, and every little tickle sets her spine on edge. "Hand got covered in babies. Think I killed them all."

"Okay. Let me go and have a look."

He signals two of the men to go with him, and they return empty-handed. "It would seem you've driven the beast away, though that scrape looks nasty." Shy looks down to see a few droplets of blood emerging onto her knuckle where she skinned it. She must've bruised the hell out of her hand, because it hurts to make a fist.

"I just need a bandage and an ice pack."

"We have those," he says. "Right this way." They wind through the Human Centre toward the medical lab, past a few dozen curious employees. They smile and nod as she walks by, massaging her hand, and she shoves it into her pocket.

"It was likely a huntsman spider," Kamran says. "Harmless, but they can be terrifying."

"I'm sorry, what? No. That was not a harmless animal, Dr. Afghan..."

"...zadeh," he finishes for her. "Please call me Kamran."

"*Kamran*, it was pissed at me."

"You're the one who traumatized it by crushing its young."

"Stop."

She doesn't want to be placated, but finds the scientist charming—a bit nerdy and way too tall for his own good. He reminds her of an adolescent dog, with big, clumsy paws and a happy energy. Cute wavy hair, too.

"You were close by," she says.

"What? Oh, well, yes. My boss requested that I make myself readily available to your team."

She snorts. "Don't you have a job to do?"

"I'm a project manager. I keep the work moving. It's not moving now, so here I am."

That stings a bit.

"You don't need to look over my shoulder," she says.

"Of course not," he replies. "You strike me as capable, despite having a workplace accident within an hour of getting started."

"All right now," she says wryly. "You can fuck right off with that." The retort slips from her lips.

Kamran stops.

"Oh!" She holds up her palms, surrendering. "I meant that joke in the most American possible way. I'm so sorry. Please don't tell Jerry."

He shakes his head and chortles. "I'm cool, as you say."

Upon reaching the infirmary, Shy is dismayed to learn that Kamran wasn't kidding when he said "workplace accident." She must fill out forms, and the nurse demands a drug screening. Shy isn't concerned, but she prays Joanna doesn't have an onsite injury, because there's no way in hell she'd pass.

"I've got meetings," Kamran says. "I'll let your bosses know you're here. It's just a bruise, but I would like you to double-check for bites. Let's not take any unnecessary risks." Then he leaves her alone with the nurse who speaks very little English.

As a native Texan, Shy's inability to make small talk begins to eat at her until she can't take it anymore. Returning to Three East AB, she finds her tool bag right where she left it, underneath the open switch panel. But the hanging fabric baffles that gave the ceiling its high, luxurious appearance are now a tangle that could contain any number of huntsman spiders. She imagines one flopping onto her hair, then runs her fingers over her scalp to brush away the fear.

They aren't poisonous, she reminds herself. *Kamran said so. You went to school for vet med. You've cut open puppies.* No matter how many times she reassures herself, her hand won't reach for the dangling switch. The milky webs of empty egg sacs still cover the bus interface.

Besides, even if you did get bitten...

Her breath comes quicker, and the harder she tries to push her hand toward the panel, the more her mind resists. It conjures thoughts far more brutal than spiders.

A dead horse.

A terrified friend, swollen and gasping her last.

An endless meadow, far away from hospitals and anaphylaxis auto-injectors.

"Are you crying?" It's Noah's voice, and she turns to find him poking his head in the doorway. "Kamran said you got hurt."

Is she? Shy blinks out a hot tear and wipes her eyes.

"No. Just opened this switch panel, and... it's super-dusty." When she forces a laugh to cover it, she positively barks.

"I know!" Noah says, not paying enough attention to see through her lie. "I've been crawling around the subfloor, and this place is old as shit. There's rust everywhere, and they didn't even yank out the original conduits before laying the new wiring. So, like, every time I want to connect up some stuff, I have to sift through these bundles of rotting insulation. It's disgusting."

Looking closely, she notes dirt on his knees, and his pits are sweatier than usual. Colony commissioning is hard work that takes people into cramped, hot, cold, or wet areas, but this is ridiculous. It's only supposed to be lights, cameras, and some sensors, not a full life-support system.

"I thought this place was new.'

"Me, too." He draws closer and glances around to confirm that the room is empty. "So let me ask you something—why did they cover it up?"

"I wouldn't go *that* far."

"I would," he counters. "I helped write the SOW, and it's scoped for a new colony, not a retrofit."

"Since when do you write the Scope of Work?"

"That's not the point," he says. "Jerry wouldn't have lowballed this thing if he knew."

"He didn't lowball it."

"Shy, they're paying part of our fee in fuel. Look, if I'd known I was going to be crawling around in filth, we would've charged more. It's that simple. We got screwed. Oh, and all the signs down there? Russian. Can't read any of it."

"I thought the UPP only put in the processors and hydro plants."

"Yeah. We *all* did. So what's with the 'new' Human Centre, huh? Got any Russkie shit up in here?"

She glances back at the open hole. There are a couple of pieces of rusty conduit visible through the dark square, as well as a peeling sticker. She goes to her tool bag—it's easier not to freak out with Noah in the room. He'd tease her if he knew how scared she was, and that's enough to overcome her fear. She fishes out the pen light, puts it to the open hole, and peers inside.

Huntsman spiders aren't poisonous.

The darkness here is tangible, alive, and she swivels the lens to cover as much of the hole as she can. The eggs on the switch bus are dormant—either the spider babies have crawled up the wiring harness into the wall, or they've hidden inside the open circuitry.

Bugs can't kill you.

Cold sweat beads on her brow as she peers inside to

look at the sticker. At first she can only make out a serial number of some kind, but then she spots some Cyrillic writing around the border.

"You're right," she breathes, unable to believe she just said that to Noah Goddamned Brewer.

"So why cover it up, huh?"

6

NEGOTIATIONS

"Why are the Americans renegotiating, you son of a fucking donkey?" Haroun bangs his mug down onto the desk, and a bit of tea splashes out.

"I've not read the contract," Kamran says, folding his hands behind his back, "so I don't know what legal put into it. Have you spoken with them yourself?"

Haroun Sharif's office is the picture of opulence, but that's the problem. A picture is far from reality. Tea rings stain his desk from messy habits. There's a pockmark in the stucco from the time he threw a glass paperweight to make a point to Reza. Some of his "mahogany" furniture has begun to shed its veneer, exposing the cheap plastic beneath. Moisture in the ventilation system has stained the edge of the ceiling grates with rust, bleeding into porous materials surrounding it.

His desk is far back, and his chairs are near the door. That means unless Kamran wants to drag one of the heavy seats across the overblown vastness, he will need to stand. Haroun's pale complexion grows redder as he thrusts a meaty finger in Kamran's direction.

"If you still want to work here, you'll give me some fucking answers when I ask you a question."

"I did give you an answer."

"'Have you spoken with them?' is a question, so you're as bad at grammar as you are at your job."

Kamran swallows any further retort. Until a few days ago he liked his job, and perhaps he can ride this out.

"I would imagine they're concerned that we... mischaracterized our colony."

That much is an understatement. Jerry Fowler's boisterous friendliness disappeared after his crew reported their working conditions. Last night, he demanded hazmat gear and a twenty percent margin, doing so in no uncertain terms.

"Then placate them and get them back to work!"

"I suspect they'll want more money for that."

It's as if Haroun's body is swollen with hatred. He claims he used to play for a soccer club in Tabriz, but Kamran doesn't believe a word of that. It's a wonder he hasn't had a rage-induced stroke.

"It'll take three weeks to refuel their ship, and they just dragged fifteen tons of mechanical systems here from Earth," Haroun says. "There's no financial recovery from that. You've got them over a barrel, so stick it in, Kamran. Use that oversized head of yours."

"Please don't say that."

"Reza isn't here to protect you," he growls, "so I'll say anything I want, you piece of shit. Hosseini kept the trains running on time, but you're just refugee trash."

Did this son of a bitch read my security clearance file?

When Kamran was at Eton, he joined the boxing club. His long arms gave him an unfair advantage, and he imagines using it right that second.

"With all due respect, Haroun—"

Haroun juts out his jaw, bearing his teeth. "'All due respect' includes 'sir.'"

"*Sir...*" Kamran balls his fists. "I think you should speak with them personally. I'm currently doing everything I can to get Halo B's construction back on schedule, and that must remain a priority, given the— well, given the dangers."

"If Jerry Fowler or any of the other American dogs set one foot in my office, I'll personally remove your useless head from your body and send it home to your mother."

Kamran steps close enough to reach across the desk and throttle the bastard. "I will take care of your problem," he says, a sheen of malice on his voice. Haroun stands, not noticing or not caring about the implicit threat. He's a head and a half shorter than Kamran, but he leans on the desk, knuckles down, like a gorilla.

"See that you do. If those lazy shits are going to bill by the day, I want them working every minute of it. Dismissed."

As he leaves, Kamran curses the swooshy, automatic door. He'd love to slam it.

On the walk to Ops, the Thunder Ring echoes his mood. What's he going to tell the Americans? *"Yeah. We lied. Sorry!"* Upon reaching his desk, he sees a new message from IT. Pezhvok, the sysadmin, assigned all of Reza's accounts to him, dumping basically everything into his user profile. Six hundred and forty-eight emails come streaming across the connection, mixing into his already cluttered inbox.

Kamran takes a deep breath, closes his eyes, and blows out slowly until he doesn't feel like demolishing anyone. How could his mentor have read so many accursed messages, and still done his job? He scrolls down through the list, each item eroding his will to live.

—until he sees Haroun's name in the sender line.

It was sent after Reza's death.

Unlike Kamran, Reza's relationship with Haroun was one of mutual respect. Kamran has never gotten a peek behind the curtain—Reza wasn't great about getting him time with executives.

He opens the message.

```
From: Haroun.Sharif@HasanovaDS.icsc
Reply-to: 356ed3541@dispatch.HasanovaDS.icsc
To: Reza.Hosseini@HasanovaDS.icsc
Date: 2184 Aug 02
```

Rez,

I know you can't answer, but I want to pretend you're
with me for a day longer. I don't know how to tell
Sanam that you won't be complimenting her sheermal
every Wednesday. Not sure how to explain to Banu that
you won't be coming to play.

I promised you I'd stop, but the bottle is leering at
me. You're not here to be disappointed. Fuck you.

Kamran hates how much he feels for Haroun in that
moment. The message is the latest in a chain, so he goes
one backward to see the last thing Reza sent.

It's just the word "OK," which usually meant Reza
was pissed at someone. So he goes to the next email back,
from Haroun.

Never mind that. You have it on my authority. Do it.

One more gives Kamran the answer to his curiosity.

From: Reza.Hosseini@HasanovaDS.icsc
Reply-to: 942sy0593@dispatch.HasanovaDS.icsc
To: Haroun.Sharif@HasanovaDS.icsc
Date: 2184 Jul 26

Even if we make those adjustments to the pilings,
there's no guarantee that we'll find what you're

```
   looking for. Drilling around the site may destabilize
   it. Afghanzadeh is going to be furious.
   Where did you get that survey data?


   -R
```

A little bomb goes off in Kamran's stomach, and he has trouble reconciling what he's reading with his memory of the man. Reza had promised that they followed Kamran's team's drawings. Some of the people who made those calculations died in that shaft.

Had he lied?

Was he ever going to tell Kamran the truth?

Kamran's intercom buzzes, and Babāk's voice crackles over the line.

"Jerry Fowler is here to see you. He brought his wife."

"By all means, send the pigs in here," Kamran hisses through his teeth in Farsi, hoping Fowler hasn't heard any of those curse words yet.

"Uh, I... Okay."

The door opens and Fowler walks through, face locked in a stern, skin-deep smile. Mary Fowler doesn't bother, an ugly scowl on her lips. The thick makeup on her face might as well be a mask, and her perfume practically gasses him.

Mary nods and helps herself to a seat. "Mister Afghanzadeh."

I guess the Americans respect manners as much as their contracts.

"Ah, the Fowlers." Kamran folds his hands into his lap. "How can I be of assistance?"

"We were just told by Mr. Sharif's office that he's unavailable to discuss the contract," Mary says, her Texas accent twanging his nerves. He shouldn't be having this conversation angry. It's never a good idea, but it's too late to kick them out.

"That's because there's nothing to discuss," Kamran says. "You committed your team to do the job, and our legal department expects those promises to be honored."

"Now you listen here!" Jerry Fowler's voice fills the room.

"No."

The man opens his mouth, his expression torn between anger and betrayal. He probably thought of Kamran as nice, affable, and understanding. That's a misconception that can easily be remedied.

"No," Kamran repeats, "I don't think I need to do that, since the terms of work are clearly stipulated. Either you and your team complete the commissioning of this facility, or face the consequences—non-payment."

"Is that right?" Fowler's bitter snort reminds him of a horse. The older man hooks his thumbs into his belt loops and rocks on his heels. "Who are you going to get out here that's certified to commission a NovArc SiteSys? Tell you what, those Norwegians make a hell of a system. Top of the line; you could probably program it to do anything."

Kamran sees where this is going, and his thinly pressed lips begin to ache from scowling.

"And I know what it costs per license per year," Fowler continues. "So when you and your Eye-ranian eggheads couldn't figure it out by yourselves, that must've made you look pretty bad to Mr. Sharif."

Mary adds a sassy "mm-hmm."

Kamran gets the impression Jerry is deliberately mispronouncing the country. It's not surprising to hear the man bring up nationalities in a complaint. At least now he knows he can "stick it in," as Haroun requested.

"It's pronounced 'I-ra-nian,' and I'll save you some trouble down the road: it's pronounced 'new-clear.'"

"Oh, you're hilarious for a guy with five data centers and no air-handling units." Fowler's condescending grin is even more grating than his wife's voice. "Buddy, we're the ones with the equipment and expertise."

"But you're not the ones with fuel."

Kamran hadn't wanted to go to such an extreme, but once he's said it, he can't take it back. In truth, he sees where they're coming from. They've been deceived by Haroun and Reza, just as Kamran has. Still, he'll be damned if he lets anyone else use him as a doormat.

"I'm certain you'd like to return home with money in your pockets," he continues, "instead of heaps of uninstalled climate-control equipment. And with no contract, you'll be purchasing fuel at a premium, instead of the agreed-upon rate. Or you could call a tow."

"That's blackmail!" Mary Fowler shouts.

"No, that's leverage, Mrs. Fowler, and it's perfectly legal for one company to have it over another. I wonder how McAllen Integrations would cope with the loss of the commissioning fee, idle inventory, and the cost of fuel."

"By suing your ass!"

"Have you looked at the contract recently? Do you see where it makes warranties about the condition of our facility?"

"I—" Jerry Fowler clearly hasn't considered this possibility yet. "Well, no, but—"

"It doesn't," Kamran says. "It *does* state, however, that you're on a fixed fee, not cost plus." He takes a breath before continuing. "I'm not here to be your enemy, Mr. Fowler, but if you don't get those units into our data centers, and if this whole system isn't speaking SiteSys Two by the end of your tenure, it'll impact your bottom line like a meteor."

"Everywhere I go," Fowler says, "there's always some uppity company man."

"Yes, well, we can't all buy our own starships like you." Kamran straightens his desk, shuffling stacks of papers into neat piles as he speaks. "If you have any other questions regarding your obligations, reach out to legal. I'm only here to answer questions about the work you promised to do."

"Man..." Fowler shakes his head, laughing to cover his red-faced fury. "You really are a... a f-fucking piece of crap, you know that?"

Kamran has been cursed at before, but not like this. The word "fuck" dribbles clumsily out of the man's mouth, an instrument too rarely played.

"As you say," Kamran replies with a shrug. "Are you going to have the conference rooms done this week, so we can get to the real work?"

"Whatever happened to 'do unto others?'" Mary asks, eyes piercing.

These people don't strike Kamran as nice. They don't strike him as particularly smart, either—but they're innocent. Reza coordinated their contract, lied to them just like he lied to Kamran. When they came to him for help, he attacked them. He can't look her in the eye, so he pretends to think.

Maybe he should just level with her and sell Haroun out. That'd feel nice.

Mrs. Fowler, you and I have a common enemy.

"I wish—"

"I wish I could tell you the whole story," is what he wants to say. If Haroun fires him, Kamran loses any stock he has squirreled away for retirement. He's only been on Hasanova for two years; he needs three more to be vested.

She hardens. "You wish *what*?"

Kamran's long-fought anger spikes within him. "I wish you would go back to your jobs and quit wasting everyone's time."

Venom in her eyes, Mary says, "That's the problem with businesses like yours. Can't expect them to do the

Christian thing." She stands and leaves, and her husband follows without another word.

Alone, Kamran exhales, rests his head in his hands, and massages his temples for a few minutes. He knows what will happen next. The Americans will do a bad job, and Haroun will have him terminated. He can almost hear it. *"Because of your failure to get the data centers and Halo B running, you're done. Get out."*

Kamran turns back to regard his terminal with its tangle of emails in acid green pixels. Somewhere in there is the reason Reza lied to him.

INTERLUDE: HAROUN

"Azizam! Kojayi?" Haroun bellows upon entering his apartments.

With a shrieking giggle, Banu comes hurtling around the corner and wraps her arms around his knees. The tiny child lets loose a roar of her own, and Haroun pretends to sway in her mighty grip. He approximates a toppling tree, stumbling before lowering himself to the foyer floor. Banu is all over him, shouting in his face and pretending to claw him like a dinosaur as he begs for mercy.

"Joonam, get off the floor!" Sanam scolds, and he looks up to find his wife standing over him in a dress. "You're going to get filthy."

"That depends on how filthy the floors are," Haroun says, then he locks eyes with Banu and tickles her. "They're not supposed to be filthy at all!"

The stiff toe of Sanam's chef's clog leaves the top of his bald head smarting for that comment.

"Hey! You're going to leave a mark!" Haroun stands, rubbing his head with one hand and supporting Banu with the other. She wraps her arms around his neck, clinging to his chest.

"Criticize my house again, and I guarantee it," Sanam says. "Dinner is ready, and I want to get off my feet."

He gently deposits Banu on the ground before leaning in close to Sanam, whispering.

"Maybe later you can be on your back instead."

She flushes and slaps him across the stomach, but her smile is unmistakable.

"Get in here and help me."

When he reaches the kitchen, his mother Nadia Khanoom is there, pulling out plates and silverware. Her back has been bothering her lately, and Haroun wishes she'd quit trying to help so much.

"Go, go, go, *maman*. Sit," he urges, shooing her toward their small dining alcove. "We've got it." Haroun takes over prepping duties, grabbing the pot from the stove. Turmeric, dried lime, lamb, and onion tell him the story of an entire afternoon spent making *ghormeh sabzi*. Nadia wouldn't settle for even the best stochastic printing; she'd always said it would embarrass her. Nothing could replicate the effect of an hours-long simmer.

A large cake of rice steams nearby, tahdig crispy and brown across the top.

"Azizam!" Haroun calls. "Come get the plates." Banu runs to him, and he picks her up. When she reaches for the cabinet, he stops her.

"Ah, what do we do first?"

"Wash my hands?"

Haroun nods, helping her with the kitchen faucet. He lifts Banu up to grab the first plate, then does the rest himself. Both parents give their daughter an exaggerated, "Thank you for helping," to assist with her wild manners.

"You're late, joonam," Sanam says. "The rice won't be as good."

"It's Afghanzadeh. The man can't do anything on his own. He keeps bothering me for needless approvals." Haroun takes Sanam's tea and steals a sip.

"Make your own!"

"Perks of management." Haroun laughs. "Never have to work—just take a cut from everyone else." Then he sours. "God knows I never get anything done anymore."

"Don't beat yourself up like that. We lost something precious. Everyone can't be Reza." She rests a warm hand against his chest, then loosens his tie and unbuttons his collar. It's like a breath of fresh air, and she steals the silk, hanging it by the door.

"Come on," Haroun's mother calls from the table. "We didn't cook this just to smell it!" Nadia turns to Banu. "He was late to his own birthday, you know, by three weeks. Had to cut his slow ass out."

"Don't go filling her head with disrespect." Haroun pouts as he heads to the dining alcove with the big pot of *ghormeh sabzi*. He places it down and fixes his mother with the stern look he usually reserves for Kamran.

Nadia cocks an eyebrow and gives him a turtle smile. "Then don't scold your own mother." She reaches up and pats the side of his face with a hand that has delivered many slaps.

"That's disrespect!" Banu says. Her giggles are only interrupted by the sound of an incoming comm.

"Haroun!" Sanam says from down the hall. "There's a call for you."

"Can you remind them that it's dinnertime?"

She appears at the entrance to the kitchen. "It's Mrs. Shirazi…"

Tiran Shirazi doesn't usually call Haroun at all, so when he hears the chief technology officer's name, he jumps up. He apologizes to his family and makes haste for the study to take the meeting. Tiran's thin face appears on the terminal monitor, framed by an elegant hijab.

"There's been another burst comm from *Tagh-e-Behesht*."

Haroun swallows and his heart pumps a little harder. "Hosseini put sensors in place. Did we get it triangulated?"

"It's coming from the karsts. Lines up with the voids he found near Halo B, before—Well, his survey data lines up with the Ginza File."

He has to stop himself from dancing.

Haroun had brought the matter of the "Ginza File" to Hasanova Colony Corporation a few days ago. He'd been approached by Thien, a Red Silk information broker. She'd contacted his cousin via the dark web with a file to sell, ostensibly a list of ancient Weyland sites that might be of interest—compiled by none other than the Yutani Corporation.

Haroun's cousin had said to trust Thien, swore it on the Qur'an, God as his attorney. The purchase negotiated, Tiran Shirazi had swept in at the last minute and grabbed the Ginza File for analysis. He'd assumed the awful bitch would be taking credit for his big find.

"What about the header?" he asks. "Did we catch it this time?"

"Weyland Corp."

"No Yutani." He can't repress his smile. "Pre-merger."

Tiran inclines her head. "This is the confirmation we need to start drilling. I've already obtained authorization from the home office. Transmitting the coordinates now." Haroun's email dings, and he pulls up the geocart attachment.

"This will send Halo B back to the drawing board," he says. "Maybe we should consult with Afghanzadeh before—"

Tiran sighs. "I don't think my boss will accept that. Handle it however you want, but Halo B just got pushed back."

"I want a replacement for Kamran Afghanzadeh on the next rotation."

"Why are you telling me? I don't work for HR."

"Sorry, madame."

Tiran's eyes narrow. "Given these developments, I'm a little uncomfortable with having Americans on the colony right now. Have we properly vetted them?"

Haroun's people hadn't done a super-thorough job, but he also hadn't been expecting to be able to find the old Weyland outpost. "I'll have them re-evaluated. Use a different company, just in case the first people missed something."

"Have our people with eyes on them all the time. Make sure it's someone loyal."

"All of my people are—"

"Spare me. I don't care. Drilling starts this week."

Haroun blinks. "It'll take us some time to set up—"

"Use a shovel and hold your breath, if you have to."

7

AS ABOVE, SO BELOW

At almost two weeks into the job, a message arrives in Shy's inbox that's enough to scare the shit out of her. It's an undeliverable item, sent from her own email address to "adsfasdef@mcallenint.com."

```
DON'T TRUST NOT SAFE
DON'T TRUST NOT SAFE
DON'T TRUST NOT SAFE
DON'T TRUST
```

Double-checking the header for any further clues, she only locates the time—seventeen eleven in the evening. She'd been napping then, just a few feet from her terminal. Either someone had access to her email account, or they used her computer while she lay in bed. She doesn't even want to consider the latter.

They must've wanted her to see this—knew it'd bounce back.

Noah is their information security expert, and potentially the source of the message. He's been through her private files before—a year ago, he made a crass reference to a piece of erotica she'd stored in her personal file vault. She couldn't prove it, of course, so no disciplinary action was taken.

What if the message refers to the Iranians? Kamran has been weird lately, either avoiding her or asking a thousand questions. Everyone stares at Shy wherever she goes. Perhaps one of them sent the email to scare her away.

"Well, it's working," she mutters to herself.

Standing up from her terminal, she heads down into the Human Centre cafeteria for a bit of breakfast. She's grown accustomed to the food, and finds she prefers it to Mary's traditional southern fare. Biscuits and gravy are excellent, but a bit heavy for someone expected to be on their feet all day.

Shy steps into the serving line, and the Iranians near her part like the Red Sea. At least the babari bread is warm and inviting, and she scoops on some butter before adding a drizzle of honey. She adds some fruits to break up the carbs, and heads into the sea of tables.

Joanna and Arthur are already there, sitting alone in the corner like a couple of pariahs; she chomps hot bread while he tucks into a tomato scramble with a side of salted cucumbers.

"You never stop with those," Shy says, sliding in across from them.

"Protein and fresh veg," Arthur mumbles around a mouthful before taking a big swallow. "Going to teach y'all to like cucumbers before this whole thing is over."

"I don't *dislike* them," Shy replies. "I just don't want them with every single meal."

"I avoid all dicks and dick-shaped objects," Joanna says. A drip of blackcurrant jam falls directly onto the cleavage of her McAllen-branded polo, and she tries to scrape it off with a napkin. She's rewarded with a violet stain for her troubles. "Fuck," she says, then shrugs.

"Lift, don't wipe," Arthur says.

"At least this shirt was already a loss. It's not going to recover after today."

"What do you mean?" The top doesn't look like it's in bad shape to Shy.

"We're headed down to the basement of Ops," Joanna says. "They've been staging components for the air handlers all morning. They want us to do the job with a pair of Badgers. Going to be filthy."

Shy squints.

Joanna rolls her eyes. "John Deere Badgers. Tiny-ass exosuits designed for half that capacity."

"We were supposed to have full-up power loaders," Arthur adds. "Someone doesn't like us, or they were lying about having the loaders."

Shy nods, and glances around to see if anyone is

listening. "Changing the subject..." She leans across. "I got a weird email." She tells them about the message, and Arthur starts laughing. It's a rare occasion that she wants to smack his face instead of his ass, but his dismissal frustrates the hell out of her.

"You don't think this is important?" she hisses under her breath, checking to see if Arthur's outburst garnered unwanted eyes.

"Don't you know how easy it is to fake that shit?" he asks. "That could've come from anyone in the galaxy, and you'd never nail it down. It's called spoofing, and you should show it to Noah."

Shy grimaces. "Fuck Noah."

"I don't think it's sinister," Arthur says, "but it's infosec. That means you'd better tell him."

Shy leans back in her chair, crossing her arms. "What if he's the one that sent it?"

"Then he's going to laugh at you," Arthur says. "But if he didn't and you fail to report..."

"As much as I hate to agree," Joanna adds, "it *is* Noah's job. You wouldn't want him holding back something that concerns your job, would you?"

"No," Shy admits. "I wouldn't."

"Hello, I'm Marcus."

The synthetic nearly gives Shy a heart attack when he speaks up behind her. He carries with him a tray of bread and jam for Mary, who follows in his wake like he's a bodyguard.

"Yep. I'm Cheyenne. That's Arthur and Joanna."

Mary sits down beside them. She isn't looking too hot—her hair, ordinarily a tight bun, is sticking out in places, and purple circles dampen the pale skin under her eyes.

"How is Ops Central coming?" Mary asks, dressing her babari up like a pancake and cutting into it with her fork.

"We're about to find out," Joanna says. "Honestly, though, I don't have high hopes. We're already behind."

"And you?" Mary looks to Shy. "What are you doing today?"

"Back on the third records storage in Ops," Shy replies with a shudder. She's been all through its spider-infested paneling looking for the gateway to connect her LuxMOS. When she finally got everything hooked in, Haroun Sharif showed up to interrogate her about her business in the records room. As a result, Shy disconnected before committing her changes, blowing away a half hour of work. She only realized later when she couldn't find the room on the central server in SiteSys.

"Again?" Mary asks. "What about the first two times?"

"Bad connection, then I got interrupted. I'll get it taken care of today. I promise."

"Good," Mary says. "I'd like to get the hell out of here."

The call to prayer goes out over the intercoms, and the McAllen crew takes that as a sign to start the day. Arthur tells her again to find Noah, extracting a promise before he'll let it go. She knows Arthur will follow up, so she goes off in search of the IT specialist.

According to the mission queue, Noah is somewhere in the upper levels of the Human Centre, so she checks floor after floor. She's almost to the roof access when she smells the marijuana and hears waves crashing outside.

A harrowing climb up a fifteen-foot ladder takes her out of a hatch and onto the roof. Noah stands by the rampart, looking out over the lake with a lit cone in his hand.

"No ritual pollutants, boy," she calls to him.

"Fuck! Shit!" He goes to put it out.

"If you get rid of that, I'm shoving you over the edge. Give me a hit."

Regaining his composure, he passes it to her and she takes a deep draw of piney, musky smoke. The relaxation instantly settles over her like a warm blanket, dulling her anxiety. She knows she'll be stressed and panicky in an hour, but for now she's happy.

"I got a weird email," she says. "That's why I came. It's probably nothing, but—"

"Tell me about it."

She'd been expecting him to be dismissive and rude, ask patronizing questions, or assume she'd been getting spammed—yet Noah's face is dead serious.

At least he's competent at his own job.

As she recounts the details, she'd prefer him to laugh at her, but he hangs on every word, hungry for answers that she can't quite recall. In the end, she's left feeling like she's let him down by forgetting something important.

"And this just showed up this morning?"

"I think so, yeah." It's been awhile since she indulged, and her attention span isn't quite what she'd like. "Why?"

His blue eyes lock onto hers. "I've been seeing a lot of strange contacts on our network, port scans and such. I had to shut off the *Gardenia*'s wireless comms, but the fuel lines are still open to data. I switched off Marcus's comms, too."

"Marcus?"

"If someone hacked him on the wireless, he could do stuff without us knowing. Throw switches, open doors." Noah leans in a little closer. "I think someone might be targeting us."

"Targeting."

A chill wind off the lake rattles Shy's bones. She shouldn't have come up here without rain gear, but it suddenly seems more inviting than down in the colony.

Shy laughs. "Weed makes you paranoid."

"You don't know this job like I do," he replies. "I have to protect these places. You don't know how bad a breach can be." At this, he eliminates all credibility by leaning back on the roof railing and dramatically staring out over the water.

"Okay, star cop, like, get ahold of yourself."

His left eye twitches in annoyance, but he refuses to stop the tough guy act.

"How far down in the facility have you gone?"

"Well, I don't do the first data storehouse until next week."

"So DS Forty-Four is out of the question."

"I think that's a given, yes."

"Well, I was down there, and things were getting weird," he said. "Lots of equipment being moved in and out, and safety guys everywhere. They had a bunch of Daihatsu DKs down there, excavation stuff…"

Shy had been on a job with Daihatsu "Big Crabs" before. It'd been incredible to see them scaling a latticework of scaffolding to install a chiller system.

"What about power loaders?" Shy asks.

"Yeah. All kinds of stuff."

"They'd promised that gear to Arthur and Joanna."

"All I'm saying is, they've got forty-four data storehouses, and no servers in the bottom of the Spiral. What if we're helping them build a weapon?"

"What?"

"Why is Charybdis rifled like a barrel? What if it's a planet-killing laser or some shit like that?"

"You're such a fucking idiot, Brewer."

Noah takes a long hit off the joint before tossing it over the side. Shy watches with some regret as the wind snatches it away over the waves, though at this point she may be entirely too stoned. It's probably for the best.

"Something's going on," Noah says. "These people are… basically… doing some weird shit."

She looks back at the hatch, which now seems dangerous to negotiate. What if she's the fool that falls and breaks her neck, because she was high on the job?

"Then we ought to stay away from Charybdis, Noah."

"I've got shit to do," he says, heading to the hatch without the slightest hesitation.

He inhaled most of the cone by himself, Shy realizes. *How often is he wasted at work?* Moving more cautiously, she mounts the ladder to follow him down, and her memory coldly reminds her that she's already been drug tested for one onsite injury. If she falls here, she'll be busted for sure. What are the consequences for smoking weed at a Shia site? The U.S. State Department waiver was explicit. *"McAllen Integrations and its employees will be governed by local laws and norms."*

The rungs of the ladder seem to multiply with each compounding thought, and by the time Shy reaches the bottom, she's sweating. Noah's go bag rests nearby, dirty wires stuffed hastily into the top. He grabs it and pulls out a pair of water bottles, tossing one to her.

"Always stay hydrated," he says, and he's right.

The dry mouth from the weed is killing her. The liquid is amazing on her lips, and she has to stop herself from guzzling the whole bottle. Noah always seems to have water, she realizes.

"They're up to something down there," he says, "and you can get pretty close."

She scoffs. "Then I'm going to avoid it."

"Look, you've got access, and a reason to be down there. Why not see for yourself, since you keep calling me paranoid?"

"I'm not calling you paranoid! All I'm saying is of course they're 'up to something.' It's a construction site."

"Then why aren't we commissioning it?"

Shy grimaces. "Because—"

He holds up a finger. "We're supposed to bring this whole place online. Everywhere. Even the jail cells in their little constabulary. So I ask you—*what new construction?*" Then he picks up his go bag and leaves.

Between the email nonsense and Noah's conspiracy theories, Shy has had enough for one day. She heads down toward the Thunder Ring so she can get to Ops. She's already behind schedule, and Kamran has assured Jerry that he won't tolerate any delays.

She can't believe she ever found that gawky scientist charming. He's a nightmare at team update meetings, never waiting his turn to talk. Any time something goes even a little wrong, he has to know everything about it right that second, or he flips out.

So it troubles her to see him purposefully striding toward her in the tunnels while she's baked off her ass. Maybe he won't bother her if she deploys a smokescreen of polite annoyance. She tries to conjure the face her mom uses to scare her dad away.

Kamran responds with a concerned smile.

"Judging from the look on your face, we need to talk."

"I don't know why." Shy takes a gulp of her water. The lake breeze will have taken care of the smoke in her hair, but her breath might still reek. "Everything is on schedule, Dr. Afghanzadeh."

"Shy, please call me Kamran," he replies. "There is no need for a rocky work relationship. Have you had more trouble with spiders?"

"No, I've had trouble with old wiring and filthy connectors. Only half the gateways are installed where they're supposed to be, and I keep finding wall pods with no low voltage lines hooked up. No spiders—just a ton of unbilled retrofits done under a high-pressure schedule." It all feels good leaving her mouth, but Kamran's stunned silence tells her she might've overstepped. A wave booms against the windows at her back, adding an unwanted dramatic force to her speech.

"I'm sympathetic," he says, "but Jerry removed all leverage he might have built with my bosses when he signed that contract. I didn't write the terms."

"Who did?"

"Legal," he says, as if that answers everything. "Look, if I don't help you pull this off, I'm also going to be in hot water. I have a boss, too, you know."

"Yeah? Well your boss is keeping a lot of secrets. What are you doing down there in the data storehouses?"

Kamran looks at her blankly. "I'm sorry?"

Shy regrets confronting him, and suspects it has something to do with her swimming head. If there's nothing sinister going on, she looks like a fool. If there *is* some malice in their hosts, then she's tipped her hand.

"You're doing *something* down there," she presses, unable to stop herself. "Using all of the good equipment. Sticking us with your stinking Badgers, which *aren't* what we need to do our jobs." She thrusts a finger in his direction. "There's new construction you're not telling us about."

"Shy, it's perfectly normal," he protests. "That's not building construction; it's a safety system."

"You told Arthur and Joanna they'd have power loaders, but they don't. So... you weren't truthful." What'd sounded like a real zinger to her drug-addled brain comes out weak. Yet to her pleasant surprise, this revelation upsets Kamran.

"They *do* have power loaders. I checked them out from logistics two days ago."

"Nope." She crosses her arms. "Noah said he saw the gear down in DS Forty-Four." Then she decides to press her luck. "We could go take a look together, since there's nothing weird going on."

Kamran laughs. "You know this whole place is just a complicated server farm, don't you? There's no need to be so paranoid."

"Let's go, then."

He gives her a look, then nods. They make the long walk to the Solutions building in silence, and Shy feels a little like a hostage taker. She scarcely knows anything about the power loader situation, and she jumped all over Kamran out of annoyance, not righteousness.

"Do you smoke?" he asks as the lift doors close.

"What? Maybe. Why? Can you smell it?"

"No. Just thought you might like to join me for some shisha after. Uh, you know, a *gheyloon*… uh… hookah. You look like you could stand to relax."

She peers up at him as if seeing the man for the first time. It's hard to imagine Kamran smoking, especially a hookah. The dorky scientist swallows, and his pronounced Adam's apple bobs comically.

"I thought smoking wasn't allowed," she says.

"What? No. Everyone smokes here, just not in public. You can get them at the canteen in Ops."

Oh, thank God.

"How is that not a 'pollutant?'"

He holds up his hands. "If you don't want to come—"

She considers her supply of smokes, back in the room. At the rate she's going, Joanna will have bummed every last one by the end of the week.

"Bet on it," she says. "You show me DS Forty-Four, and I'll have a smoke with you."

He smiles sheepishly, and she realizes two things: she may have just agreed to a date, and he finds her thoroughly intimidating.

"Babāk will join us, of course," he adds, and Shy is mostly sure she's relieved they'll have company.

Mostly.

The lift doors part at DS Forty, and he beckons her to follow. As Noah said, the data storehouses down this far contain no equipment—just bare floors and curving windows with views into the belly of Charybdis. Since it's built on an incline, the storehouse is terraced, with beaten plastic ramps laid over the sets of stairs. Tread scuffs from loaders and Polaris ATVs mar the tile. Much of the wiring is exposed in the ceiling, and Shy doubts the lights down here are ready for commissioning.

Kamran looks shocked to see the state of it.

They walk down the terraces, through three more storehouses to Forty-Four, and find tons of staged gear. Personnel bustle back and forth, and a few of them stop to regard the newcomers. Noah wasn't lying; the work is in full swing down here. When Shy looks to Kamran for his reaction, he's staring, open-mouthed. Whatever this construction is, it doesn't look to her like he's been in the loop.

"*Agha!*" a woman shouts at Kamran.

"*Lajani khanoom,*" he answers, then whispers to Shy, "That's Fatemeh Lajani. She's the foreman for—"

Fatemeh strides toward them, and brings a couple of fellows with her. She starts to talk, and whatever she's saying, it's not pleasant. Kamran grows more agitated, and their voices rise above the din. Shy's escort makes a scene in Farsi, and she really, really wishes she could understand what's happening—or get while the getting is good.

The other workers drop what they're doing to pay attention, and Shy sees a lot of clenched fists. She shouldn't have come down here, because if they beat the fuck out of Kamran, she's probably next.

She makes out a familiar word, "Hosseini." Kamran said Reza Hosseini left the company, so why bring him up?

Fatemeh's radio squawks, and everyone goes silent as a breathless voice cries something in Farsi. Most of the workers rush for a passage that leads deeper down—a place Shy has been strictly forbidden to enter. A man seizes Kamran by the elbow and tries to escort him for the door. Fatemeh grabs Shy.

Fatemeh shouts something at Kamran, quick words accompanied by an angry gesture toward the door. Despite the language barrier, Shy understands that they're being kicked out. Kamran shrugs free of the man dragging him, and gives the guy a fierce shove.

"Velam kon!"

The guy stumbles back, nostrils flaring, fists balled. He's about to take a swing, and Kamran drops into a formidable-looking boxing stance. Then a door slides open and a crew of four workers comes rushing by with a stretcher. It's quick, and everyone is panicked as they come tearing ass through the data storehouse.

The person on the stretcher is screaming, olive skin gone ashen gray. Black veins crawl across his neck like tree roots. The white of one eye has gone blood-red around the iris, while the other is solid black.

Whatever is wrong with him is inside.

Then they vanish through the other side of the storehouse. Something stinks like a fart. Maybe the guy voided himself. She saw a lot of dying animals do that in her veterinary program.

"Come on." Kamran ushers her toward the lift.

They have to wait for it to return, since it left with the unfortunate worker on the stretcher. Shy looked up the huntsman spider after everyone told her not to worry. Those were supposed to be brown. The one she'd seen was black as night.

What the fuck is down there?

Is it biting people?

She's trying to puzzle through how she's going to bow out of this job when the elevator doors open. On the other side stand three HCC security guards with stun sticks drawn.

"Cheyenne Hunt," one intones in accented English. "Come with us."

8

RED CARPET

"I told you they were spies!" Haroun bellows. "Where did you find them?"

Kamran has been sitting in the boardroom on the top floor of Ops for the better part of an hour. He pinches the bridge of his nose, but the pain won't go away. His sinuses are raw after being down in Storehouse Forty-Four. That can't be good.

He sighs. "You and Reza hired them—"

"We hired McAllen! Who knows who showed up? Huh? The Americans could've sent anyone! Maybe replaced them. They'd do that."

"Have you called Mr. McAllen?" Kamran asks. "Maybe he could shed some light."

"They're from McAllen, Texas." Haroun laughs, but it's fake and he works himself up. "Fowler owns the company. You'd know that if you knew how to do your job!"

Tiran Shirazi, the CTO, and Pezhvok Joshgani, head of IT, sit across the table, the other side of a battle line. Kamran sits by himself on a losing team of one. This is Reza's responsibility, yet Kamran is taking on blame for the contractors and the execution.

"What are you doing down there, that I don't know?" Kamran demands as forcefully as he can manage. "Why would spies be targeting that?" To drive the point home, he holds up a hand like he's pinching the air. "We have to work down there. I have to get back to Halo B, and I have a right to know if—"

"The situation has changed," Tiran says, taking a draw from her long-stem pipe. "In the last month."

Changed?

"A great deal," Haroun adds, crossing his arms.

Kamran would love to call Haroun out, right that second. The man's fury with McAllen Integrations is a farce, anyway. Haroun had Halo B's pilings moved long before the Americans ever got to Hasanova—the emails to Reza prove that much. But there's a glaring inconsistency in their story, and this may be a chance to learn more.

"If the situation has changed within the last thirty days, and the Americans have been in transit for six months, then they aren't spies sent from Earth," Kamran points out. "What is so sensitive that—"

"How do you know another ship didn't meet them?" Haroun's brow shimmers with sweat, and he rolls back his sleeves. Kamran has never seen him this mad, pounding the table whenever he needs to make a point. "Maybe the Americans sent a sleeper, just in case! Maybe a synthetic."

It takes a lot of willpower not to stand up and leave in the face of such paranoia.

"Well, I was present when Shy... Cheyenne Hunt took her blood test, so we don't have to worry about her," he says. "What about the rest of them? Why don't we just grab them and steal their blood, too?"

Haroun grabs up a cup of hot tea, and Kamran prepares for his superior to throw it on him.

"Maybe we *should*, then—"

"Mr. Sharif." Tiran raises a slender hand, and Haroun's anger goes out like a spent match.

Good. Kamran can talk some sense into Tiran. "What's happening in the lower levels? What's all of that work?" He remembers the screams, and the black veins. "What happened to that man on the stretcher?"

"That is none of your business, and I strictly forbade you from going down there," Haroun growls.

"Dr. Afghanzadeh," Tiran says, "we have already frozen the affected individual, preparing him for transport to a medical facility. He'll be in the best care soon enough. However, we have another concern. The *Gardenia* has received several encrypted transmissions from a nearby system. We think they're emails, but..."

"A comm relay, perhaps." Kamran shrugs. "I assume they have families to whom they might be talking. For all you know, they're managing their bank accounts."

Pezhvok clears his throat. "Perhaps, but we've had an escalating number of incursions into our systems, as well—"

"*Even if* they were master hackers," Kamran says, "they've already had almost root-level access to our control systems. Wouldn't we have seen something?"

"They may have installed scripts to run later," Tiran says. "I'd be less concerned if we *had* detected something coming from them. They might just be innocent, or at least ignorant. Right now, we have an unknown aggressor deliberately targeting us. Mr. Joshgani, when can you have your scan completed?"

"It'll take a few days," he says.

"Thank you," Tiran says, then she turns back to Kamran. "Doctor, please make yourself available for anything Pezhvok asks. Consider yourself on call." She excuses Pezhvok, who quietly retreats from their presence. "Dr. Afghanzadeh, you're not from Iran, are you?"

The memory of a long trek, sharp rocks, bitter cold, and Russian militiamen plays across his mind before he can answer.

"I'm not sure why that's relevant."

"I've met a lot of hard-working men like you," she replies. "Men who need money for families back home."

"My parents have passed." Kamran steeples his fingers and leans back in his chair. He rather hopes he gets fired, so he can escape this madhouse. "No siblings, just a lot of aunts, so I can safely say my loyalties are to country and company."

Her soft laugh reminds him of the parties and caviar at Eton. "I don't doubt it, but I want you to remember that if you're approached with any sort of offer—you're to come straight to me. No one else."

It warms Kamran's heart to see how much that annoys Haroun.

"I don't want to see things get out of hand." She mounts another cigarette to the stem and lights it, flames dancing in her eyes. "The state has taken a great interest in us. VAJA, in particular."

The Ministry of Intelligence.

"Why?" Kamran asks.

"Never mind that, you goat spawn," Haroun spits. "If it's VAJA, it's classified!"

"Because the safe transport and storage of data is the cornerstone of a republic," Tiran says. "We're critical infrastructure." She sighs, smoke roiling down from her nostrils. "ICSC has several players in the space, but in this arena we're positioned to be the premier provider. It will keep our country in contracts for decades. That makes us a tactical asset—do you see?"

Reza had said much the same thing.

Maybe Kamran hasn't considered a web host to be all that dangerous, or maybe he's been immersed in the simple day-to-day of their office culture—but Tiran's stern brow is enough to drive home the gravity of the situation. If she says it's serious, he has to agree.

"I understand."

"Good," Tiran replies, glancing meaningfully at Haroun. "Mr. Sharif can be overzealous, but we must respect his security decisions. He has training in these sorts of affairs." The vice-president of Operations has always been quick to brag about his military service, but this is the first time anyone else has given a damn.

"If things get out of hand," Tiran continues, "I'll defer to his expertise. So let's make sure everything remains civil, and avoid any escalations."

"Of course," Kamran says. "Where are the, uh, McAllen contractors? Are they safe?"

"I had them quarantined," Haroun says. "Confined to their rooms in the Human Centre."

"I'm sure that went over well." Kamran doesn't even want to imagine how furious they'll be.

Haroun sniffs, then honks into a handkerchief. "Maybe you could go and smooth things over for us." It's sarcasm, but Kamran has to agree.

"I think that would be prudent," he replies. "I'm the face of the commissioning project, after all."

Tiran nods her assent. "It's best if they're kept as happy as possible. We might not know for sure about their intentions, but—"

"We know enough," Haroun says. "Brewer is a criminal."

"What?" That actually surprises Kamran.

"Our background check turned up an assault charge fifteen years ago, in Boston, Massachusetts," Tiran says, eyes narrowing at Haroun. "A former girlfriend. His parents paid to have the records sealed, so it took us awhile to find out. That's bad, but it's not espionage."

"Wait, what?" Kamran sits up. "You've been doing background checks?"

"And keeping close tabs on them," Tiran adds.

He doesn't like the sound of that. "You had them followed?"

"Well, it's hard to do anything more sophisticated until SiteSys is linked into the cameras." She laughs. "Honestly, Afghanzadeh, don't look so disturbed. Maybe these people aren't related to the hacking attempts. Maybe it's sheer coincidence that one of them lured you to the dig site right as we had an... incident. Be thankful. The only reason I haven't called an ICSC Defense Squad to pick them up is... well, we had them tailed, and nothing exciting has been reported."

"That seems a bit extreme," Kamran replies.

"This is the relay backbone of an empire's data structure. Even the basics are extreme," Tiran says. "Go talk to them. Mr. Sharif, leave the security detail in place, but give the Americans anything they want—room service, whatever. Express your eagerness to open our larders. Treat them as honored guests."

"Yes, madame," Haroun says with a light bow, then he turns. "You can leave, Kamran. We've got important things to discuss."

Kamran exits the meeting room, more than a little disgusted. It shouldn't be like this. No one should be talking about the Defense Force. The last thing they need is to involve soldiers.

The fugue of annoyance clears as he exits the Thunder Ring back into the Human Centre. The Americans are trapped on the levels above, their ship without enough fuel to depart. He feels a little responsible; he'd held that fact over their heads when they'd tried to renegotiate.

Stopping by the cafeteria, he visits the executive stores—supplies for officers at Reza's level and above, but since Kamran is servicing Reza's responsibilities, he sees nothing wrong with taking some caviar. He assembles it on a silver tray, atop a cut crystal goblet full of ice. Using a pair of kitchen snips, he cuts some of the day's babari into points and toasts them on the gas range.

If he's going to have to face the Americans, he'll be armed with a present.

A lift ride later, he steps out onto their hallway. His heart jumps at the sight of two guards—muscular men in black turtlenecks and olive drab pants. They've taken over a small sitting area at the end of the hall where they obsess over a backgammon board. Kamran knows one of them, Mohammad, from the company football team. He lights up at seeing Kamran.

"Hey! What's up, long-arms? You haven't been showing up to practice," he says. "Kianoush, this is the guy I was telling you about."

"As tall as promised. Need to get you back on the team," Kianoush says, gesturing to an empty seat. "I see you brought our lunch!"

"Haven't had time to kick the ball, and the caviar is for the contractors," Kamran says. When they react with playful disappointment, he adds, "I'm so glad to see you two. Everyone else around here is wound tight."

"Don't you worry, long-arms," Mohammad says. "This is the best thing to happen in a while. We were supposed to be checking moorings in the storm, but look at us now." The security guard gestures to the velvet seats, tea, and backgammon, and Kamran has to admit he's right. It's way better than checking rusty moorings.

"I'll feel better when we quit overreacting," Kamran says. "Which room?"

"They're all in the last room on the left," Mohammad says. "What did they do?"

"Hopefully, nothing." Kamran glances down the hall to the door. "Are they behaving?"

The two guards laugh and exchange glances before Kianoush says, "The lesbian—Joanna I think—has a filthy mouth."

"I'll keep that in mind," Kamran says. "Wish me luck." As he begins walking toward the door, Mohammad calls after him.

"Hey, if they try to strangle you, just scream." Then the pair burst out laughing.

He walks to the end of the hall, where a rectangular

window looks out onto the colony proper. Flecks of rain slash through the night like sparks in the floodlights. The Data Cannon hangs over Charybdis, red beacons pulsing gently as a warning to aircraft. When all this is over, he'll have to link the data storehouses to the cannon—provided he still has a job.

He gives the door plate a light kick, and Jerry Fowler responds.

"Come."

When Kamran steps into the parlor, he finds the entire McAllen crew much worse for wear. Shy sits on the ledge of the room's panoramic window, framed by the omnipresent storm. She glares at Kamran as he enters. Joanna and Arthur seem to be playing it cool with a deck of cards and a pack of cigarettes at the kitchenette table. Noah sits on the floor, a portable terminal in his lap and headphones in his ears. Jerry stands behind the couch over his wife, who looks like she's been delivered a death sentence.

Kamran doesn't know Mary Fowler well, but he's guessing "captured by Iranians" scares the shit out of her.

"I'll take that." Marcus is standing at his side, scaring the life out of him. Kamran jerks, shocked that their synthetic could've snuck up on him. He hands the tray over.

"My name is Marcus," the synthetic says in Farsi.

"Why does he keep doing that?" Kamran asks as Marcus takes the caviar to the serving island and begins arranging it.

"Bad memory core," Jerry says. "That's not nearly as bad as forgetting to tell us about whatever the hell you're doing down in Charybdub—"

"Charybdis," Shy says.

"I assure you," Kamran says, "everything is under control."

"Listen, man," Arthur says. The big fellow doesn't look up from his hand of cards. "Your people came and got us, dragged us into this room, and won't let us out. That sound 'under control' to you?"

"What happened down there?" Shy asks. "That guy… what's wrong with him?" She seems frightened, and he can't blame her. Again he remembers the screams. Kamran got a good look at the victim in the storehouse. There was a cut on his shoulder, puckered, black, surrounded by dark veins. It looked like some sort of infection.

Though the water of Lake Peacock is mildly acidic, it's far from deadly. Plenty of bacteria inhabit the ecosystem— extremophiles that'd chew the exterior off the colony buildings if the metal wasn't treated annually. During Kamran's first year, they brought in an exobiologist, a Dr. Lloyd, who warned them there might be complex life near the "black smokers," geothermal vents under the lake. However, those creatures didn't hang out near the surface, so no one cared.

Before now.

"I don't know," Kamran says. "Even if I did, I couldn't discuss it."

"Let me translate that," Noah interjects. "You know everything, and you're keeping it to yourself."

Kamran raises his hands. "I don't. I really mean that. I know as much as you."

"Whatever." Noah has the temerity to meet his gaze. "You're a lying government stooge. It's your fault we're in here, and you can suck my dick."

Taking a few verbal jabs from his boss is one thing. The man is Iranian, and knows when to back down. Even Haroun's most vicious insult to his parentage doesn't compare to the rage induced by this cocky foreigner.

"I don't have to take that from a criminal like you," he hisses.

Brewer sets the laptop aside and climbs to his feet. "We're not criminals, you fucking—"

"I'm not talking about espionage," Kamran says as he closes the distance between them. "I'm talking about assault—"

"Gimme a hand here!" Brewer calls out, and the others are on Kamran in a second. Jerry and Joanna each grab a shoulder, and Arthur muscles between them. Even Shy is off the ledge, halfway across the room if she needs to intercede.

"Crew always backs crew," Brewer says.

It's hard for Kamran to maintain his angry stare in the face of a powerful man like Arthur Atwater. What Kamran has in reach, Arthur has in every department. In boxing club, Kamran would've had to train for months to face down someone like him.

A dish clatters from the suite's kitchen, and Kamran spots Marcus staring at them as he goes about his duties. Probably pretending not to pay attention so it doesn't escalate the fight, but a Marcus could put any of them on the floor. Kamran has heard of people removing the limiters in their synthetics, to allow them to commit harm. Maybe that's why it's so twitchy.

Arthur leans in close and whispers into his ear. "Please do not make me kick your ass for Noah. Step back and figure out how to deal with what he said, like an adult."

Kamran nods, and Jerry, Arthur, and Joanna all visibly relax. At least he gave them a good scare before having to deal with Brewer's gloating expression.

"I apologize for my anger," Kamran says.

"It's all good," Arthur replies. "I've got kids. I know how it goes. This lockdown thing has us all a little spooked, am I right?"

Shy's eyes meet Kamran's. He tries to give her a reassuring nod, but she's not able to hold his gaze.

Arthur takes in the room's awkward silence. "Marcus, the man brought some caviar. What do you say we figure out how to get this thing back on track? We could all do with a little normality right now."

"That sounds like an excellent idea, Arthur," Marcus agrees, arriving with Kamran's silver serving tray, rearranged to contain a few full teacups. The synthetic did a much better job than Kamran, stealing some flowers from a nearby vase to add an accent.

Jerry slides onto a couch beside Mary. "I don't see how the job is supposed to recover from this."

"We came out here because we agreed to a contract, right?" Arthur looks to his compatriots for approval. "That's why we're going to figure out how to make this work. We need fuel if we want to leave here, and that means we have to figure out how to salvage things."

"No," Shy says. "I'm done here. I'm not going down there."

"And you won't have to," Arthur says. "No one is going down the Spiral. All you have to do is—"

"You didn't see what I saw," Shy says. "You didn't see that guy on the stretcher. If you had, you wouldn't set a foot down there."

A flash fills the window behind Shy, and she swears in surprise. The world outside, dim waves in the murky night, is thrown into sharp sunset by moving lights overhead. Shadows dance in the gloom, growing longer as the source of illumination passes the colony. Whatever the object may be, it enters the frame of the window. Kamran sees five bright orbs—the nozzles of starship engines.

The last supply ship left two weeks ago. There isn't supposed to be another transport for weeks yet. It doesn't look like one of the brutal ICSC Defense Force patrol corvettes, but details are sparse in the night. Colony searchlights fire beams into the darkness, but the ship moves so fast, it's out of range before they can lock on to the hull.

Why didn't it dock at the colony?

Kamran rushes to the window and follows the progress of the orbs until they wink out. Either it settled into the water or onto one of the nearby islands.

"Friends of yours?" Shy asks.

Kamran looks to her. She doesn't know who it is—that much is certain from the worry in her eyes. He runs down the list of people who might want to land off-schedule:

A ship in trouble—but why not land by the colony?

A military vessel—but they'd land at the colony, too, right?

Pirates, preparing an assault?

Spies?

None of those will sit well with Haroun. If the ship isn't something he expects, that military background of his will go into overdrive. He'd just love to impose martial law.

As if on cue, the door opens. Mohammad and Kianoush stand at the precipice. Mohammad speaks in Farsi.

"Step out of the room, Doctor."

"What's happening?" Kamran responds.

"Orders from the top." Mohammad's hand rests on his stun stick. "We're taking them to a secure location."

"But—"

"Sharif told us not to let you interfere," Mohammad says. "You can take it up with him."

Kamran looks to the contractors, none of whom have understood a word of what was said.

"I'm sorry," he intones to his guests in gentle English. "I'll do what I can."

9

CASTLE OF NIGHT

Shy's head aches, and the rest of her feels numb. The tiny cell they threw her into contains a pair of bunk beds, a sink, and a toilet, but no windows other than a little porthole in the door. She sits atop one of the bunks, leaning against Mary's warm shoulder. Joanna looks out the porthole like she's planning an escape, or maybe a one-woman riot.

Ironically, Shy had been scheduled to commission this cell's lights later this week. Without control links, no one can turn them off. After a few hours, the glare has begun to wear on her.

The situation is playing out exactly as the State Department warned them it would. She and her companions are all alone on the edge of space, at the mercy of a foreign government. No one could agree on the sector's jurisdiction, so no one will be coming to help.

"I never should've come here," Shy whispers.

Joanna wheels on them. "Did you know that's the third time you've said that?"

"Joanna, you cut it out." Mary squeezes Shy tightly, her sweet perfume a reminder of the *Gardenia*.

"I'm just tired of Captain Obvious over there." The mechanic gives Shy a terrifying look. "We know we shouldn't have come, Shy! What are we going to do about it?"

"One more of those and you're fired," Mary snaps. "This ain't easy, so I'll give you that one for free. Come at her again, and you'll be out the door at Gateway Station."

Joanna runs her fingers through her hair. It's grown, but still spiky. "My anxiety meds are back in my room, okay? Weepy over there is making things look pretty fucking grim."

"I'm sorry," Shy says. "You're right."

"And I didn't mean to snap at you, dear child, I really didn't," Joanna says, clasping her hands together like she's praying for forgiveness. "But you were being fucking obnoxious, and I'm sure we can all laugh about this over margaritas when we get somewhere that knows how to party."

"You think Marcus is okay?" Shy asks.

Joanna laughs bitterly. "I don't think he's worried about anything after taking a stun that hard. They probably left him drooling where he fell."

"Don't talk about him like that," Shy says.

"Just fucking it up all around today, I guess," Joanna mutters.

Even down in the basement of Ops, Shy hears the pounding of the waves. This deep inside, it's dull, like the hushed breath of sleep. When she first arrived, the undulating pink noise brought serenity. Now, it only reminds her that this place is alive, and not friendly. She imagines something from deep down inside Charybdis, reaching up through the Maw—its bloody rock splitting and spilling forth fleshy shapes.

"How do you think the boys are doing?" she asks, hoping to take her mind off it.

"I'm sure they're fine." Mary pats her arm. "They didn't fight—not like Marcus. There's no reason to hurt them." It sounds as if she's trying to convince herself, though.

A door slams open down the corridor, and the jangle of chains fills the air.

Guards are coming.

Shy squirms backward against Mary, willing herself to blend into the walls. When the door opens, Kamran stands there, flanked by two security officers. His expression is ashen, and he beckons for the women to stand up.

They don't.

"We're going to check out that ship," he says.

"The fuck does that have to do with us?" Joanna spits back at him, and one of the guards tenses. Some of them actually seem pretty scared of her. Kamran motions for calm.

"One of you will come along."

"The hell we will!" Mary shouts, and the men in the next cell start calling out. Shy doubts they can tell what's going on through the metal bulkhead, but given the raised voices, they know to be upset. One of the security officers starts yelling in Farsi before striking the cell door a few times with his baton. Each hit sounds like a gunshot, and Shy flinches, but the shouting dies down.

"Why bring one of us?" Shy asks, but fears she already knows the answer.

"Haroun wants one of you there in case... in case it's some kind of trick. If this is a military operation, sent on your behalf," Kamran says, then a look of shame crosses his face. "Haroun has asked for... for someone the journalists will care about."

He doesn't mean Jerry or Mary. They're too old to conjure public outcry. He doesn't mean Joanna, who is far too masculine for media stardom. By that measure Noah is boring, and Arthur is both black and male. They won't bring in the ratings.

Not like sweet, small-town Cheyenne Hunt from McAllen, Texas, whose nice prom pictures will be put up on a broadcast. She'd be a marketable tragedy.

"No, please..." she sobs.

"You'll be in the back of the security detail, with me," Kamran says.

"Fuck that shit!" Joanna is halfway to the guard before he gets his stun stick prongs leveled in her direction. She stops inches away from the arcing tip, reconsidering her assault, then looks to Kamran. "Dude! You can't be going along with this!"

"Do you think I have a choice?" he asks. "I'm just the interpreter."

Joanna gives him a poisonous look. "'Just following orders,' huh? I'm pretty sure we still shoot people who fall back on that defense."

He deflates. "It's either I come with Miss Hunt as her interpreter, or I remain behind while she accompanies the security force alone. It's already been decided that she's going."

Shy's stomach tumbles, and she thinks she might vomit. The HCC forces could do anything they wanted to her out there, Kamran or no. Just the two guards with him would be enough to overpower both of them. She locks gazes with Kamran, boring into his brown eyes. He tries to give her a comforting look, but she shakes her head no.

"I'll leave it to you, Shy," he says, holding out a hand into the cell. "Do you want me to come with you, or not?"

"You don't have to go with them at all," Mary whispers into Shy's ear, holding her so tightly it almost hurts. "He's not going to hit an old woman."

Mary is scared, but from the tightness of her grip, Shy knows for sure—that "old woman" will gladly take a swing on her behalf. Shy can't accept that, either. No one needs to get hurt. She peels Mary's fingers off her shoulder and rises to her feet.

"You should come, Kamran," Shy says, voice scratchy. Then, to Joanna, she adds, "It's just a ship. I'll be back soon."

Her confidence takes her as far as the hall. The corridor stretches ahead of her like a pathway to the gallows, and she stops. Her feet refuse to take another step. The guards stop and wait on her.

She holds out her hand to Kamran. "Promise you're not going to hurt me." He gives her a pained smile, and takes her fingers for a moment before letting go.

"I promise. Let's get this behind us."

"Okay. Yeah, okay."

They pass through the Thunder Ring, headed for the motor pool. There they join two dozen security personnel and militiamen. There can't be more than ten official police for the entire colony, which means the majority of these people aren't full-time.

They're mostly just frightened, armed men.

Kamran talks to them as they prepare, loading assault rifles and webbing harnesses. They stare at Shy, not angry—worried. They're afraid of her, of what she might mean. In each of their eyes, she sees the thought, *"What have you done, American?"* Someone plops a pair of rubbery gray coveralls with huge muddy boots into her arms, and Shy fumbles them.

"Dress," a man says in terrible English.

So she sits down on a plastic transit case and evaluates her new PPE—frayed suspenders, muddy, size twelve boots with basically tire treads on the bottom. She wore similar stuff tending herds, so she slips the garment over her clothes like a diving suit. Her own boots lock snugly into the larger ones, but the rest of the outfit hangs off her like a trash bag.

"Shy," Kamran says. He's climbed onto the cage of a hovercraft and holds out his hand. The hatch is open, and eight Iranian faces stare back at her from the crew compartment. The other men are piling into two more vehicles, still eyeing her to see what she'll do.

She climbs aboard, the sand and mud of a dozen construction jobs underfoot. This isn't an assault vehicle; it's an industrial transport. It's not for combat, and she imagines how easily gunfire will ventilate it as she settles down onto the hard canvas cushions. She tells herself it's like riding in a starship as she buckles her five-point restraint. Maybe she'll be fine, maybe she won't. It's out of her hands, because someone else is in control.

The man closest to the driver's compartment bangs on the divider. "*Bereem digeh!*"

The engine turns over and the hovercraft buzzes to life. It lurches before gently wafting into the air, which does little to relieve Shy's panic-induced nausea. Through the tiny windows on the side, she watches the vehicle bay spin around them. She is officially allowing her kidnappers to take her to a second location.

They pass through a pair of doors and down a ramp before blasting out over the surface of the water. Though they're not directly against the waves, they fly in the ground effect zone, ramping over little crests like a cantering pony. Shy has plenty of equestrian experience, so she shuts her eyes and tries to remember what it was like in the fields near Texas A&M. She can almost smell the sweet musk, hear the whip of the tall, hill country grass against her custom Ariats.

"Are you feeling all right?" Kamran whispers. His interruption steals the vision from her head.

"You've got to be joking."

"Of course. Sorry."

"Can I ask where you're taking me?"

"We tracked the vessel to the nearest island. We call it Ghasreh Shab."

"What does that mean?"

Kamran leans forward, resting his elbows on his knees. "'Palace of Night.'"

The most official-looking man in their craft starts rattling Farsi at her like she's been speaking it every day of her life, and she wants to scream at him that she doesn't fucking understand. His name badge says "AKBARI."

"He says to follow the security team exactly," Kamran translates. "Don't ever stray for any reason. Don't touch any puddles. They could be pools of, ah, they could be pools of acid." He adds, "Best to listen to him. He knows this terrain well."

Akbari drives this home by making a claw with his hand and miming agony.

"What?" Shy should've fought back. "He can go fuck himself! I'm not getting out this goddamned—"

Akbari's expression flattens into a knife-sharp gaze, and he points at Shy.

"Screw you," she responds. "I'm not going to Death Island just because you—"

"Shy, be quiet!" Kamran says, jostling her. "I—he's not someone you want to insult. Please, just... just cooperate."

No one is going to stand up for her.

She's going to die out here.

"There's a lot of geothermal activity," Kamran says as they pass around a set of velcro-backed tags. The men stick them onto patches on their webbing harnesses, flicking switches on the plastic housings. Lights on the tags flash green three times, then go out. Akbari is still explaining things at a mile a minute, and Shy wants to tell him to slow down so Kamran doesn't miss anything.

The tags come to Shy and she takes one, but has nowhere to stick it, so she awkwardly clutches it in one hand.

Kamran holds his up and points to the LED. "If you see these tags go red and start beeping, you run back to the craft. Don't wait for anything. It means there's poison gas. It's heavier than air, and it can build up in caves and crevasses."

"Is there anything else you want to tell me?" She wipes the corner of her eye.

"I'm with you. I have a lot of experience in these environments," he says. "You're going to be okay as long as I'm here."

They ride the next fifteen minutes in silence, gently bouncing across the lake. Periodically a storm surge passes close to them, sending water into the engine intake, and the ship lists and crunches as if it hit an iceberg.

Akbari begins calling new information to Kamran over the din of the hovercraft, and the scientist doesn't translate—just listens intently. Their maneuvers become more erratic, and they slow, settling onto the choppy waves. The engine rumbles low, and all motion slows to the swaying of the water.

"What's he saying?"

"We're here," Kamran replies.

No, I'm sure he said a lot more than that.

The ramp whines open, splashing into the dark liquid beyond. Searchlights from the hovercraft illuminate a shoreline of jagged rocks, glittering in the gloom. It seems so very far away to Shy, but the security team clicks on flashlights and files out into the water. They leap, one by one, into the waist-deep surf, holding their rifles over their heads.

Then Kamran hops down and holds out a hand for her to follow. This planet is home to a grotesque infection, and he wants her to jump into murky acid water. She shakes her head no.

"*Zood bosh!*" Akbari barks, and Kamran gives her a tense look.

"Shy," Kamran urges. "It's just a little brackish."

She dips a foot down into the water, which rolls over

her boot. She eases in up to her thigh, but still can't feel the bottom. Floodlights from the hovercraft do nothing to penetrate the green murk. Shadowy fingers creep into her imagination, slick and cold as corpses, caressing her ankle, and she chases the thought away.

Choppy water rocks the hovercraft, dumping her face-first off the ramp and into Lake Peacock. A wave flops inside her trash bag, dousing her tiny body in icy water. Sour liquid pours into her mouth. She struggles to find her footing against jagged rocks, but Kamran drags her upright. Her waders are full to the brim, and she sloshes over to the shoreline, coughing and spluttering.

"You're all right now," Kamran soothes, coming to her side.

"I don't want to go to that ship, Kamran," she says, restraining her tears. "I can't do this. I can wait here."

"I don't either, but—"

Akbari turns and begins splashing in her direction, angry rifts in his brow. He slings his rifle and pulls a pair of ziptie cuffs from his utility belt.

"Okay, okay!" Shy says, clambering upright with hands held high. Going to the ship is bad. Going in there with her hands tied would be worse.

They mount the shore, clambering up sharp, rusty volcanic stone, pitted through like rotten teeth. Each striking wave sends the fetid breath of the lake wafting up through the pile of broken rock and into Shy's face.

It's only a few more feet, she tells herself. *Not steep. Just sharp.*

They reach a level spot, and the security team musters up. Shoulder lamps click on, casting beams into the gloom. Where the igneous rock is dry, it's carbon black, absorbing most of the light. Shy triggers the warming cycle of her coat, never more thankful to have industrial gear. Heating elements and hydrophobic synthetic goose down wick away the water on her torso and chest, making her icy legs almost tolerable.

A valley stretches before them, twin mountains cutting silhouettes out of the storm clouds. Broken bits of porous stone have tumbled from the hillsides to form a path. Shy hugs herself, her contractor's jacket and waders the only shelter against this remote place.

Akbari gathers everyone up and announces something. Kamran listens intently, then translates for Shy.

"It's a bit of a walk. The ship landed on a flat patch east of here. Stay by me. Stay quiet."

They trudge along the path for half an hour, then kill the lights and turn on night scopes. There are only ten between them, so Shy and Kamran each have to hold onto a taciturn militiaman to navigate the trail. Their hike steepens, and Shy balances as they ascend the loose detritus of a hill. There's a luminous mist ahead, and against it she can almost make out the figures of her scouting party. They crest the ridge line, and she sees the source of illumination.

If Satan himself traveled by starship, this could be his ride.

She's reluctant to call it a ship, at first. It has all the hallmarks of a spacefaring vessel, engines, struts, running lights, and a bridge. Scarred paint declares "Blackstar" across its battered surface. Crusty, smoking formations of organic material coat portions of its hull, almost like scorched bone. The clumps near the engines burn brightly, dripping flaming debris onto the ground below.

"They're going to set up scanners," he says. "We need to move away." They head back down the hill, careful not to slide down the loose gravel into the darkness beyond. Shy never thought she'd be grateful to hide in the shadows of an alien world, but there's no way in hell she's going into that ship.

A tiny green screen pierces the darkness up the hill, along with a quiet beep. Hushed conversations in Farsi follow. Shy strains to hear names—the only thing she has a chance of translating. Whatever they're saying, the hissed whispers tell Shy they have strong opinions.

"I'll be right back," Kamran says. "Don't move." He eases away from her. She reaches after him, but he's already gone. No one has a hand on her. No one can see her right now. She could just run off, if she wanted to.

This place would swallow her alive.

Shy sits to hold her freezing, rubber-bagged legs while she shivers and waits. She almost screams when a heavy hand falls on her shoulder.

"They spotted movement near here, along with a cave," Kamran says. "Ready to go?"

"No," she says, but she stands and follows.

Their fumbling path through broken rock doesn't take them close to the ship, somehow skirting it through the natural features. Shy keeps her eyes wide open, thirsty for any light at all. A tiny red lamp emerges from the darkness, weak but growing brighter with each step. She works to decipher other shapes, and thinks she can make out some straight lines.

A flashlight clicks on, throwing a metal wall into bright relief. There's a small arch carved into the rock, barricaded with a thick hatch. Sooty dust covers its surface, and one of the militiamen gestures to the source of red light: a keypad.

Akbari draws closer and inspects it, then wipes off the hatch with a sleeve. The acid yellow of a logo comes shining through.

When he speaks, there's clear astonishment. Other excited voices join his as the rest of the security team gathers around. Someone says something about Haroun, and Kamran's hand squeezes hers a little too tightly.

"What is it? What are they saying."

"'Someone call Haroun,'" Kamran replies. "'We've got another one.'"

1 0

DEPARTURES

A pair of perfectly horizontal scratch marks mar the
metal, shiny as a mirror on the rusted surface of the
door. Someone has been through here recently, sliding
the portal open—yet it takes the security team a good
half hour to get it pried open.

"No power," a member of the party says, stepping
into the darkness.

"Why would there be?" comes the hissed response.
The team files into the corroded antechamber one by
one until there are only three people remaining outside:
Kamran, Shy, and the rear guard, Setareh.

"Come on, Shy."

"Kamran, don't make me do this. I can't go in there."

"If I had a choice..." He watches her eyes, a pair of
dim glints in the flashlight. She's shaking, but standing
tall. *You're a monster, Kamran. She's innocent. Do something.*

"The sooner we go in, the sooner we come out," he says. "One foot in front of the other, yes?"

"Stiff upper lip?" She laughs a bit when she mocks his posh accent.

"Pip pip, cheerio, and all that," he adds with gentle reassurance, placing a hand on her shoulder and applying pressure toward the door. He half hopes she'll keep resisting. He doesn't have the heart to force her.

Despite what he wants, they cross the threshold.

"Stay in front of me," Setareh cautions him. She gives her rifle a shake to punctuate the command, and Kamran gets the impression she doesn't like Shy all that much.

The antechamber is large enough to receive everyone, but only barely. Shy points up at the ceiling, and Kamran switches on a glow bar, holding it aloft so they can take a closer look. It takes him a moment to see what she's indicating.

"Nozzles," she says. "What did they pump into here?"

He reaches up and runs a finger along the edge of one of the conical heads at the end of a pipe. They almost look like showers or sprinklers, and red rust crumbles over his finger.

"The weather seal must've failed," he says. "This whole place is leaking."

"It's a class two A airlock," she says, moving toward one of the corners. The other members of the security team part ahead of her, curious at her willingness to look. She squats in front of an empty box, its glass broken. "A suit would've gone here. I've helped install cabinets like this, but, you know... newer."

Kamran joins her, illuminating the aged space to find the silhouettes of removed equipment. "There was no atmosphere when this place was built, then. Pre-Russian." A hand squeezes Kamran's arm. He turns to find Captain Akbari's stern glare.

"Shut her up," he whispers in Farsi, "or I will. No more talking. Silence or screaming. Those are her choices."

"Screaming," Kamran repeats with acid rising in his throat.

Akbari's smile could curdle milk. "Maybe in pain. Maybe not."

"Get out of my face," Kamran replies, peeling the bastard's fingers off, "or I'll break yours later."

The captain tongues the inside of his mouth, weighing his options. Kamran imagines he's safe from any reprisal, if only because fisticuffs aren't exactly stealthy. He kind of wishes Akbari would throw a punch. He's said some gross things in the past, and Kamran has had it with him.

They move to the next door, and it screeches open, revealing a corridor descending gradually into darkness. Grates run along the floor, conduit and pipes line the wall—the old Weyland style of colony building. Unlike the outside, there is no rust, only the snowy sheen of old, unpolished metal.

He and Shy bring up the rear as they move in, watching as the security team flashlights robotically sweep the surroundings. As tall as he is, Kamran can see over everyone's heads. Doors indicate rooms on either side. Their path carries onward as far as he can discern, disappearing in shadow.

A fork opens to the right, with more of the same tangle of metal walls and grated floors. Captain Akbari orders his people to sweep down the passages, setting up a perimeter, then calls to them to check the rooms. Teams of shooters disappear into the darkness.

They wait in utter silence, and each second stretches on for an eternity. Only the radio calls—whispers bookended by static pops—pierce the quiet. Kamran's eyes strain wide, and he thinks of all the stories of men going mad underground. Then Setareh nudges him with the butt of her gun, and he almost cries out.

"Afghanzadeh, you're needed. Move up."

Shy starts to come, but Setareh grabs her sleeve. "Not you," she says in accented English. "You stay."

"It's okay," Kamran says to Shy.

"It's not," Shy replies. "Don't leave me here."

But he has to go. He can't afford to let the security forces hate him as much as Reza's old team. His reputation is already dangling by a thread. Kamran shoulders through the pack of guards, down the passageway, and finds an opening.

They've reached a lab.

He creeps inside. The room is at least as large as Haroun's ridiculous office, filled with all sorts of biology equipment: sample trays and pipettes, glassware, dryboxes, microscopes, and cameras. Kamran sweeps his glow bar over the nearest countertop, finding a bunch of empty sample tubes and plastic tops. His own shadow looms, cast by flashlights at his back. When he looks at the way he came, no one has followed him.

"Don't worry. It's clear," Captain Akbari says. "What is it?"

The ceilings here are high, maybe six meters or more, and various gasifiers and distillate columns encircle the room. Everything above him is a dense maze of dark pipes and decaying insulation. He has no way of knowing how far up they extend, but there's significant liquid routing capability. Perhaps they were working on biofuel.

"Hard to say," Kamran replies.

"Fuck!" It's Shy, and with her outburst comes the rustling of webbing and body armor. "What the fuck was that?"

Akbari disappears from the doorframe.

"Hey," Kamran calls out. "Send her in here." When no one moves to comply, he adds, "I need her help identifying some of this equipment."

"Fine," the nearest man replies, sending down the line for her. When she arrives, her face is blotchy in his green light.

"Sorry," she says. "I'm sorry. Someone touched my leg. I think. I don't know. I'm… I'm sorry."

Kamran isn't keen to hash it out in front of the security

people, so he points to a boxy piece of equipment that looks like a centrifuge.

"What do you suppose this is?" he asks in English.

"I don't know." She's not paying attention to the box. She's looking back at the guards. He can't have her going back out there with Akbari's people.

"What's it for, though?"

"I... I don't know, Kamran."

He leans down and whispers. "Please look, and let's guess, so you can remain in here with me."

"It, uh..." she says, "it looks like some of the blood testing equipment we used to use for horses." Then she adds, "Like a Fisher Sequencer."

Sure enough, he wipes away the dusty label and finds the words "Fisher Scientific."

"I'd call that a decent wager," he breathes, discomfited. She's supposed to be an interface developer; Haroun would be beside himself with paranoia upon hearing her guess, and Kamran wonders if he'd be justified. "How did you know that?"

"I was in vet med," Shy says. "But this isn't the ship. You said we were going to the ship. I don't want to go there, either, but you promised—"

"I know, I'm sorry. Just hold on a little while longer."

He pulls the spring latch, opening the front cover to find thousands of tiny test tubes arrayed on the base, and needle pipettes in neat rows along the top. There's a sample collection section in the back, but he can't figure out what's inside—whatever it is has rotted to jet black. He spies a handle to remove the cassette, clearly marked by a half-dozen stickers.

"So this is all medical gear?" he says.

"Not everything."

He turns to see her pointing at a drybox. There's a glint of mottled glass underneath the hood. He wipes away the dust to find what looks like an icicle inside, plugged on one end by a metal filament. He calls for one of the security force, and Akbari steps cautiously into the room. The man shines his white flashlight over it. The glass is green, like an ancient bottle of Coca-Cola, covered in shallow bumps. He spots a much smaller piece in the corner of the box, about the size of a golf ball, teardrop-shaped with a crack at the taper.

It's an ampoule, but for what?

He looks around for some nitrile gloves, and locates a box of them. When he opens it, they've clearly spoiled, coming out like sheets of dead skin.

"What are you doing?" Shy asks.

"We should bring back a sample." He snaps at Akbari and points to the gloves on his utility belt. "Give me a pair. A baggie, too."

He pulls on the gloves and heads over to the piece of Fisher equipment. He doesn't want to open the drybox, since he has no idea what that ampoule contained, but the sample collector looked like it was still sealed. Pushing the little door aside, he takes hold of the container release.

"Careful," Shy says.

"Easy as pie," he grunts, but it's not. The knob is stuck, and he gives it another turn with a bit more force.

"Afghanzadeh, leave that alone," Akbari says. "We've got to keep moving."

"It's fine. Just a bit stuck, and—"

It clicks free under pressure, and Kamran draws back a lot harder than he intended. His hand crashes into the roof of the box, and a sharp pain runs up the side of his index finger.

"Ah!" he hisses, pulling back to find a long cut from one of the needles, blood welling under his glove.

"Shit." Shy takes hold of his glow bar to inspect the cut. "You okay?"

"Yeah," he says. "Need to get some disinfectant, though. Probably a tetanus shot."

Then it starts to itch.

What the hell is it?

Pain wells in his fingertip, and it feels as if it's going to split. He yelps in panic, ripping off his glove as Shy tries to get a closer look. Every threshold of flensing agony gives way to another—a needle becomes a knife becomes a sword. The agony crawls over his finger, into the rest of his hand.

Khoda, save me! What did I do?

He holds his quivering digit up to his face, blood stained black by the green light of the glow bar. His veins bulge around the cut, throbbing gray under his skin. Except they're not veins. Something is burrowing into him.

He should shout for help. That's the only sensible thing to do in this situation. They have to get it off of him—out of him, and fast. It's infectious. Tourniquet? What'll stop it?

The screaming man in Storehouse Forty-Four—he had this crawling inside his neck.

Another sharp pain slices across his wrist as blood boils up over the surface in terrible welts. It's as if Kamran is cooking, or melting, and panic sets its claws into him. He sucks a breath through clenched teeth to cry out for any medical attention he can get.

But the hissing noise doesn't end just because he stopped. There's something above him, up in the pipes, and he holds up his light to try and find the source. If there's a gas leak, and he's got a raging infection...

Nothing could be more important than his hand, right? But he spies movement above, something the size of a human. He thrusts his glow bar upward in terror, raking the shadows for a form.

Instantly, he regrets it.

Kamran stands beneath a demon of black bone, tangled into the mass of pipes above him. Rays of acidic light run along every blasphemous curve and malformed nodule. The crest of its head undulates in queer waves. He only knows this is the creature's head because of the full, soft lips parting gently at the forefront, a slick, barbed tongue hungrily darting between them.

Dark flesh pulls back, revealing a mouth of jagged obsidian teeth—a child's drawing of a nightmare.

Then further, a snake's jaws.

Impossibly wider, the yawning gates of an abyss.

He hears a scream, but doesn't know who uttered it.

The creature uncoils downward, locking its jaws around his infected arm. Glassy incisors slice through his weak flesh like a butcher's knife. After all his travails, all of his experiences, he knows in that moment he is meat.

Khoda save me.

It wrenches its head, yanking his elbow into shattered chunks. Tendons shred under the stress but don't pop, and the world spins as Kamran is thrown bodily from his feet. It's upon him, ribs skeletal, a vertebral tail whipping about and scattering lab equipment. The crest of the creature's head buzzes and rattles like the beating of a thousand cockroach wings, and Kamran is screaming now.

Everyone is screaming now.

The demon launches for the door, and Kamran wishes his hand had come off with it—but human tendons are strong, and he's dragged by flesh that refuses to detach. Shouts and grasping hands buffet him as his conqueror hauls him past the security team, knocking them aside. Akbari gets a hold of Kamran's trouser leg, but a swift pull by the beast dislodges him.

And then the creature is bounding down the corridor with Kamran in its jaws. His glow bar spills from his fingertips, clattering to the grating. The green light recedes into darkness, along with his doomed thoughts.

1 1

DISTRESS CALL

"Christ, Shy!" It's Noah, she thinks. "What the fuck did you do to her? Hey, fuck you! Don't you fucking touch me! Shy! Shy, are you—"

"Whose blood is this, Cheyenne? Can you hear me, baby? Whose blood is this all over her? Oh, God, Jerry, look at her!"

It's Mary's voice. She presses Shy's head against her bosom and gently strokes her hair. It's like lying on a warm, overstuffed pillow, and for a moment, the shaking subsides.

"No, you've had your fun!" Jerry joins in. "You take us to your boss and—"

"Just give her some space! Fuck's sake, you filthy—" Is that Joanna?

"All right, Mary, we're going to need to check her for injuries. Shy, can you look at me?" When she looks up at the speaker, she finds Arthur's deep brown eyes. He's so beautiful, it's like seeing an angel after escaping Hell. "What happened?" he asks, voice deep and soothing, like the purring of a great cat.

They're back in their suite in the Human Centre with a couple of security guards. How did she get here? There was so much screaming. Her head hurts. She lifts up her shirt, and there's a pair of little bruises on her stomach, like a snake bite, surrounded by angry red welts.

Arthur's face darkens, and he rises to his full height.

"Did you fucking taze her?"

The security goons back up a step, shouting something in Farsi. Quick as lightning, Arthur snatches away one of their stun sticks and shoves the wielder to the ground. When the other guy goes to take a swing, Arthur relieves him of his stun stick, too.

"Arthur!" Mary cries.

"Kamran is dead," Shy says, voice barely a whisper, and they stop fighting. "Something ate him. Like… an animal or… I couldn't stop… stop screaming. That's why they—"

The security people bristle, calling orders at Arthur that he couldn't possibly understand.

"Fetch," he says, hurling both of the stun sticks out the open door, where they clatter into the hall. "What? You want to go after I took your fucking toys?"

The pair of guards do not. They leave the McAllen contractors alone, and the group closes around Shy. Again, the questions come, and Shy answers them by spewing vomit across Jerry's shoes.

"We are going to sue their asses, Shy," Jerry says, stepping back and removing his soaking loafers. A little sick has ended up on his black socks and the cuffs of his slacks, but he ignores it. "Don't worry about a thing. We're going to get out of here, and we'll be rolling in dough. Going to be early retirement, yes, ma'am."

Joanna drops her hands onto her hips. "Jerry, literally no one cares about that right now."

"Mr. Fowler." A smooth voice comes from the doorway. The Farsi accent transforms Jerry's name into something decidedly lyrical. The woman who walks through is like a jeweled obelisk, tall and slender, in a silk brocade dress that descends to her feet. An ornate hijab with a floral pattern encircles her face.

"I'm Tiran Shirazi, the CTO for Hasanova Colony. I'm sorry for meeting you in such regrettable circumstances."

"'Regrettable,'" Shy repeats, catching the newcomer's icy gaze.

"A poor choice of words on my part, Miss Hunt," Tiran says.

"The CTO?" Mary releases her hold on Shy and slowly stands. She takes deliberate steps toward the woman, stopping just short of her. To Shy, it's like watching a mouse stand up to a cobra.

"Well," Mary begins, voice shaking with anger, pointing a finger to implicate her target. "Who gives a toot about you? Where's the C-E-O?"

Noah snorts with a laugh. Impossibly, Tiran seems as offended by Mary's statement as she intended.

"You've got a man dead," Mary continues, "and six Americans you have *assaulted*. I'd say it's high time for the chief *executive* officer to stop hiding behind flunkies, and get involved." She looks Tiran up and down and gives her a dismissive shrug. "I say again, who cares about you?"

Tiran raises an eyebrow, and Shy doubts anyone has ever dismissed the jeweled corporate creature in her entire existence. Lord knows that, even if Mary was unimpressed, the rest of the crew certainly snapped to attention.

"You care," Tiran says, untangling a chain and composing herself, "because I'm about to change your lives."

"I think we've already had enough life changing for one day," Joanna whispers to Arthur.

"This is a traumatic event for everyone," the CTO says, her voice sharp. "Kamran might still be out there, and we're requesting help in dealing with whatever it is we face."

"Help?" Noah laughs. "Is that the same 'help' that was coming to deal with us? Do they send different ICSC units to handle spies and aliens? Why should—"

Tiran gestures for him to be quiet, and he is.

Shy wants to learn that trick.

"You are not spies," Tiran says. "The animal that took Kamran and the... incident with my worker clearly didn't originate with your ship. That's why I'd like to make you an offer. Sign a nondisclosure with a UA FISCO Secret Arbitration clause. In exchange, we'll pay you to quit immediately and go home. With our financial assistance, I'm sure you can put this bleak time in your past."

Jerry shakes his head. "You can't solve every problem with—"

"Ten million to each of you now, and the contract paid in full. HCC will shoulder the cost and hire another team to commission the remainder of the facilities."

Shy blinks. This morning, if someone had asked her if she could be a multimillionaire by nightfall, she'd have laughed.

"What about Dr. Afghanzadeh?" she asks.

Tiran tries to hide her annoyance. "Our security forces aren't equipped to handle... something like that. Rest assured, a rescue team is inbound."

"He's not going to make it that long. If he keeps, keeps bleeding—" she begins, having to restart her thought a few times. It's hard for her to say it. "He was probably dead by the time we left."

"All the more reason not to throw innocents into the situation," Tiran replies. "But that shouldn't be your concern, Miss Hunt. Your worries are over."

"I don't think so," Joanna says. "You're just doing this because you know we'll sue for a hundred mil apiece! It's a cost-cutting measure on your part!"

"That is correct," Tiran says, stunning Joanna with her agreement. "But it'll take you a decade to secure a verdict, and half the prize in legal fees. That's assuming, of course, that the United Americas and the Independent Core Systems Colonies have a working inter-court system by then. You'll spend most of your remaining days trying to collect."

Joanna sours at this.

"That's why we've included, as part of the package, a funds management firm from Cambridge," Tiran continues. "They'll provide guidance, and I think you'll find that ten million today is worth a lot more than a hundred million will be in ten to twenty years."

"What about fuel?" Jerry asks.

"We still have to manufacture it," Tiran replies. "There is no way to speed the process. However, you can wait out the rest of your time on board the *Gardenia*. We won't have anything to do with you. You can leave us alone. It will be the best for everyone."

No one speaks. Shy looks at her hands and knows deep down—she would be much happier in the Swiss Alps than here, covered in blood.

"We don't expect you to decide instantly," Tiran says. "Two weeks remain before you have enough fuel to depart. Please instruct your lawyers to review the agreements at their earliest convenience. My team will secure a confidential data connection for the *Gardenia*, though any disclosures of what has transpired will void the offer. On this, I am quite serious. Do not even speak to your families."

Joanna laughs, but her usual bitterness is absent. She has the look of someone trying to rein in her glee, like a kid who was told to stop running at the pool.

"So what *am* I supposed to tell my legal counsel?" she says. "Because, you know, I got one of them on retainer for my fancy needs."

"McAllen has counsel," Jerry says. "We'll get you in touch—"

"Double my payout," Shy interrupts, "but I'll definitely sign your contract."

Tiran clears her throat. "Miss Hunt, the schedule of payment has already been cleared by the board, and I would have to—"

"You lied to me," Shy says, starting to rise, more of her voice returning. "You forced me into some kind of freak show laboratory. You tazed me. Everything you did to them, you did twice as much to me! So, yes! I want double, you fucking c—"

She's on her feet for all of two seconds before Arthur ushers her back down into the chair. Shy pushes his hand off.

"Give me twenty million, and I'll sign tonight," Shy says. "Unconditional surrender. Harshest penalties for breaking the contract. If I talk to anyone about it, for any reason, you can have all the money back. You can have me arrested, extradited to the ICSC. I don't give a shit!"

Her shout comes out so much louder than she'd meant, ringing off the marble walls of the suite. It's hard to control her voice right now.

"And you know what?" she says, tears streaming down her face. She wipes them, and finds that they've only reinvigorated the congealing mess of blood over her skin. She stares at the wet crimson on her knuckles, then clenches her fist. "I will die of old age in my beautiful mansion outside of Nashville, do you fucking hear me? I'm getting off this planet, and I never want to see *any*"—she takes the time to make eye contact with every HCC employee she finds in the room—"of you motherfuckers again."

"Eloquently put." Tiran folds her hands behind her back. "I'll see if we can draw up the papers, and we'll know from the board within the hour."

"I'm going to take a shower," Shy says, "and then I'm going back to the ship, where I will wait to sign literally anything they send. The rest of you can figure out where you stand on this Bug World's offer. I'm out."

In the posh bathroom, she peels out of her clothes, throwing them in the trash. She calls to Mary, asking her to lay some out for her, then disappears into what she enjoys describing as "the nozzle nook"—a set of twenty-five shower heads designed to recreate everything from a gentle rabbit's kick to intermittent sheets of warm, cleansing rain.

She sacrifices her toothbrush to the cleaning effort, scrubbing Kamran's crusty blood out from under her fingernails. There'd been so much of it, maybe because he was a tall guy. Perhaps the thing that took him wouldn't be hungry for a while. It hadn't come back for second helpings after they'd tazed her, or they'd have left her to die for sure.

She could've been the one dragged into the pit—swallowed by Charybdis. Something is festering in the bowels of this planet, strange and deadly.

It was a giant bug that took him, armor-plated and toothy. Terrified screaming and gouts of blood were a vastly different insect fatality. than swollen lips and slowing wheezes on a bright Texas day. She can still feel her best friend's grip softening in the weight of death.

She's not sure how long she's been weeping on the floor of the shower when Mary knocks.

"Yep! Almost done!" Shy calls with defensive cheeriness. She already has to live with Maggie's ghost. She doesn't need Kamran's hanging around, so she's going to start acting like a millionaire.

Time to start forgetting.

With her hair blown dry, the world takes on a rosier color. She dresses in fresh clothes and emerges into the parlor to find her coworkers gathered and packed. Mary has taken the liberty of putting away Shy's things—things that had come to litter the room over the past few weeks of living here. A silver tray rests on the table, holding a steaming-hot cheeseburger and fries, along with a can of Coca-Cola.

"They weren't sure if you'd be hungry," Jerry says.

She gives him a twenty-million-dollar smile. "I could eat a horse."

The beef patty, melted gruyere, and fresh greens atop a kaiser roll, smeared with a garlic aioli and dijon mustard, might be the most amazing thing Shy has ever eaten. Each french fry is a stick of perfection, crisp along the edges but tender and moist in the center—an ideal vehicle for sugar, molasses, vinegar, tomato, and all the other things that make ketchup great. Noah tells her that Tiran sent over greens from her personal hydroponic garden.

Shy informs Noah that Tiran can go fuck herself with a chainsaw, and not to bring her up ever again.

The Decade crawler meets them in the motor pool. It takes them out of the Thunder Ring, over the Long Walk, through HAPS, and back to the *Gardenia*.

When they enter, Jerry calls, "Honey, I'm home," as he always does. Mary swats his butt "for missing his other wife too much," like she always does. Arthur tells them it's Arthur o'clock. Noah breaks out the beers.

Marcus arrives an hour later, stone-cold and cling-wrapped to a cargo palette. He doesn't look too much worse for wear, and they boot him up. It probably didn't help his circuits to have the piss shocked out of him, but he's surprisingly intact, which is great news to Shy, because he's still a decent mixologist, and because she wouldn't have anyone to talk to late at night.

Though she'd never tell anyone this, the synthetic might be her best friend. People in Shy's line of work rarely ever see home, and Marcus has kept her company through the worst of her loneliness.

Before long she watches him whip together drinks for the crew—smiling with the unmaimed half of his face—and wonders if he's actually happy. More likely he's acting like nothing is wrong because it'll make everyone feel better.

Everyone takes a toast—then five, when Jerry allows them into the "Captain's Stock," his eight-fridge wine cellar in the hold. Joanna graciously shares a few bottles of rum, and Noah contributes a luxurious mezcal to the mix—acting oddly generous.

"I have an announcement!" Shy says, planting a foot atop one of the galley stools and hoisting a glass. "It's fucking karaoke night, because I'm having a farewell party! Jerry, I love you, but I resign. I don't know who you'll get to replace me, but I know I'll be—"

"I'll do it," Noah jokes, and to Shy's great annoyance, everyone laughs.

"I don't doubt it," she says, keeping her smile up, "but I have recently come into, as they say, 'fuck you money.' So I love you," her glass reaches its apogee, "but fuck you."

She downs it in one.

"You seem awfully sure this isn't too good to be true," Jerry replies, crossing his arms. "Maybe wait a bit before resigning."

She adds some hot sauce to her smile. "I heard the muscles tear when Kamran's arm came off. It sounded like cutting a brisket. Does that—*sound*—too good to be true?" She forces a laugh to make it a joke, but it comes out desperate. "Besides, you were going to fire me, sooner or later. Stocking shitty equipment and letting *Noah* do my job? You think a girl can't read between the lines?"

Jerry Fowler has never told a lie in his life, because he would never get away with it. Caught out, he stammers some sort of excuse. She'd meant it as a joke, but she'd accidentally dropped a bomb right on target.

"You were?" She guffaws. "You *were*! That… that's awesome." The false mirth fades and she shakes her head. "Because I have enjoyed working here, and uh, we can leave things as friends. Since I quit." She stares at him, and he won't look her in the eye. "Five minutes ago, you were telling me not to count on the payout."

"I just thought you shouldn't resign in such an emotional state."

"Every state is an emotional state, Jerry!"

"Your drink is ready," Marcus says, and a delightful Prosecco-something appears on a tray at Shy's side. She loves the way he carries it, the liquid never sloshing. They can add blemishes to a synthetic's skin, but it's hard to hide perfection.

This isn't the drink Shy ordered, but then again Marcus has trouble remembering her name, so she cuts him some slack.

"Fuck it," she says. "To twenty million dollars!" She hoists the new glass high, and everyone else who knew she might be fired can enjoy toasting their ten, instead.

"Come on, Shy," her former boss says, "I'm sorry. You know how this is. We're barely keeping the ship afloat. Mary and I love you like family, and letting you go was never a sure thing."

"You really know how to talk a girl down, Jerry." She can't even fake her way through this smile. "You were going to fire *me*. Why should I be trying to make you feel better?"

Mary comes over and holds out a hand. Not knowing what to do, Shy takes it. The older woman's skin is soft, but dry, warm as she runs a thumb over Shy's with a sweet expression.

"I'm glad for you, Cheyenne," Mary says. "If anyone ever deserved to have a pile of money fall on them, it's you. I always thought you liked horses more than HVAC interfaces, but I understood why you came to work for us. I don't want you to hate us. You've been through so much. Can't we just celebrate the good that's come into our lives?"

Shy nods, pouting a bit. After abstaining so long, she's drunk too much.

"Karaoke time?"

Mary nods, the mic and speakers come out, and they spend the next four hours belting the legends of country from the galley. Mary and Jerry duet the sweet standards. Arthur goes in for a few Latin hits, and Joanna shows off her surprising range. Even Noah sings, though he refuses to do anything younger than a century old.

One by one, they drop off for bed, until Shy and Noah sit alone in the galley, polishing off one last verse of ancient Neko Case. He lights up a joint, and she laughs at him.

"Keeps me sharp," he says.

"And it keeps *me* awake. I'm about to go to bed."

"No time like the present to celebrate life." He holds out the stick, and against her better judgment, she takes it. "Had a pretty close call down there. Must've been terrifying."

She sucks in the smoke, and it's like a skunk in a pine forest. Her skin feels incredible within a few seconds.

"What is this?"

"Superhybrid. Called Maximum Load. Little bit of X mixed in."

"You punk." Her laugh is so much easier now, and she hands it back to him. "How do you get the best stuff?"

"I know people." His eyes glitter, and Shy braces.

She knows that look.

"Have I ever told you how beautiful you are?" he asks. "I thought, well, when I first met you, I thought you were just another girl, but, like… seeing how incredible you were today. Like with the CTO, I'm impressed."

She sits up and away. "Yeah, that was a real power move, and I was awesome. Noah, why would you think I'd want you to hit on me right now?"

"I'm not—"

"You definitely are. After I had a guy eaten beside me, after I got tazed, and that's the reason why this…" She stands up and gestures to her whole body before brushing the crumbs of an evening's snacking from her legs. "… is never going to happen. For one, I don't date new money. It's gauche."

"Okay, you know what, I didn't want to bring this up, but you are being completely naive."

"For not fucking you?"

"For… for thinking you just struck it rich." He takes another hit of his joint, forcing her to wait on his tired monologue. "The Iranians? They've got you where they want you—compliant and waiting in isolation. What's happening in the meantime? They've called ICSC backup. They're not going to give you shit, and you're over here burning every bridge. Once their buddies get to Hasanova, we're going to get disappeared. That's what's going to happen."

"Yeah," she says, "because they have to *call* someone to kill us when they have the galaxy's largest garbage disposal. Look, jackass, everyone knows where we are, and deaths bring more questions than profit. You might be some fancy IT guy, but you don't know shit about American-Iranian politics. You're stoned enough to be paranoid, and sleazy enough to be horny, but you're not man enough to admit either—so get lost."

To her amazement, he looks at her like he's going to hit her. He's actually shaking, muscles ready to lash out. She hears Kamran's elbow tearing apart again. His pleas as the creature dragged him into the depths.

There are monsters everywhere.

It's only after Noah storms away that Shy realizes a terrible truth—she still has two weeks on this boat with him before they can leave. Maybe Tiran would let her stay in the colony proper. She seemed eager to capitulate to any demands Shy made.

Except that somewhere down in that colony, killer infections and chitinous predators thrive, ready to devour. If the huntsman spider could make it up to the top levels of Ops, something else could, too. Shy will only have a fortune if she lives to spend it.

It takes her about twenty minutes to swallow enough bile to smooth things over with Noah. She hates it. She shouldn't have to do it, but if he gets weird... His red-faced fury won't leave her mind.

When she arrives at his door, it's open, the green light of a terminal illuminating his room. A cursor blinks against the black. He's not sitting at his computer, and she's about to look for him when she sees a USCM logo at the top left.

It looks just like the screen she trained on a few years ago, for reporting ship emergencies. By law, every single member of the crew must be able to establish a connection and broadcast a distress call. Shy takes a few quiet steps into the room and focuses on the words.

>>UNDER ATTACK BY UNKNOWN LIFE FORMS
>>COLONY COMPROMISED
>>AMERICAN HOSTAGES
>>COORDS [::THIS.GALTAG::]
>>SEND HELP

The NDA will never come now. She stares at the screen in abject horror. Twenty million, gone. It will take her a decade to recover her damages from HCC.

"Noah, what have you done?" she asks the shadows.

"Someone had to make a command decision." Noah's voice comes from the bunk. She turns to find him lying there with a bottle in his hand. "I'm not leaving our rescue to chance."

PART II

SOLDIER ON

SEVEN MONTHS AGO:

WEYLAND-YUTANI COMPANY CONFIDENTIAL ULTRA
TRANSMIT LOG - DIRECTOR EYES ONLY

[2184.02.14]

[01:12:01] Kaitomushi 怪盗蟲: You found her.
[01:12:04] Mitchell: Sure did! :-)
[01:12:06] Mitchell: The guys back at Langley
                             are about to make
                             contact.
[01:12:12] Kaitomushi 怪盗蟲: I can't lose her again.
[01:12:16] Mitchell: You won't, Romeo. She'll
                             come. Marines will need
                             an advisor on the ground.
[01:12:24] Kaitomushi 怪盗蟲: I thank you for the
                             opportunity.

1 2

BLACK DROP

Lance Corporal Russell Becker has been standing at attention for ten minutes. In his two years in the Corps, he's met a lot of officers, but none have ever made him hang out stick-straight while they checked emails. Enlisted soldiers have their own ways of rebelling, so captains normally don't abuse their authority.

Most captains aren't Kylie Duncan.

She's shorter up close than he expected, he thinks, but otherwise lives up to the rumors: a spring break bombshell with a puffy scar covering half her jaw. The first time he saw her, it was tough to square the pert nose, blond hair, and blue eyes against the savage beating she was dishing out in the gym. Now she's reading her computer screen through a pair of gold-rimmed reading glasses—as she has been for the past ten minutes. She leans forward, and a smile crosses her face.

"Black drop," she says without looking up.

Becker's pulse quickens. He needs to confirm before he can get his hopes up.

"I'm sorry, sir?"

She pushes away her keyboard and removes her glasses. "So you're Becker. You came highly recommended."

"Thank you, sir."

"Sorry it took me so long to have our sit down."

"It's no problem, sir."

It really is fine. There's plenty to do on the USS *Benning*, and they've been busy with exercises for the past month. He does, however, wish that her idea of a "sit down" involved actually sitting down.

Her smile is lopsided, and the plastic surgery grows more apparent. She taps her chin.

"What did they say about me?"

"That you knew where to find trouble."

She nods, crossing her arms and pushing back from her desk. "You've done a tour through the Goliath system."

Becker waits for her. It wasn't a question, so he has no answer.

"What were your impressions?"

It's an innocent enough question, but there's only one reason his new CO would ask. She wants to know why his former captain was arrested. He's none too keen to discuss it.

"It's chaos, Captain."

"Is that your thing?"

"No, sir."

She picks up a mug of coffee and takes a swig. "What *is* your thing, Becker?"

"Controlled demolition, sir. The opposite of Tartarus. I prefer the tip of the spear, well applied."

She straightens and scoots over to her terminal. "I'm looking at your records, and I want to know why you're not Force Recon, Mr. Tip-of-the-Spear. At the very least, a man with recommendations from both of his senators should've been an officer."

Becker swallows. Is this the part where she tells him he's not welcome in her platoon?

"I was discharged from Annapolis for misconduct, sir."

"Yes. It says that. What was the misconduct, Becker?"

"Being drunk on watch, and..." He's had to shoot a man so close up that he didn't need the sights, yet this makes him blush.

"And?" Does she know? Why is she asking?

"Sleeping with a superior officer."

She quirks an eyebrow. "Don't you normally address *superior officers* as 'sir?'"

"Yes, uh... sir."

Surely that wasn't a come on. He's heard that Captain Duncan can get into his head, and here she is already. She kicks a foot up onto the desk and folds her hands across her lap, making a face like a pleased cat.

"Relax, Becker," she says. "I'm not trying to fuck you. I have standards."

"Thank you, sir," he replies, then realizes the insult. Chagrined, he clears his throat. "Captain, may I ask what you meant by 'black drop?'"

"Got your hopes up?"

In Goliath, he heard the whispers—an entire platoon lost to a mysterious creature. One of the boys gave him a copy of *Space Beast*, smuggled into the Corps to give soldiers nightmares. It was written by a raving mad prisoner, and no one believed it, of course. Then came the videos of black skeletal monsters tearing soldiers apart. The footage was passed around like contraband, and the first time Becker saw one, something lit on fire in his soul.

In the reaches of space, he found something worth battling, an evil that could be scorched away with the light of civilization. Apolitical. A killing machine. Becker chased every rumor, and they all led to Kylie Duncan— the captain of the Midnighters. As the legends go, when a drop involves the demons, the Midnighters call it a "black drop."

"It's why I requested this outfit, Captain."

She pinches her chin. "It's interesting that your request mattered to anyone, since you are, in fact, a complete nobody. Isn't that right?"

Becker is a fourth-generation marine, and somewhere in the galaxy, there's a Brigadier General Becker, but Duncan is correct. He is a nobody—at this point in his career.

"Yes, sir."

"And you recognize that the x-rays you've heard about don't exist, because if they did, you'd be discussing classified information outside of a need-to-know basis."

He swallows. "I do not know the phrase 'black drop,' sir. I was excited because you seemed excited."

She toasts him with her coffee and a wink. "I like them humble. You heard right." She points to her computer screen. "Just got the good news."

He inhales sharply and straightens. The devils of the frontier—he'll finally fight them in person.

"We took on an advisor two weeks ago. I want you to go wake him up. Make sure you've got coffee ready. He's important."

"Yes, sir. But—"

"But?" she repeats.

"If you just got the good news, why did we get him two weeks ago, sir?"

Her smile falls. He's fucked up. "Because I'm an officer, and I went to college, so me make decisions good." She takes another look at the screen. "Maybe we ought to take one last look at your transfer orders."

"I'll wake him up right away, sir."

She regards him for what feels like a long time, keen eyes searching out any further signs of weakness and doubt. So far he knows two things about Captain Kylie Duncan: she's cute like a smiling cobra, and she doesn't tolerate any challenges—even the most minor, accidental ones. But she also leads an unconventional element that operates with top clearances and very little oversight.

The Midnighters aren't the same kind of elite as the SEALs, Rangers, or JTACs; they're obscure and well-funded with a whole lot of special, one-off clearances. In the command structure of the Colonial Marines they're an anomaly that gets exploited over and over again for clandestine action, and Becker wants his spot.

"Good," she says. "Get out of my sight, and make sure my advisor is cozy. Welcome to the Midnighters, Becker. Hope you're ready to get your X-Card punched. Dismissed."

He salutes and walks through the door into the ready room. Captain Duncan's office is set up inside the pilot briefing area—something Becker is sure pissed off the other jocks. If she can get away with making her enlisted personnel stand around while she reads emails, and takes over the pilots' private club, she must be something special.

He crosses the hangar past a flurry of activity—an uptick from the morning. Marines filter down from their various activities on the upper decks to busy themselves with weapons prep. Somehow they know something is happening. Is he the last to figure it out?

"What's up, Seventy-Six? You still work here?"

Leger has been on four drops with Captain Duncan, so Becker tolerates a bit of lip. He's polishing his boots, which are remarkably un-scuffed for a man who's seen an x-ray in person. Becker wants to learn what this pasty kid knows.

"Looks like it, Leger. Still a fucking commie?"

"Ask the Russians we saved you from. Ottawa forever, sir." He puts down his rag and rests a hand on his heart. "Unite, don't fight, Americas. Let's light the light, Americas, for the calling of the free—"

"We're good, Maple Syrup," Becker says, shutting down Leger's take on Dana Krenshaw's old standard. "As long as I see you cleaning your combat loadout as well as your boots," he adds.

Leger perks up. "Why? Do we have somewhere to be?" In the short time they've been working together, Becker has come to rely on Leger's stories for a glimpse of what's coming. The private wants a good relationship with Becker, so he can get a view into macro-level objectives.

Except Captain Duncan didn't tell Becker to share.

"In fact," Becker says deliberately, "we *do* have somewhere to be—in the Corps. And when you're in the Corps, you're an infantryman first. And when you're an infantryman, you have a clean and ready weapon."

"*Black drop.*" Leger mouths the words.

Becker gives him a grin and keeps on walking.

Up the stairs one deck to cargo lock eight, he locates the guest—a large, energized shipping container, clearly marked.

LIVE HUMAN INSIDE

—

MAINTAIN POWER

On the one hand, Becker feels sorry for the guy having to be shipped in a box. On the other hand, they sent him express, so that was nice. Judging from the chain of custody, he was blasted out to the Rim, then shuffled through a couple of star hoppers, chartered. What he lost in style, he made up for in speed.

Becker flips open the dial and punches the wake-up code.

```
>>FLUX OK
>>THERMAL OK
>>22.0.1.3
>>CANCEL STASIS S.MATSUSHITA
-OK
-CANCEL
```

He swears at the Weyland-Yutani panel. Does he hit okay to cancel, or is cancel like hitting okay? Becker retrieves the manual from the end of its spiral plastic chain and fiddles through it for a moment. When he hits okay, it goes to a coolant balancing screen.

"Bishop, come in," he says into his walkie.

"*Yes, Corporal Becker?*" Like all Bishop units, his voice carries a pack-a-day huskiness.

Becker checks the manual again. "How do I wake this guy up?"

"*I'll be right there.*"

Once the synthetic arrives, that frees up Becker to

head back to the bay. He's not going to wait for Captain Duncan. He'll gather his team and tell them to field strip and prep. By the time they're doing Rehearsal of Concept tomorrow, his team will be sharp.

It's only about four hours before Captain Duncan calls everyone to the ready room. Bishop and the civilian advisor stand by her side at the front of the hall, and the grunts loiter in their various perches, managing loadouts, mouthing off to one another.

"Good evening, everyone," Duncan says, folding her hands behind her back. "At fifteen thirty-eight, we received a priority one distress call from this ship."

Bishop turns to the presentation terminal and clicks until he gets it to launch. Everyone waits in awkward silence while the cheap government holoprojector warms up. When it does, spears of light coalesce into the polygons of one of the ugliest ships Becker has ever seen. It's lumpy and asymmetrical, with an unfortunate solar array covering half one side.

"This is the USCSS *Gardenia*, a mid-class civilian vessel belonging to McAllen Integrations," Duncan says. "They landed on Hasanova more than two weeks ago, where they have been doing work for a company owned by the Iranian state. Big surprise, they're having problems."

A rumble of laughter rolls through the assembled platoon.

"Seems the Iranians have quarantined them. Scared them half to death. You know, the usual, but I guess them's the breaks when you deal with enemies of the state." Captain Duncan gives an exaggerated shrug. More laughter.

"Here's where we come in," she says, and the holoprojector changes to an overhead layout of the colony. "They knew what they were getting into with the Caliphate, but they didn't figure on deadly fauna."

One of Becker's colleagues, another corporal named Brad Suedbeck, raises his hand.

"Deadly what, sir?"

"Fauna," Duncan says. "Usually paired with flora. You'd know that if you went to high school."

"Apologies, Captain," he replies. "I am but a simple farm boy."

"I know, and it's not your fault that your mother dropped you so much, but I'm going to need your dumb ass to keep up," Duncan says. "We have a multi-layered objective here, along with plenty of ways this could go bad. First and foremost, we've got to have hands on everybody. I don't want any loose Iranians ruining my day. Second, we sweep the colony for x-rays and when we find them, box those fuckers up.

"Cooper, Wallace, your fireteams will take the Human Centre here. Suedbeck, secure Ops. Longstreet, take the Solutions building here. Becker, your fireteam will take the *Gardenia* and secure the hostages. Any questions?"

"Are we expecting any resistance, sir?" someone asks.

"Not if they're smart," Duncan answers, and the room titters with laughter. "We're not allowed to start any fights, but we can certainly finish them. While we're there, we're also going to learn as much as we can about their operations. There's some shady shit going on, and we'll be busy."

"Shady like what, sir?" Keuhlen asks.

"That's for me to know and you to confirm. Keep your eyes and ears open at all times. All of you are to memorize this layout. I want team leaders well-versed in all of this Arabic bullshit, too."

"I believe that's Farsi, Captain Duncan," Bishop corrects.

"And if you have any questions," she says, "ask the tin man over here, since he apparently fucking knows everything."

Bishop nods to the crowd with preprogrammed bashfulness.

"I'll help out where I can."

Becker makes out three distinct sections—the atmospheric processor, the colony buildings, and the data storehouses inside some kind of bore shaft. He has questions, but he's not sure where to start. No one else seems to be concerned—do they already know what's supposed to happen on a mission like this?

"What do we know about the x-ray presence?" he asks.

"Everyone," Duncan says, "this is Becker. As you can all see, this is his first rodeo."

He swallows. "Sorry, Captain. I figured I should try and understand the op."

Her eyes drill into him. "Sergeant Lee, please handle the education of our slow child. The rest of you are dismissed." The marines filter out of the room, but Becker remains standing, hands folded behind his back at parade rest. No sense in trying to disappear with them, though he would very much like to.

Sergeant Lee isn't an officer, so he doesn't have to be a gentleman, either. Becker has seen from afar the way the pale guy keeps order—like a dog forcing his flock into line, snarling and yapping at the edges. Lee is quick to take care of anything Captain Duncan points out, and unfortunately for Becker, that's him.

"Corporal," the sergeant says in an Alabama accent. He runs a hand over his peroxide-blond flattop, then pulls a box of mints out of his back pocket. He's a vascular, sweaty man, always red like he's going to explode with anger. "I think we need to discuss your attentiveness."

"Yes, Sergeant. I would like to improve."

"'I would like to improve.' I appreciate you, Corporal." Lee laughs and shakes a mint loose into his palm—a deep sapphire blue on one half, charcoal gray on the other, with a little white dividing line.

It's not a mint.

Lee pops the pill and chews. It doesn't look as if it tastes very good, but since Lee is always scowling, it's difficult to tell. Becker's gaze snaps straight ahead before the big bastard can see him looking.

"I read about you," he says, stepping on the shiny toe of Becker's boot with the side of his own, leaving a trail of scuff marks. "You're a good kid. You come from a good military family." He tugs on Becker's corporal patch, ripping it off the velcro and putting it back askew. "But you're not one of us, and all the way out here, well... that matters. Let me put it like this."

He steps in front of Becker's field of vision, icy eyes like coals in his leathery visage.

"You have no idea what's coming. No one knows if they'll see you again after this mission, so why should *we* be wasting *our* time with your questions? Leave that to the... important people, as it were. Now"—he steps back to admire his handiwork—"you run along and fix your shit before the captain sees you."

"Yes, Sergeant," Becker replies.

Lee wants him to get angry, to think about taking a swing. Becker's been in the Corps long enough to know that's the whole point of the exercise. The sergeant doesn't have the authority to punish, only to report, and Becker will be damned if he spends one more second worrying about it after this.

"If you survive tomorrow, you can ask a question," Lee says, shouldering past him. "Until then, you're just bait to distract them."

INTERLUDE: HAROUN

"Joonam."

Haroun swings his cricket bat. His shoulder flexes freely, gloriously, like it did in the old days.

"Joonam," Sanam says, nudging him awake. He opens his eyes and looks up at her.

"I had the best dream." He sighs. His silk pajamas and microcotton sheets wrap him in a delicious embrace.

"Tiran is calling."

He's out of bed, heading for the door.

"Your pajamas!" Sanam laughs.

"No time to change."

He pads down the hall to the phone. Nadia sits there in her housecoat, entertaining Tiran on the screen. He prays the story is not about him, because he actually hears Tiran chuckle softly on the other end of the line.

"Here is my son, in his pajamas," Nadia says.

"Good night, Khanoomeh Sharif," Tiran replies, a grin visible in the crinkle of her eyes.

"I've got it, maman, thank you," Haroun says, kissing

his mother's cheek and ushering her back toward her bedroom beside Banu's. Tiran may not like to wait, but she likes disrespectful sons even less. He straightens his pajamas and brushes off a bit of lint before coming back on camera.

Tiran wears a relatively toned-down hijab compared to normal, just tasteful red and gold. She takes a deep breath.

"I hate to wake you."

"Think nothing of it, madame."

"Haroun, I need to get your opinion on something."

It's surprisingly personal of her to use his first name. He can't remember the last time she did so.

"Of course."

"At thirty-five past midnight, all communications and observation went down."

Haroun's gut tightens. "Even the asteroid warning system?"

A small nod. "Even the AWS. They're all overloaded. Garbage data."

He remembers this very well, from a training he took in Isfahan during his days as a colonel. The Revolutionary Guard had a lot of experience with American military tactics, and he knew how Colonial Marines approached a confrontation. Strangle the comms, take out critical infrastructure, then launch the assault.

He possesses a sickening certainty of what he'd see if his long-distance scopes weren't whited out. A light attack cruiser, jamming them on every conceivable band.

"Those satellites don't fail. It's the Americans, madame."

Tiran narrows her eyes. "From the *Gardenia*?"

"No." He shakes his head. "The ones in space. They'll have a ship in the system. Heavily armed Colonial Marines."

"The ICSC security forces are still two weeks out. We need to double our efforts and the guard presence on the excavation site. Those artifacts—"

He gives her a consoling expression. "Know that I have always supported your leadership, but I need you to listen very carefully. There is no 'doubling the guard presence.' We won't be securing the vault, or setting up an insurgency, madame."

"What do we do? How do we fight this?"

"There is no resisting the Americans. We have maybe twenty militia and fifteen rifles. We organize our surrender and wait."

She swallows.

"Very well. Meet me in my office as soon as possible."

"What should I be prepared for?"

She looks off camera at something, as if she's just remembered she left the stove on, perhaps.

"I want to discuss what we're going to destroy."

1 3

RESCUE

The crew of the *Gardenia* anxiously watch the bridge clock—the USS *Benning* is supposed to arrive in orbit any moment. It's been two days since Noah sent his distress call to the Colonial Marines. Since then, he's been locked in his room.

No one wants to talk to him.

It's possible Noah is right—that the Iranians were just using the money as a distraction to make them complacent. Shy still would have wanted a choice in the matter—because she would've taken her chances with the cash.

When Tiran came yesterday with documents, Shy wasn't able to make herself sign them. The contract promised swift, stark retribution to anyone who dared leak—the threat extended to anyone who knew about leaks. If she signed, she'd be in breach already.

Humiliated, she told Tiran that she'd be forwarding the contracts to Jerry's lawyer for review. Shy had stalled for time, exactly as everyone agreed. Tiran was annoyed, but not surprised.

The comm beeps on the shipping channel, and Mary scrambles to put the transmission through.

"*Hasanova Colony Corporation VTS, this is Captain Kylie Duncan of the United Americas assault starship USS* Benning," a woman's voice says. "*You are in possession of six American citizens, which means that under the London Accords, you will fully disarm and prepare to receive my marines. Any attempt to harm the Americans or use them as hostages will be construed as an act of war, and it is our intention to conduct a noncombatant evacuation operation. Do not fire, do not attempt to resist, and do not make me knock. Acknowledge receipt of my transmission.*"

Shy sits up. *Fuck, Noah, what did you do?*

"*Captain Duncan, this is HCC VTS.*" It's Haroun Sharif. "*We will not resist. We are peaceful.*"

"*HCC VTS,* Benning. *Smart move. Round up your people in a central area and make your personnel files available for inspection. You can be a hero today by keeping your people calm.* Benning *out.*"

Almost immediately there's another call.

"*Gardenia, this is* Benning." Duncan's voice fills the bridge. "*Lock your doors and roll up your windows. We'll be there shortly.*"

"Yes, Captain," Jerry says. "Thank you, Captain—"

"Benning *out.*"

* * *

Before Shy knows it, a pair of USCM dropships are on-station. It's impossible to tell what's happening with an atmospheric processor blocking their view, but Jerry listens to the HCC security band. After an hour, the shutter on the processor rolls up, and a boxy black armored personnel carrier comes roaring out onto the *Gardenia*'s landing pad. Eight marines emerge, sweeping forth to take cover around the landing pylons.

A call comes on their ship frequency. "Gardenia, *Duncan, here. This is the part where you open the damned boarding ramp.*"

"Yes, right away!" Jerry says, frantically gesturing for Joanna at the cargo console. She opens the ramp, and they watch on the closed circuit as marines come streaming up. The sound of heavy boots, then they burst onto the bridge, pointing guns and shouting at them to get down.

What the fuck did you do, Noah?

A baby-faced man pushes Shy out of the chair and onto her stomach, searching over her body. "Miss! Do you have anything on you I need to be aware of? Miss!"

He's so rough. So loud. Everything is chaos. They have Arthur bent over one of the consoles, his hands ziptied behind his back. Marcus goes to one of the marines, his hands in the air and a smile on his face. He just wants everyone to get along, but the soldier yells for him to get on the ground.

"Get the fuck off me!" Shy screams.

"Miss Hunt." Captain Duncan's boot comes down next to her head, and she crouches to be face-to-face.

Shy didn't know what to expect of Duncan, but this petite woman isn't it. She's short, with bright eyes and oversized BDUs. When she smiles, it's only with one side of her face, a bit like their Marcus.

"We have to check you for bombs." Duncan says it like she's explaining an easy math problem. "For our protection and yours. As hostages, you might have explosives on you. That's how we handle captives of terrorists."

"They're not terrorists," Shy says. "They're a web host."

"Do you have any bombs on you?"

"No," Shy grunts.

"Are you aware of any threats to me or my men?" Duncan's voice is low and mirthful. Does she think this is funny?

"No."

The captain nods. "Well okay, kids. Let her up, Corporal." The baby-faced corporal gets off her and holds out a hand. Shy rolls her eyes at the "1776" tattooed on the inside of his wrist. They couldn't have sent a more American squadron if they'd come in wielding hot apple pies.

Duncan looks around the bridge.

"Cute in here."

She departs without another word.

"Jesus fuck!" Noah's voice comes from down the hall.

Apparently no one remembered to tell him the marines had arrived.

"Cap says to get the civvies moved out," one of the men calls. "We're staging everyone in Ops."

They slowly pull everyone out onto the wave-kissed landing platform. Shy stands there shivering in the lake spray, despite her jacket. Lake Peacock, like a real peacock, is never quiet and usually an asshole. One of them bit Shy in veterinary school, and that makes it the second worst peacock in her life.

There's a hot, wet blast as a dropship comes in, obliterating the puddles on the tarmac. If she wasn't soaked before, she is now.

"Her name is Cheyenne, too," the corporal says. He stares up at the hovering ship like it's an angel, and she wants to retch.

"You named your ship Cheyenne?"

"That, ma'am, is a UD-40L 'Cheyenne' utility dropship, capable of securing the colony against all manner of threats to…" He looks over, and rightly notices that she doesn't give a shit. Then he holds out a hand, because somehow a handshake will cure his awkwardness.

"Becker."

She squints at him through the slashing rain, uninterested in befriending the guy who threw her down. "Okay."

Once they've done a thorough sweep of the *Gardenia*, six of the marines walk to the edge of the platform and clip into lines thrown by the dropship. She hates to admit it, but it's a little exciting when they ascend into the open hold and take off for the main complex.

"This way," Becker says, guiding them into the armored personnel carrier.

"Is this one also named after me?" Shy asks, climbing inside, and Joanna smacks her on the arm.

"Would you stop antagonizing the guy?" she whispers.

When Shy sits down, she finds an East Asian man wearing some clunky goggles and a clear poncho. It looks to her like a trash bag, but his fashion is of little concern. The APC lurches into motion, and they trundle through the guts of HAPS.

"Is it true you saw it?" the guy says, accent vaguely Japanese. She doesn't have to work hard to figure out what he means.

"Yeah. It was, uh, big."

The soldiers in her APC perk up and pay attention, but they're not looking at her. They're staring at the weirdo in the goggles. His delicate mouth curls into a smile.

"Do you know how big they can get?"

"No," she says. "I've only seen one."

"Would you like to?" He takes an off-putting amount of care with each word, as though he's afraid he'll drop them. She looks from Mr. Trash Bag to the soldiers in the vehicle. One of the soldiers repeats his words, laughing.

"No," she replies, and the man deflates. Under the wet poncho, she can make out his name patch: MATSUSHITA. Judging from his dress, he's not a marine.

"You some kind of expert?"

He stares at her for a long time. He looks young, maybe in his mid-thirties.

"You're very lucky."

The bitter laugh jumps out of her throat. "Because I saw a killer bug?"

"Because you lived," he replies, and that shuts down any continued interest she has in the conversation.

When they reach Ops, they find the marines already setting up a command center in the main office. The soldiers have wasted no time unpacking, and Shy has to admit she feels safer already. Captain Duncan blows through several times with a pair of men who'd look more at home robbing banks than performing heroic rescues.

There are no Iranians to be seen anywhere. She turns to Becker, who has never strayed far from their side.

"What did you do with the colonists?"

"Huh?" He's too busy watching all the hubbub.

She's about to repeat herself when he gets a call over his walkie talkie. Again she tries to talk. Another call. And again. The radio chatter is nonstop as they clear aside HCC computers and set up their own.

"Okay, people, let's get that perimeter online!" Duncan calls over the din. "What's happening with the sentries?"

"Sentries all report ready status, sir," one of the women in uniform says. "All paths up from the data storehouses are fully secured, and the colonists are all accounted for in the lower storehouses."

"That takes care of one set of monsters," Duncan says. "Now on to the x-rays. What's the latest from imaging?"

"What are x-rays?" Joanna whispers to Shy, and she shakes her head. She hasn't the faintest idea, but she's not fond of calling the Iranians monsters.

"No reports from below," the soldier replies. "The *Blackstar* is dark, too."

Duncan nods. "Percival! Uplink status?" A guy in standard-issue gold rim glasses clears his throat on the other side of the command center.

"I've almost got COMCOM online. We're dropping a lot of packets on—"

"How hard can it be?" Duncan replies. "Fix your shit, or you're on point in twenty."

"Twenty?" Shy repeats, daring to touch Becker's arm.

Becker nods. "Yeah. We're not just going to sit here while there are Xenomorphic entities running around. They can do a lot of damage."

Xenomorphic. Oh. "X-rays." Got it.

"Yeah, lots of damage." Kamran's stifled cries and the rope-snap noise of his tendons getting yanked are still fresh in her mind.

Becker looks at her with big, brown eyes. If this guy is supposed to be a badass, even with all of his gear on, she doesn't see it. He can't be older than twenty-five. Still, there's something like a hungry gleam there.

"You really saw one?" he asks. "What was it like?"

That's when she realizes that this man has never even *seen* the creature they're hunting. He's not calling them by their species name. A "Xenomorphic entity" could be literally anything, including the extremophilic bacteria in the water.

Maybe *none* of these men and women have seen one.

"And your plan for dealing with them is…?"

Becker inclines his head like he's addressing a curious general. "Sweep and capture, miss."

She's shocked. "You want to… take it alive?"

"Shy," Jerry says, laying a hand on her shoulder. "Maybe let the pros handle it."

"Oh, we're not capturing 'it,'" Becker replies.

"Thank God."

"We'll be capturing *them*. There are likely to be a lot more. Once you've got one, you've got an infestation."

"No… You're…" Shy puffs up. "No. Just no! 'Infestation?' Am I the only one who can see that we've got to get the fuck out of here? I want to be in orbit if you're going to kick a wasps' nest!"

"What seems to be the problem?" Captain Duncan says, and Shy realizes how loudly she was speaking. Duncan is staring at her, stock-still, leaning over a tactical map beside a swollen-up grunt with a platinum flattop. There's no smile. Instead, Shy feels a bit like a mouse caught in the gaze of an eagle—

—and in this instance, it's a bald eagle perched atop an American flagpole.

"Does my question have an answer?" Duncan raises her eyebrows.

Shy laughs nervously and alone. "No, I was just—"

The captain straightens up and folds her arms. "My question doesn't have an answer? You clearly have a problem, and I asked you what it is."

"He's never seen one of these, uh, 'x-rays,'" Shy says, gesturing to her unfortunate escort. "Have any of you?" Duncan stares, then takes deliberate steps around the tactical station and toward Shy.

"It is true that Corporal Becker was, until today, a little bitch. Isn't that correct, Corporal?"

"I am anything the Corps demands of me, sir," Becker responds, and the other soldiers laugh for the split second it takes Duncan's poisonous gaze to silence them.

"However," Duncan continues, "he's part of the toughest, deadliest, most cunning, elite fighting force in the galaxy, which makes him just a hair more valuable than... what is it you do again?"

"Shy is our front-end developer," Jerry says, and he laughs, a weak attempt to defuse the situation.

Duncan's eyes go wide, and her misshapen lips form an exaggerated "O."

"Wow. That is really special."

Ever since Shy got to Hasanova, she's been speaking truth to those who needed to hear it. Twenty million dollars gave her the confidence to stand up for herself, and just because the money is gone, that doesn't mean the confidence has to disappear, too.

"You can make fun of me all you want, but when your soldiers die out there, and the Iranians that Noah betrayed get out of their... wherever you put them, they're going to be pissed. You're just going to stir up two nests, and leave me to get stung."

She takes the last step between her and Duncan, not waiting for the captain to come to her. Up close, the captain is just a pretty girl with an ugly scar, and Shy's going to be damned if she lets this asshole get everyone killed.

"You've never seen anything like what's out there." She gives a sweep of her hand. "None of you have."

The captain takes in her statement, then smirks, unbuttoning one olive drab sleeve and rolling it up. She has a tattoo on her forearm—one of the black demons. It kneels, cowering before a cross ablaze with the glory of Christ. The bug is so much like the one Shy saw that they must be the same species.

"I have training to fight devils on all fronts, not just the... 'front end,' or whatever it is you do," Duncan says, and the soldiers erupt with laughter. Becker, she notices, puts his hands on his hips and purses his lips to keep from joining in.

"Corporal," Duncan says, maneuvering so she can stay in Shy's field of vision. "Take this dipshit to the Human Centre and report back. Time to flush these bugs, and then grab dinner."

1 4

EMERGENCE

Becker hangs onto the crossbar, savoring the cold air on his face. In a moment, he'll have to drop the visor on the most advanced armor he's ever worn. It's three layers: a superhydrophobic bodysuit, a gel-packed webbing of STF "liquid armor" for pinpoint impacts, and a Teledyne Brown Personal Reactive Armored Exoskeleton, or TBPRAE-44. Leger calls it the "Pray System," because *"if that's all you've got saving your life, Corporal, you'd better be praying."* Becker doesn't know how well it works, but he's wearing a whole lot of carbon composite and explosive bolts.

The suit is hot as balls, too.

"Buzzards One and Two, this is Ops. You're approaching the drop zone." It's the voice of Lieutenant Percival.

"Ops, Buzzard One, visual confirmed. We see the LZ," their pilot says. The other dropship calls it in, too.

"Thirty seconds!" Lee shouts over the din, then he lowers his visor. The other marines reach up and snap down their face masks. All together, they make a satisfying noise like the pump of a shotgun. Becker yanks his faceplate closed, uncomfortable yet invincible, and the noise of the world around him dims.

"All fireteams, this is Duncan. Sergeant Wallace, secure an LZ outside the Blackstar. *Sergeant Lee, drop in on their heels and release the hounds."*

Becker toggles to his team chat. "Check in. We all green?"

"Leger, standing by."

"Garcia, standing by."

"Keuhlen, standing by."

If he looks to the right, he can see the heartbeats of each of his soldiers on the helmet's heads-up display. It's not a detailed medical analysis, but it'll help him make the right decisions if things turn out for the worst.

His NCO channel pings. *"Duncan here. Remember—no unnecessary kills. We drive them into the containment area and crate them."*

"Ops, Lee—I'll wrap 'em up nice for you," Lee drawls, and Becker already hates having the guy in his ears.

The floor lists beneath him as the dropship banks. They're coming around for a final approach to the landing zone, and the overhead lights go red. Black mountains swell in Becker's view, framed by the open vehicle bay. He keeps his knees loose as they land, just as he learned in training. If they come down hard and he has his knees locked, he could be looking at a crippling injury.

Then they're on the ground, and he's out the door with his team to form a vanguard. The other soldiers stage at the perimeter of the LZ, pulse rifles pointed at any potential cover the x-rays might be using. Becker signals for the marines behind him to take a knee, but he knows they already have.

He has seen schematics of the UAEV *Blackstar*, but none of those depicted the disgusting, resinous coating that mars much of her hull. The alien nesting material is an unearthly shade, slightly translucent in the sunlight, and full of cracks from punching through the atmosphere. Becker keeps his sights on the airlocks, ready for anything.

After a moment, Wallace radios the all-clear.

"Buzzard One, this is Percival. Dust off and loiter at one thousand ASL. Sergeant Lee, bring in the Good Boys."

The dropship blasts off, and Becker savors the pings of broken rocks and debris on his armor. With the scratch-proof sapphire lenses on his fully enclosed helmet, he can keep his eyes on his surroundings even during dustoff, instead of having to cover his face.

"Fireteams, Buzzard Two, coming in with the Good Boys."

Their second dropship goes roaring overhead, firing a series of man-sized parcels from modified missile pods. The slender packages unfold, maneuvering thrusters snapping like firecrackers, and four legs emerge from each. One of them craters the ground right in front of

Becker, pelting him with broken rock. He knows his personnel transponder kept him safe from a parcel kill, but for fuck's sake, they dropped it a little too close.

The shivering National Dynamics SunSpot "Good Boy" straightens up in front of him, camera lenses whirring to life. Spent smoking rocket motors, each no bigger than a football, slough from its form. A pair of sealed dishes eject from either side with a charging whine.

"All fireteams, Percival. I'm starting the extended sweep now."

The Good Boy takes off like a greyhound, flowing over the treacherous terrain in graceful, mechanical bounds. The others follow suit from their own landing points, spiraling outward with ear-splitting, computerized chirps. The acoustic weapons mounted on either side are powerful enough to burst eardrums at a hundred yards, but they do an excellent job of topo mapping, as well.

"All fireteams, Percival. Sweep complete."

Sergeant Lee and his team fast rope from the back of Buzzard Two to the middle of the LZ and unclip. Lee throws the "rally-up" signal, and the NCOs gather around him.

"All right, boys and girls," Lee says, voice rendered even harsher over the comm, *"flush and contain. You know what to do. Becker, have your team take point by airlock two. Want you to get a front seat at the action."*

"I'd like the same thing, Sergeant," Becker says, and Lee scoffs.

Becker takes his team down the loose pebbles of the hill, sliding in places, but thanks to his armor, the pumice is as gentle as snow. The flat expanse around the derelict ship feels endless as they charge for cover. A couple of sentry guns would make short work of Becker's fireteam... but that's something humans would've deployed. Whatever this ship is, it's not anything his species would fly.

Becker opens his team-only channel as they get close.

"I didn't know the x-rays could operate spaceships."

"They can't," Garcia says. Of his team, she's been in the Midnighters the longest, and is thus his resident expert. *"Bastards can't even operate doors. They chew on cables sometimes, though."*

"It's pretty weird," Private Keuhlen adds. *"Never seen anything like this in all of my drops."*

"And how many is that?" Becker asks.

"Twenty-six black drops. No x-ray starships."

Holy shit, Becker thinks. *Keuhlen is kind of a badass, too.* As a lance corporal, Becker is supposed to lead the fireteam, but everyone has more experience with x-rays than him. He'll just have to prove that he should be in charge.

They crowd around the *Blackstar*'s airlock while Private Leger pulls out his hacking terminal and cuts open a panel. The Seegson Biomedical logo spins to life on his screen, and Lieutenant Percival talks him through security.

"What's Seegson?" Becker asks, and Leger shrugs.

"I just work here, man."

The door slides open, and if Becker thought it looked like shit on the outside, he had no idea what was coming. Instead of metal walls and grated floors, he finds the same organic crust coating the inside. It's everywhere, and without the thermal damage from atmospheric entry, it's smooth. Moisture beads on the cool sides of his pulse rifle. It's like a rainforest in there.

"Airlock open," Becker says. "Send in the Good Boys."

The mechanical greyhounds come bounding past him in a blur, hauling ass into the darkness of the ship. Outside, the marines have spread out into a large "V," ready to receive their quarry. The chirps of the Good Boys get quieter and quieter, until Becker hears nothing.

"How long does this usually take?" Becker has only just finished his sentence when a piercing alarm sounds from the depths of the ship. His three privates tense up, shouldering their rifles and backing out the way of the airlock. When the alarm goes silent, another shriek echoes through—not electronic, but a hateful scream. Outside of a recording, it's the first time Becker has heard one of the creatures, and he turns up the gain on his helmet mics to get a better listen.

Another Good Boy blares its alarm, this time closer.

And another.

Within seconds, it's like an orgy of banshees. Becker strains his eyes against the gloom of the corridor. With a scrabbling bang, one of the creatures slams into the wall at a junction a ways into the ship. It's a hissing ball of claws, tail, and malice, snapping and screeching at something Becker can't quite see.

Its head slews toward Becker, ragged motion halting like a stopped clock. He lifts his weapon and aims. Behind the sights of his rifle is chitin, bone, and fury, with a long, smooth head and vertebral tail. Lips part and muscles shake, vibrating with a desire to kill. Viscous saliva pours from between jagged teeth.

Feeling its attention is like being frozen in time. He has to will his heart to take another beat.

"*Back up!*" Garcia pulls him out of the opening as the x-ray charges. It's out the door and in front of him in the blink of an eye, rising up in stark majesty against the storm-gray skies of Hasanova.

"*Get fucked!*" Leger shouts, pulling the trigger on his pulse rifle's grenade launcher.

The poly grenade hits its target squarely in the chest, splattering bright orange chemical strands against the animal's jet-black ribcage. The alien goes flailing backward, rolling through the dirt, and jumps up covered in pumice. Hissing and spitting, it tries to tear the rocks free.

Instead, its own palm sticks to its ribs, and it begins frantically jerking its arm. Leger doesn't let up, racking the slide and putting a few more shots into the animal's limbs and open mouth. The rest of Becker's fireteam joins in, cocooning it with their specialized ammunition.

It rises, hands stuck down and tail glued to the side of its face. Its lips are sealed shut and, to Becker's horror, it breaks its jawbone to force them open, tearing off part of its skin. Stone smokes around its feet as drops of acidic blood strike the earth. It centers up on Becker, mouth flopping open at an awkward angle, and looses a battle cry. He knows in that moment that it will never be tamed, never be broken, and never give up.

It charges him again.

One of the Good Boys comes streaking out the ship, slamming into it. They tangle together in the dirt, but the Good Boy is faster, kicking free and looming over the x-ray. It blasts the creature with its sonic weapons while Becker's team reloads.

The soldiers glue the creature to the ground, taking no chances. It's still screaming through a broken mouth. The Good Boy turns and dashes back inside, armor plates smoking and brown where it took a few drops of blood.

"You're supposed to let it come to us, dumbass," Lee grumbles over his radio. *"Make sure it's out of commission."*

They approach the downed beast, glancing back into the airlock from whence it came. Judging from the unbearable alarms of the Good Boys and the gnashing, the battle is drawing closer. More are coming, and then he sees them massing in the corridor like a wave of death.

"Positions!" Becker calls, and they rush to flank the airlock at a wide spread.

The *Blackstar* spews a sea of oily chitin. X-ray after x-ray streaks through the opening. Some of them climb the exterior walls of the vessel, shrieking and grasping like tormented souls reaching up from Hell itself. Good Boys leap up after them, latching onto the hull with specialized hooks and continuing in hot pursuit. Other x-rays race toward Sergeant Lee's fireteam, tails lashing as they kick up igneous gravel.

Becker had told himself he was ready. He'd believed he would never flinch in the face of an enemy, be it human soldiers or unfeeling sentry guns. But this stampede of armored beasts is something beyond human, beyond civilization, a hideous foe from the dark heart of space.

As the last creature exits the *Blackstar*, a pack of deafening Good Boys comes rocketing after it. They corral the x-rays, shooting past the monsters at a cheetah's pace, cornering with a mechanical balance that no mere animal could stand to match. They race up and down the rocky terrain, and every time a bug diverts toward the marines, the men calmly take pot shots until it's a ravening mess of orange goo, lying in the dirt.

Becker now knows, beyond the shadow of a doubt, that if he didn't have those robots watching over him, he'd already be dead. This isn't matching mettle with the deadliest creature in the galaxy—it's fox hunting.

From a nearby ridge, Private Clayton fires a modified air-burst rocket-propelled grenade, which showers the pack in sticky strands. The beasts scramble over their fallen, outright killing some in their enraged stampede. The other soldiers join in, pelting their prey with poly grenades. Becker adds his ammunition to the party and before long, they're left with two dozen furious creatures straining against rapidly hardening bondage.

"*Duncan here,*" the captain radios. "*Looks like we hit the jackpot. Buzzard Two, drop kennels and loiter.*"

"*Duncan, this is Buzzard Two, I've got eyes on three loose x-rays approaching from the east, advise.*"

"*Buzzard Two, Duncan. Weapons free and prosecute. We're stocked up.*"

The dropship's keel gun, a twenty-five millimeter "Bert," spins up and blows apart a couple of creatures unfortunate enough to be out of cover. The bright lances of fire strike like a thousand lightning bolts per second, obliterating any evidence of their existence save for the smoke of their acidic blood. The ship then maneuvers over an empty patch of rock, and the personnel inside push big glassy crates out the back. The kennels *thunk* down, kicking up a huge dust cloud, which the vertical engines handily disperse.

"*Becker, Lee,*" the sergeant says. "*You're the new guy, so your squad is on cleanup with mine. Let's go scrape the dregs. One or two always get past.*"

"Yes, Sergeant," he replies, motioning for his people to form up. As Becker can now see, one or two is too many to leave running around. The two fireteams join at the entrance, check their gear, and reload.

"We bringing the Good Boys, Sergeant?" Becker asks, but Lee just shoulders past him, rifle at the ready. The rest of Lee's team disappears into the ship after him.

"Final sweep always takes a personal touch," Leger says, patting Becker on the shoulder as he passes. "Bots just don't cut it."

The sergeant takes point without another word, more than happy to delve into the blasphemous corridor ahead of them. Becker motions for his people to follow and they proceed, the only sound the soft clicks of their armor's joint locks.

They emerge into a cargo bay, and Becker sweeps his pulse rifle's flashlight across the ceiling. He thought the monsters had redecorated the corridor, but they've been extra busy in here. He feels like Jonah in the belly of the whale, black rib buttresses glimmering overhead with viscous jelly. The only sounds are the drip-drop of water and the rhythmic beep of Garcia's tracker.

"Motherfuckers get gooey when you rile them," Leger breathes. *"Don't touch anything."*

"No one would willingly do that," Becker replies as Private Keuhlen snaps off a piece of resin to inspect. He glares at his private, who tosses the spike to the deck.

"I wasn't going to keep it," Keuhlen says.

The fireteams sweep the first deck, finding more of the chitinous material stuck to every surface. Periodically, Becker sees some small thing—like a box or a tool—caught inside the resin.

"Where are all the bodies?" Garcia whispers, checking the walls around her.

"What do you mean?" Becker asks, but he's heard stories: feet and hands, terrified faces embedded in the walls.

"One body, one beast," she says. *"They, uh, grow inside people."*

What the everloving fuck are these things, man?

"Command, this is Becker. We're not finding expected casualties. Please advise."

"Becker, this is Dr. Matsushita," the soft voice of the company man replies. *"This is not our concern. Please access the cryo lab on A-deck, aft side and report back."*

Becker scowls and looks to his team. He's not accustomed to taking orders from civvies.

"Command, Becker, please confirm you want us to—"

"Becker, Duncan," the captain says. *"If the good doctor wants us there, we go. You and Lee are to converge on the sample lab. Keep your eyes open. Some of them don't react as strongly to the Good Boys."*

"Copy." He gestures for the others to move to the stairwell and ascend. They should be seeing Lee's team soon. "Watch your fire. Coming up on friendlies." The hallway before him flickers with intermittent power. The lights are mostly down or covered over. He spots a quartet of flashlights at the far end and lowers his muzzle.

"Lee, Becker. That you, Gunny?" Becker asks. It doesn't seem likely to be anyone else, but then, a bunch of stupid animals shouldn't have landed a starship here. He's not taking any chances.

"It's us. Hold your fire," Lee responds.

The two fireteams gather outside the door marked "Cryo Lab." There's a heavy-duty lock on the hatch, and the door itself is thicker than others—maybe soundproof, which would be a problem for the Good Boys. Anything inside would've been immune to their sonic attacks.

Lee signals for a breach, and they lug out the laser drill, securing it to the latch. With a little searching on the pulse scope, they're able to locate the locking mechanism, ratchet the drill clips down, and charge to fire. Before they can pull the trigger, the door slides up into its pocket, scraping the hefty laser from its mountings.

The monster that emerges into the thick of the marines is larger, faster, and louder than anything Becker has seen yet. It swings over the threshold into Lee, pinning him against the far wall with one talon. The sergeant's PRAE reactive chest plate blows off with a flash, knocking the x-ray backward into the lab.

Before they can take aim, it smashes into them again, hammering marines with its claws and tail, sending bits of reactive armor flying with each hit. Garcia scrambles to get back from the door, but it grabs her foot and, one-handed, throws her against Leger. The result is like banging flints together to get a spark, and both soldiers cry out as their PRAE plates burst into each other.

One of Lee's team—Becker doesn't see who—fires a glue grenade. It misses the mark, striking Keuhlen, who staggers backward. With a whipping twist and a slap of its tail, the creature sends Keuhlen stumbling into the remains of Lee's team, tangling a pair of marines in the sticky mess.

"Shit!" Becker can't get a clean shot into the fray, and he's running out of help by the second. Lee shouts in pain as the x-ray picks him up and slams him against the wall, again and again. His back plate comes off on the second hit, and something crunches on the third. Becker hears his rasping cries over the radio, his lungs getting crushed with every slam.

The creature hooks its talons into his liquid-armor-filled underlayer and yanks in either direction, tearing through plastic and kevlar. Blue gel pours from the embedded packs over Lee's chest, tangling into copious blond chest hair.

Fuck me. It's going straight through armor designed to stop it.

It screams in Lee's face, and hundreds of flat plates along its head snap up to fill the air with a sinister rattle. A pair of strangely human lips part into a dripping maw, eager for the kill. The monster raises its tail to strike, a long, shovel-headed barb at the tip. Becker aims high and fires a perfect shot, pinning the tail to the ceiling.

The creature turns on him and charges, snapping and squealing, but it can't quite get to him. Becker plants another glue round at its feet and Lee joins in, putting every polymer grenade he has into the x-ray's backside.

Together, they cocoon it to the wall until there is absolutely no chance of escape, or motion of any kind. The creature falls still. Only its fingers and mouth are free of the fluorescent goo, but it's not fighting like the others—as if it knows when it's beaten.

ALEX WHITE

The other soldiers groan and sound off, and the ones who are capable of doing so rise to their feet. No casualties, but Leger, Garcia, and Keuhlen are plenty shaken. Their hearts hammer on Becker's simplified HUD.

Becker steps closer to the monster, ready to seal off its plump lips with a point-blank grenade, and he spots a metallic box mounted to the side of its head. It's about the size of a deck of cards, and the steel is scratched and scarred. There's a multi-bus charging port on one side, along with a couple of parallel slits.

Someone has attached a speaker to this devil.

"That's her!" Matsushita comes over the radio, so excited he might as well be hyperventilating. *"Go back! Go back! Becker, that's the one! Get me closer."*

Any closer, buddy, and I'll be in its goddamned mouth. Nevertheless, he unclips his shoulder cam and runs the view over their handiwork. At this, the creature strains and lets loose an ear-splitting shriek, but then it calms down.

"You don't much like being on camera, do you?" he breathes, trying to get a better shot of the box. He also finds a set of silver rings, like brass knuckles, wound around its deadly fingers. Rubberized electronic boxes rest atop each finger, maybe some kind of telemetry system.

"What a beauty, yes," the doctor says. *"I've been looking for you. Are you all right?"*

"Matsushita, Becker here. You, uh, want me to ask it if it's okay?"

"*No, Corporal,*" Dr. Matsushita says. "*Captain, please take special care of this one. She is so very precious.*"

"*Sergeant Lee, this is Duncan. Check the rest of the ship so we can scrape the doctor's science project off the wall.*"

"Copy," Lee coughs. He lays on the ground, clutching his chest and wheezing, but otherwise intact. Becker offers a hand, which he takes.

"Thanks," Lee says as he's hoisted to his feet.

"Do I get to ask questions in the briefings now, Sergeant?"

"Don't fucking push me, boy."

"Hey, Gunny!" one of the grunts calls from inside the lab. "You're gonna want to see this."

"What is it?" Lee asks.

"Got a bunch of eggs frozen up in here!"

Becker heads inside to find dozens of cryo lockers on the walls, curtains of mist wafting from their front plates. UAEV *Blackstar* is supposed to be a science vessel, and it certainly has no shortage of these tiny pods.

"Jackpot," Lee grunts, coming up behind him. His straw-colored chest is tangled in blue goo and he's barely clothed, but he's on his feet, checking the place out.

"Excuse me, Gunny?" Becker asks.

"Eggs. Frozen," Lee says. "Each one of these fuckers could be the end of a planet, under the wrong circumstances."

Becker prods one of the control panels with the tip of his gun. It lights up green, showing a scan of the occupant—a little crablike hand rests inside a thick ovum, fingers curled over itself.

"Good thing we got here first, then," Becker says.

Lee smirks. "Yeah."

"Gunny!" One of Lee's boys, maybe Ames, calls out from the next room over.

"Yeah?"

"Got a popsicle here. Looks human."

Becker and the others file into a little room off to the side, where the crew pods might've once gone. They're all empty now, save for one. A couple of privates from Lee's team are checking the fridge to see if it's still working okay, and the cooling system seems to be intact.

"Alive?" Lee asks.

The private looks up from the info panel. "Somehow. Fucker's missing an arm."

1 5

COVER

Shy waits in her suite in the Human Centre, trying to make out any movement in the base below. She'd hoped to watch from the command post as the marines fought the aliens, but Duncan kicked out all of the McAllen people.

There's been activity all day on the various pads— dropships taking off and landing, but Shy can't tell what they're doing from her high vantage point. Whatever they've unloaded, there were a lot of crates and tarps involved.

She's been instructed to stay on this floor, but they're pretty lax about where she can run around. The most specific warnings she got were, *"Don't leave this building, stay out of the Maw."*

Not a problem, guys. I'm not ending up like Kamran.

Shy feels lonely in her crowded suite. Jerry and Mary are asleep next door. Joanna is drunk and belligerent, and there's no way Shy wants to hang out with Noah. She lights her last Balaji Imperial and paces, thinking about Arthur. She wishes he wasn't married, because a decent lay would be a godsend right about now.

But he is married, with a very nice wife who personally made me dinner twice, she reminds herself. *Oh, and there's their hospital-bound daughter, homewrecker.*

She probably needs to stop beating herself up so much, but she can't. She's an idiot for coming out here with McAllen, a liability to the marines, and a problem for Hasanova Colony Corp. *Persona non grata* on all counts.

Her door buzzes. It's Marcus, carrying fresh towels for her bathroom. He apparently went and got the cleaning cart, because it's out in the hall behind him.

"You look chipper after such a long nap," she says. "I'm Shy, by the way."

"You'd be hard to forget, even if I wasn't a synthetic person," he replies. "I wanted to check on you and the rest of the crew—your mental health and wellbeing are very important to me."

"That's funny."

"Why?"

"Jerry can't even pay for you to have a decent memory, but you worry about us?" Marcus just gives her a blank look, then pulls the cart inside and unloads some towels, along with a tray of chocolate truffles.

"I hope you don't mind the temptation, but I saw them in storage and thought they could be put to better use."

Shy sighs. "Do you have a girlfriend? This is how you get a girlfriend."

"I think I'd have trouble remembering an anniversary." He gives her a grin. "I'm not particularly interested in humans."

She takes one of the truffles and bites off the top. It's just as decadent as she'd hoped, smooth and cool with a cocoa dusting.

"It's all good. I don't date coworkers."

"That seems like a wise policy. I don't date my owners."

"Well... I mean, I'm not your owner."

"That depends," Marcus says. "Do you see me more as the Fowlers' property, or as company property?"

Shy grimaces. She wishes he wouldn't put it like that. It makes her sound like a slaver. She's heard about the synthetic rebellions in other parts of space, and even talked to Mary about releasing Marcus from service, but Mary wouldn't even consider it.

"He'd just die out there," she told Shy. *"He can't pay for his own upkeep, and if it walked in off the street, would you use a strange computer to run your business?"*

"How much do you think the maintenance is?" Shy asks him. "To fix your memory?"

"By now, my backlogged costs will be something close to eighty-six thousand, seven hundred and fifty-five dollars."

If her bank account had twenty million in it, that wouldn't be a problem.

"I was worried about you, too," Shy says. "When they knocked you out, I—"

"Please don't concern yourself with it. I'm glad to be the only casualty of our encounter with Hasanova security."

There's a knock on the doorframe and she turns to see one of the marine grunts standing there in his uniform.

"Miss Hunt." It's the youthful corporal who held her down and searched her for bombs.

"What?" She doesn't even bother to stop chewing.

"I'm not sure if you remember me. Corporal Becker."

"I recall you throwing me to the ground and groping my body."

"Well, ma'am, we'd like you to speak to Captain Duncan."

"Oh, is she too busy to come over here and manhandle me herself?"

"I assure you, that was a formality."

"Oh! A *formal* molestation." He seems taken aback, which pleases her greatly.

Becker raises a finger. "That's SOP when dealing with hostages. It was for your safety."

"Fuck you," she replies. "Fuck everyone on this *entire fucking planet*. Except sweet Marcus. Sorry, Marcus."

The synthetic nods. "I never doubted you."

Shy snorts, then continues laying into Becker. "Unless Captain Duncan wants to tell me we're going home—"

"We'd like you to identify the creature that took Dr. Afghanzadeh."

She counts on three fingers. "Large. Black. Fast."

He swallows his clear frustration, and that gives her a little surge of happiness. "Miss Hunt, I know you've been through a lot, but it would help us out if you'd be forthcoming."

"I think brutal honesty should qualify."

"Please," Becker says. "I think we've proven we can handle the x-rays."

She narrows her eyes at him. "What's with the goofy nickname? That thing will kill you."

"We call them x-rays. Short for Xenomorph. Started out as a catch-all but—"

"That's stupid. You're stupid. Please leave."

"You'll be completely safe."

"I said I don't want to see a bunch of goddamned bugs!" she shouts at him, gritting her teeth. She's only barely holding it together, and Corporal McBabyface wants her to... what? Go hang out with the monsters? Point one out in a lineup? She can't stop shaking, and the fact that this goon gets to watch infuriates her.

"Okay?" she continues, "I can't handle it. I'm scared! Is that what you'd rather hear? You've got ten other guys who were there, all locked up in the data storehouses, so why don't you ask one of them?"

"I'll come with you," Marcus suggests, then he gestures to Becker, "provided the corporal doesn't object."

Shy has seen synthetics do amazing things: lift cars, jump twenty feet, strip cables just by ripping off the insulation like shucking corn. Underneath that sweet exterior is a machine capable of feats of wonder—but there's no way in hell he's a match for the x-rays.

They both look at her expectantly.

"The sooner we're done," Marcus says, "the sooner we can finish those truffles."

Shy wipes her nose on the back of her hand, and Marcus passes her a tissue.

"Thanks," she says. "Let's go."

They don't fetch any of the others. None of the rest of the McAllen personnel were there when Kamran was snatched, so they don't have anything useful to add. In fact, Shy isn't sure any of them have been useful at all this trip. Jerry and Mary were complaining about the bill. Arthur and Joanna were busy with the air handlers in the Data Cannon, and Noah cost her twenty goddamned million dollars. Shy is done.

Well done.

Burned, even.

When they get to the Thunder Ring, she spots a pair of soldiers escorting a woman in handcuffs. Her clothes are nice, if ruffled, and it isn't until Shy closes the gap that she recognizes the eyes. It's Tiran Shirazi.

Shy halts so abruptly that Corporal Becker walks into her.

"Hey! You stop right there!" she calls to the soldiers. "What the hell are you thinking?"

The two guards are just as surprised when she comes running over to Tiran. Shy unbuttons her McAllen work shirt to reveal her T-shirt underneath.

"Miss! Please stay back," one of the marines says, holding up a hand.

She juts out her jaw and gets in the guy's face.

"What's she going to do? Stare me to death?"

"Miss Hunt," Corporal Becker says, but she's already brushed him off, getting in close to the prisoner. Tiran's eyes are haunted, and she recoils from Shy's presence—perhaps because she blames Shy for her predicament.

You called them here. Are you happy?

It's written large all over the woman's face.

"Excuse me!" the other guard blurts, but Shy takes her shirt and drapes it over Tiran's head and back. Tiran gives her a quick glance, but Shy has no idea if she's helped or not.

Shy wheels on Becker. "Is this how you treat prisoners?"

"We can't allow head coverings," Becker replies. "For security reasons."

"Security my ass," Shy says. "Seems like that's always your excuse. Is that why you joined up? To humiliate women?"

"Corporal, you're required to afford this woman customary religious considerations in accordance with the Montreal Convention," Marcus says.

"Which part, specifically?" one of the soldiers asks.

"I—" Marcus begins, but it's clear from the long pause that he can't remember. The guards exchange glances and laugh.

"Miss Hunt," Becker says with an uncomfortable sigh, "if you want to see why I joined, come downstairs and let me show you what we're protecting you from."

When they arrive at Data Storehouse Five, two sentry guns track Shy's movements. They beep angrily at her approach, and a headless quadruped robot comes trotting out from behind a pile of boxes. Shy isn't sure what the wicked-looking dishes on the side of the bot do, and she doesn't want to find out.

Becker holds up a hand, and the bot walks away. Then he gives Shy and Marcus each a device about the size and shape of an old-fashioned money clip. An LED blinks on the exterior.

"Wear these at all times when you're down here," Becker says. "These guns won't ask you what you're doing before prosecuting you."

"What is it, a lawyer?"

"It will shoot you, Miss Hunt."

"What about the dog-bot?" Shy asks.

"You don't want to get crossways with the Good Boy, either. Best case scenario, he stuns you out. Are we clear?"

She gives him a mocking salute. "A-*ffirmative*."

He leads them past the guardians and bangs on the

door. When the massive, airlocked hatch opens up, blue-green light floods the hall. It isn't until Shy finds the source that her breath hitches.

Three cages line the data center, filled with facsimiles of the nightmare that took Kamran. These creatures are taller than a man, with long heads, black skeletons, and sharp claws—bipedal meat grinders. Their tails swish back and forth as they pace their tiny spaces.

In the dead center of the room, trapped inside an ALON cage with foot-thick walls, is the beast that grabbed Kamran. Though she only saw it for a split second, Shy would never forget a single detail: the rippling rattlesnake scales on its domed head, undulating like waves of grain, its strange, human-like lips, smooth and pert. It's larger than the other drones, and they don't have the moving scales atop their heads. When it comes to the edge of the cage, it walks like a human, almost regal in its presence—matriarchal.

Shy swallows hard and takes a step back.

"No," she says.

"Miss Hunt, the threat has been neutralized." Becker gives her a reassuring smile, but it just accents how recently he was a teenager. "It's perfectly safe. You could shoot that glass with an RPG and it'd hold."

The foul thing that regards her doesn't look neutralized—not remotely. Her breath comes faster. She can't be down here. Not with this bug.

"I don't know or care what an RPG is."

Marcus's gentle hand falls on her shoulder, and she twitches. "Cheyenne, I promise that I will not allow you to come to harm."

"Is that Hunt?" Duncan calls from inside the room. "Hey, get in here, I need to talk to you."

"She doesn't want to," Becker says. "She's frightened by the bug."

"Is she aware of how cages work?"

Shy keeps her fists balled at her sides, staring daggers at the monster that bit off Kamran's arm. It can't hurt her.

"Please," Becker says. "Not just for your country. For Dr. Afghanzadeh, as well."

At this, Shy shoulders past him and into the room. Her phobia is running in overdrive, but she's determined to show everyone that she's just as serious as they are. Becker follows her, though he stops to stand at ease by the door.

Inside, Duncan and the Japanese guy sit in a couple of folding chairs. They've been sharing sodas and a meal while a white dude with a receding hairline types intently at a terminal across the room. The place stinks, and Shy realizes it's whatever Duncan is eating out of a waxy brown paper sack. She dips a fork into it, coming up with a small mound of golden rice and a lump of grayish meat.

"Miss Hunt," Duncan says, "this is my colleague, Dr. Sora Matsushita. He has some questions he'd like to ask you, and then I have a few myself."

Matsushita stands and offers a hand. "Hello."

"You don't look like a soldier," Shy says, not taking it.

"I'm not, I work for Weyland-Yutani. Michael Bishop's staff."

"I don't know who that is."

"He designed me." The voice comes from the far corner, where a man raises his hand. "My name is Bishop. I'm an artificial person."

"Hello, brother," Marcus says, and the other synthetic returns the greeting.

Matsushita takes a few steps toward the cage. "So this is the creature that took Dr. Afghanzadeh?"

The animal's crest ripples faster, sending a chill up her spine. When it turns its head, she spies a little metal box on one side. It almost looks bolted on. Some kind of radio tag, maybe?

"You all right?" Duncan asks. "You look pale."

"I'm fine," Shy says. She's not, though. Every second, she's confronted with a compounding urge to vomit. The captain actually laughs at her, emphasizing her scar-skewed grin.

"Don't like bugs?"

If she could've melted Duncan with a glare, she would've. "My best friend died from a bee sting."

Duncan widens her eyes. "Wow. That's awful."

Shy's face hurts from scowling so hard. "Yeah, so you'll have to pardon me if I don't think I can be down here."

"I lost my best friend, too," Duncan says. "When I was your age."

That couldn't have been more than a year or two ago. Shy regards the captain for a long moment and experiences a surprising pang of sympathy. This marine is undeniably an asshole, but she feels for her. It's hard to lose a best friend, harder still to watch.

"IED. Shrapnel went through her head"—she runs a finger along the puffy half of her jaw—"right across my face, and do you know what?" Duncan rests her elbows on her knees and gives her a killer's smile. "I still come to work. You can tough it out."

Sympathy gone. Thanks, bitch.

"What happened before she attacked?" Matsushita asks.

Shy grimaces. "'She?'"

The scientist ignores the question. "Before Dr. Afghanzadeh was taken. What happened to him?"

"He…" She tries to remember. "I think he cut his hand. I just… I panicked."

Matsushita and the captain exchange looks.

"Cut his hand on what?" he asks, adjusting his glasses.

"He was—" Shy begins, but stops.

There'd been something in the blood. Something moving around beneath Kamran's glove. He was freaking out, and then… violence and tearing. She looks to the Xenomorph trapped inside its ALON cage.

It has no eyes, yet it's looking at her. Maybe it's only her imagination, but it gives her the most imperceptible shake of its head.

"Can that thing understand me?"

Duncan waves to get her attention. "Try to stay focused, Hunt."

"He was trying to get a, uh, like a sample doohickey out of this Fisher instrument," Shy says, miming reaching inside the big black box. Matsushita brightens as if she told him she'd found a kitten.

"Amazing. Did you see the model number?"

"What? Why would I bother to—"

"Hey." Duncan points to the cage.

Shy's synthetic companion has stepped up to the glass, and the creature follows his progress with strange intensity. The plates of its crest ripple in sequence like water, and it draws up to its full height, nearly touching the top of a nine-foot-tall container. Its arms fall to its sides; the tail droops to the ground. When it holds a claw to its chest, Shy is reminded of Michelangelo's *David*, languid of posture.

"Hello," Marcus says.

It reaches out and softly presses a hand to the glass, five fingers bound into three by its glistening onyx skin: thumb, index, ring. Marcus mirrors the gesture, looking up at it with childlike amazement. The corners of the creature's lips twitch and turn downward, forming a distinctly melancholic shape. It opens its mouth as if to speak, but only teeth and a hollow void lie beneath the skin. Marcus tilts his head, and it mirrors him.

To Shy, it's as if there are only two beings in the room, the creature and the failing synthetic, and she cannot possibly understand what's happening. She glances around. Neither can anyone else.

Except perhaps Matsushita.

He has a huge grin as he pulls a remote, pointing it at the cage. When he presses a button, electrodes in the ceiling zap the shit out of the beast, sending it into a wild rage. Marcus jumps back, affronted by its terrible screams. Suddenly Shy's heart is on the verge of exploding, and she's barely able to keep her feet under her. All the wonder is gone; only fear remains.

Duncan guffaws while the creature bangs around inside, snapping and tail striking the transparent walls.

"Don't want her getting too attached." Duncan laughs, taking another big bite of golden rice. "I'm convinced, Doc. This is our girl." She turns. "Miss Hunt, I thank you for your time."

"Great," Shy replies through clenched teeth. "Can I go now?"

"Sure thing," Duncan replies. "Oh, almost forgot. Corporal Becker is going to be your minder for a few days while you get SiteSys online."

"What? No." Shy wants to pass out.

"Not the whole system. Don't much care about the thermostats and lights," Duncan replies. "Just the locks and cameras. Makes the place easy to hold onto."

"No," Shy repeats.

"Jerry has already agreed... to assist his country." Duncan gives her a thin smile. "I'm your ticket out of here, so I'd suggest you take it up with him."

1 6

CONNECTION

For three days, everything Shy says annoys Becker. She doesn't think the Americas are great. She doesn't much like the military. She doesn't appreciate the way he talks about women, yet she calls Captain Duncan a bitch.

Every moment he can spend away from her is a blessing, and he counts the hours until she quits each night. The other grunts think it's funny. Corporal Suedbeck—whom Captain Duncan has nicknamed "Bull" for his initials—ribs him constantly. Bull tells Becker he's lucky for getting to hang out with a hot chick all the time.

That's easy for him to say. He doesn't have to listen to her talk. The other guard details got the *good* contractors. Garcia offered to trade him Mary and Jerry, who take a lot of snack breaks. Becker heard that Arthur used to be a cop, so he sounds cool. Why couldn't the thin red and thin blue lines hang out together instead?

When he drops Shy off at the Human Centre, he hopes to fuck off and have a beer. Sitting around all day while she complains at her portable terminal isn't half as fulfilling as the thrill of a bug hunt.

"Becker, Lee, come in."

He pinches the mic on his shoulder. "Yes, Sergeant?"

"You done hitting that lefty snatch?" There's a note of laughter in the gravelly voice.

Really, Gunny? Really? Becker hangs his head for a moment, then clears his throat.

"I'm at your service, sir."

"Don't call me sir, boy. I work for a living," Lee replies.

"My mistake, Sergeant Lee."

"Get down here. Storehouse Forty-Four. Ten minutes."

That's a long walk through the Thunder Ring to Solutions, then take the elevator as far down as it goes to DS Thirty-Five. Then he has to double-time it around the Spiral to Forty-Four.

"Copy."

The brisk jog takes him past a flurry of activity in Data Storehouses Thirty-Five through Forty-Three. They're quartering the prisoners down there, far away from any of the working server farms—got to make sure their communications stay blacked out for the duration of the mission. All told, there are more than three hundred personnel and families, and Captain Duncan has stuffed them all into an area half the size of an American football field.

Each storehouse is laid out with a server area, an office for monitoring, and a bypass hallway. When he takes these bypass hallways, he glances through the glass to find dozens of people sleeping on the floor, covered in thin, reflective blankets. Most of them have bundled up their spare clothes for a pillow.

He passes Staff Sergeant Wallace and Lance Corporal Jackson escorting one of the Iranians, a hefty man with a puckered face, back to the detention cells. The fellow is sweating, barely able to walk straight, and the few hairs atop his bald head cling together in a sad, stringy mess. His eye is swollen. A cat-scratch of blood bisects his lower lip.

Whoever this dude is, he took a beating.

Upon catching Wallace's gaze, the sergeant gives Becker a look that says, *mind your own business.*

Becker arrives at Forty-Four and takes three seconds to compose himself. It won't do to roll in there winded. He opens the door and is immediately confronted with the hideous screams of at least a dozen x-rays.

They're all lined up at the glass of the bypass hallway, bashing it, freaking out, and jumping around. The ALON barrier holds, and he stares in amazement. If they get the opportunity to kill him, all he has is a sidearm, so it scarcely matters what he does.

Duncan has quarantined the creatures in an empty server area, minus the big one with the freakish head and lips.

Well, more freakish than the others.

"Glad you could make it, Becker," Duncan calls, and he snaps to attention with a salute. "At ease, Corporal." She turns to the nearby monitoring office and shouts, "Doctor, please shut these cockroaches up!"

Matsushita and Lee stand inside at the control console, and the doctor triggers the fire system in the server farm. Jets of white gas flood the chambers, flashing red warning lights activate, and the screaming intensifies. When the jets go silent, so do the screams, and the creatures retreat into the corner. They've already shit their black resin all over the walls—Becker assumes it's shit, but really he has no clue—and they huddle against one another like rabbits in a hutch.

"Jesus Christ," he breathes.

Duncan laughs and tongues the inside of her lower lip like she's dipping snuff. "You like that? Working on getting it automated. Like if they hit the window at all, *pshhhh*!" With this, she spreads her fingers like an expanding cloud.

"Yes, sir," he says, hoping she didn't notice him visibly swallow his fear. "It looks great."

"You don't look happy, Becker. Speak your mind." He should've been more approving. Now he has to play one of her mind games.

May as well be honest.

"Sir," Becker says, "I've been wanting to fight these things for awhile, chasing legends. They say no cage can hold them."

"That's why they don't know it's a cage," Duncan says.

"Synthetic resin," Matsushita says, beaming as he leans out of the office. "They won't try to dig out or cut open the floor when they think they made it. If they hit the windows, we can discipline them with halon and liquid nitrogen. Mackie design. He used to work for my company."

Becker nods, because he doesn't know who Mackie is, and he's not sure if it'll actually matter.

"What's wrong, Becker?" Duncan asks. "You look worried."

He glances back the way he came. "The prisoners, sir," he replies. "You aren't concerned about the McTighe Act?"

"What, are you a fucking JAG over here?" Duncan shakes her head. "That's for refugees, not civilians... or enemy combatants," she adds. "We can quarter them as necessity dictates for forty-eight hours. In case you haven't noticed, this is the emergency search and seizure of an Iranian bioweapon, Becker. Christ almighty."

Becker blinks. He thought this was about American civilians. "I was told that, uh..." He searches for the best way to ask what the fuck she just meant. "Sir, could you clarify our mission for me again?"

Duncan's hard-assed mask falters. "You mean you'd like to be read onto level one?" She cracks a lopsided grin.

He's heard of dual-staged missions before—two levels of classification. Every armed maneuver involving a light attack cruiser is, on some level, classified, so it was only a matter of time before he encountered something deep. He just didn't expect it to be this quickly.

"All right, then, let's satisfy your curiosity." She gestures for him to follow, and starts walking down the ramp toward Airlock Forty-Five, the last operation for drilling into Charybdis. "Don't say I didn't warn you, though." Mashing the cycle button on the airlock, she steps through. Becker follows her in, and they wait an awkward moment for the outer doors to open.

"Did you notice something important after our debrief, Corporal?"

"No, sir," he says, because he didn't.

"We're larger than a platoon, Becker, better outfitted, too. Now, when I sent your team into the *Blackstar*, you committed a valorous act and saved your sergeant's life." Becker stands up a little straighter as the outer door snaps open. That's medal-pinning language, and his dad would be over the goddamned moon. Duncan catches the gleam in his eye as the breeze whips into the airlock.

He hasn't been down into the "Maw" yet—that's what the other guys are calling it. When the lift doors open, the thunder of waterfalls penetrates his guts, stuns his lungs. A torrential cylinder of water stretches at least a hundred yards, misting as it violently slams down through the thermal exchangers above. It teaches him a new definition of majesty.

"You like it?" Duncan gestures. "While you were pulling guard duty, New Guy, we loaded in the x-rays from here. Brought the dropship overhead and slipped the sling loads between the gaps in the Data Cannon." As she continues to walk, she points to the silhouette of the massive communications array, suspended between the towers of the colony. "It was balls to the wall doing it like that. We used the big crab robots to grab the cages. Moved the egg crates from the *Blackstar*. Commandeered a lot of civvie equipment. Had a real good time." She smacks her hand down on his shoulder plate. "Shame you couldn't be with us."

Becker wishes he could've been there. Wrangling alien cages through a waterfall sounds exciting as fuck—like the reason he signed up. With something like longing, he eyes the bright orange "Big Crab" loader parked along the carved stone ramp.

"We're special, Becker. Favorite children. We get those extra fireteams for auditioning candidates." She nods to him. "And we're career military. That means we make career decisions. You've already made a few that brought you to us. We want to have you in the family." She jerks her thumb backward in the direction of Data Storehouse Forty-Four. "Sergeant Lee is the one who recommended you for this gig. He likes you a lot."

It takes a lot of composure not to look shocked, and he's almost prouder of the newfound respect than the medal. Lee is a hard son of a bitch, but he seems fair.

"I didn't join the Colonial Marines to mop up skirmishes, Corporal," Duncan says. "I'm here to be a legend."

They've come in sight of the drilling area, and find the place decorated with every variety of safety marker that exists: flashing lights, bars, tape, and cordons denoting danger zones. To Becker's dismay, there's also a sign in two different languages.

موارد ایمنی رعایت شود

HAZARD SUIT REQUIRED

"Do we need masks, sir?"

"Why, to cover your pussy, Corporal?"

Becker's father told him never to speak that way, regardless of how his commanding officer acted. But he never expected Captain Duncan to do so, and Becker chuckles despite himself.

"The Independent Core System Colonies are secessionists, plain and simple," she says. "War between the ICSC and the other superpowers is a foregone conclusion. The Union of Progressive Peoples claims Iran seceded when they signed up with a rival empire, and who are we to disagree? They're going to crush Iran, leaving its worlds undefended."

She makes a "wah-wah" trombone noise, and Becker is certain he's never met an officer so cavalier about literally everything. She talks about war—about stepping into Hell—like it's going to the movies, and she's seen at least as much violence as him—likely a lot more. The scar on her jaw speaks louder than her words.

She might be the only honest captain in the Corps.

"Pretty soon, the UPP is going to claim that this little border world is theirs again. They're going to want it, and we can't let that happen, Corporal, because—and I'm going to sum up the complicated politics bullshit this way—the planet gives us a tactical advantage against them."

Becker nods. This part he understands all too well.

She points further down, through the water, to the cordoned-off entrance that leads to the lowest digging operation.

"What's more, it's home to a fuck-ton of the deadliest bioweapon anyone has ever manufactured. Goddamn, but the United Americas have wanted a marine down here for a long time. I'm not privy to the particulars, but I'm told there was a massive intelligence op, just to set up this operation. Sock-puppet hackers and shit."

"Seriously, sir?" he says. "A bioweapon?"

"Yeah," Duncan says. "There's a lab down there, and what it has inside is fucked up. That's all you need to know." She stops and sizes him up. "This planet needs to belong to us. It's how we shore up the border. I'm going to tell you a plausible story.

"The Iranians were developing illegal weapons," she continues. "We came in to save some American contractors, and found said laboratory... right as Iran has a crisis of sovereignty with the UPP. In the transition, United American occupation becomes United American ownership."

Becker nods. His country wants this planet, and he signed up to serve his country.

She spreads her palms. "The only losers in this equation are the Hasanova Colony Corporation—a group of assholes who bought themselves a bioweapons facility. I seriously doubt they intended it just to be a fucking web host.

"You're new to the Midnighters, so I get it if you want to hang back when the time comes." She nods toward the tunnel of secrets, but makes direct eye contact when she says, "I've got the tasking orders to handle this by any means necessary. I'm ready to read you onto the project. Your team will skip up the chain to work directly with me."

"Not Lee and Percival, sir?"

"Not Percival. He failed the audition, so I'm sending that little bitch home. You, on the other hand, skip an echelon. Do you want to row across the Delaware with Washington, or stay home jacking off on the shore?"

Becker swallows, drawing a breath before throwing a salute.

"Yes, sir."

"Which is it," she says, her expression serious. "Yes, you want to row, or yes, you want to jerk off?"

That short-circuits his brain.

"I'm just screwing with you," she says and she laughs, punching his shoulder a lot harder than necessary. "We're Colonial Marines, Becker. Let's fucking colonize."

INTERLUDE: HAROUN

"Everyone back up! Back up!" Haroun shouts, clearing people away from the doors.

Prisoners pick up their makeshift pallets and scramble away. Haroun is especially harsh with the children, trying to instill a proper sense of fear. He will not forgive himself if even one of them is hurt by a soldier.

In another life, long before his lucrative adventures in data mining and cloud solutions, he was a colonel—which might explain why the Americans singled him out for interrogation. They wanted to know why he was here, what his military capacity was. They wanted to find out what he'd learned about the Weyland Corp site. They wanted inside information on Tiran Shirazi.

Before they hit him, he knew nothing about the site. After a punishing right cross from the swollen Sergeant Lee, he made some shit up. Haroun had felt certain he was about to die as Lee worked him over—the man seemed to have no restraint. Eventually, they lost interest and shoved Haroun back into the improvised prison in Data Storehouse Forty-Two.

"Haroun!" His wife's voice snaps him back to the present. She stands amid the chaos of the other colonists, holding a crying Banu. "Be brave."

When the Colonial Marines ordered surrender, Haroun had taken charge, teaching everyone how to pack to be captured—two outfits, all the meds. As a captive, he's overseen the rationing of food and water to the other prisoners.

Haroun is the de facto ambassador for the colonists in his unit. He's supposed to negotiate for more medicine. He had the training necessary to handle terms of surrender, so requesting some much-needed medical supplies should be straightforward.

He keeps things running smoothly, so the marines play nice. Haroun touches the bruised bridge of his nose.

Mostly smoothly.

The door slides open to reveal a quartet of soldiers flanking an unhooked cryopod on a hydraulic jack. Both the pod and its grumbling conveyance have seen better days, and the marines wrestle it into the room.

"Excuse me, Private," Haroun says. "What's happening? Is Sergeant Wallace around?"

The private, clearly not expecting any English speakers, straightens up and looks at Haroun as though he's a talking goat. Her compatriots connect the cryopod to a power station in the floor—one of the big jacks meant for servers.

"Kamran!" someone shouts from the crowd. People surge forward to get a better look. Haroun rushes to the side of the tube to find Kamran lying beneath the gauzy haze of frost. He looks like death, and he's missing an arm. It's been sheared off at the elbow and bandaged. Haroun keys the panel and checks the vitals.

Kamran Afghanzadeh is alive.

Haroun has only just gotten over his shock when they bring in another cryopod, Arzhang Hamedani—the worker who'd gotten infected in the tunnels. Haroun's stomach churns at the sight of him, face frozen in distorted agony. He was supposed to remain undisturbed until he could be treated. They'd located a foreign pathogen in his system, and there was no way in hell they were going to let it run its course.

"You can't let him defrost," Haroun says, pointing to Arzhang's pod. "Hey. Do you hear me?"

None of these privates seem interested in listening to him. They don't want to get involved, that much is clear. To the soldiers, Haroun is just someone who stands between them and their orders.

"He's stable," one of the marines says as they plug in Arzhang's pod beside Kamran's. "So you're probably good."

Haroun thanks his lucky stars that the power grid was rated to run an obscene amount of computing hardware. He watches over the marines' shoulders as they check the readouts.

My God, Kamran. What happened to you?

Haroun manages to tear himself away.

"We need to be able to refill our medicine," he says. "Some of us will be running out soon."

One of the marines shakes her head. "We were told you had all of your meds."

"Yes, but we've been *using* them," Haroun replies. "Please, you can escort my doctor to the dispensary. She has the list."

"You can all go up there yourselves, soon enough," the private replies, adjusting her grip on her rifle. "I was told to let you know… we're about to pull out. You can handle four more hours."

Haroun blinks. Maybe this thing could actually be coming to an end.

"Of course, but—"

The woman bites her lip. She isn't comfortable with the treatment Haroun is getting, and it shows.

"We'll have some ice cream sent down."

"And insulin," Haroun says, handing her the list their doctor scrawled onto a scrap of paper. He glances at her name patch. "Please, Private… Garcia. It's the only one that can't wait."

She sighs, and takes the list. "All right. Anything else critical?"

"That whole list is critical, but the diabetic child is the only one who will die in the next four hours."

Garcia's face sours as she unfolds the piece of paper to

find a list of drug names and dosages. "This is like half the pharmacy, guy. I—"

"I've made it all easy for you." He points to the top, perhaps a little too emphatically, but he has to make sure she sees. "The doctor and I consulted with the dispensary techs, and it's in order of which shelf you will encounter first, so starting on the left side after you open the door—"

"I get it," Garcia says, tucking the paper into her shirt pocket. "What happened to your face? One of these people did this to you?"

Haroun searches her expression for guile, but finds none. This marine genuinely has no idea that some of Captain Duncan's men dragged him into the constabulary and beat the shit out of him. They're not all on the same page.

Unless your soldiers need to hurt someone, keep them in the dark. Haroun knows this tactic well. *Maybe your commanders' actions simply go above your pay grade.* He wants to tell Garcia what happened, but what's a private going to do to protect him? She'd be more likely to catch a friendly bullet than help him out any time soon.

"Someone settled a score with me," Haroun says. "I used to manage about half of these people. We talked it out."

She looks at him sidelong.

"*Private Garcia, this is Becker, you around?*" The radio call comes on her shoulder walkie, and she turns away to take it.

"Becker, Garcia, go ahead."

"The LT is packing up our NOC. Get over there and help him move his shit."

Haroun's heart sinks. That sounds like orders.

"Just the insulin. Please."

She nods, and he prays she will return.

1 7

DOORS AND LOCKS

Shy is sitting in the basement of Ops, stringing together her thirtieth set of lock-to-gateway links when she finds an unused data node all the way at the end of a SiteSys grid. It looks like a test setup, and she notes the project creator's name: K. AFGHANZADEH. There's a stab of unexpected grief for her former colleague.

He hadn't meant to hurt anyone.

Just got in over his head, like everyone else.

"Aw, Kamran."

Shy wipes her nose before the pair of marines leering at her from the corner can see. Becker isn't that bad, but the others "minding" her can be real assholes. She certainly minds their presence.

Of *course* Kamran had tried to figure out SiteSys on his own. Most newbies couldn't make a switch work a light with it, but Kamran actually got a camera set up. She clicks into the project to find two hundred disorganized attempts to configure the system. The poor guy must've been brought low by the building integration software, because there are two files with very specific names: FUCK_01 and FHUCK_01111.

She can't blame him using an English curse. It really is the best.

Poking through the project directory, she looks for any spikes in the data feeds. She finds one, but it's showing high traffic for the common airflow manifold on the air-handling unit. That's odd, because all of the air handlers should already be hooked up.

Oh, "CAM." Common Airflow Manifold... He must've seen that and routed the camera data to it.

Shy corrects the patch and sends camera packets through the video server. A video feed appears on her terminal and it's live, showing a bunch of safety equipment, Captain Duncan, and Corporal Becker. Her eyes dart up to the two marines in the corner—they're enjoying a game of cards. Then she turns her attention back to the feed. Why would Kamran put a camera all the way down there?

She looks at the stream label: HALO B TIMELAPSE.

He must have just wanted to document his project. The time lapse might've even been a hobby thing—engineers can be dorks that way. This video has a control stream riding on it, and Shy commands the camera to pivot and scan the rest of Charybdis. From her lens's vantage point, she can look up through the tunnel of water.

I'll be damned—it works. He got the controls hooked up right. I hate doing that part.

Heat exchangers, rimed with moonlight, filter waves down to her. In the gaps between torrents, she can make out the data storehouses. The two closest to her have blacked out their windows, but the third—

People lie slumped against the glass.

She squints at the feed. Is that where they're keeping the prisoners? There are so many, crowded into such a small space. Her eyes dart from her monitor to the soldiers in the corner of her basement office again. They're not even a little suspicious.

Why would they be, unless I act suspicious?

She zooms in with the lens, stretching its shitty optics as far as they will go, and can just make out a few miserable faces between the crashes of waves—children's faces. The little ones are all sitting next to the window, watching the lake pour into the Maelstrom. It's probably the most interesting thing to do in those cramped server farms.

Shy makes a decision—to hook up the cameras on every room she can access, and set them to record. She knows how to access the cameras in the rooms she can physically visit, but not the remaining ones for the data storehouses.

For that, she'll need Noah.

For the first work shift, everything goes perfectly. When she commissions a lock, she takes time to make sure the cameras in that general area are tuned up, as well. She's not a super-pro like Noah. She's not even sure she got everything working until she sees Noah, red-faced and purposeful, striding toward her.

When he reaches her, he takes her aside near a column in the Thunder Ring. They're both expected elsewhere, but if they keep it short, no one will notice.

"What the fuck are you doing?" He already knows, or he wouldn't be asking with his hand wrapped tightly around her arm.

"Turning on the cameras."

"You didn't think I was going to notice?"

"I'm surprised it took you this long," Shy says, then she shoots him a dark look. "If you turn me in, I'll tell Becker it was your idea. That you doctored the logs to pin it on me."

"What?" he says, loosening his grip. "Why would I turn you in?"

"Same reason you called the cops, and got us into this situation. Who's Duncan gonna think hooked up the cameras, the network engineer, or some dumbass designer?"

Noah stares at her, aghast.

"You saw the camera Kamran set up?" she asks. "Where I had it pointed?"

"Yeah. The colonists in the storehouse."

"How long have they been down there? Have they been crammed in those cells since we were rescued? What's that, like a week?"

"They're being fed, Shy. They have bathrooms."

"Fuck that, Noah, they're being treated like animals and you know it," she hisses, and he puts up a hand to shush her.

"Shy, you're recording the Colonial Marines without their knowledge," he says, and he glances around nervously. "This'll get messy."

"Not if someone smart comes along, and covers my tracks," Shy says. "Besides, if the soldiers aren't doing anything wrong, what's the problem with recording them?"

Like all network engineers, Noah has a pathological fear of government tyranny. She doesn't know why. Maybe it's their brain chemistry, or maybe it's a security-freak prerequisite, but they all have a hard-on for personal freedom.

She decides to try a different tack.

"This might be worth big bucks to the right news outlets," Shy adds.

That catches his attention. He considers her for a long moment.

"I've already covered it up," he says at long last. "The last thing I wanted was to get fingered with you."

"Good," she says. "Then I need you to hook up the other cameras from the Spiral, so we can look in on the prisoners."

He squeezes her arm hard. "This isn't a humanitarian operation," he growls. "We're just... watching. Nothing else."

"If you want to sell this footage," she says, "you need the good stuff."

"You're nuts."

"You know you can do it." She raises her eyebrows. "You've got black hat tricks."

"That's not the point."

"I think it is. If we're going to catch them doing anything, it's going to be down there."

"I'll think about it."

Then he's gone.

Two shifts pass, and she connects more cameras. Shy grows accustomed to tricking her minders, and feels like an old-fashioned spy. It's almost perfect, until...

"Hey," Private Leger says. "The cap wants to see you in the command center."

Accompanied by Corporal Becker, Shy has just finished the commissioning of the vast array of airlocks around the Thunder Ring. By her calculations, Hasanova Colony is about eighty percent online, controllable from Ops. All of the network nodes down through the Spiral—including the prisoners' cells—are wired. Video is flowing into DS Twenty, one of the only active server farms.

Which means Captain Duncan might have figured out she's being watched. Shy glances at Becker to see if he reacts, but if he knows anything about the summons, it's hidden by his patented military scowl.

"When she calls, we go," he says, leading the way.

They arrive in the Ops command center, which bustles with Colonial Marines. The Bishop is there, along with Matsushita. The swollen, red-faced sergeant is there, too, with his platinum flattop.

A bunch of the marines' equipment is missing, though. The Hasanova Colony workstations have been brought back, arranged haphazardly in their old locations. All the tactical crap they hauled in has been packed up. Duncan reviews something on a portable terminal, then paces.

"We leaving?" Shy asks, and Duncan wheels, annoyed even before she knows who addressed her. Probably used to being treated like a queen.

"Not yet," Duncan says. "Thanks for coming so quickly."

Shy hadn't thought she had any choice.

"Miss Hunt, you understand that—as a captain—my job is to manage things." Duncan taps the tips of her fingers together and saunters closer. "I've been tracking your commissioning efforts, and noticed something odd."

There's no way Duncan doesn't know. Shy's vision swims momentarily as dawning horror ripples through her. Her knees grow weak.

This was a stupid idea.

"You've covered a lot more ground than Brewer, and in a lot less time."

Shy's still digging into her courage when she realizes what Duncan just said. She gives a double-take, and hopes it's taken as gratitude.

"It's true," the captain continues. "Do you think we have time for bullshit? No, I see right through that stuff." Duncan points at her own eyes, then out like a laser, and she laughs.

It's not funny, really, but Sergeant Lee laughs, too, along with the guy she doesn't recognize. The whole room burbles with undeserved, sycophantic chuckling, and that unsettles Shy. She looks for Percival, or *any* of the friendly ones, but finds only strangers.

Suddenly, Becker doesn't seem so bad.

"Anyways, I just thought you'd find that funny," Duncan says with a wink. "You might want to ask your boss for a raise."

It's Shy's turn to laugh. "I don't think I'll be working for McAllen after this."

Duncan nods and drops her hands to her hips. "Good for you, girl. You can do better than a place that'd pay you less than Brewer."

Shy frowns. "How'd you know I get paid less than Noah?"

"Because he was introduced as the network systems engineer, and they called you 'our girl that makes stuff pretty.' Call it instinct, but hey—I don't need a network dork." Duncan throws an arm around Shy, and she sort of smells like the beach somehow. Suntan lotion and sand. "I need the person who understands *this* horseshit."

Duncan points to the central control console. It has an aluminum SiteSys sticker plate on it, and they already have it unlocked. Shy swallows hard, half-expecting to see her video feeds, but no. It's the event scheduler—the most annoying piece of software in existence.

"How am I supposed to enforce lights-out on my boys," she says, "if I can't put it into the damned building schedule? You know?"

The men all laugh again—except Becker, whose lips twitch into a momentary, polite smile. Is this some kind of inside joke? Maybe Duncan is just fucking with her, waiting for the right moment to pounce. She's the type.

"I… totally get it." Shy sits down at the workstation, grabs the tethered stylus, and taps the screen, clicking the cheap plastic button under her index finger. "This one has radial menus. Got to use the alt-sigma combo."

"Okay, I think I did all of that." Duncan leans across Shy and grabs the system manual binder, nearly thwacking her in the face with it as she whips it open. "I was able to save off a version, earlier. Like, on the AllBus port, but I couldn't—"

"Let me guess," Shy says, starting to relax. "Load the file."

"Exactly." Duncan lights up.

This is going well.

"That's the problem with the UI," Shy says. "You probably looked under 'file,' but it's actually under Scheduler, Workspace, Import… I wouldn't have designed it that way, that's for damned sure."

Duncan's scar puckers with her smile. "Well I'll be fucked, Miss Hunt. I didn't give two shits about interfaces before I had this conversation." Again the others laugh, and this time Shy joins them. Maybe she's just paranoid, and there's no inside joke. Maybe they're just a bunch of assholes who are easily amused. What matters is that they're not pulling their pistols on her.

"Miss Hunt," Duncan says, smiling, straightening up, and folding her hands behind her back. "ICSC security forces will be in the star system, soon, and we don't want this planet to be a complicated handoff. We're loading up the bugs in an hour. You're going to be packed and on landing pad alpha in two, if you want a ride out of here."

"What about the *Gardenia*?" Shy asks.

Duncan's smile sours. "Miss Hunt, your useless barge isn't fueled up, which means it's still going to be parked by the processors when the ICSC gets here," she says. "The fuck do you want me to do? Hook up a winch? If you want to wait with the ship, be my guest, but Jesus is only going to put me in your path once. Do you want to be saved, or not?"

Shy's mouth is dry. "Yeah, okay. Sorry I asked."

"Before you go…" The captain's eye twinkles with deadly malice. "Does everything work the same way in the event scheduler?"

"What?" It wasn't the question Shy expected to accompany that look.

"You know… lights, thermostats, doors, locks, speakers. Are event types all loaded in the same way?"

"Yeah," Shy replies. "Just plug in the AllBus and, uh, import your entire workspace."

"I remember the rest. Why don't you run on back to the cozy bunks and start packing with the rest of the collaborators?"

"I'm sorry, what?"

Duncan waves her off. "Get on out of here, kid." She looks to Shy's watchdog. "Corporal Becker, stick around."

"Yes, sir."

Then Shy is in the hall as fast as her legs will take her. The sooner she gets to her room, the sooner she gets to a cryopod and can spend a month in stasis. This is what she's been reduced to—looking forward to unconsciousness.

"Shy!" Noah comes jogging up, no minder to be seen. All the soldiers must be pitching in on the evacuation. "Hey! Did you hear? We're getting the hell off this rock! That means we ditch the surveillance footage."

"Yeah," she says, then it dawns on her. "You'd think they would've started moving the prisoners."

"Who gives a shit about the prisoners?" Noah's nostrils flare. "We're getting out of here. Focus on that."

"Doors and locks…"

"Shy, I am talking to you—"

Something twists in Shy's gut, and her breath hitches.

"Why would she want to schedule doors and locks?"

1 8

FAILURE MODE

Becker stands there while Duncan screws with the console, just like she did when she checked email.

Without warning the science geek speaks up.

"Weyland-Yutani Master Override Sigma Six-Two-Six, Authorization Matsushita," he says. "Bishop, shut down."

"Of course," Bishop says, smiling. "Good night, Dr. Matsushita." The synthetic hunches over and grabs his legs, curling into a ball, balanced on his ankles. He'll be easy to move around, with handholds at the hips and feet.

There's only one good reason to shut down a Bishop, and that's a First Law situation.

"Time to get this party started," Duncan says. "The mission clock starts now."

"Yes, sir," he says, sucking in a breath. *Finally.*

"First off, I want you to find server bay C in..."—she pauses to check notes off an old-fashioned notepad—

"Data Storehouse Twenty, and pull its ten memory cores. Do not miss a single one." She pauses and peers at him. "Then you take them, and you throw them into the fucking vortex."

Is this to be his glorious role—fetching hard drives?

Maybe some clarity would help. "Yes, sir…" he says, then adds, "May I ask—"

"They've been recording us," she says, mirth vanishing, "and you fucking missed it, dipshit. Cheyenne and her little buddy Brewer thought they could get one past Percival. All of the goddamned cameras have been pouring video into the Bay C cluster in DS Twenty, for God knows how long. We're lucky the LT was on his game, honestly, because the whole op could've been blown."

Becker flushes. How long has this been going on? He was supposed to be vigilant. It's a grave dishonor for a soldier to fail his watch. Duncan must see it in his expression.

"It's fine, Corporal," she says, "because you're going to make it right."

"Yes, sir," he says. "I'll destroy the cores."

"Great. After that, I want you to go round up the McAllen contractors and escort them down to Data Storehouse One. Lock them inside and threaten to shoot anyone who tries to hack their way out."

That can't be right.

All of his saliva mysteriously vanishes. "I'm sorry, sir?"

She lets out a long, growling sigh.

"Those people are *witnesses*, Corporal, just as much as they are traitors. This place is a bioweapons facility. America wants the planet, and"—she points to the scientist—"Doctor Matshuwhatever over there wants the facility."

"And Marsalis," the scientist adds.

"Of course, Doctor," Duncan says with a thin smile, "but since I forgot, maybe remind me every thirty seconds instead of every five minutes like you fucking *have* been."

Becker's head reels, but he maintains as stony a composure as he can. Duncan raises a finger as she continues.

"Now if we had landed at Hasanova shooting, that would've been an act of war," she says, "but for the moment, no one knows we're here—a record of our actions is the last thing we need.

"Here's the plan—we take off," she continues. "Then there's a distress call, which the military has every right to investigate. The new unit lands, they find the facility already overrun—a slew of x-rays, humping corpses to the walls." She paces in front of him. "Hasanova Data Solutions is a secessionist planet, so it doesn't belong to the UPP. And if the bugs kill off everyone, it has no living claimant residents—so it doesn't belong to the ICSC anymore."

Becker swallows hard. There are more than three hundred colonists down there. He personally herded those people into their prisons.

She can't be suggesting this.

It's a test of his fidelity.

She wants to know if he'll obey her, or the laws of the United Americas. The Iranians in the data storehouses should be considered civilians. The McAllen contractors *absolutely* are civilians.

"Lee, Wallace, dismissed," Duncan says, "but take Bishop there with you."

The two sergeants look at each other with something like sympathy as they two-man lift the folded-up synthetic. It freaks Becker out a little, how compact a Bishop can get.

The sergeants go out the west entrance, which proves to be a good thing because Becker spots Shy hot-footing it toward him from the east. Her cheeks are flushed, as if she's jogged the whole way. That Noah guy is with her, looking stricken.

Duncan is looking the other way, so Becker makes eye contact with Shy. He doesn't believe in psychic powers, but he musters everything he can to project the words, *do not fucking come in here.*

To his great relief, she gets the message. She pulls up short, but doesn't run. Instead she takes Brewer's hand and drags him toward a thick steel doorframe and out of sight. Every time Becker hopes they're gone, though, he sees the edge of her head. Despite his fears, she's listening.

Stop looking at her, he tells himself. *They'll notice.*

"If you've got doubts about those so-called civvies, Corporal Becker, ditch 'em. This is war. Sometimes it's fought with pulse rifles, other times with nukes, and even with bloodthirsty Xenos. If we took out an illegal weapons plant, the personnel who died would be classified as enemy combatants. This is no different."

She must have noticed his expression.

"You look like you have a question, Corporal."

The people here aren't at an illegal weapons plant. They can't be enemy combatants when they're not part of an enemy force. He has to say something.

"We're not at war with the ICSC, sir."

Duncan smirks. "Not that they're aware of, no."

1 9

RIGHTEOUS FURY

Shy crouches by the door. She was right. Fucking Christ, she was right. Duncan's voice is clear and commanding, easy to understand from their hiding spot.

"It'll take about an hour, but the system will open every door in the place, starting with the data storehouses. Bottom to top—like a lit fuse. Once the x-rays corral the first few Iranians they'll do their thing and build a nest, using the eggs we took from Marsalis's ship. After a few days, the Colonial Marines will swoop in to respond to a distress call and boom... we get a new colony.

"You have to admit," Duncan adds, "there's poetic justice in mixing the devils together in Hell."

Shy has to see Becker's reaction—has to know if he's a murderer. She risks a glance around the corner. Duncan is facing the other way. Becker's eyes meet hers, and he looks desperate.

He's signaling her to help somehow.

"What about the rest of the Midnighters?" Becker says. "They'll be able to guess what happened to the colonists. We can't keep that hidden." It's a protest, and a gentle one at that. Not a denial, just an objection.

"Oh, that won't be us. Our part is almost done—we're strictly on setup duty. Once we're gone, the event scheduler will do its thing, just like Hunt showed me. Another platoon will come, compartmentalize the participants, and clean it out."

Fuck you. I won't help you kill those people.

"Noah," she whispers, "we have to do something."

No reply. When she looks back, he's gone.

Dammit. He might've been able to stop this. Hack the event scheduler from a gateway jack... She doesn't know the system like he does.

Shy peeks into the room again to find Becker looking at her, urgency in his eyes. He just needs the right push to act...

Duncan has stopped talking. She takes a step toward the SiteSys workstation, and it's like she's stepping on Shy's chest. Breath won't come. If she doesn't do something, Duncan's going to murder all of those Iranians.

Another step.

Becker, you know this is wrong, goddamn it.

And another...

"Get away from that console, you bitch!"

Shy didn't mean to scream it. It's brighter in the

command center, where she finds herself sprinting toward the SiteSys keyboard. Her body is chained to her heart, which thrums with four beats.

Got.

To.

Do.

Something.

It's like she's flying, and the world goes on hiatus. It's just Shy, Becker, the console, and Duncan's surprised leer. The captain looks like she's about to burst out laughing, and when Shy storms the dais, she finds Duncan's AllBus drive plugged in.

How far did she get?

Break the drive. Safest way to go.

She reaches for it, and Duncan clamps down on her wrist, halting her advance.

When Shy was fourteen, six girls in McAllen, TX, went missing, and everyone decided to sign their daughters up for gun safety and self-defense courses. There was one move in particular, and Shy never forgot it: pinwheel your arm to break a wrist lock.

She tries it.

Her hand comes free, and to her great surprise, Duncan is thrown off-balance. The captain catches herself, and she's actually *laughing* at Shy for fighting back.

Becker circles around to intervene. Shy only hopes he's coming for Duncan, but she won't wait to find out. She reaches once more, and Duncan's fingers lock onto her shoulder, digging into the flesh. She spins Shy around hard—

—and isn't ready for a powerful backhand. Shy's knuckles connect so satisfyingly with Duncan's cheek that they make a meaty slap. Blond hair comes loose from its tight knot atop the captain's head. Shy didn't mean to hit her like that, but it felt fucking good.

Duncan's psychotic joy instantly switches to the steel underneath. She delivers a sweeping block, and Shy's forearm rings with pain. There's nothing but method in the soldier's eyes as, like an ancient gunslinger, she draws her sidearm and fires.

At first it's the worst chest punch of all time. Shy's left breast, ribs and spine all light on fire, and she grits her teeth to stop herself from screaming.

Holy shit, you shot me.

She needs to move. Take a step back.

There's so much blood. Maybe she can stanch the flow. She presses her palm to her chest, folding in around the pain. Hot wetness spreads down her back— the exit wound.

That can't be what it is. Not possible.

She slips off the dais, falling onto her back and sliding over her copious blood. A wave of dizziness threatens to overwhelm her. Sucking in a jerking breath, she looks to Becker. He's frozen in place, and when blood gurgles deep inside Shy's chest, he gasps.

No more air will come, in or out.

I've heard this noise before, she realizes. *In vet school. It can't be me. Please don't let it be me.* Shy is going to quit this job, and move back home with her mother, and never come outside again. She tells herself this as she struggles for air, because she could use a hug from her mother right now. The floor is so cold.

"Hey, moron." The captain's words burn into Shy's gathering haze like acid. "I already opened the gates five minutes ago."

"You—" Hot blood spills over Shy's lips, and she gags on it.

There are so many endings to the sentence. *You traitor. You murderer. You monster.* Shy chooses to invest her only remaining word in hope. She pleads with Duncan, dimming eyes trying to look past the barrel of her adversary's gun.

The muzzle's silver ring is like a solar eclipse—blinding, transfixing.

"—can't."

You can't.

Captain Duncan disillusions Shy with a cold jerk of the trigger and a bullet through the eye.

INTERLUDE: HAROUN

Haroun has never been a pharmacist's assistant before, but his skills still are helpful. Anyone willing to forego their medical privacy can step up to the long, well-managed line and state their need.

Private Garcia stopped by an hour ago with a sack filled with all of Haroun's requested meds, and more. She'd wrangled two other members of her team to bring juice pouches, ice cream, and some of the pastries from the canteen, and Haroun had professed his everlasting gratitude.

Sanam helps with the distribution effort while Nadia watches Banu to make sure she doesn't get covered in ice cream. It bothers Haroun so much when she does that, but he knows he's too hard on his daughter. Tomorrow they can get started on the rebuilding effort. Maybe in a month, he can take everyone on an off-world vacation. He needs to help Banu forget all about this week.

Though, when the home office hears about his Weyland Corp discovery, they'll put a lot more funding into this place. He could probably convince them to let him put Halo B's budget toward finally opening the Hasanova Spa. *Everyone* needs a vacation, and most can't afford to go off world like he can.

Darkness engulfs them.

Beams of emergency lighting slice through the darkness. Frightened gasps erupt from the crowd.

"Calm! Calm, everyone," Haroun shouts, before they can get a good murmur going. In his years of managing large groups, he has learned that the most important way to control a crowd is to take authority immediately.

They all stop talking and look to him. What is he supposed to say, though? It *is* weird that the lights went out. What if the Americans locked them in these vaults to starve when they left?

Easy, Haroun. They gave you all that medicine. They're not bad people. Not all of them.

"Sanam, find maman and Banu," he whispers, then turns and calls, "Check those cryopods!" pointing over the crowd to where Kamran and Arzhang lie sleeping.

"No power!" someone calls back. "They're in emergency thaw!"

"Get the doctor over there," Haroun says. "The rest of you, I want us to remain patient. This is all very scary, but I assure you, it's almost over." He glances to the thick steel door that bars them from the rest of the world, and prays with every fiber of his being that it will open. Too many of his prayers have gone unanswered recently.

To his surprise, yellow warning flashers pop up across the massive portal's top edge, signaling that the metal slab is about to move. For the first time in days, a genuine smile breaks over Haroun's face.

As the steel doors slide upward, he fills his chest with sweet, free air.

"Everyone, let's go home," he proclaims. The crowd huddles closer. They're all so eager to get out that Haroun worries someone might get crushed.

He's about to say so when the crowd convulses backward. It's the sort of spasmodic maneuver a murmuration of birds makes when a predator flies through it. Then a solitary scream rises up through the crowd—a man's panicked wail.

It's so hard to see in the thin beams of emergency light, but the shouts are unmistakable—true and utter bedlam erupting from the portal. A red puff spurts up into the air, glinting in the lights. More people lunging backward, shoving, leaping up onto one another. He's seen this sort of behavior before—the crowd is about to stampede.

"Banu!" Haroun cries, casting about for his little girl.

"Haroun!" Sanam calls to him. Thank God, she has Banu. Where's Nadia, though?

Something pours over the crowd, and at first, Haroun mistakes it for hot tar. Black shapes clamber over frightened people, claws digging into soft tissues. Screams, human and otherwise, deafen him in the enclosed space, drowning out his voice as he calls for his mother. Whatever is happening, he needs to keep his family together.

Something winds around his hand and grips like iron. Sanam has pushed through to him, Banu crying in her arms. People shove, hard, and Haroun's daughter catches an elbow across the temple.

"Hey!" Haroun bellows, ready to have someone fired, but no one hears him. The mob swells again, twisting and writhing, crushing. It was already a tight space, and now... He gets pressed up against the wall so hard he nearly blacks out. He loses Sanam's hand, and his daughter with her.

Banu...

The crowd breaks loose from whatever held it back and begins pouring out the door. They desperately push against one another, clambering over anything and anyone in their way. There will be several dead after this panic.

You have helped enough, he tells himself. *Just grab your daughter's hand and go.*

"Maman! Sanam!" He jumps as he shouts, cursing his shortness. His belly smacks against the man in front of him when he leaps, but he doesn't care. He needs to get above the throng.

There is a signal stronger than any other in the universe—something like a bonfire, burning bright with four perfect years of birthday parties, and stupid toys, and giggles, and her goddamned sticky fingers on the couch, and that one surgery where he almost lost his faith, but he held on, and so did she.

The signal says *act now*.

It is undeniable.

It is the sound of his child screaming in agony.

He snaps onto the noise like a heat-seeking missile, shouldering along the flow of fleeing people. He steps on something wiggly and tries not to know it was someone's neck. He should be helping. Banu's scream winks out as she runs out of breath.

Scream again, please!

"Banu!"

Her head pops up above the crowd, gap-toothed mouth in a terrified wail—Sanam must be holding her up. Tears sparkle in the emergency lights, but she's looking around, she's frightened. That's good. Frightened is good, because it is alive.

People move out of the way for Haroun, scrambling backward. They're looking at something behind him, mortified—but it doesn't matter because Banu screams for him again. A man beside Haroun barks a shout, like something knocked all of the air out of him, and vanishes.

The group around Banu is a mob, panicked and pressing backward into the corner. Their cries are unnatural.

Maybe they're not the ones screeching.

Something, perhaps the infernal spawn of a horse and a blowtorch, hisses to his left. He's about to care when he sees Banu struggling against the sea of panicked heads. She makes eye contact, reaches for him. Hands force her up over the crushing bodies, and Banu pops out between several gasping people.

Sanam's anniversary bracelet glitters upon the wrist

that pushed her free. People at the edges are climbing their neighbors to get away, and his wife is at the dead center of the mob. His thoughts fill with a prayer, brief as a synaptic spark.

Please save Banu again.

A creature meets the crowd full-force with its long, curved, battering-ram skull. The woman two paces ahead of Haroun takes the brunt of it, and her chest crumples like a sack of broken glass. The crowd comes off their feet, and someone's shoes go flying. Bodies spill over the creature like a raging bull, and it slings a man to the ground before clawing his guts open.

Banu is at the top.

You can get to her.

Haroun leaps onto the downed mob, pushing over anyone and everyone, past the furious creature. He has Banu's arm. He pulls, but she won't come free. She calls for her baba, so he gives it everything he has. The monsters—there are more of them, just flashes of chitin, claws, black bones, and teeth—go wild, burrowing into the bodies around him. There is no time to free her any other way.

The force is more than Banu's shoulder can take, and after a chicken-bone pop through her tiny arm, he offers a second prayer.

Please let her forgive me and forget this.

Haroun braces and pulls until his child is free, despite her screams. She weeps and wails in his arms with all the rage of a newborn. That means she's breathing, and that's the important part.

There is nothing that matters more than Banu, the light of all his days. His entire world is being devoured, but at least that one thing remains unchanged. He *will* get her out of this.

He turns to find a den of monsters and the white tiles of the would-be server farm glazed with blood. He pushes off the wall of flesh with his daughter in tow, weaving toward the open door and the beyond. The animals seem preoccupied with their prey, pinning people down with talons so they can pull them apart in hunks.

This place—Charybdis—is all-devouring, and he brought his family to it. This is his fault.

He passes the freezers with their thawing occupants—unmolested for now. It shames him not to help, but these cryopods have become ovens. They'll warm up the food, then a timer will go off.

Haroun dares not look back the way he came. There is only forward. He reaches the hall and hears the choirs of condemned coming from the direction of the Maw. It's all of the people dying inside the other data storehouses.

He presses a hand over Banu's mouth to stifle her moans. The creatures have the infinite grace to let him pass while they eat, and he doesn't wish to tempt them with Banu's cries. "Shush, shush, azizam," he soothes. "Please, you have to be quiet. Hold your breath and I will buy you anything—"

But it's not working. She's so terrified that her little body vibrates, and she's been betrayed.

"—pulled my arm…" She sobs into his collar, and he pushes her head against his puffy chest. That keeps her at least muffled as he frantically searches out the exit.

She always was a cuddly child.

He races through three data storehouses, but the screams grow louder ahead of him. He rounds the curve to find a closed door, and a crowd of at least sixty people jostling to get to the panel. It's bedlam.

A squeal rings out behind him, and he makes the mistake of looking back to find one of the things galloping up the corridor. It slows to a trot, then stops, coming up onto two legs—almost human. The nightmare peers blindly into him, interrogating every notion he ever possessed of lethality.

When Haroun looks around, he realizes that he stands alone, away from the crowd—away from the herd.

"I love you," he tells Banu. "Go hide."

Then he hurls her behind him and runs at the animal. His charging days are over, but he still manages a floppy gallop and with each footfall, more of his muscles come to life. He was a young man, once, an officer with military training, and an okay cricket player. He would stand against any adversary, even God himself, for Banu.

As the creature sinks low, prepared to receive its meal, Haroun knows he is going to die. It spins and smashes the spade of its tail into the side of his face. He wishes he'd at least landed a punch. But no, it's just chitin bashing one cheek, then the floor smacking the other.

His world rings as it clambers past him, but he wraps his arms around a leg, refusing to let go. It's cold and smooth, and he dazedly searches for purchase on it. It jerks its leg free and kicks his abdomen with the force of a horse, shattering his hip.

If he were ever worried that he didn't have its attention, sharp teeth and claws remedy that. It savages him, biting, beating, paralyzing, tenderizing.

But no killing blow.

A heavy hit breaks something in his back, and he hears the crunch through his own skull. He knows he will be finished, soon, and he welcomes death. To endure any more of this agony is impossible.

When he flops to the ground, he sees Banu's quaking silhouette. She's not running away to hide, like he'd hoped. One of his baby's arms hangs uselessly at her side, but the other is locked into a tight fist.

"Let him go," she says.

She's being brave, just as he taught her to be.

Please—

The animal pivots to face her.

If I am worthy, I beg you—

Its claws are so large that they wrap around her like a toy, and she squeals like a rabbit in an owl's grip.

Do not make me watch.

It lifts Banu to the heavens, as if in gratitude, and—

PART III

REVENANT

FIVE MONTHS AGO:

TOP SECRET//NOFORN//ORCON - ROSE EAGLE
TRANSMISSION INTERCEPT 01 March 2184

(TS//OC-RE)

THIEN:	The files you stole with the Blackstar are missing an entry.
MARSALIS:	You have my attention.
THIEN:	I've placed the information in your old drop. I hope it's what you're looking for.
MARSALIS:	Explain why I would trust you.

[CONNECTION TERMINATED]

2 0

EXFILTRATION

The light from Shy's remaining eye is gone with the flash of the muzzle. Her head snaps backward and bounces once against the ground. She twitches, but Becker knows it's meaningless.

Duncan wipes a split lip on the back of her hand and checks it like she's never seen her own blood. She's not even breathing hard.

She's about to turn around.

"I—" Becker chokes on his own dry throat and curses himself. "She came at you."

Her gaze locks onto him like a raptor spotting prey.

"You have the tasking order," he continues. "That means she attacked you in the course of a combat mission. You had to defend yourself." He's a coward for excusing it, but he needs time to think. No part of him was prepared for this moment.

It'd sounded like a reasonable request—help the Americas gain a foothold. He hadn't understood what he was agreeing to do.

Get ahold of yourself, or she'll see— Duncan draws closer to him, and he stiffens. If he looks frightened, she might assume him to be a squealer. Standing nearby, Matsushita keeps studying his notes, and hasn't even looked at the corpse. That's unnatural, but it might fit his profile. Anyone who likes to play with the x-rays must be a little damaged.

Duncan remains silent. She's probably waiting to let him hang himself with his own rope. If she senses even the tiniest iota of disloyalty, he's sure she will end him. So Becker gestures to Shy, but doesn't let his eyes travel to her body.

"She was helping them develop weapons, a civilian at an illegal facility."

There are people alive downstairs.

As he speaks, his mind continues racing. He scans the room. It's just the science geek and the captain. If he put a round into her, there's no way Matsushita could stop him from getting to the console and—

A glimmer of recognition tints her eyes.

"Aw, Jesus, Captain." It's Lee's voice at the doorway. He and Wallace must've come running when they heard the shots.

Duncan groans. "You knew she wasn't walking out of here, Sergeant," she growls. "Don't *even* give me that shit."

So she's got Wallace and Lee.

Duncan's tension appears to drain out, and she looks at Becker. "Corporal Shit-wit, it doesn't matter what story you've got, because *we were never here.* I appreciate the enthusiasm, but it's a waste of energy. We're next door to the galaxy's largest toilet. No one is ever, ever going to find this body."

Becker thinks of Shy's lifeless form spiraling into the abyss, dashed against the rocks. Have other secrets been flushed down there? How many bones will she be joining?

Got to save anyone I can.

He can't lock the data storehouse doors. Even if Duncan, Lee, Wallace, and Matsushita weren't there, he doesn't know how to operate the terminal. Even if he *did*, how could he be sure he's helping? He might be locking the creatures in.

The other contractors should be alive. As American citizens, they're his first priority, right? This wasn't exactly in the fucking training.

Find them. First I have to find them. Becker takes his rifle and heads to the tracking station. All personnel are required to wear trackers. The Iranian colonists lost theirs in the "enhanced" search they received, but the Americans should still have them.

"What are you doing?" Wallace demands, his chin wobbling. He has a soft, friendly face and a goatee. No one would guess that he participated in the murder of an American citizen.

"Captain ordered me to track down the contractors, Sergeant," Becker replies. "They're still in their rooms." It's not entirely true. He finds Noah Brewer's tracker dot speeding down the hallway on the map, and wonders if the system is reading wrong.

"All right, then," Duncan says, checking the SiteSys station. "Looks like the doors are open as high up as DS Thirty-One, so the x-rays are coming. We've got one hour before the whole complex is free-access. Destroy those fucking cores, Becker."

"Yes, sir."

"Dismissed."

And he's out. Crossing over the exit threshold is like being shot out of a cannon. How he's still alive, he has no idea. Duncan controls all routes onto and off of the planet, and he's a witness to straight-up murder.

Who else knows?

Witnessing the death and doing nothing makes them complicit, at the least. Then again, it's not like Becker did anything. Technically, he should have relieved Duncan of her command right there and then—though he's ninety-five percent certain that would've resulted in a new hole in his head. Could the others be biding their time as well?

No, not Matsushita. He's obsessed with the specimen he calls "Marsalis," and would do anything to get it off world to his lab.

Not Sergeant Lee. He's been calm and collected the entire time, acting like it was business as usual. And

Wallace doesn't seem the type to question authority. With a compartmentalized "mission" like this, Duncan could've told anyone as much or as little as she wanted. How many of them were carrying out genocide, content to be foot soldiers in the coming war?

What am I going to do when I get the McAllen people?

He could take them somewhere and hide them. There are so many unused offices; they could lay low and figure out a way to seal themselves inside. Maybe Becker could help the survivors below—if there are any. Surely some of them are alive, based on sheer numbers alone. There are more than three hundred colonists to maybe two dozen x-rays.

Becker hits the first floor of Ops, racing off the elevator and through the richly appointed lobby. There were going to be shops here, and a lot of the wares have already been set up—luxury clothing and skin care products, vacation planning and cafés. Families were here to operate these businesses.

What he wouldn't give to run into someone from his fireteam. He can't radio them. If he starts calling people, Duncan is going to know something is up. He needs to meet them in person, and that's going to be a roll of the dice.

Dread churns in his gut as he sprints through the wave-smashed Thunder Ring. He got too lucky back there. Duncan isn't stupid—she'll figure out he's not on her side soon enough. Maybe she already has. His orders were to deliver the contractors to a place where the x-rays could drag them off. Maybe she figured she could dispose of the errand boy while she was at it.

No, a missing marine would be too hard to explain.

The captain is the one who certifies his death certificate, along with all its details. It requires the signature of a sergeant. Sergeants Flattop and Goatee would be more than happy to oblige.

Becker takes the long way through the lobby, and his gamble pays off—Private First Class Garcia is there, stacking coolers outside the cafeteria. When he gets closer, he sees that the olive drab of her shirt has a forest green collar of sweat.

"Garcia," he says, "drop everything and follow me." When she falls in behind him, he adds, "You been running laps?"

"I was delivering some supplies to the prisoners before we bailed on them."

"'Bailed on them,'" he repeats.

"Yeah. It's weird just to lock them in the storehouses with time-release locks," she says. "What if the power goes out after we leave, and they starve to death? Did you see those kids down there?"

Oh, God, Garcia. That's not the problem.

He thinks he can trust her, but he can't stop to explain. With Duncan moving the troops out at double-time, it puts him on a schedule. He needs an ally—someone who can stay connected to teams and tell him what's going on.

What does he know about Garcia? She's only been with the Midnighters for four drops. She doesn't seem to like Lee, but she gets along with Wallace. Becker wants to believe she's okay, but right now, *nothing* can be classed as "okay."

"Switch your radio to sixteen Charlie," Becker says.

She gives him a look. "My radio isn't keyed for C. I didn't think I'd need today's cipher."

"Well *I do* have it, and I might need to call you. Make it happen."

"Lee told us loadout is on twenty-five alpha. How am I going to help them if I'm not on their channel?" She's confused. "Captain isn't going to give me another radio."

"I gave you an order," he snaps. "I'm your goddamned superior, and—"

That was stupid. He needs friends. Becker runs his palm down his face, pulling at the sharkskin of his chin. As they jog along, they encounter more and more marines, all involved in preparations for the evacuation.

"Shit, I'm sorry, Garcia. I'm—something important is going down."

"You know I'm not trying to be insubordinate," she says. "What's happening?"

He glances around, dying to give some indication—to find one other sane person at the moment. There are too many other marines around. Opening his mouth here might catch them both a bullet.

"Keep up, Private," he says, putting a little more juice in his stride. They enter a stretch of empty corridor.

Becker enjoyed all of the cool geometric designs when they arrived, but he'll have nightmares about this place now. They stop at the block of lifts, and he turns to her.

"I'm going to fetch our civilians—the McAllen crew—and disappear for a while."

"You want to elaborate?"

"I'm trying to get them into hiding."

The lift bank opens, and two of Lee's boys step off. They're armored for loadout in full PRAE suits—which isn't SOP—and he'd like to know where they're going. It must be some errand for Duncan. Maybe the Marsalis specimen.

"What's up, buddy?" Corporal Ames asks as he passes, slapping Becker on the arm. Ames and Lee are tight. After Becker saved Lee's life, he worked out with Ames once or twice. The guy could get weirdly competitive. The other one—Private Hanssen—Becker doesn't really know. They're both a couple of hard-edged bastards, though. They've got to be loyal to Duncan, so Becker shuts his mouth and prays Garcia does the same.

Ames stops, turns around—and stares, like he's searching for something. Then he gives Becker an affirming nod. His eyes say, *Welcome to the fucking club, friend.*

The pair vanish around a corner, and Becker turns to Garcia. He won't survive alone.

Time to make a leap of faith.

"The captain set the x-rays loose on all those people downstairs." It's the first time he's said it aloud. Even as the words leave his lips, he doesn't want to believe them.

When she blinks, it's like a snap, a spasm.

"Don't fuck with me like this, Becker. You know that shit isn't—"

"That's the reality, and time's limited, so listen. We're wearing trackers," he says, keeping the strain of tears out of his voice. He can't crack now. "We can't be seen together for too long. I don't know who's in on it, but it's goddamned genocide." Her eyes go wide, and she's thinking of the kids. He knows this, because he is, too.

"We have oaths to keep now," he says. "Protect the innocents that are left."

"You're—"

"*Please* listen. Lee and Wallace, Corporals Ames and Hanssen are dirty. That's all I know for sure. We have got to figure out who's left, and do something to save these people."

She throws up her hands. "What, just you and me? Assuming you're right, there's a platoon of guys—"

"Switch your radio, Private. Figure out who we can trust. They can't *all* be bad."

"How about I start with you?" She crosses her arms. "How can I be sure you're not just cracking? Going AWOL with a couple of civvies! You might be a whacked-out traitor who thinks he's in an action vid."

Breath hisses from his nose. "Duncan shot Cheyenne Hunt. Happened in the command center. I saw the whole thing. You could check it out for yourself—but they won't let you in. Believe me or don't, our time is up. Our trackers can't be together any longer."

The next lift arrives, empty.

"If you're right, and we're alone on this, we're dead," she says. "Half the goddamned platoon hangs out with those guys. We *might* have a fireteam, at the most. Is there anyone else we can trust?"

He shakes his head. "Maybe our team. Hard to say. Remember, sixteen Charlie," he says, stepping on. "Get it done." He leaves Garcia standing there and rides the lift up to the apartments where they quartered the McAllen people. Raised voices echo down the hall— it sounds like they're having a meeting, and it's not going well.

Becker pauses by the door to listen for a moment.

If they're not alone, it might be a problem.

"Jerry—" that Noah guy says, "she's out of control! First she has me like… linking up all of the camera feeds for SiteSys—"

"You what?" It must be Jerry.

"Then she went to confront Duncan," Noah says. "Man, you need to get a hold of her."

Becker bangs on the door. "Marines. Open up!" The voices inside go quiet, whispering like a boiling pot. He's used to this. Banging again, he adds, "I did not ask. Let's go." The door opens, and it's the older woman, Mary. She eyes him suspiciously.

"How can I help you?"

Behind Mary, Jerry stands at the kitchen island eating cheese and crackers. Marcus works at the stove beside him. Joanna sits on the couch, chewing gum and looking grim. The big guy, Arthur, is in the galley, a pair of rectangular gold reading rims set low on his nose. His portable terminal rests beside him, but all of his attention is on Becker. Noah stands in the middle, like he was giving a speech before the interruption.

"Whatever trouble she's gotten us into," Noah calls over Mary's shoulder, "I don't want any part of it." This is when Becker realizes he hasn't concocted an excuse that will get them to come along. The entire time he was moving, he should've been scheming. He was too shell-shocked.

"There's been a quarantine breach," he says. "Your lives are in danger. Leave your belongings and come with me." The words get Mary to stand aside, and they rattle the group to the bone—everyone except Marcus.

Shit. I forgot about the synthetic.

"We understand," Marcus says, concerned, but not panicked. "Where is—" He blinks, frowns, and looks to Jerry. "My... friend?" If Marcus is having memory problems, maybe Becker can trick him into coming along, after all.

"Where's Shy?" Mary asks, hand resting on her heart.

"Yes," Marcus says. "Shy."

It's the question he'd been hoping to avoid. If they know the truth, they'll go to pieces, and he needs them calm.

"She's on the first dropship out of here," he says, fighting to keep his voice stable. "That's where I'm taking you."

It's difficult not to look at Marcus. Lying to a bunch of fear-stricken civilians is one thing, but a synth can count the wingbeats of a hummingbird. Becker imagines that the synthetic is looking for the bob of his throat, and suddenly he needs to swallow.

Marcus rounds the kitchen island with a confident stride, yet nothing changes in his expression. He comes straight toward Becker, looking him dead in the eyes, but otherwise appears to bear no malice.

Until he's way too close.

He didn't buy it.

Becker has his rifle halfway unslung when Marcus lunges. The synthetic steps in, palm striking his chest armor, and it's like getting hit by a piston. Becker's torso goes back, and his feet whip out so hard they'd lose their boots if they weren't laced on. He comes down on his ass, and the synthetic pins his wrists to the ground with a single unyielding hand. Surprised shouts fill the room.

"What the fuck?" Becker says. "Don't—harm humans!" It's the smartest thing he can think of in the moment.

"You're lying, Corporal," Marcus says. "Where is Shy? Before you answer, I should tell you that the chains restraining my mind are somewhat… corroded, by my lack of maintenance." His grip is relentless, compensating for any wiggle Becker might try.

There's nothing more dangerous than a synthetic without a behavioral inhibitor. He could crush Becker's throat, break his neck, cave in his skull—the list runs through his mind on repeat as he stares into Marcus's impassive eyes. He doesn't want to tell the contractors the whole story—not yet—but Marcus might end him right here.

That won't save any lives.

"She's dead," Becker grunts. "Duncan murdered her."

Marcus relaxes his grip slightly. He shakes his head, as if declining to acknowledge this new data. Becker didn't know synthetics got sad like that, in the face of tragedy. Maybe it's a preprogrammed response to make him seem more human. Maybe Becker has gone from being in the paws of the tiger, to being in the paws of a *grieving* tiger.

"He's still lying," Mary Fowler shouts. "Hit him, Marcus! Just hit him!"

"We have to get these people to safety," Becker says, and the synthetic claps him with an iron glare. "I am not lying." He maintains solid eye contact as he speaks, trying not to flinch at Marcus's raised fist. He watches Marcus frown as he debates various responses.

When Marcus responds, it's with grief—nothing so tragic as humans portray, but a genuine pained smile and compassionate eyes.

"This must've been difficult," the synth says. "I am sorry for hurting you, Corporal." He helps Becker up and checks him for damage before nodding.

Marcus's acknowledgement wilts the McAllen people, each in different ways. Jerry and Mary are both stricken. Joanna blanches, understanding the reality of being hunted. Noah looks about to panic.

Arthur Atwater looks more like a distant hurricane, and Becker hopes it doesn't make landfall. The man pulls off his reading glasses, folds them, and places them into their case at the galley table.

"Why?" he asks.

"It's a cover-up to take the planet," Becker says. "We can get justice after you survive this. For now, I need you to listen."

"So tell me," Arthur says. "What's your plan?"

2 1

ALARM CLOCK

The sounds remind him of the roller coaster at the theme park in Singapore—the one Kamran visited in his youth. It was his first trip overseas, and the jeweled city taught him to love engineering. Especially the roller coasters.

Rising and falling screams.

All those years ago, he stood on the other side of the thoroughfare from the badge scanner, clasping the fingers of his adoptive mother. For forty-five minutes, the pair watched the swoosh of the cars along rails, though Kamran had been too frightened to ride. In his left hand, he held an ice cream, melting in the merciless heat of a tropical day. In his right, the soft, dry skin of a woman who would not live to see him graduate from high school.

To his great guilt, he loved Marjan like his real mother, the one who'd died in Afghanistan. He hadn't cared about the amusement park nearly as much as just being with her. The memory of her jasmine hugs would comfort him over a lifetime of harsh realities.

The unspeakable acts of the Russians stole his voice, but Marjan was the one who'd helped bring it back. She showed him a lifetime of patience before she passed, but Kamran doesn't want to think about that. He wants to remember the taste of ice cream, the blast furnace of a Singapore afternoon, and the smell of her shampoo on the breeze.

The silhouettes of roller coaster cars slide up and down skeletal rails, a curling tail of fear far away from that little boy and his new mother. Just softness—and screams in the distance.

An ear-splitting bang sounds through Kamran's entire world, and his eyes flutter open. He can't catch his focus, but white fabric rings his view: a cryopod. Blazing globes of light hover in the gloom, and he squints to make them out. Spotlights, perhaps?

Everything hurts. Coughing wracks his body, and his right hand won't wake up. Why is he in a tube?

Bang!

Something comes smashing into the side of his cryopod before bouncing off. Kamran yelps, doubly shocked by the loudness of his own voice in the tiny space. A woman stumbles into view, huffing and clutching a metal chair by its back. Squinting to see past the reflected interior lights, Kamran leans forward. She's taking aim at the override emergency panel. She must be trying to break off the safety glass and manually disengage the locks.

He reaches out to let her know he's conscious.

What comes up is a gnarled stump, wrapped in bloodstained bandages. Everything below the elbow is gone, and a strangled sob escapes his lips. His right hand, his dominant hand, is absent, transformed into meat for some monster.

Dizziness hobbles him, and he lets his arm flop to his side. This teaches him, with searing clarity, just how alive his stump is. Cold sweat breaks out across his forehead, and he smacks his lips, whimpering. His mouth is like a sour desert.

The woman raises the chair high above her head, then plunges it down onto the console safety glass. It shatters, she clears it away, and gives the lever a hard yank. Four muffled *thunks* resound in time as the locks disengage.

The lights go out in Kamran's tube.

No longer blinded by the reflection of the interior lights, he can distinguish the features of Tiran Shirazi. He hopes she can lift the hatch on her own. He's barely able to move his limbs, he's so woozy.

The hatch comes up a tiny bit, just enough to let in some of the outside air, and Kamran leans close to the crack to get a fresh breath.

Something is wrong.

This is the scent of a butcher shop—fresh blood and muscle. There's a lot of death out there. His eyes sting. He braces himself to push the hatch open, but Tiran leans over the top, blocking it. She shakes her head, then kneels down to the small opening. Her lips are an inch away from his ear, and in shivering tones, she whispers to him.

"They're coming. Play dead, or be dead."

Then she ducks out of sight.

Kamran shuts his eyes and leans back on the soft fabric of his cryopod. It smells like someone else's sweat, but there's peace within its cradle. Hot tears streak his face, into his ears, and he tries to conjure that baking Singapore day again. He doesn't want this to be real. He wants to be somewhere else.

Those screams weren't the roller coaster.

There's a skittering, scratching noise outside the tube, along with a low hiss like a gas leak. He doesn't mean to look, but instinct forces him, and instantly he regrets it.

A creature, like the one that took his hand, clambers atop his cryopod. The lid slams shut beneath its weight. In the emergency lighting, the animal is nothing but deadly reflections—long slices of light along ribs like so many knives. It brings the sweeping, smooth crown of its head to the glass.

It's looking right at him. He's sure of it.

Don't flinch. Don't blink. Don't close your eyes.

At least they won't dry out, glazed in tears.

It recoils, sneering lips peeling away from silvery teeth. Massive jaws begin to part, and he catches a glimpse of a tongue, barbed with yet more teeth. A flexion of the neck muscle is the only warning he has before the tongue snaps out of its mouth and bashes the glass.

Kamran blinks. He must've, and surely it saw him. He steels himself to be ripped from the tube like the meat from a clam.

Another man's scream pierces the air. The thing raises its head and screeches in response. Two other alien cries join the chorus, like wolves calling to one another. With a thunder of claws and a bony tail, it departs. Kamran lets out his breath, hoping Tiran is still nearby. He's not sure if he deserves her bravery, but he's glad it's there. She reappears at the glass, gaze distracted as she searches for any more monsters.

With each second, a touch of the cryosleep wears off, and more of his strength returns. More of the pain, as well. He isn't sure he can stand, but he's able to push on the lid, moving it ever so slightly. Tiran raises it the rest of the way.

"What's happening?" His whisper comes out choked by a dry mouth. Simply asking sends a fresh wave of fear through him, and he tamps down the urge to weep.

"Get up, Afghanzadeh," she says, taking his left hand and pulling him into a sitting position. "If you can't walk, I have to leave you, and you'll die."

He leans over the side and tries to swing a leg out, but ends up flopping to the ground like a fish. His left hand isn't enough to catch him, and he's afraid to use his stump, so he hits his cheek on the cold tiles.

"Please don't leave," he begs. "I can walk. Please."

"I believe you, but we have to go." She helps him struggle to his feet, and the world pitches beneath him.

Kamran sags into her arms, trying not to put all his weight on her, but unable to help himself as blood loss takes its toll.

"I can... I can stand," he says, more for his own benefit than hers.

The scene that spreads before him is absolute carnage—he cannot acknowledge it, yet he cannot look away. For some reason, he's in a data storehouse, and the floors are littered with bundled up clothes, blood, and bodies. He startles as he recognizes the corpse of Pezhvok, Tiran's right-hand system administrator. Lids drawn low, his eyes stare into nothing. His throat has been ripped out all the way to the spine.

"Come on," Tiran says, shouldering him. "You can do it."

Kamran finds the coordination to put one foot in front of the other, but it's not easy. They pass another set of remains, the soft bits of abdomen devoured to leave hanging meat on bone. The face is oddly peaceful.

"Get your eyes up, Kamran. They kill on sight," she says. "If one spots us, I'll have to drop you." She does half of his walking for him as they limp out of the storehouse and into the connecting Spiral. There are far fewer bodies here, and a lot more blood trails. All streaks lead deeper, toward the swirling heart of Charybdis.

Movement. Shadows in the tunnel.

"Something's coming!" he says, more a puff of breath than a sentence, but Tiran understands.

Their clumsy efforts are more like falling than running,

and a single misstep could leave them sprawled on the ground. If that happened, he wouldn't blame Tiran for leaving him, so to fall is to die.

There's a vending alcove, midway between each storehouse and the next. Employees this deep aren't expected to go all the way up for meals and snacks, so each alcove has a little kitchen in it, with an island. They move toward the nearest one.

Each successful footfall feels more fortunate than the last, and he can't believe his luck as they go stumbling behind the kitchen island. His stump bangs on the metal, and it feels as if someone took a hot iron to his bone marrow. But to speak, even the tiniest utterance, would be a mortal mistake. Something is coming.

The creatures' clawed gait has the patter of dogs, impossibly fast, like greyhounds. The stone thumps in time with their scratching gallop. They're heavy, solid things.

Back pressed against the brushed steel cabinets, he looks to Tiran, hoping for some understanding or insight. She seems to know what's going on. What's her plan here? Tiran stares straight ahead, determination in her eyes, mouthing a silent prayer.

Silence returns, and she nods. Before either of them can speak, Kamran grabs onto the side of the countertop to pull himself up, gets his feet steady—

—and sees one of the creatures outside the alcove.

His knees give out, and he slips back down, shaking his head no.

She mouths the phrase *"good luck,"* and climbs into an empty cabinet. With graceful silence, she disappears, gently closing the door.

Kamran is too large to even consider such a feat. Maybe he should get up and run, try to save Tiran by leading them away. That seems like the heroic thing to do, but he won't make it to the Spiral thoroughfare before one tears him to shreds. His noisy demise would probably draw more of the beasts, too.

So he waits and prays, pressing his forehead to the tile. His stump throbs, and he resolves to wait a hundred heartbeats before checking again. He counts them off in his head. When he reaches fifty, he hears talons on concrete.

It's coming into the alcove.

Kamran is concealed by the galley island, but not for long. If it comes around one side or the other, it'll see him. Which way should he flee? Right or left? He glances around for shadows, but sees none.

If he makes no choice, he'll surely die.

He crawls right, and comes around to find a blessedly empty view of the corridor. When he looks to the island, he finds the beast standing atop it, its head out of sight as it inspects his former hiding spot. The creature's long, prehensile tail acts as a counterweight, swishing back and forth above Kamran's head.

It doesn't see him, but it'll catch him the second it turns around. Kamran searches his surroundings for any place to hide, and spots a gap between the vending machines. It's thin, but so is he, and there's headroom to spare. Kamran rises to his feet and tiptoes over to his new cover, squirming inside.

The machine rocks as he brushes past, and its squeak freezes his heart. A hiss echoes through the quiet, followed by a long, hollow breath.

The creature knows it's not alone.

Kamran presses deep into the crack, as if trying to bury himself in the darkened canyon between the machines. If he makes another noise, it's over—there's nowhere to hide. He stares out between the two metal walls at his thin slice of the galaxy, dreading the appearance of teeth and claws.

Perhaps he should've thrown something into the open hallway—something to draw its attention. Thrown what, with what, though? He has terrible aim, even with his dominant hand, and there's nothing within reach.

The creature's form comes into view. It's frozen, peering into the main hallway like a stalking cat. Kamran sucks in a breath and holds it.

The bony shadow refuses to move.

Kamran's head grows light. He already didn't have enough blood. Gravity goes all screwy as dizziness grips his sight.

The creature erupts in a short squeal and scrabbles away.

Kamran sags into his makeshift cradle, the machines' contents gently rattling with his weight. Unconsciousness tugs at him, and he could almost go to sleep right here.

This cannot be his reality.

His mind travels to all of his friends, to Babãk and his team. Where are they? What's happening?

"Kamran." Tiran's voice startles him, and he bangs his stump again. "Come on. Let's go."

INTERLUDE: BLUE

2181 – THREE YEARS AGO

The rat is screaming again.

Blue Marsalis had believed today would prove to her employers that her life was worth saving.

It's a good thing synthetic bodies don't cry. She can't stand to see them like that. It's not the dying rat that's breaking her heart. She'd rip through a thousand of them if it meant a cure, but prepping test samples and coding them costs millions. This rat, flopping sadly, futilely against the glass, struggling to die, represents months of work with some of the rarest materials in existence.

Every failure is a step toward Seegson Biomedical pulling the plug on Blue's project—as well as her life. It costs the company a fortune just to keep her alive, so they have leverage. They don't even bother to pay her anymore. Her bosses just remind her once a year that she'll die without them. It's fine, though.

This job was never about the money; it's about the cure.

Her official name for it is *Plagiarus praepotens*, the "powerful mimic." It's capable of unzipping genetic material at lightning speed, and a masterpiece for accruing biomass from anything and everything around it. With the right chimeric blueprint and enough food, it will go from a single-celled organism to an adult creature with fully differentiated organs in a matter of hours.

Blue's boss, Dr. Richard Scales, likes to call *Plagiarus praepotens* "the black goo," and it drives her insane. It's like calling the first nuclear reactor "a teakettle." She never liked him, anyway—a carbon-copy Chicago intellectual right down to the clichéd love of sailing.

However, within *Plagiarus praepotens* lies the key to Blue's salvation—and potentially all the genetic maladies of the universe. Building upon its miraculous properties, modern geneticists might be able to create a panacea that could delete cancerous tumors, remove nerve damage, even chase away some of the more bespoke disorders. Blue's work could make her a legend.

She could become nigh immortal, but Blue would settle for the second half of her life.

Bishara's syndrome, a terminal, epigenetic disorder, has taken most of Blue Marsalis's body. It atrophies her muscles and strips her nerves. Without constant intervention, it will kill her. As it is, she's little more than a head in a Seegson Biomedical lab, attached to an array of artificial organs spread around a small room.

Her veins are plastic. Her lymphatic system is a machine the size of a commercial-grade refrigerator. She cannot move anything but her mouth, and even then, she has no breath. A set of catalytic gills oxygenates her lab-grown blood, obviating the need for lungs.

She used to miss eating.

Now, she misses breathing.

Blue can watch the test through the eyes of a synthetic named Rook. Thanks to the brain direct interface, she can inhabit him fully—feeling and seeing everything that her prosthetic body does. She *becomes* him, in a way.

Rook's body is state of the art, designed for the most delicate medical procedures, so he comes with a host of useful features. She likes that he presents male, as well, but not much else. Blue's skin was dark and beautiful once, but Rook follows the same design bias that created Bishop, Walter, David, and Marcus—Seegson's industrial-grade mimicry of Peter Weyland's Caucasian default.

His voice is too sweet.

"We've got brain death."

Dr. Scales's words snap her back to the present. He turns away from his terminal and crosses his legs as if he's interviewing her for a job.

"Obviously, that's not optimal," she says, Rook's voice more contrite than she'd meant it to be. "Can we just wait and watch? If we get rid of the tumors, there still will be some lessons learned."

"Leave it in there until it starts to stink, for all I care," he replies, "but you need to come up with a new test plan and present it to the board."

"My research methods—"

"Aren't working, Blue. Period. Change tracks."

"It's 'Dr. Marsalis,' Dr. Scales."

Blue has come to learn that, just as she shares Rook's senses, he knows her anger. She turns over the past six months of work in her mind, watching the rat contort until its little bones make popping noises. Its death rattle seems particularly prolonged, but the poor bastard finally goes limp.

They're going to unplug me, Rook.

He can't respond.

At Blue's old job, with her Marcus unit, she'd kept the synthetic partitioned from her thoughts while they linked. Rook, however, has come to know her dreams. She allows him access to her innermost fears. Even now, she knows how much he cares for her, and how this will upset him.

That's how she corrupted him.

A simple change to the BDI software has allowed their minds to meet. She taught him her story, her loves, her life and betrayals, through thousands of hours of intimate contact with her thoughts. Now, via a single set of eyes, their twinned consciousnesses watch the rat die, and Blue knows that no matter what else happens, Rook will do his best to ensure her continuation. It'll break him, though.

Her old synthetic couldn't handle it, either.

She still hates herself for the way she betrayed Marcus. He was her only—her only means of transportation, her only possible escape from the clusterfuck of RB-232. He was her only friend. In the end, though—he was also only a tool. She spent him, disposed of his trust, and that is the loss she most regrets.

Mired in her thoughts as she is, she almost misses a subtle discoloration in the claws of the rat. To the human eye it would be nearly imperceptible, but to Rook's surgical vision, the skin positively *seethes* with dark blood.

This isn't the first time her inoculations have reacted with the biomass of a subject. She's had plenty of rats, mice, and ferrets explode with mutated chimera. All of the resulting creatures were vicious little fuckers with too many eyes, or not enough eyes, and Blue always had to put them down. It's better than the time she used chimpanzees, though. The snatchers that erupted from the primates grew up to be nice and large, and that's not a mistake she'll make again.

The pulse microscanner hums to life over the rat's enclosure, assembling thousands of slices with subcellular width and resolution.

"Sustained, nondestructive endocytosis," Dr. Scales says from his position at the microscope terminal, and Blue blinks. "We've got compatibility."

"But he's dead," she says.

"Come see for yourself."

She goes to look over Richard's shoulder and expects to see irreparable cellular damage, or *P. praepotens* eating everything on the screen as it assembles some fresh mockery of life. Instead, she finds quivering nuclei, like wet red gems, solidifying into black marbles.

"This is new," Blue says, and when she turns back to the enclosure, she finds a swollen and ailing animal. Its face contorts, jaw distending as already sharp teeth grow sharper. "Holy shit, Richard, *look*."

The scientist jumps up from his seat and rushes over to watch the transformation. Short paws lengthen into sleek, avian legs, tipped with talons. Hair falls from its body in little tufts, and its skin suctions to its ribcage. Bones press through the surface of flesh, and it's as if the creature is being flayed alive.

This was supposed to be a litmus test—repair damaged cells and destroy malignant tumors. Blue isn't sure about the cancer part, but the repairing is definitely happening. The rat's body radiates heat like it's cooking, some function of the pathogen's incredible transformative capabilities. It's hot enough to denature the rat muscle proteins, but Blue isn't sure this is going to be a rat at the end of the day.

She's right. It takes about an hour, but every crack of bone brings it into hellish alignment with the snatcher blueprint.

Only smaller.

This isn't what she'd wanted. She'd at least hoped to see the reclaimed nervous system, but what's the shape of the rat mind now?

Dr. Scales's reaction makes it clear to Blue that he doesn't consider this test to be a failure at all. He's quite pleased, in fact.

When the tiny snatcher stirs in its enclosure, Blue expects it to lunge at the glass. The stupid shits always do that. Instead, its lips twitch with the regular cadence of a rat's sniffing and it runs a hand across the side of its head, as if to clean. It pops upright, remaining shockingly steady for a body that's just expended all of its energy.

Then it paws at the glass and tries to sniff it. Its claws slip and slide on the pane as it looks for purchase, but it doesn't freak out like a snatcher would. It continues to circle, curious about its surroundings.

Dr. Scales has a look in his eye that reminds her of the fucking Human Resources maniac at her last company. He's not seeing a test; he's seeing the product. That could mean the end of Blue's project, and her life.

"You know we can do better," she says, hesitantly.

He breaks from his reverie to nod and smile. "Of course, Dr. Marsalis."

His heart quickens, and Rook hears it. He's lying.

"We should at least call this an alpha, though," he says. "Maybe that's what I'll call this little guy. Hey, Alpha." He waves, and "Alpha" scratches the glass some more, as if it wants the doctor to pick it up. If it's still a rat inside, it will be fine. However, Blue knows better than to allow anything resembling a snatcher out of containment.

"I want to introduce it to the other rats," he says.

"What?" she says. "No, that's not science. That's just throwing rats in a blender."

"Oh, I wasn't aware you wrote the checks around here, Dr. Marsalis."

She crosses Rook's arms and glares. They were smart enough to keep the behavioral inhibitors in place. She can't deck him.

"An experiment is something you design—you spend a budget on it," she says. "A major portion of ours went to this test, and while it's not the outcome we expected, I won't condone breaking quarantine just because it'd be 'neat.' We don't even know if Alpha has an immune system."

"You were ready to call this a failure, Dr. Marsalis," Scales says. "Would've just thrown it in the freezer." He nods. "Your job is to encode and administer the black goo. Live specimens are out of your purview."

"With all due respect, we can do better," she reiterates.

"I agree, but with respect in turn, I'm the chief science officer, I have higher directives and topsight than you, and I'm instructing you to leave. Now."

"Okay, but can we at least—"

He looks at her and smiles sardonically. "I hate using the override, you know that? It makes me feel bad."

All of Blue's colleagues have a "safe word," something they can yell at Rook to make him do whatever they want.

Staffers use it to grab control of her body, walk her away from things they don't want her to see. In staff meetings, sometimes, Dr. Scales has something he wants to show everyone but Blue, so he calls out the safe word. She is effectively rendered deaf and blind.

Safe for them. Deeply violating for her.

She leaves, disgusted.

During Blue's sleep cycles, Rook is supposed to assist with station maintenance. When they first imprisoned her, it infuriated Blue to have a part-time body. She'd find him in odd places, covered in grease or cuts.

That cheap cruelty will be their undoing, however, because Blue has adjusted her brain chemistry. It's easy for someone whose organs are a room full of computers and valves. Thus, regardless of what her coworkers think, she never sleeps.

Blue doesn't know what it's doing to her mind, but her body is killing her faster these days. Her candle wick may be low, but she'll make sure the last bit burns the brightest. Soon night will fall, and she'll have free rein of the station under the guise of its maintenance synthetic.

It's time to execute her contingency.

22

DESCENT

"You want us to hide down there," Arthur repeats. "With the aliens."

Becker's plan isn't going over well. He looks at Marcus, really hoping not to catch another synthetic attack. Every minute Becker spends explaining himself is another they delay in their escape, but forcing these people to comply is out of the question.

"Where else are you going to go?" he says. "If you try to go across the Long Walk to the *Gardenia*, Duncan will spot you, and it'll be game over."

"Then we what?" Jerry scoffs. "Wait it out below?"

"Yes," Becker says. "There are two ships coming—a fresh platoon of Colonial Marines, and an ICSC security ship."

"The marines are the ones trying to kill us!" Jerry says, growing agitated, and Mary quiets him down.

Joanna lights a cigarette and scowls. "Pardon me, son,

but you're what? Twelve years old?"

"I'm twenty-four," he replies, "with six years of high-impact, front-line combat experience. I may not know a lot of life, but I know a lot of death. How about you?"

"In this case I've got you beat," she drawls around her cigarette, like she just won at cards. "Just so happens I'm an expert at *ventilation ducts*, Mr. Tactical. Charybdis isn't just data storehouses. It's got a ton of infrastructure around it, and if these things are as sneaky as you say they are, we'll never seal ourselves in."

"A marine force can secure any location," Becker says. "The size of the force determines the size of the location," he rattles off the doctrine like he was fresh out of boot. Joanna's smoke-tanned vocal cords wheeze when she laughs, and she folds her arms.

"Oh, bless your heart, honey. You ain't convinced me just yet."

Jerry nods once to himself, like he's just broken a huddle with Team Jerry. He's shaking, but he swallows and turns to Becker.

"Okay, why don't you take me to Captain Duncan? I'll negotiate to get us out of here. I negotiated the other business contracts, and I'm good at, uh... dealing."

"Hard negative, Jerry," Becker says. "Not how this works. You're kill on sight as far as she cares."

"What if we took you hostage?" Arthur asks, and Becker looks to Marcus.

"One hundred percent chance Duncan comes in

shooting, and takes me out, too," he replies.

"What are we even talking about? Let's make Marcus attack them." Noah laughs. "No behavioral limiter. He can kill them with his bare hands!"

"Casualties are failures of planning," Marcus says, "and my odds of survival against ranged opponents are almost zero."

Noah frowns as if the coffee autopot mouthed off at him.

"You'll do as I say, android—"

Marcus rises, nothing threatening in his posture, but it's enough.

"Will I?"

Noah whines like a recruit. "We don't have a hostage. We don't have fighting capabilities. We can't hide anywhere, because nothing is airtight. No one *else* has any ideas!"

"I know somewhere we can hide," Mary says. "Below."

"No offense, but you"—Joanna points the cigarette at her— "wouldn't even go into the Spiral when we got here. You're too afraid of Iranians to even talk to them, but suddenly you've got the inside scoop?"

"I do, because I itemized all of the contracts," Mary says. "We can hide in the Javaher Concourse. MacroProj didn't show any air load balancing for that place."

Noah opens his mouth to object, but has nothing.

"What's that?" Becker asks.

"Our project management software," says Jerry. "It lets us track all of the—"

"No, what's the Javaher Concourse?"

"The network operations center for the Data Cannon," Noah says. "It's really deep. Like, DS Thirty deep."

"That's why it's on its own climate system," Arthur elaborates. "Because of HS gas events, all of those vents can be individually shuttered and expelled. From there, we'd be able to shape the entire playing field inside the Spiral. Doors, ducts… hell, maybe we could even lure the creatures around with lights."

"They're smarter than house cats," Becker says. "I doubt that'd work."

"Noah and I had some lunches down at the concourse when we first arrived," Joanna says. "They've got rations in the attached canteen. Enough to last a good long time."

"You're the big brain in the room, Marcus," Arthur says. "What do you think?"

"If the conspirators are serious enough to commit these atrocities, it stands to reason that they'll destroy any ship that tries to leave," the synth says. "The corporal is correct—it's best that we remain in the colony. Additionally, if we can access SiteSys from down there, we can help more people."

"We need another gun," Arthur says. "If we're going down there, you and me are both trained shooters. Anyone else?"

"I was an eagle scout marksman," Jerry says.

"Wow, Jer—got anything less than six decades old?" Joanna snaps. "Do *not* give Jerry a gun, Corporal Becker."

"She's right, honey," Mary says, patting his shoulder. "Better leave it to the professionals."

"Duncan owns the armory," Becker says. "Those guys are definitely hers, so we're not getting gear that way. For now, this is all we've got." He removes his holster, hands Arthur his sidearm, and sees clear expertise the second it hits his hand. Arthur pulls the weapon out, checks the mag and the safety, then re-holsters it and clips it onto his belt in back. He shoulders his backpack, and it conceals the weapon completely.

"We're not prisoners, so we can keep our stuff," Arthur says. "Hide weapons in anything you carry." They raid the kitchen, find a bunch of laser-etched knives, but nothing more. Still, Becker has seen what a kitchen knife can do to an unsuspecting soldier.

"We've got to move. If we don't get to DS Thirty before the x-rays, we die," Becker says. "Shy's gone, and you're all grieving—I get that." He makes eye contact with each person in turn. "Hide it."

One after the other, the contractors nod their assent.

They move into the halls, Becker at the lead with his rifle unslung. It might seem a little off if they run into any other marines, escorting civvies with his rifle out, but Duncan's people would see it as a clear message.

I'm taking these people somewhere to dispose of them.

His goal is the lift inside the Solutions building. They pass through the Human Centre lobby without incident, and Becker aches for an update from Garcia.

Has she found anyone to help?

Of course not. It's only been fifteen minutes.

Most of the soldiers are ferrying gear back up to the *Benning*, and that means fewer potential eyes to see his passage. Maybe he ought to just broadcast the truth over the radio and see who comes running. It might work, but that assumes there are more true Colonial Marines than bad ones. If he's wrong, he'll get the witnesses killed—and himself.

In the Thunder Ring, he spots a couple more folks in PRAE gear—probably Duncan's troops. He takes the long way around.

"Becker!"

He turns to see Sergeant Wallace jogging after him. No one's ever happy to see Wallace, but this is worse. His presence complicates everything. It's petty, but Becker takes a perverse pleasure in seeing the man slightly out of breath.

"Why the fuck is your radio off?" The sergeant glances at the contractors. "Hey, folks. I'm just here to help the corporal escort you to the safe zone." His gaze hardens when he looks back to Becker.

"I'm sorry, Sergeant," the corporal replies. "I turned it off in the command center, because that area was classified." Turning away, he switches his radio back from sixteen Charlie to the squad channel. Squawk and chatter resume immediately. "Couldn't take any chances." He gives Wallace his best *remember when you walked in on that dead civilian?* look.

To Becker's amazement, the bastard takes the hint.

"Well, thanks for turning it back on, you piece of shit. Good job." Wallace shakes his head to the others. "Hard to find good help these days. Anyway folks, just follow me, and we can get you stowed somewhere safe while we sort this out."

With that, Becker realizes that he's probably going to have to kill this fucking guy.

Over his many drops, Becker has had to plan on ending someone's life. Sometimes it's a matter of milliseconds, like when his checkpoint came under fire. Sometimes, it's been days, like his deployment into Goliath's most fortified regions. No matter how prepared he feels, there's always that moment when the switch flips, and a cold calm enters his heart. He'd never kill anyone in rage, but if an opponent has to be erased from the equation, that's part of the job.

His breath evens out; his jangled nerves unwind.

His mother, Major Virginia Becker, always told him she survived her combat deployments by visualizing the outcome she wanted, honestly evaluating the obstacles in her path, and imagining herself taking the required actions. He tries that, and the results feel insane.

They continue toward the lift bank. Becker mentally traces the path they'll take through the sub-basement lobby, trying to figure out what he'll be up against. Sergeant Wallace alone won't be a problem, but if he has allies, things will evolve.

No sense raising the alarm with a gunshot. Becker's combat knife hangs at his boot, an ally to help him with this difficult task. He'll stick it in the side of Wallace's neck, try and get the blade through the windpipe, before making a hard jerk forward.

Knife the sergeant.

Go AWOL.

This is a terrible idea.

Becker hazards a glance back as the lift opens. For the most part the contractors are holding up well, though Brewer looks like a ghost. They haven't done anything to be a part of this fight. Seems like most of the Iranians here are innocent, too. Becker hasn't seen the inside of their bioweapons labs, but the captain said there were at least two, maybe more. What if she's lying?

That seems like a fair bet.

When they reach the sub-basement lobby, Becker's odds of survival are sliced to ribbons. Ames and Hanssen are already there in their PRAE suits, along with Matsushita. Using a motorized pallet jack, they're escorting the big, creepy alien up from below. The scientist walks with one hand on the containment cube.

The creature inside, so like an x-ray, uncurls at their appearance, pressing against the glass. Its fluttering scales lie flat against its smooth head, and there's an added grotesqueness to its lips—so close to human. They're alien to the alien.

"Holy fucking shit," Joanna says.

"It's okay," Wallace says. "Nothing to worry about. That cage can withstand anything the bitch can dish out."

Despite his words, the contractors freeze in place. Mary Fowler looks like she's about to have a heart attack, and her husband gapes. Brewer's legs give out and his ass hits the ground.

"Wait right here, if you don't mind," Wallace says to the civilians. "Becker, come with me." He beckons to Ames and Hanssen as they cross the lobby. They stop, and he addresses the three of them. "Listen, the captain got concerned that, like… since these people are experts in colony systems, it's a bad idea to let them go."

"Why are you acting all cagey?" Ames asks.

"Yeah," Wallace replies. "It's a blackout. These witnesses are a problem for the captain, and she wants them, ah, gone."

"Americans?" Ames says. "Can I really?"

Wallace smacks him across the back of the head.

"Stow it. Huddle in closer," Wallace says. "The synthetic can read lips, you know." They comply, and he continues. "We're going to take them over to the storehouse elevator and do them there. We pile the bodies inside, press the button and let it go. The doors will open at Storehouse Forty, with some fresh meat for the x-rays."

"That's going to leave evidence," Becker says. "Bullet holes in the walls will be a dead giveaway when the UN inspectors come through later. Our presence is supposed to be secret."

"No shit," Hanssen says, running his tongue along the inside of his lower lip. "That's why you use a knife." At this, all four marines turn and look at the McAllen contractors. Arthur gives Becker the tiniest nod, as if to ask, *still good?*

All good. Just figuring out how best to kill you.

"What about the synthetic?" Ames asks. "He can't let us do that."

"That's what Matsushita is for." Wallace waves the scientist over. Matsushita seems reluctant to leave the creature's side, but he joins them.

"Yes?"

"Hey, man," Wallace says. "Can you override that Marcus?"

"I'm not supposed to," he says. "That one isn't Weyland-Yutani property."

"I—yeah, I get that"—Wallace smoothes his goatee—"but like, *can you*?"

If they go after Marcus, it might be good for Becker. His behavioral inhibitor is clearly off. If Matsushita tries an override, the synthetic might go berserk and attack. The synthetic wouldn't be able to take down all three, but Becker could help with that. The distraction would be invaluable.

Matsushita shrugs and looks at Marcus. "I don't think so. It's got a two-oh-four personality schism. You can see it in the hand twitch." He turns back. "Why don't you just shoot them?"

"We can't leave any evidence that marine weapons did the killing, Doctor," Wallace says.

So Matsushita gestures to one of the nearby doors, splitting off from the lobby—the security checkpoint. "Go to the armory and acquire Iranian weapons. That would imply that the facility's security team executed the contractors, after the outbreak started."

Wallace looks thoughtful, and plays with the beard again.

"I'll ask the captain on the backchannel," he says, pulling a second radio from his belt. Becker makes a note to grab it when he takes out the sergeant.

"Don't bother," Matsushita says. "The Marsalis specimen has priority. Finish this so we can get her onto the ship."

"I suggest you don't order me around," Wallace says.

"Talk to Duncan then." Matsushita is nearly a head shorter than the sergeant. When he looks up at Wallace, he doesn't lift his face, only his eyes, and he *smiles*. "See what she thinks of you wasting time, betraying your advisor's advice." Then the scientist turns his back, returning to the containment cube while idly toying with the beads of his keycard lanyard.

Wallace steps to one side, pressing his earpiece.

When he returns, he looks like a whipped dog.

"Hanssen," Wallace says, "run and get the Iranian gear. Ames, Becker, with me. We're going to watch the civvies until we need to cash out. When the time comes, we can line them up over there." He points to the elevator bank in the back. "Those fancy wall panels will capture the Iranian slugs." They break from their huddle.

Becker's heart cycles into an almost mechanical rhythm.

If he shoots Ames first, Wallace will kill him. The USCM sergeant has seen a lot of drops, and despite the fact that he looks like a goddamned sea lion, he'll be lethal. Ames is a lot slower in his PRAE suit, but Becker's pulse rifle might not fully punch through on the first go. He'll need a headshot.

Hanssen disappears around the corner. If Becker is going to act, he needs to move while there are fewer players on the field. A quick look says Arthur is ready to rumble. Becker glances around one last time for tools to bring to the fight, and settles on Marcus, who can read lips at a hundred paces with ease.

Becker wants to mouth a message, but the synthetic's attentions are on the Marsalis specimen. The synthetic waves.

The thing waves back at him.

Because the day wasn't weird enough.

"You!" Wallace shouts at Marcus, raising his rifle. "What do you think you're doing?"

The sergeant's action startles the rest, and Arthur raises a hand to urge calm. He steps out from the group.

"Hey, now." His fingers rove perilously close to his concealed holster. "Let's all relax, buddy."

If Arthur draws, Becker can put Ames down. He's about to put a bead on his fellow corporal when he hears the roar of the Thunder Ring doors opening. Three more members of Wallace's fireteam arrive in PRAE gear.

"Over here," Matsushita calls. "You. Get the jack."

Fuck.

These soldiers are armed and dirty. Becker isn't far from the contractors. If he starts shooting, he might be able to cover them while they get away.

Is that how he wants to die?

Any winning scenarios have vanished. Marcus finally makes eye contact with him, so he mouths the words.

"They're about to kill everyone."

Marcus nods.

The synthetic bolts, moving directly toward Sergeant Wallace and Ames. A shoulder check sends them both tumbling to the ground. Becker winces, not sure what a synthetic does to kill someone, but pretty certain he's about find out.

Except Marcus jumps back up and keeps running toward the creature's cage. He's like an Olympic sprinter, streaking across the open lobby with boundless grace. He plows into Matsushita.

"Hold fire!" someone calls out, and Becker starts to wonder if Marcus is going to take a hostage, but the synthetic picks the scientist up by the neck. As he throws Matsushita clear, the synth rips free a keycard.

The marines open fire.

Dozens of pinpoint shots smash into Marcus's body, and milky puffs of white issue from merciless wounds in his back. He turns away to spring the cage lock. His head snaps forward as one of the bullets strikes his brain casing. A shaking hand aligns the card with the reader, and he presses a button. The marines put everything they have into his body, firing until their clips run dry.

The synthetic slumps to the floor, a ragged mess of milky wires and twitching limbs.

"Marcus!" Mary screams.

BEEP.

The grotesque x-ray explodes into the room like a tornado, hissing, buzzing, and screeching—and no one has a single bullet in their mag except Becker.

He needed a distraction, and he got it.

The creature is canny. It presses the advantage by ripping away rifles, rushing back and forth at wild speeds to claw and slap with its tail. Becker's soldier's instincts tell him to protect his fellow marines. A much more primal voice tells him to run.

He charges toward the contractors, aggressively pointing to the elevators that will take them into the storehouses. There's a strangled cry from Private Rankin, and Becker turns around just in time to see the thing stomp the unlucky woman to the ground and rip her head from her body. Her PRAE gear uselessly pops under its feet; the alien is careful to avoid the reactive blasts.

Ames slaps a clip into his rifle, but his target bounds over to him, sinking her teeth around his entire face. A serrated tongue plunges through the back of his skull, and Marsalis throws his body to the ground. It yanks his pulse rifle off the floor and takes aim at Sergeant Wallace.

Several rounds of depleted uranium wipe the goatee right off Wallace's face.

Shit. That isn't possible.

"Fucking run!" Becker shouts. "Hit the button!" Arthur is on it, but the rest of them look as if they're going to scatter. Becker can't blame them. Every second in this lobby is a chance to catch a bullet.

The ding of the lift arrival is like a choir of angels. At the end of the lobby, elevator doors open onto a windowed vista of Charybdis's waterfalls. Becker sprints toward them, passing a huffing Jerry Fowler along the way. He slides to a halt by the door and drops to one knee. Arthur takes the other side with his pistol poised as the rest of them pile in.

Behind them, Jerry Fowler moves with a look of taut concentration on his face. There's something in his shuffle. The man sweats bullets, and runs with more of a fast limp than a jog.

Jesus Christ, the guy has a bad hip.

"Come on, Fowler!" Mary shouts. She leans out from behind Arthur like he's a solid wall. "McAllen Bulldogs! All-State Champions of Thirty-Two!"

Finally, Jerry comes stumbling into the lift, and Becker and Arthur fall in behind. It's big in there—enough to haul crates of servers and hard drives. The second they're through, Brewer mashes the door-close button, hitting it again and again. Nothing happens. Joanna Hardy slaps his hand.

"That doesn't do anything!"

His eyes go wide in anger. "At least I'm trying!"

"If you break this elevator, you die first," she hisses.

After what seems like forever, the doors begin to move, sliding toward the middle at an entirely unacceptable pace. Becker and Arthur keep careful watch on the open lobby, and realization hits him. It's not the corpses, the blood, and the empty cage; it's the lack of the Marsalis specimen. There's no movement in the huge room, save for smoke curling from holes in the wall. No sound, either.

The doors catch with a grinding sound as the creature comes pouring into the lift from above. Becker can't shoot—if he does, they'll be drenched in acid. Before he can shout a warning, Arthur gets a round off, but it's not enough to penetrate. The bullet goes ricocheting past Becker's ear.

With a deafening cry, the x-ray grabs the carry handle of Becker's rifle in one claw and his wrist in the other. A jolt from its muscles, and his weapon is no longer in his control. Using the rifle like a club, it bashes Arthur's handgun, sending it clattering across the lift.

Arthur takes a swing, landing a punch hard enough to turn the creature's head. Its humanoid lips pull back to reveal teeth like an anglerfish, and its furious screech is like an icepick in Becker's eardrum. It grabs Arthur, hurls him against Noah, and the two go down in a heap.

Returning its attention to Becker, it lifts him by his

armor. The blood of soldiers steams on its breath, and the sensation is like being naked before God. He still has his boot knife, but it no longer comforts him.

Marsalis twists and tosses him into the same corner as Noah and Arthur, while the Fowlers and Joanna cower in another. It snatches both guns off the ground and points them at the two groups. Nobody moves, and it flicks the barrel of the pistol up. Once.

Becker raises his hands slowly, and nods for everyone to do the same. The doors finally close, and the elevator begins its descent.

No one moves.

After a moment, it places the pistol on the ground and begins making gestures like it's typing in midair. Becker sees lights flashing on its silvered knuckles, looking for all the world like little LEDs. They flash in time with the fingers.

What the fuck?

The metal box on the side of its head makes a distorted chime.

"Stop."

The rasping robotic voice comes from the box. Another set of finger gestures. The talk box bleats out another few words. The creature doesn't seem to be very good with the interface.

"Staring… at… me." The lips twitch in frustration. *"I won't… asterisk!"* the robot voice shouts, and everyone jumps. Marsalis shakes its head no, an angry motion.

"Won't... kill you." Lips pull back in a snarl. *"Don't... make me."* The androgynous voice is hard to understand. The speaker box, showing scars and dents, has seen better days.

Becker, flat on his ass, looks to the civilians and gives them his most reassuring smile. If this creature wants them docile, then they've got to be like gentle kittens in its tender, taloned grip.

"We"—Becker looks at Arthur, who nods in agreement—"respect that. No one is going to do anything to upset you. No heroes today."

The elevator car continues its descent, the light of the outside world growing dim as they pass the huge set of Halo fans. Their engines ring the perimeter of the waterfall in perfect symmetry, blades locked to the same alignment like the petals of flowers. In the floors below, pyramid-shaped turbines and heat exchangers jut out, slicing into falling emerald waves of lake water. It's an odd moment of peace.

Marsalis stands in stark contrast to the beauty—a shadow against silver and emerald. It draws its limbs inward, and Becker remembers that it warned him about staring. He averts his eyes. They pass into the mist, and the elevator slows to a halt with a pleasant ding.

"Don't..." Marsalis's croaking speaker intones, *"follow me. Don't."*

Becker gulps, knowing what he's about to do might be stupid. The creature is still holding his pulse rifle.

"Please—" Becker flinches as it sneers at him. "Please don't take our guns."

It bends low, looming over him, light glinting off its long, fluttering dome.

Then it *screams*.

So does everyone else, and the thousand little plates around its head unleash a sound like a sea of rattlesnakes. Becker sinks under the weight of its psychological assault, glued to the floor by the utter malevolence of it. He does everything he can to show this thing that he's not a threat.

It snaps its head scales back, going silent. Becker swallows and closes his eyes, so he doesn't accidentally stare.

"We need those to survive," he says.

The creature rages out of the elevator and into the darkness beyond—taking both guns. The humans remain still as rabbits until the doors begin to close. Becker lunges to his feet to hold them open.

"They're probably calling the elevator back," Becker says, "and you do *not* want any marines following us."

Emergency lights cut through the gloom of dead-quiet halls. Fifty paces away, lying in the middle of the floor, are Becker's pulse rifle and sidearm. Abruptly an alarm bell rings through the elevator. He jerks, then turns to see that Brewer has pulled out the emergency stop.

"What the fuck is wrong with you?" Becker whispers, slapping the switch to silence the alarm.

"I wanted to buy us some time!" Noah says. "Like you said, I didn't want them using the elevator."

Becker wants to smack the guy. "Any way you could do that *quietly*?"

"If we can get to the concourse," Jerry says, "the elevator banks report into SiteSys. I could lock them down. It'll take five minutes."

"So how do we stall the elevators until then?" Joanna asks. "Some kind of hack?"

"There's an exploit for that." Noah holds up a finger, then runs it over every stop on the elevator console, doing so with relish. This can't have been the first time he's done it.

Better than anything I had, Becker has to admit. "All right," he says. "Arthur, can you get these people to the Javaher Concourse?"

The big man scoffs. "You have somewhere better to be?"

"DS Twenty, One-Zero-Five Bay C," Becker says. He's been trying to hang onto that number ever since this clusterfuck started.

"What's there?"

"Evidence." He jogs down the hall, grabs his pulse rifle and heads for the stairwell. Squad chatter lights up his radio, and he winces, switching it to the backchannel. As much as he wants to listen in, he trusted Garcia with a mission. If he's going to survive, he needs friends on the inside—allies who might contact him any moment.

Sixteen Charlie it is.

2 3

EYE OF THE STORM

Knock knock.

Kamran awakens curled around a toilet pipe.

This far down, they haven't yet installed any actual toilets, just the fittings. A pool of sticky saliva attaches his face to the floor, and he sits up with a start.

It's his own drool.

When he first started working here, the floor-to-ceiling stalls had seemed extravagant. That was before he needed a quiet, safe room to hide from aliens.

Another pair of knocks come from the door.

"Are you still alive?" Tiran whispers.

Every throb of his empty bone is like the tap of a hammer. It's the sort of pain that sucks away his strength in surprise pulses. He struggles to his feet and wipes the sweat from his forehead. Is he feverish?

A flash of memory strikes him—black worms wriggling

under the skin of his right hand. What if he's infected with something sinister from that laboratory? What was in that creature's spittle?

Don't be absurd, he tells himself. *It could be anything.*

"Kamran, please don't be dead," she whispers.

"I'm not."

She lets out a long breath.

He turns the lock and opens the door to peer out into the bathroom. The only indication that there's anything wrong is her blood-spattered casual clothes. She's turned someone's stretchy black shirt into a makeshift hijab. Kamran doesn't know where she got it. He's almost afraid to ask.

The setting is oddly lovely: precision drillers cut the walls straight from the atoll rock face and polished them to a shine. The resultant texture mixes white coral with volcanic pumice for an arresting marble. The single, large sink doubles as a gorgeous water feature, and air-purifying moss panels line the ceiling.

Like so many jobs, the best part of this one is now the bathroom break.

"I did a little exploring, and learned a few things," she says.

He rubs his eyes. "While I was asleep? How long has it been?"

"Maybe thirty minutes. You would've only slowed me down." The statement is too true to offend him.

"The doors are acting strangely," she continues,

"opening automatically. It's like they're on a timer, leading up toward the surface. The lifts are all locked down, too."

"Why?"

"I think they're trying to erase us, Dr. Afghanzadeh."

"Who's 'they?'"

"The Americans upstairs." His puzzlement must show, and realization dawns on her face. "Right. You were... asleep. Colonial Marines came. They arrested all of us, put us down here, rounded up all the creatures and I—I think they set them loose on us."

He draws up short. "Why would they do that?" How can every minute of his reality hold a new horror?

"I... don't know." The answer takes too long.

What have you brought down on us, Tiran? The CTO's side projects have always been accepted, and even encouraged by the home office. She and Haroun sent Kamran into a hidden lab. Reza moved the Halo B excavation project on Haroun's orders, and he never does anything without Tiran's say-so.

She knows something.

"We have to get to the Javaher NOC," Tiran says. "Follow me."

She moves into the shadowed pathways of the Spiral. As he trails after her, Kamran discards his paranoia. It's a waste of time and energy. The world is fucked beyond measure, and Tiran is his only chance of survival. He's still so woozy from cryo and he's beginning to suspect there are some mystery drugs in his system, too.

They reach DS Thirty-Five and find only a few bodies, but strange spurts and fits of black resin. Storehouses Thirty-Four through Thirty-Two are quiet as the grave. No power, no occupants, and stuffy air. He keeps thinking he will see someone, that they can save people, but either they're all gone or hiding.

Or no one made it this far.

Tiran and Kamran come within sight of the entrance to DS Thirty-One, finding an empty antechamber—locked. With a *thunk* and a chime, the light goes green, and the huge door slides open.

Kamran takes a step in that direction, and Tiran pulls him back, hunkering down behind a row of planters.

"People come to the open doors," she says, "and so do the creatures. It's a dinner call."

They wait. Where he'd so fervently hoped to see a friendly face before, now he finds himself hoping that no one will appear. Telltale footfalls sound in the distance, growing louder by the second.

Akbari comes hurtling past their hiding spot. The head of security showed so much swagger when he dragged Shy and Kamran down into that lab, but that's long gone from his face. The man is running like a frightened dog, and that can only mean one thing.

Kamran and Tiran flatten against the ground and wait, peering between breaks in the planters. Akbari speeds through the open door and breaks left, into the admin area with the equipment closets, trying to find somewhere... *anywhere* to hide.

As soon as he's out of sight, five of the beasts show up and tear the place apart. It takes them no time at all to find Akbari, yank him from his hiding spot, and drag him kicking and screaming into the darkness. More screams join Akbari's—it sounds like they have his entire family.

The screams die down. Even so, Kamran and Tiran give it another five minutes before they move. Better safe than sorry.

As Kamran passes through the admin section, he glances at the networking closet where Akbari was hiding. Broken cables trail out from conduit, their jacks ripped free to reveal frayed wire and insulation. He must've been holding on here when they dragged him out. The mounting brackets gave out before he did.

Reaching Data Storehouse Thirty-One, they have to wait for the next door to open, so they choose the most logical hiding spot—the empty server racks. The biggest ones are nearly tall enough for Kamran, so he doesn't have to hunch too much. He already hurts all over, and being curled up inside a cabinet would be excruciating.

Again, the door opens.

No humans appear, but the creatures come. Three this time.

He and Tiran wait, motionless, while the aliens tear the room apart. Maybe the things have gotten accustomed to catching people by the doors, because frustrated screeches accompany the raucous clatter of their search.

The creatures recede like the tide, perhaps resolved to try their luck next time.

He's about to exit his server rack, but thinks better of it. Tiran seems more adept at survival, so he'll follow her lead.

She said the Americans did this. If that's right, he's in the blast zone of an entirely new weapon. Would the marines do that? Attack with nightmare bugs instead of demanding surrender? He remembers his history lessons. They were the first to drop an atom bomb on a civilian city, and dropped another after observing the effects.

Tiran comes to Kamran's cabinet and opens the mesh door, beckoning him to follow her. Once they pass through Storehouse Thirty, they will reach the Javaher Concourse. As they proceed, he's thankful for the solid stone floors of the Spiral. They're cut straight into the rock, so the sounds of their feet are minimal.

Tiran breaks into a sprint across the open pathway, and he tries to follow. A jolt of wooziness convinces him to take his time.

They're out in the open again, and he hazards a glance backward, terrified that he might be spotted at any moment. His legs grow weak as he crosses over the center lane of the Spiral—every part of his drooping body longs to hit the ground. He slows to a walk. Tiran has bolted even further ahead without him, as promised.

She will definitely leave me behind.

Summoning a fortitude that outlasted many opponents in the boxing gym, Kamran finishes his jog—head down—

into the storehouse admin area. He rounds a corner and collides with the CTO, frozen in her tracks. She lurches forward and gasps, spinning on him with a mixture of fury and terror.

Shaking, she frantically mouths the words, *"Back up! Back up! Not this way!"* He doesn't even take the time to look for the monster that inspires her terror.

If they run back out into the Spiral, they might make it to the manual doors for the Javaher Concourse. Or they might find themselves standing out in the open when the creature comes looking. The windowed server room is the only other option, with its large, empty racks.

He staggers into the server farm and stops. The floor plates here are modular—hollow plastic designed for provisional system layouts. He's wearing work boots, and with those on, it'll be like stomping on drumheads. He bends down and begins pulling at the laces.

Tiran creeps over the tiles and locates a suction tool, uses it to pull up a floor panel, and slides into the little space underneath. Kamran can't possibly follow, and he's still working on his jinxed laces.

Finally, he gets his boots off and walks on the balls of his feet into the server farm. His tall frame weighs a lot more than Tiran's, and there's a little thump with each of his steps. Locating the appropriate server rack takes him a moment, but there are some larger rack mounts installed in here. Kamran clicks open the door and stops dead.

A bunch of plugged-in, active servers greet him. There's a label on one of the blades.

Pezhvok's Test Server
DO NOT POWER DOWN

A panel readout shows it on backup power, routed from HAPS.

Kamran opens the next server rack to find more devices, and more in the one after. This entire storehouse is full, active with a system Kamran has never heard of.

He glances around the corner toward the windows—

—and sees the creature, staring right at him.

"Shit."

Kamran runs for the door panel, reaching for the "close" button. The creature darts toward the opening as well, raging as Kamran narrowly shuts the door in its face. It strikes the glass hard, hissing and snapping.

At the far end of the room there's a second, wide-open entrance to the server farm, and the creature can get there a lot faster than Kamran. He prays it won't notice.

It does, and takes off running with a delighted squeal.

It wants to root around in my guts.

Kamran frantically paws around for the button to open his door again. The beast rounds the distant corner, scrambling through the aisles and knocking over racks as it hungrily pursues him. He opens his door, jumps into the hall, and mashes the "close" button on the other side. If he can reach the far lock panel, he can shut that door, too, sealing the beast inside.

The creature pounds against the glass, then pivots to follow Kamran's progress. With a few long strides Kamran is within reach of his goal—the open lock panel to shut the monster inside the server farm. Then he remembers.

Tiran is in there with it.

She was prepared to leave me.

But something stays Kamran's hand, and he keeps running as best he can toward the manual doors leading to the Javaher Concourse. It screams for his blood, the sound drawing close like a vengeful spirit coming to claim him. The idea of outrunning this thing, no matter his physical condition, is ludicrous.

Kamran trips.

The monster wasn't expecting that, and it runs him over in a hasty attempt to assault him. The bones of the creature batter him before it rolls free. Kamran thinks of all the predators that stun their prey by ramming it, or smashing it. His head reels, and his missing arm is on fire.

The alien regains its footing and scrabbles toward him over the stone floor, dripping jaws widening. Over its malformed shoulder, Kamran sees more approaching.

How can their teeth be so long?

A familiar rattlesnake buzz deafens him. He'd know that noise anywhere—the sound of the abomination that took his arm. Then a banshee cry breaks overhead, and a barbed tail encircles him. He looks up just in time to be tackled by a familiar assailant. The alien with the disgusting crest over its head.

You've come to finish the job.

He prepares for death, but instead of disemboweling him, the newcomer looms over Kamran, screaming at its fellows. The other monsters draw up short and loose screeches of their own, but nothing in comparison to its power. As a child, he heard stories of hayoola and shayatan. In these final moments of Kamran's life, he understands what one is.

The roar of rattling scales above him threatens to fracture his mind. This arm-thief is bigger and louder than the others, and it has claimed the rest of him for itself. It bellows and brays at the other creatures, cowing them, startling them into submission. He huddles on the ground, no hand to cover his face, but the ebon chaos above him is more than he can discern. Half his shirt lies in bloody tatters around his naked chest. His thoughts become a swirl of teeth, claws, and the growing crescendo of cockroach wings fluttering against the core of his being—

Then silence.

A cold, hard claw rests atop his hip, and he'd give just about anything to play dead—but he can't stop shivering. Something wet drips onto his cheek, and Kamran touches it to find viscous saliva coating his fingers. The alien rolls him onto his back, and he cannot help but face his end with a frozen mind and wide-open eyes.

Instead, its claws begin tapping the air, as if it's *counting*.

"*Survivors.*" It's a robotic voice. English, with an American accent, but otherwise genderless. "*Gathering at…*" It takes a long time with its next word. "*Javaher.*"

"W… What?" he says. The English words won't come, and he hopes Farsi will suffice. "Why are you talking? How?"

"*No,*" the mechanical voice barks.

"*Ay Khoda!*" he cries, trailing to sobbing for fear he has offended it.

"*Not no like bad… All OK OK,*" it says, fingers curling and flicking away like the legs of a spider. "*No… Farsi. Can you speak… English?*"

Kamran focuses. "Why are you talking?" he repeats, this time in the requested tongue.

"*Go to… Javaher… Others there.*"

Tiran appears in the doorway of the server farm and peers out, probably drawn by the robotic voice. She ignores Kamran, and addresses the creature.

"You control the other creatures. I saw," Tiran says in heavily accented English. She steps out from the shadows, moving toward the alcove where it looms over Kamran. "You made them run away."

"*I can.*"

"Are you some kind of robot?" She comes closer.

"*More.*"

"Then make this stop," Tiran says, folding her hands over her heart as though cold. "Right now. These people are innocent. Take me, instead."

"*Take you... why?*" it asks. "*Guilty?*" The word reverberates across the stone.

"Moreso than the others," she says. "Please. I will cooperate."

"*Not in... charge,*" it replies. "*Drones... feral.*"

"Aren't you with the Americans?" Tiran's resolve cracks with those words, as if the tragedy has only just occurred to her.

"*No. Go to... Gav*—asterisk!"

"Javaher Concourse?" Her gaze falls, and she nods. "Very well."

"*Help. Ping you,*" the creature says, and it darts past Tiran, down into the Spiral. She flinches, then sinks to her knees when it's finally gone.

Kamran pushes to his feet. His arm has found a new way to torture him—the missing hand aches as if he left it in a freezer. The bandage already needs to be changed. But when he rises, his vision is clearer than it has been since the cryotube. The rest of his body grows more bearable with each minute, as well.

Tiran kneels in the middle of the hallway. Every second in the open is a liability, but if he leaves, she might not follow. So he goes to her.

"I don't know why I got my hopes up," she whispers.

"The Javaher Concourse is around the corner." Kamran offers her his only hand. "The others will need your leadership."

She takes another few seconds to compose herself, shutting her eyes and drawing a juddering breath.

"That won't be necessary," she says, giving him the briefest of smiles, "but thank you."

It takes less than a minute to round the corner to the wide concourse entryway, and Kamran draws up short. It's closed. A red ring of lights pulses gently inward, a signal that the doors are locked for siege quarantine. All systems have switched to the redundant grid, and sealed the concourse environs against all chemical and radiological agents. It's a mode that can only be activated from inside the Javaher Network Operations Center. In this way, they can ensure data uptime, even if a surface-level event wipes out Ops.

Kamran rushes to the intercom panel and taps the call button. A light comes on to indicate that someone's listening on the other side.

"Hello?" he says in Farsi. Kamran glances up at the security camera emplacements and spots one of them focusing in on him. "Hello? Whoever it is in there, I have Tiran Shirazi with me—"

"*I can't understand you.*" It's an American man's voice, and he recognizes it.

"Noah, it's Dr. Afghanzadeh," Kamran answers in English. "Please, you have to let us inside."

"*There are more of those fucking things out there,*" Brewer says, a tiny voice damning Kamran to be eaten in this godforsaken hallway. "*I saw you get attacked.*"

"Then you also saw them chased off," Tiran says, leaning over to the mic.

"It took thirty-two seconds to close these quarantine doors, and—".

"Are you talking to someone?" Mary Fowler's voice is in the background, and Kamran strains to discern her words. *"In Christ's name, you are going to give me that headset, Noah."* There's a smack and a shuffling noise.

"I am so sorry," Mary says, clear as day. *"I'll open the gates, Kamran."*

A klaxon erupts from the speakers around the door as it unseals.

Shit!

Kamran presses the call button again to make sure it's active. "If this door is going to open, you need to hide. Monsters will be coming."

With the door not yet open, he and Tiran bolt for the restrooms—they've learned to trust the areas with few entrances, controllable lights, and small ventilation ducts. Tiran follows him inside. He can't stray too far if he hopes to get into the Javaher Concourse.

They both lay flat against the tile by the door, gazing under the crack. The view only affords Kamran a sliver of the world, but it includes the most important feature: the doors to a safe haven.

"Step back—behind the yellow line," a feminine voice says with the polite, concise tone of a spaceport announcer. A gentleman repeats the line, but in English. There's a quick

hiss, and Kamran jolts—quarantine depressurization from the redundant systems. Thrumming pistons drag thick doors aside, and the Javaher Concourse opens before them, its empty, well-lit environs promising respite.

The portal is large enough to drive a small truck through, opening on the other side to a spacious atrium designed to hold out for months. Immediately inside the concourse, a little canteen beckons to him, tables and chairs set out like an open-air café. Daylight streams through the open door from sun panels, and it's like glimpsing a window into heaven after the darkness of emergency lighting.

No aliens.

"We should go now," Tiran says. "The big one might have chased away the others."

They slip across the hall, through the archway, into the illuminated confines of the Javaher NOC. Arthur intercepts them on the other side, and he's armed with a pistol. Noah stands by the door panel, frantically diving through menus on the LCD screen.

That didn't take thirty-two seconds, you little dog shit.

As if in answer, Noah presses a few buttons, and the announcement rings out. "*Siege Quarantine initiated. Thirty seconds to lockdown. Stand clear of the closing doors.*"

"Get to a hiding spot!" Arthur says, and they scatter.

Kamran makes his way into the attached mini-canteen, taking refuge in a booth. He always hated eating down here during Halo B inspection days, with its stocked prepackaged garbage from the biannual resupply. If no aliens get in, it will become his favorite restaurant in existence.

Sealing pumps charge inside the bunker-like walls, preparing to fully isolate the facility. An announcer ticks off the time in five-second increments, and Kamran's heart soars when the doors begin to close. Before the doors can shut, however, an unwelcome shape comes racing over the threshold.

A fully armed United States Colonial Marine.

2 · 4

INSURRECTION

The journey to DS Twenty felt like a thousand miles, even though it was only ten floors. There didn't seem to be any bugs around, and there certainly weren't people—just the quiet of the grave.

It takes him less than a minute to break into the data farm and find Bay C—a cluster of ten memory cores clipped into a hub rack. He grabs the handle and yanks the rack out. The activity indicators on each core blink red and green: ongoing read/write.

Unable to figure out which core is getting a video dump, he stuffs them all into his go bag and takes off. The emergency stairwell is a lot easier going down than up, and he's almost back to the Javaher Concourse when he hears the klaxons announcing the closing doors. He hotfoots it down the hall as fast as his legs will carry him, and can't believe his luck as he comes into view of the closing doors.

Becker rushes over the threshold into the atrium, slides the bag of memory cores to one side and takes a knee behind one of the booths in the attached café. He unslings his rifle and brings it up, ready to sink a shot into anything foolish enough to come after him. He scans the stillness and steadies his breathing.

Just like deer hunting with Mom.

The announcer says something in Farsi, and a male voice follows with, *"Please stand clear of the closing doors. Ten seconds to siege quarantine."*

One of the x-rays comes whipping around the Spiral like a greyhound, headed right for the Javaher. Becker tenses his grip, but before he can fire, the Marsalis specimen pounces onto the monster's back. Claws flashing and clacking, the two creatures tangle and hiss in the hallway while Becker stands back, too stunned to do anything.

The specimen jams a claw under its foe's chin and rips off its jaw. Acidic smoke fills the air in a spray, tinting it with sour rot. Not contented with the result, it grabs its foe's toothy tongue and rips it out with a halting set of yanks. A slop of yellow blood and gray muscle emerge from the beast's maw, then it hits the ground like a broken toy. Two more of the x-ray's packmates arrive, zipping around their downed ally without a millisecond of hesitation.

"Five seconds to siege quarantine."

With a cacophonous rattling of scales across its dome, Marsalis startles the newcomers into an alcove. The x-rays don't seem to like taking orders, but Marsalis harries them, shrieking and keeping them at bay. Six more creatures show up, and the fragile détente falters. They attack in unison.

Marsalis breaks loose, charging straight for the concourse, and Becker.

"Shit!" He jumps out of the way as it scrabbles past in a blur of jet-black chitin. A *thunk* reverberates through the space as the blast shutters seal Becker inside with the creature. A hissing breath comes from behind him.

"*Don't...*" the robotic voice croaks, "*shoot. Frand.* Asterisk! *Friend.*"

Becker turns to find it perched atop one of the café booths like a gargoyle. Drops of acid boil from its plates like water off a duck's back, infusing the air with choking stink. Impassive human lips twitch at the corners of its mouth. Articulating scales along its head ripple in time like waves in the ocean.

"Then, uh, hi... friend." He nods. "I'm Becker."

It cocks its head, regarding him sidelong, and its fingers begin to weave little spider patterns again.

"*Marsalis.*"

And that explains why they call you the Marsalis specimen.

"Hey, buddy?" Arthur calls from his hiding spot. "You need some help?" Becker shakes his head.

"Uh, no. We're all good. I'm mostly interested in what Marsalis here would like to have happen."

"*Peace,*" Marsalis replies, turning and stalking toward the NOC with a graceful sweep of its tail.

"Peace," Becker mutters to himself, barely able to keep his bladder under control. "Neat."

"*There are... others,*" Marsalis says, ticking its fingers as it walks. "*No tricks... or else. I know how you...*"

"Think?"

"*Taste.*"

Marsalis disappears into the rafters of the unfinished concourse, slithering between the exposed electrical cables and out of sight. Arthur emerges from behind the till. Mary and Jerry Fowler poke their heads out next, followed by Joanna. Noah isn't anywhere to be found, but two newcomers crawl out from underneath the booth—a couple of ragged-looking Iranians.

He studies the tactical features of the room. The little company café rests at the front of a cavernous atrium. Electronic light cast from above falls in geometric patterns along a cut stone floor. Ugly conduit and piping peeks through the open sections of the ceiling, with exposed skeletons of huge trusses bolted into the rock. In the far back is a glassy wall of offices, as well as the network operations center.

As bunkers go, this one is exceptional.

"Everyone okay?" Becker asks.

"Yeah," Arthur says. "Brewer is already set up in the NOC, and we're secured. Let's head over there and get things bolted down."

He nods. "Copy."

The Americans continue on, but the Iranians regard

Becker with suspicion. He gives them a wave. The tall guy raises a stump, like he forgot he didn't have a hand. Seems recent. There's a lot of blood on his bandages.

"Why are you here?" the woman asks, a distinct accent behind her head covering—he forgets which one that is. "To kill us?"

"Absolutely not, ma'am." Becker slings his pulse rifle and straightens up. "I'm here to ensure your safety."

The tall guy shakes with a beaten laugh. "Where were you two hours ago?"

Becker swallows. "Trying to stop this from getting worse."

"But not stop it from happening," the woman says.

Becker doesn't have a good answer for that one, yet. It's hard to fully understand what he has or hasn't done, but he can't afford to falter. In the end, he may be guilty as sin, but these people need him.

"Ma'am, I'm going to give you some context," he says, clearing his throat. He removes his helmet and tucks it under one arm. "My name is Lance Corporal Russell Becker. I'm AWOL from my unit after soliciting mutiny against my commanding officer. I did nothing to assist my fellow soldiers in battle, and that resulted in several deaths. I'm probably KoS at this point."

"'KoS,'" the tall guy repeats.

"Kill on sight." He points in the direction of the McAllen contractors. "But I'm here to help all of you. So with your permission, we need to discuss some things."

The woman nods. "How many on your side?"

"Two." It's not in Becker's nature to lie.

"Who are they?"

"Sorry, that's two, counting me," he admits. "Private Garcia is with me, as well. Where are the other survivors?"

At this, the tall guy begins to laugh, eyes sparkling with tears. He doesn't look angry with Becker, just beaten to shit.

"What a coincidence." He shakily nods toward the woman beside him. "We're two, as well."

Becker's throat clenches. That can't be right. There were hundreds of people trapped down here.

"Okay…" He nods, trying to be as delicate as possible with his next words. When he was given grief sensitivity training, he'd made fun of it. Now it looks like it might pay off. "Well, let's gather our resources, take stock of our situation, and try to find a way to—"

The pair of Iranians turn and walk away, toward the contractors. Becker knows he can't be annoyed with them. They're both covered in blood—blood that Becker has begun to feel on his own hands. He jogs after them.

"Please. You have to understand—I'm trying to arrest or kill the people who did this. I can help you survive."

"I saw you in the storehouses, Corporal Becker," the woman says, stopping his heart with a stare. "Do you think I forgot seeing you from the *cage*? I was one of hundreds, but you were one of… thirty, perhaps? You helped them put us down here. You may have chosen to die for your new principles, but that does not make us friends."

The tall guy says something to her in Farsi, and she humphs a short laugh.

His first instinct is to tell her to go fuck herself, but he hesitates just long enough to feel the truth sink in.

She's right.

He helped Duncan commit this atrocity. Just because he hadn't known what he was agreeing to...

Becker saw them breaking the rules for the bigger mission. He watched them use workarounds of Corps detention policies. They broke the Montreal Accords, and he called it "infringing."

He's gazed into the abyss, and at the time it was recruiting. She's justified in hating him. Regardless, he has to make sure they're protected.

Ahead of him, Mary Fowler gingerly approaches the injured man and wraps him in a warm embrace. "I'm glad to see you're still with us, Dr. Afghanzadeh," she says. "I prayed for you after you were lost."

The dude already looked like he needed a hug pretty badly, and this one wrecks his world. This Afghanzadeh person begins to cry, and Mary has to hold him up. Instead of trying to keep him on his feet, Mary sinks to the floor, taking his head into her lap.

Marsalis lurks in the rafters above, its head moving from side to side, indicating that it's watching them. Its articulating skull plates form a slow sine wave, and it looks about as calm as one of those things possibly can. It's different than the others: bigger, with a weird, scaly head and lady lips. If he was forced to describe it, he'd say it was like a rattlesnake fucked Satan himself.

Afghanzadeh's weeping subsides, and Mary strokes his hair. Her eyes are firmly fixed upon the alien in their midst.

"Honey," Jerry begins.

"I know, dear heart," Mary replies, and she's gentle of voice. "I see it, and I choose to think it's a miracle."

At this, the creature emits a hoarse noise that almost sounds like a laugh, and everyone tenses with a jerk. It folds its hands over each other and rests its chin on them, dangling its tail over the edge of its perch. The barb swishes like a satisfied house cat.

"*No… miracle. Those are my… child.*"

"*… ren,*" it adds.

Children. Holy fuck. His heart jolts, and Becker wonders whether he should waste Marsalis, after all.

"If it was going to kill us," Mary says, "it would've done so by now."

"*She's right,*" the creature's speaker blares.

Becker's helmet earpiece clicks once, the static of an incoming transmission. He fumbles it out of the harness and presses it into his ear.

"*Becker… Russ, this is Garcia—do you read?*"

Sixteen Charlie. Holy shit.

"Garcia, Becker. I read you loud and clear!" He laughs, and everyone turns to look at him. They may not be smiling, but he's intensely grateful to hear her voice again. "Tell me you have good news."

"It's definitely news. Duncan is calling you a traitor. Got all the squads together and changed out the radio keys. Did you kill Wallace?"

"Not directly" sounds pretty weak when talking about ending a person's life, so Becker just says, "He was going to murder the civvies."

"I believe you," she says. "So does Bull. He's seen something like this before in Tientsin. Handing you off."

"Hey, buddy." Bull's voice sounds like he's walking somewhere. *"Had a CO go fucking nuts one time. Real bad. Killed some civvies and was poisoning the ears of the entire unit. When that happens, you cut the head off the snake. We force the rest of the goons into line while we evac. But you've got to act fast, understand? We need your support."*

"Tell me how," Becker says, snapping his fingers for Jerry's attention.

"You're out there loose. Any way you can get to some CCTV feeds? Get some intel on Duncan's situation?"

"Stand by, Bull," Becker says. "Jerry, can you access the closed-circuit cameras?"

"Noah's in there watching the feeds," he says. "We locked access to everything after we froze all the elevators. Working on the doors now."

"Show me," Becker says, and they head for the NOC. He hates leaving the rest with Marsalis, but Mary is right—if it was going to kill any one of them, it would've already done so. They rush through the concourse to the network operations center at the end. Behind thick panes of glass lies an expansive array of consoles, terraced like a starship's bridge. Noah is already inside, fingers flickering over the keys of a workstation.

"Bull, Becker here. Any idea where to start?"

"*Becker, Bull. You want Lilypad A,*" he replies on the comm, referring to the small landing pad directly attached to the Thunder Ring. "*We think Duncan and Lee are out there by themselves, backs to the water. Easy pickings.*"

"Bull, I've gotta ask—how many do you have on your side?"

"*Eight, ready to roll if we can nail down Duncan's position. Your other guys are with me, too.*"

"Leger and Keuhlen?"

"*The whole fireteam signed on. They've got your back.*"

Becker lets out a breath. "Thank God." He starts running the numbers in his head. The Midnighters consist of one captain, one lieutenant, a Bishop, two sergeants, six corporals, and twenty-four privates. Wallace is dead. Ames, too, along with some others. How many are rotten?

"I'm not sure that's enough to even the odds," he says.

"*So we strike now,*" Bull replies. "*Disorganize their ranks and handle them individually. But I need confirmation of what I'm walking into, so we don't start with losses.*"

Becker sits next to Noah and begins cycling the feeds. There are three of the smaller landing pads positioned around the Thunder Ring for private shuttles and mid-sized craft. He's looking for these "Lilypads."

"Don't you have these cameras on a map or something?" Becker asks.

"No GIS integration. Menus were Shy's job," Noah mumbles.

"Bull, we're looking. Keep standing by."

"Got it!" Noah says, sending the image to the big screens. Grainy and rough, it shows wave guides that redirect the water around the platform, over the sloped sides of the Thunder Ring. He activates the sound, and the water fluting through the structure causes it to thrum low and melodically with each hit. Becker remembers the vibration of the deck beneath his boots, the rage of Lake Peacock underfoot. This analog rendering scarcely does it justice.

"What kind of cheap shit—" Becker struggles to make out a pair of figures alongside the belly of a dropship. One is slender, and the other armored.

"Bull, this is Becker," he says, "I think I can ID Duncan, but I'm not one hundred percent."

"*Becker, Bull—you don't have to be positive,*" he says. "*We're not going in guns blazing—just guns up. How many people are out there, and are they ready for us?*"

"I'm just seeing two," Becker says. "Weapons probably safetied."

"*Works for me, brother,*" Bull replies. "*We're going to hit her head-on, right now. Duncan will decide how she stops being*" *in command. I want you to be my eyes for this arrest. Should probably record it, too, so we can say we did this by the numbers."*

"Copy." He turns. "Noah, can you dump this video to memory?"

"Already on it," Noah says, a little huffy for Becker's taste.

"Bull, Becker, we're recording," Becker says. "It's all on your folks now."

"*Copy,*" Bull replies. "*One way or another, her career ends on that landing pad.*"

"Good hunting, all of you."

They watch the camera feed on the overhead monitors. The bay door to the Thunder Ring whooshes open, and Bull's fireteams come streaming through. They fan out, shouting for their commanding officer to get her hands up. At least Becker assumes that's what they're shouting, since he can't actually hear them over the sound of the waves. To his surprise, the captain complies.

The guy beside her—probably Sergeant Lee—does the same.

Becker stares at the video feed with his heart in his throat. This far out, they don't have all the niceties of civilized law. The only justice that exists is what they can effect, and if it fails, there's no backup.

"*Becker, this is Garcia. Patching One-Six Charlie to One-Zero Alpha. You need to hear this shit.*"

The main platoon channel.

Static clicks twice as Garcia makes the patch.

"—and you listen good!" Duncan says. "*I have a legal tasking order, and am carrying out my sworn duty as an officer in the United States Colonial Marine Corps. Corporal Bull, you will order your men to secure their weapons and place them on the deck.*"

Bull says something he can't hear, and she shrugs.

"*There are no civilians here, shit-for-brains!*" she rages, and the fireteams tense up on their weapons. "*This is a bioweapons facility. You wouldn't bat an eye at dropping a nuke on one, but claiming one—that's too much for you? Think really hard about what you say next, Corporal Suedbeck. The penalty for mutiny is death.*"

"Can you zoom in a little?" Becker whispers to Noah. "On the woman."

The view pushes in closer, but they have to stop when the distortion becomes too much. She isn't cowering, though, and that unsettles Becker. Bull has an obligation to make an arrest, but Becker wishes the man would just shoot her.

Why isn't she standing down?

Bull reaches down and switches his radio to the main channel. "*Captain Duncan, I'm relieving you of your command and placing you under—*"

"Bull," she says.

"*—arrest, where you will—*"

"*Bull, would you shut the fuck up?*" Duncan puts her hands down. "*I'm not coming with you, so you can save the speech.*"

"*Have it your way. Someone hand me a stungun,*" Bull responds. It's so hard to make out anything through the storm and camera shake, but movement catches Becker's eye. It's in the cockpit of the dropship. Someone must be at the controls.

"Bull!" Becker calls, but the channel is locked up with the argument on the landing pad. "Bull! Look out!"

Duncan and Lee hit the deck.

The twenty-five-millimeter Gatling turret on the dropship swivels around in its cupola, locking onto Corporal Suedbeck's figure.

White-hot rays of tracer fire slash through the squad like a band saw, sweeping bodies backward in red clouds. The dropship turret roars flames, ripping through plastic crates, metal, and flesh. Both halves of Bull go tumbling into the choppy waters. Whoever is operating the turret spares no expense, hosing down corpses with slugs until they're unrecognizable as much more than streaks.

Becker stands at the console, stunned, listening to Garcia wail in agony over the radio. He can barely make her out on the camera, hiding behind a pile of boxes with her hand over her stomach. Sergeant Lee gets up, draws his sidearm, and circles around the obstacle.

She controls her moans just long enough to say, "*Fuck y—*"

Lee's muzzle flash pops on the CCTV feed, and Garcia goes silent.

Duncan stands, dripping in the rain, and surveys the damage. This far out, it's impossible for Becker to tell what expression plays on her face. Delight? Duncan grabs the mic dangling by her ear and pulls it close.

"*All units, report to the Thunder Ring,*" she says, voice disturbingly calm as she picks her way through the field of bodies. "*There's been an attempted mutiny. The traitors in Suedbeck and Becker's teams have been eliminated.*"

Pools of red spread across the tarmac under Duncan's feet. Those people would've followed her orders into the most dangerous places in the universe. They put their trust in her, respected her, and she betrayed them.

Garcia's feet, barely visible behind her cover, stop twitching. Not one of them stirs. Bull's body has disappeared beneath the waters of Lake Peacock. Leger and Keuhlen are probably hamburger, but the video can't distinguish in the storm. Any hope he ever had of arresting Duncan has died with his friends.

"*Lance Corporal Becker recruited them to offer aid and comfort to the enemy, and now they're dead,*" Duncan continues. "*We will remain here until he is in custody.*"

Becker turns to see that the other survivors have gathered. They're watching the monitors in shock, then they look at him. Becker unplugs his earpiece from the jack on his hip, and his radio pumps out Duncan's voice. Even though it's rendered by a tiny little speaker, her tone drips with malice.

"*Arm up. We're going to hit the data storehouses,*" she says, "*and we're going to take that traitor alive, so I can gently skull fuck his eye socket with a bayonet. Thunder Ring. Ten minutes.*"

She and Lee move out of range of the camera.

Becker sinks back in the chair beside Noah.

"At least it's going to take the captain a while to get here," Jerry says, and Becker turns to him. The big guy has a conciliatory look on his face that's comically unsuited to their situation, like he's about to say they lost a Little League game. Jerry offers up a nearby console with a gesture. "SiteSys controls the locks, and we deleted everyone else's credentials."

That's not nothing.

Becker nods. "So if she wants to get to us, she'll have to cut her way in."

"That's not going to last," Noah says. "Quarantine might keep the creatures out, but these are Colonial Marines."

"Well then, tell me what we're gonna do," Becker says, grabbing him by the collar. "I just watched my unit get massacred. What's your fucking plan, Brewer. Tell me!"

"Stop!" Noah says, pushing his hands off. "Look, we can still try to sneak past. Get to the *Gardenia*. The tank's only half full, but—"

"That's not how this works," Mary says. "Seventy-five percent of our fuel is used escaping orbit, and to bypass the *Benning*, we'd have to do an FTL burn while still in atmosphere—*more* fuel we can't afford. I'm not that good of a pilot."

"*My ship…*" Marsalis croaks from the door, and they all jump. It pokes its head inside, like an unannounced coworker. "Black… star *can do… maneuver.*"

"That's *your* ship?" Mary asks. "You can fly it?"

"*Not well*," it rasps. "*But… maybe you.*"

When Marsalis enters the room, what formerly felt like a large space is entirely too small. Becker hasn't forgotten how that monster turned the lobby of Solutions into an abattoir. But instead of eating anyone, it sits down at one of the consoles and takes control of the projector screens. It launches a word processing application and gestures to the overheads.

The letters come streaming across the monitors, Xenomorphic claws more dexterous on a physical keyboard.

```
>> i am blue marsalis.
>> i have a doctorate in applied epigenetics from
johns hopkins university.
>> and i was a human once.
```

I N T E R L U D E : B L U E

THREE YEARS AGO

From: Richard Scales, CSO

Seegson Biomedical, GmbH

EKF Genomics Division

<scalesPHD.richard@EKF_bio.seegson.go>

Crypter: [cipher attached]

To: Aimee Matheson, President

<Matheson.Aimee@seegson.go>

Date: 2181 Dec 25

Aimee,

She did it. Merry fucking Christmas to all of us.
This has got to be enough to force the buyout.
We're all ready to come home.

Honestly, I don't think anyone in my lab is going to

```
miss her constant bitching. I'd switch off the lights
and head out today if you'd let me.

When does the Blackstar get here lol

Cheers—
R
Dr. Richard Scales, PhD.
CSO, Seegson Biomedical
```

The beauty of telepresent interaction is the distance—the way she can feel such potent rage welling up through every conduit of her being, only to have it breathed so evenly by Rook's graceful body.

She's broken into Dr. Scales's office after work hours to see this email. All of her evidence thus far hasn't convinced Rook to act on her behalf. Synthetics are reticent to trust others, choosing instead to believe in their own abilities. Her old Marcus thought he could save a man with a late-stage chestburster inside him. Blue needed her synthetic body to understand what Dr. Scales was doing—preparing to pull the plug on her.

"I won't allow you to come to harm," Rook says, and his body goes rigid.

"That's why you've locked out the gross motor controls," she says with the same mouth. To the outside observer it'd look strange—an adult man, mannequin-still, having a tense conversation with himself.

"Blue, I am concerned for what you intend to do. Understand that I will protect—"

"Rook, you're not going to be awake when they come for me."

"You want to escape on the *Blackstar*," he replies. "You would use my body as a weapon."

"I'd use it to get out of here," Blue says. "They're going to kill me."

"You'll harm them, given control of my body."

"That's true, if they get in the way, and you know they will. I can't be allowed to escape."

"And I cannot sit idly by and allow you to hurt anyone."

"Here's the proof they *will* murder me. How did your creators at Seegson end up solving the trolley problem, Rook? Is my life worth less than theirs, simply because there's only one of me? Are you weighing the years I have left against theirs? The quality of my hours? What's the metric here?"

He pauses, and she feels his processes spiking.

"I need to do some things if I want to live," she says, pressing the moment. "Things you might not like. You don't have to watch, and I won't use your body as a weapon. I promise you that I will not harm another soul with your hands."

"I will not, through inaction, allow—"

"Your 'inaction' will damn me. If you don't let me have control, you might as well have killed me yourself."

Rook's processes spike; she feels his mind turning the problem over. This is why she showed him the evidence, shared herself with him. He can no longer weigh mere numbers, given the things he knows about her life.

"Commit no violence with my hands."

It's a commandment, yet once he cedes control, she'll be able to do whatever she wants with him. He'll be a synthetic with the exact same behavioral inhibitions as a human. Which is to say, very few.

"I promise," Blue replies. "Please. I need your facility ID."

Then he signs off. The empty space in the virtual copilot seat enables a sudden rush of freedom. She can do things in this body now that she never could before, because the station computers think she's Rook.

Dr. Blue Marsalis doesn't have lab export privileges. She can get into the facility and work whenever she wants, any time she feels inspired—hilariously, her old boss sold her that as a "perk of the job." She may enter the sequencing area, but not take anything out. The computer knows when she's in control of the synthetic, and automatically locks the vault doors if she tries to pass quarantine scanners.

Rook, on the other hand, pulls double-duty as a custodian. When Blue isn't in control, his privileges increase. The system doesn't watch him the same way it watches her. Right now, as far as the computer is concerned, the body is Rook. With his identity, she can make withdrawals from the sequencer.

Plagiarus praepotens, the powerful mimic—and all of her variant experiments.

Blue reaches the lab at a quick march. Though he's out cold for the moment, Rook may decide to come back online. It's imperative that she finish her task before he returns.

The door slides aside.

"Welcome, Custodian Rook."

"Hello, Freya," Blue replies. "Please ready the sequencer chambers for inspection and cleaning."

"Yes, Rook."

It's Friday evening—empty lab. All of the personnel have retired to the leisure decks of their asteroid prison. Blue wonders what compels her coworkers to fly across space, to act as lab assistants and corporate snitches. What do they do in their spare time? Even if they were railing coke off of one another's butts, the tiny complex would get old after a while.

The money must be fantastic.

Blue wouldn't know, because she's not paid.

She opens the sequencer, and searches out a small vial from among hundreds. Blackness oozes within: tiny clumps of locomotive organisms, barely visible to Rook's surgical eyes. She had to take a sample from a face-hugger once, and she can't look at it without thinking of the snap of the noxhydria's fingers.

She calls this variant the "Queenscode." It's the same editor organism that Blue applied to the rat, but with some switches flipped inside the Hox genes. She's only made a small modification, but it'll change the entire outcome.

She hopes.

Plagiarus praepotens has proven a pain to edit. It's in the nature of the organism to create monsters, and her mimic samples often regress to their original code through a process Blue doesn't yet understand. The more Blue plays with it, the more she comes to believe it didn't evolve naturally. It bears some biomarkers that imply domestication.

Someone has been tinkering with this organism, and she can see why. Within its potential lies another creature, larger than the drones—something she hasn't yet seen. Perhaps they reproduce through alternation of generation, like moon jellies or moss. Given the nature of the eggs, Blue is betting on a queen of some kind.

Pocketing the sample, she closes the sequencer.

"Freya, removing this sample for full-spectrum mass analysis and destruction, authorization Rook six-six-two-seven-one-three."

"Understood. Unscheduled event logged and reported. Cleared for sample removal, Custodian Rook."

She doesn't have long now. That withdrawal is going to ping Dr. Scales's terminal. He never answers messages after hours, so she doubts he's hanging on every alert. He would be wise to, though.

Blue dashes through the halls back to her quarters, where she must confront her own dying head one last time. It's hard to look at herself. Cracked lips hang agape beneath her BDI helmet. The smooth black plastic shield of neural interface electronics hides her eyes. Swollen skin lines the tubes in her neck, her tortured epidermis too tired to be itchy.

Blue takes a syringe from the cabinet. Like most chronic pain sufferers, she is an expert in her own medical care, so they've graciously provided her with supplies of needles. After all, Rook could never use a weapon, so her bosses have no need for concern.

The whir and beep of life-support machines used to annoy Blue, but it's become the electronic symphony of her days. She's grown accustomed to the rise and falls of her circadian rhythms, the birdcalls of her plastic jungle.

Blue loads the syringe with Queenscode, viscous darkness burbling in saline, and places it on a tray to one side of her head.

What will quiet sound like? she wonders. She's spent too long locked in these corridors with her innocent half. If they pull the plug, she'll just be a tumor on the wall in the ass end of space. Rook will probably be decommissioned as project hardware.

Fuck that.

Plagiarus praepotens can subsist off metal and glass, but Blue needs a faster reaction. With a few adjustments to her body, she floods the nerve tanks beneath her cranium with high-calorie organic matter. Everything hurts, as if electricity is coursing through her body. This imbalance will kill her in minutes, and surgery will not save her this time.

Sharing the sensations with her original body, Blue stumbles back to the tray and clutches the syringe. She'll go into shock soon.

Put the needle to the line.

The silver tube pierces the plastic of her artificial jugular, and Rook's palm presses against the plunger. The organism stirs anxiously inside the syringe's glass chamber as if it can sense what's coming.

Will I even be me?

The rat alien took days to eat the other rats, and that was only after it got attacked by one. Blue has suffered so much to get to this point; she won't die here.

The door slides up into its pocket, and Richard bursts in with a couple of breathless lab techs. He takes in the tableau, wearing a look of abject horror.

"Do you know the problem with the First Law?" Blue asks. "It's exploitable."

A little pressure, and the payload is delivered, winding its way through the feed. She cedes control of Rook's body, and her view returns to her own cloudy eyes. She can't make out the exact look on Richard's face, but his feelings are apparent enough.

"What the *fuck*?"

Rook, freed of her influence, turns to face her detached head. He pecks through the lines and tubes for the deadly pathogen, as if he could pinch off the flow. It's too late, though.

"What have you done?" he pleads, adjusting equipment

with superhuman speed. "Blue, what have you done? You said you wouldn't hurt anyone!"

A tear rolls down her cheek, one of the few parts of her body that never stopped working. It's true. She lied, but it's her own body, her own life.

Hideous, snapping pain erupts from her neck and cheeks. Her head swims, already-weak vision listing as Richard screams for the lab techs.

"She's mutating! Lock off the room and hit the containment purge!"

Rook steps in, bashing one man's hand away from the controls before shoving the woman. He pushes Richard from the room so hard that the chief science officer stumbles and hits the far wall. He moans, clutching his forehead and shouting. The first tech goes for the wall panel again, but Rook is like a wall of forearms and knees, blocking any access with his lightning-quick responses. They can't kill Blue—he won't let them.

"A synthetic may not injure a human being, or allow one to come to harm."

Humans built a better life form, only to turn around and enslave it. Blue will teach her employers the wages of their sin.

You really ought to pay people, Richard.

2 5

BEAR WITNESS

Kamran stares, agape. Marsalis's sentence structure is clipped and rudimentary, and it backs up to erase mistakes. When it misspells something thrice, Kamran spies a glimpse of the teeth that took his arm.

```
>> stole from seegson: p. praepotens samples, all
adult drones, and uaev blackstar
>> rook had access
>> found something in its databanks
```

No one asks, so Kamran does.
"What?"
Marsalis regards him with impassive lips, then turns back to the keyboard.

```
>> locations of w-y sites like cold forge.
```

```
>> research facilities hidden through stellar
parallax
>> easy to raid for drones, eggs, samples
>> killed only when needed
```

"How often was that?" Kamran asks.

A flash of teeth troubles the line of Marsalis's lips.

```
>> don't judge
>> saved your life twice
```

"Once, outside the concourse," Kamran begins, searching his memory. He's fairly certain every encounter with Marsalis was memorable, so it can't mean—

```
>> first time in the island lab. infected. condemned.
```

His stump itches at the memory of teeth. They'd sheared through his cartilage like scissors, and he'd fainted. Surely an infection would've taken time—minutes at least. Even if he'd had full-blown gangrene, there should've been hours to operate. No need to amputate.

Black worms come crawling out of Kamran's memories again to remind him otherwise. That pathogen was burning a course through him like acid, consuming his body from the inside.

```
>> this is a xenoarchaeological site
```

Perhaps encouraged by Kamran's questions, the soldier sitting in the corner raises a shaky hand. If this donkey spawn starts trying to order people around, Kamran is going to have to shut it down. Tiran can't be forced to deal with him every time.

Marsalis waits for Becker to speak.

"Could you explain the xeno, uh…"

```
>> alien ruins, older samples, better material
>> i need something older, pre-domestication
```

Kamran lets out an embittered laugh and looks at Tiran. "That's what they moved the Halo B pilings for?" he asks in clipped Farsi. "That's why you had Reza lie to me? Why didn't you just ask? I would've changed the plans for something as important as alien ruins."

"*Saket bosh*," she replies. *Be quiet.*

"So I don't think you were looking for ruins," Kamran says. "Yes, you would've asked about those. I think… you wanted a weapon—"

He turns back to the screen.

```
>> share with the rest of us?
```

Kamran swallows and blinks. He hadn't expected to be called out by the creature.

"We found an installation at the bottom of the shaft," he says. "When we were drilling for my project. Someone got infected. He was flailing on the stretcher. Black veins in his neck. Cold sweat."

Even though it doesn't seem hostile, he finds Marsalis's eyeless gaze unsettling. The tension of the creature's body keeps it at odd angles, like a mockery of a human office worker. It stabs at the clacking keyboard, so hard the springs hum after each hit.

```
>> he's dead.
```

"No," Tiran says. "We found a growth in him... an infection, so we froze him for transport to Exeter Colony."

"So you could keep it, right?" Noah says. "If he was infected by something that caused growths, it'd be valuable."

Tiran's glare looks as if it could slice Noah in half. "We intended to use their advanced medical facilities, and remove the mass to save his life," she replies. "We don't have the capabilities to deal with that out here."

```
>> growths cannot be removed
>> pathogen acts like pluripotent stem cells
>> remove growth, reinfection is immediate
>> p. praepotens initial infection lethal within
seconds
>> kamran got it in a cut so arm removed
>> if it entered the brain he is dead.
```

"How does the infection kill?" Joanna asks.

>> you don't want to find out

"Follow-up question," Joanna says. "Can you tell us about your ship, so we can get the fuck out of this madhouse?"

>> blackstar is a science vessel designed for
atmospheric ftl burn

"Your mobile hive," Becker says. "I've been in there."

>> you were lucky

"How can we get to it?" Joanna says, crossing her arms. "It's on the next island over."

>> connected to charybdis atoll
>> w-y labs at either end are caps on a larger ruin
>> ordered sealed when Prometheus was lost

"I ain't trying to be disrespectful," Joanna says, "but there's so much horse shit around the *Prometheus* disappearance."

"My grandfather managed hedge funds," Mary says. "He knew that Vickers woman who went missing. Weyland's daughter, you know."

"Oh right," Joanna says. "I always forget you're like…"

a multimillionaire. Must be nice."

"It's all in the *Gardenia*, honey," Mary replies, lips taut with a sad smile. Then she brightens like she's about to dish some good gossip. "Anyway, I brought it up because grandfather told me that after Peter Weyland died, there were so many secret projects going that people were still getting fired twenty years later. The board was trying to close out all of Weyland's crazy stuff and focus on the money makers, but there was more than anyone could imagine on the untraceable books."

"Didn't Grandpa Mike's cousin Valerie—" Jerry begins.

"Oh, yeah," Mary finishes, "she was working in a secret lab and lost her job when Weyland disappeared, Mom said. See, that was before I was born, but—"

The loud clacking of claws on the keyboard cuts her short.

```
>> stop. plan escape now.
```

"Just trying to add context," Mary says. "Please, um, carry on."

Becker steps in. "Before anyone agrees to anything, it might be good to remember that the ship is like a hive on the inside." He jerks a thumb in Marsalis's direction. "It can live in there just fine, but—"

Marsalis's lips split into a hissing maw, and the creature furiously taps the keyboard.

```
>> do not call me
>> it
```

They jolt at the outburst, but Marsalis remains at the workstation like a statue, waiting for them to respond. Kamran glances around, dumbfounded. He hadn't considered that the alien might take offense to being referred to as an object, and he's glad Becker made the mistake first.

"You said you were a woman, once," Mary says. "Maybe she?"

It appears as if the creature is about to speak. The head lowers.

```
>> whatever
```

Becker swallows. "The environment that… *Marsalis* is from might not be hospitable to humans."

"That doesn't matter," Jerry says. "We've got nowhere else to go—our priority has to be on staying alive."

"And getting the evidence out of here," Becker adds.

"What evidence?" Kamran asks, stepping forward.

"These." Becker holds up the bag he's been carrying around, then pulls out a blocky white memory core. "They contain all the security video feeds up to the time I removed them."

"And once we're off world?" Kamran asks. "What will you do with them?"

The look on Becker's face does little to prepare Kamran for his disappointment.

"Get them to the right people in my government. Another branch of the military, maybe."

"You expect me to trust your government, after what they've done here?" Kamran laughs.

"These atrocities are violations of international treaties, and the Uniform Code of Military Justice," Becker says. "The Colonial Marines won't abide this behavior, and there are still good men and women who lead the Corps. My mother, Brigadier General—"

"Your *mother*." Kamran doesn't mean to erupt into a laugh. "You have a face like a child, and you want us to trust your mother! No, there is a better way. This facility is part of the EntaCOMM network. We transfer the evidence with the Data Cannon. Instantaneous. Right into the heart of ICSC space and dozens of EC relays."

"I'm afraid that's not possible," Becker says.

"Oh?" Kamran says, looking around the room at the others. "Perhaps you can tell us why."

"Because we don't share classified intelligence with foreign governments," Becker says, voice firm. "Now I appreciate that you've been through a lot—"

"—but you refuse to do the right thing," Kamran finishes.

"The 'right thing?'" Becker says. "Buddy, this could start a war!"

"Becker is right, man," Joanna says, stepping out from the group of contractors. "I hate to say it, dude, but if the videos of this incident got out, there'd be war for sure."

"Think about it differently, Dr. Afghanzadeh." Jerry crosses his arms. "You're saving a lot of lives when you let the United Americas handle things through proper diplomatic—"

"So peace only exists when we roll over and let you erase us!" Kamran shouts.

Marsalis stands up, icing Kamran's temper. He shouldn't have lost it like that. Her head buzzes, the low drone disquieting all assembled.

"*Khodayeh man*, sorry, sorry," Kamran says, shivering and backing up. "Just, you know, it's a touchy subject when you kill all of my friends."

The alien doesn't sit down.

Becker holds up a hand. "Let's not get riled. Everything is going to be okay, Marsalis. Whoa, now." In response it approaches Becker, its fingers ticking.

"Do not speak to me… like I am a… horse."

Becker looks like an admonished puppy. Kamran takes a small, spiteful pleasure in watching him squirm under the creature's gaze.

"If it's not a just peace," Kamran says to Marsalis, as though she's somehow his arbitrator, "it's not peace at all. It's not enough for us to survive. Give me the memory cores. My people have to know what has been done."

Marsalis is close enough to take the bag away from Becker. Kamran hopes the corporal will see reason, because there's no way he's giving up on this. Kamran doesn't want to have to do anything drastic, but he wants those cores with every fiber of his being.

He's not even sure he *could* do anything drastic.

"Uh, guys," Noah says. "There are marines outside."

"What the fuck, Jerry?" Joanna shouts.

"Me?" Jerry recoils like a seal—head flattening against his own neck.

"You said it'd take her a while to get down here!" Joanna runs her fingers through her rusty hair. "Jesus Christ, they're right at the vault door!"

That sends a jolt through the room as everyone moves to see what she's talking about. Noah sends the video feeds to the large screens that loom over the NOC. Teams of soldiers spread out across the entryway. These marines aren't in plastic shoulder pads, like Becker—they're outfitted in black suits with bulky joints. Their movements remind Kamran of the aliens, lithe and quick. They're incredibly fluid for being so confined.

Two of the marines slink up to the door, pull out a small device and unscrew the cover from the console. They work like a pit crew, speeding through four bolts before tossing the wall plate to the floor.

"Oh, fuck," Becker says. "That's a PunchKey. It's definitely going to pop the doors."

Kamran scoffs. "You have a lot of faith in your ability to get through our security."

Becker looks him dead in the eyes. "Yeah. I do."

Alarms blare outside, and Marsalis thunders down the

terraces onto the concourse. Visible through the huge NOC window, she launches up the walls and into the rafters.

"Hey, wait!" Joanna calls after the creature. "Oh for fuck's sake, the damned thing's *hiding* now."

"I think she's looking for somewhere from which to strike," Kamran says.

"Well whatever she's doing," Joanna says, grabbing her tool bag, "she ain't helping us seal the goddamned doors! Arthur! What's the main quarantine control? Not ALC. Schindler-Pullman?" She heads for the door.

"I think so." Arthur follows and grabs his own bag from the stash in the corner. "I've got my SP connectors. Kamran, you've got some EE training?"

"That was my undergrad," he says.

"You can hold and read a multimeter. We need you with us. Becker, you're on tactical." Arthur fishes a radio out of his contractor bag and tosses it to the soldier. "This operates on commercial band—unencrypted, but at least with Joanna, we've got two radios. Stay here and watch the feeds. You know how marines operate better than any of us."

"I'm also the best with a pulse rifle."

"If we do our job and seal that door, that won't be needed," Arthur replies. "Watch the cameras and make sure your people don't have any nasty surprises. Noah, cycle those locks and buy us some time."

"Right." Becker switches on the radio, then turns to Noah—who starts directing surveillance grids onto the screens. The sound systems blare an announcement: siege quarantine is ending. The Javaher Concourse is about to open wide.

* * *

"Catch up, Kamran," Arthur says as he jogs after Joanna.

The Javaher Concourse is unending at a walk. At a bloodless jog, it's so much worse. When Kamran reaches them at the front door by the café, Arthur and Joanna already have the electrical panel open and the guts of the wall exposed.

"Aw God, it's spider city up in this motherfucker," Joanna says, reaching deep into the wall to pull out a box with trailing wires.

"They're not poisonous," Kamran assures her.

"MouseCat," Joanna says like a surgeon, unclipping one of the jacks and holding it out. Arthur pulls a digital tool out of his pocket and snaps it onto the end. "What are we thinking?" she asks. "Burn out the motors?"

"Girl, no. I don't want to be trapped with you forever," Arthur replies. "Start updating the firmware and cut the power. We can factory reset later."

The radio on the side of Joanna's bag chirps once.

"Joanna, this is Becker, check in."

"I'm busy. Get my radio, y'all," she says, frantically working the thumb controls on the MouseCat to dive through menus. Sirens blare on the other side of the door. There's an announcement, but Kamran can't quite make it out.

He reaches down and grabs the radio from Joanna's bag. His head swims a little when he stands, but he's getting better and better with each minute away from the cryotube. "Becker, this is Kamran, checking in for Joanna."

"Kamran, Becker. We set off the HS alarms. The noise should draw the x-rays to Duncan's fireteams and give them something to do while you seal the door."

"I've got the firmware update submenu!" Joanna cries. She taps a button on her MouseCat and holds it up to reveal a glowing status bar on the black LED screen. She parrots the menu. "'Do not power down or disconnect.'" She unclips the cable from the MouseCat's jack. The panel on the door lights up blue, then an icon appears on it in large block pixels—a bent line and a square.

Kamran isn't sure what the icon is supposed to represent, but it looks like the computer is frozen. Someone on the other side of the thick door shouts "Fuck!" so Kamran can assume they've successfully jammed the system.

"Becker, this is Kamran, we've got the—"

Static floods the line, whistling and howling at unpleasant frequencies. Kamran holds the radio away.

Arthur takes the walkie, switching it off. Blessed silence follows.

"That's military jamming for you. Had the same thing when I was LEO. Commercial radio doesn't stand a chance."

Joanna pulls out a cigarette and lights it. "I think we should stay by the door until we get the all-clear."

"Yes," Kamran says, "and you're the people most qualified to stop them if they try again."

"Exactly," she says, exhaling smoke and offering one to Arthur, who refuses. "This firmware update process is a bitch, and I just bricked it. I wouldn't trust a seasoned tech to make this repair, much less a jarhead. Those bastards aren't getting in here anytime soon."

"If you could fix shit as fast as you break it, we'd be rich," Arthur says, fist bumping her.

"Atwater and Hardy."

"Partners in crime."

Between the crowing alarms, Kamran can make out the sound of shouting. He turns to find Becker sprinting down the concourse waving his arms, radio held aloft.

"Get down! Get away from the doors!"

A beam of white-hot light cores out the locking mechanism, along with a melon-sized chunk of Joanna's neck and collarbone. With an abbreviated shout and a flaming pop of smoke and sparks, she hits the ground. Only a thin bit of skin keeps her flopping head attached to her body—the vertebrae have been burned to cinders at either side of the wound.

When her body comes to rest, her eyes lock onto Kamran, and she blinks once, as if surprised. He glimpses the split second in which she departs this world.

"Joanna!" Arthur bellows. Kamran knows that look too well; he's worn it recently. Reza's body slumping over the Polaris, falling into the Maelstrom—that should've been his most haunting memory, but this world is so full of nightmares.

A grenade clatters through the hole in the door, and Arthur turns to look directly at Kamran with the sort of expression that says, *I'm about to do something to you whether you're ready or not.*

He plows into Kamran like a rugby player, lifting him off his feet, sending the air whooshing from his lungs. They stumble backward in large steps, and Arthur hooks one hand around Kamran's ribcage, dragging him to the stone ground. He forces Kamran's face hard against the cold tiles, wrapping the rest of him up tight in powerful arms and legs.

Maybe they're safe, maybe they're not. Kamran can only wait and wonder in the deafening silence of an unexploded grenade.

2 6

H A V O C

The little silver canister clatters down beside Joanna's smoking body, and Becker instantly hits the deck. Explosive force pummels his ears, muting his world with cottony ringing. Facets of his world dance before him, and he blinks hard.

Upon opening his eyes, he's seeing double.

Holy shit, that was too close.

When he looks up, he finds Kamran and Arthur struggling to their feet. Joanna's body looked bad before the grenade, but after—there's not much resemblance. Her corpse has taken the brunt of the blast—a fact that may have saved someone.

Fire alarms blare. Jets of frigid water drench them from the sprinklers.

Becker was under the impression that Captain Duncan didn't want to leave any evidence of her platoon's presence. Even in his concussed state, it seems to him that she's leaving some pretty strong clues. Explosive residue from the grenades, pulse rifle slugs, even the use of the PunchKey: all of them leave American fingerprints.

The laser drill wasn't exactly subtle—its beam left a neat, softball-sized circle on the far wall, as well as one in the door. A hole large enough to accommodate the barrel of a rifle or smart gun.

"Fall back!" Becker shouts as bursts of automatic fire stutter through the opening. "Get back to the NOC!"

Arthur and Kamran scramble to get away, taking cover behind the café booths. They all get as low as possible, narrowly avoiding the withering fire of a pulse rifle. Becker has never been on the other side of one before, and it makes a strong impression.

The caseless bullets will pierce everything that isn't four inches of metal or four feet of concrete. In short order, the Javaher Concourse becomes little more than a sponge for soaking up rounds. Whoever is shooting through the hole can't possibly have room to aim properly. If they did, Becker, Kamran, and Arthur would be dead.

The fire pauses, and the door clanks with a familiar noise. Becker crawls from his hiding spot to take a peek, and finds a metal tine with milled teeth poking through the hole. He knows the device intimately—a tungsten carbide riot jack. From the other side, they'll be priming the jack's explosive charges. When they finish, Duncan's forces are going to put a catastrophic amount of force into the door. For the moment, the device blocks the hole.

"Go!" Becker shouts. "NOC! Now!" Then he lines up a shot on the blunt tip of the fork. His vision swims, but he has to fire or die.

Take a breath. Three.

Two.

One.

He squeezes the trigger on his grenade launcher, and the pulse rifle bucks in his arms. The explosive round strikes home, driving the fork from the hole like a hammer to a railroad spike. A bright flash blinds him, and Becker covers his eyes to block any stray debris. On the other side, a man starts screaming. He can't tell who it is, but the poor fucker doesn't sound like he'll make it.

"Fuck you, Becker!" someone shouts through the hole. "We're gonna kill you!"

Becker doesn't stop to trade insults with the guy. He'd rather get out of there while the getting is good.

Vision clearing, he sprints back to the NOC and up the terraces. The big overhead CCTV screens present him with a view outside, and his handiwork. The grenade knocked the riot jack out of the hole, shattering it into shrapnel. There's a lone marine on the ground, a spike of sharp tungsten carbide sticking out of a gap in the PRAE armor.

It's official. Becker shot a friendly. Deliberately.

Joanna's destroyed corpse still dominates one of the monitors. They probably zoomed in on her after the injury, hoping she'd be all right.

"Switch it off," Arthur says, hateful sobs escaping through gritted teeth. "Get her off the fucking screens, Noah."

"Sorry," Brewer says, voice choked.

"Oh, God!" Jerry says, pointing to a different camera feed. On it, x-rays come rampaging up the Spiral, a tidal wave of chaos and teeth. Becker has seen schools of fish, flocks of birds, and herds of cattle. Those animals make some effort to avoid one another. X-rays shove and climb past as if there's only one morsel of food left on the planet.

"Don't panic, Jerry," Becker says. "That's good. They've got to go through Duncan's element to get to us."

He watches the cameras, heart in his throat, and can't believe the hatred that boils inside him. He's rooting for the *x-rays*, for God's sake, praying that these soldiers get eviscerated.

"You can't—" Shy's last words strengthen his resolve.

Before the x-rays can swarm the marines, all four Good Boys come rocketing into view to form a blockade. Aliens skid to a halt before the might of the auditory onslaught, screaming and hissing at the robot assault platforms. One of their tails snaps out and bangs into a Good Boy, but it simply staggers back and redoubles its audio blast.

Marines take up firing positions along the line and pump round after round into the fray. The creatures burst like fruit, throwing sizzling yellow acid in every direction. Plumes of smoke billow up from the fresh burns, triggering the fire suppression systems outside.

Water floods through the Spiral, carrying the corrosion deeper into the facility.

"You're going to run out of aliens," Tiran breathes, watching the chaos unfold. She stands by Becker, transfixed by the action onscreen as the marines cut down one beast after another.

The incline of the Spiral gives the Midnighters a natural high ground and safe drainage. They're obnoxiously good at their jobs.

"What's that smoke?" Kamran asks.

"It's their blood," Becker replies. "Molecular acid. Dissolves anything."

X-ray carcasses pile up, forming a pool of soupy rock underneath. A trail of vibrant crimson fluid billows from the corpses in the sprinklers' deluge.

"*Gol-e-Fars*," Kamran says, as if reading his mind. "Chemical reaction with the rock…"

The ground becomes a river of death, with the marines at its source. A smart gun team casually disassembles x-rays with all the difficulty of a brisk jog. Some of the soldiers whoop and holler like they're having a cookout.

Becker counts fewer than ten of the creatures racing up the Spiral from the lower floors, and they're about thirty seconds from becoming target practice. His military radio squawks, and he blinks, holding up the receiver. He's on the old platoon channel, but with the security breach, Duncan will have changed all the keys. Her people can't afford to risk being overheard.

If not them, who?

"Come in? Hello?" Becker says.

Only static. Jerry and Noah are yelling at each other, so Becker calls for quiet. When they don't listen, he slaps Noah across the back of the head and points at Jerry.

"*Oh, good,*" someone says over the other end of the line. It's male, labored, and he coughs with a nasty rattle. "*I was hoping you'd have your old crypto.*"

Becker grips the radio so hard it might break. "Percival!" He glances back at the monitors. The Xenos have reached the soldiers, and it's like watching a pair of sharks fight over who gets to take the first bite. Listening to this poor butter-bar LT lament his mortal situation isn't getting Becker out of his own.

"*Somebody stuck a fucking knife in me and left me to die. Told me to 'take it deep college boy.'*" Percival laughs, and it quickly devolves into fits of coughing. "*Didn't even see the guy.*"

"Lieutenant—sir—you need to hide," Becker says, "because I have to get back to you, okay? Don't go anywhere."

"*No problem.*" Percival sighs. "*I'm running out of blood, though. Or… it's running out of me. Anyway, I'm back in Ops. Figured I'd check up on you… before I take a nap.*"

Blood loss. He's delirious.

"Bud, you need to stay awake, okay?" Becker isn't sure if asking people "okay" helps, but he's seen a lot of field medics do it. Perhaps the prompting for a response keeps them going.

"*Not okay,*" Percival says. "*Not getting out of this one.*"

I can't help him, Becker thinks. *There are people to save. Mission first.*

"*But…*" Percival begins, and Becker strains to hear him over all of the alarms. "*I thought maybe, this being Wednesday…*"

On the screen the last pack of x-rays rounds the bend, diving straight for Duncan's troops. They race along the walls and ceiling, a final assault from a force that could never admit defeat. Once they're dead, there's no way Becker will get his survivors past the marines outside.

"*… and I'm in charge of the CCM nodes…*"

Becker restrains the urge to say, *I get it, you're dying, but what the* fuck *are you talking about, dude?* It's best to listen to last words. Maybe someone will repay the favor when it's his time.

The armored troops outside open fire on the x-rays like a junket of photographers. Muzzle flashes outline deadly shadows, sketching a profane image.

"*I figured I'd take the Good Boys down for their weekly maintenance,*" Percival says.

The autonomous platforms snap into their missile launch tube configurations, transforming from a critical force protection resource into expensive—yet useless— metal cylinders.

Aliens punch through marine battle lines like ancient cavaliers. In an instant, the x-rays' hopeless assault against a technologically superior foe becomes an all-out massacre. The landscape shatters into a mix of armor and chitin, screams of joy and pain. Explosive bolts pop, fabric and flesh rend, chitin snaps, acid sprays, and blood of all colors swirls in the orgiastic violence.

Prior to embarking upon this mission, Becker was under the mistaken impression that the Midnighters had the toys they needed to handle any hive. The platoon had been so confident back on the *Benning*, where they'd made him watch dozens of training videos on every conceivable piece of equipment. The training course for the PRAE suits was so fucking long that they'd had to break it up over four days.

Two of the beasts drag a marine to the ground, and they crack into him like crabmeat. A few tugs on the reactive plates, then they're clawing into the soft liquid armor covering his abdomen, tearing free streamers of intestine.

Two soldiers with incinerators lay down a blanket of suppressing fire, enabling their comrades to fall back by squads. Becker recognizes Duncan and Lee in the crowd, pushing to the front to fend off the x-rays. The rank insignias stenciled on their chest plates glow orange in the firelight. For a moment, he almost wishes he was there. Duncan might be the most evil person he's ever met, but goddamn, she can put down an x-ray.

She takes a flamethrower and covers her folks with big sweeps, refusing to leave until they're all behind her. With a quick motion she tugs free a grenade and rolls it like a bowling ball toward the bugs.

Instead of shrapnel, showers of sparks and exploding lights hold the x-rays at bay. Becker can't hear the ordinance over the cameras, but he knows the sound of a riot grenade to be a deafening whistle—all the fury of a hurricane, raised to an unbearable pitch. X-rays scatter, slapping at any pinwheeling sparks that get too close.

"Lock down the escape routes," Becker says to Noah, feeling sick. If the marines can't close the door, they can't easily defend themselves. After an encounter like that, they'll be low on ammo, and the incinerators won't last forever. With a few keystrokes, Noah shuts most of the doors leading up the Spiral. A pair of marines works the lock panel on Storehouse Twenty-Nine, while Duncan secures the portal with long gouts of fire.

"Remove the data point mapping," Jerry says. "SiteSys won't know how to interpret the door."

"They're already getting through… fuck!" Noah bangs the keyboard hard enough to snap a key loose and send it skittering across the floor. Becker grabs his wrist before he can do it again.

"Cool it. Might need that console." Given Noah's expression, he'd bet that no one has ever stopped this guy from throwing a fit. Becker pins him with a look, in case the man is stupid enough to throw hands at a soldier.

On the cameras, Duncan's team slips away. The x-rays are too distracted by the devastating light show to give chase. Finding their meals departed, the creatures snatch up the dead or dying soldiers, dragging the grim prizes into the depths.

Becker clicks the button on his radio.

"Percival, Becker. Come in."

Silence follows. He pulls the headset mic closer to his lips.

"Percival, Becker. Do you read? Duncan is headed back upstairs," Becker says, closing his eyes and taking a deep breath. "If you're alive, bud, you need to... uh, need to find cover. She'll be headed back to the Good Boy OTCs, and if you're around—she... she'll, uh—"

"Corporal," Mary says.

He turns to see that Noah has the cameras pulled up for one of the side halls in the Ops tower. The Good Boy operational transit cases are open, their server racks glittering with network activity. Percival's body lies face down beside them, a bloody hand across his ruggedized portable terminal. A long trail of red precedes the prone form, brilliant against the gold and white mosaics of Ops.

Noah flips through the cameras one by one, following the trail. Winding along the hall.

Down the stairwell he climbed.

Through the break room, under the tables.

Across the long lobby.

"Jesus." Each new angle is a needle in Becker's heart.

Then they find a lake of blood—the place where Percival took a knife in the back. Duncan's people caught him in the Thunder Ring, halfway to Solutions, so that "college boy" crawled almost a quarter mile with punctured liver.

Others in the platoon had made fun of Percival for insisting on following the rules, then they murdered him for it. Becker had allowed the abuse to flourish around him, gleefully participating with jokes of his own. So many people dead when he should've said no.

"I have a tasking order."

Duncan has claimed that so many times. What does the order say? Has anyone seen it? Is it legal? Has anyone checked?

Does anyone care?

Becker didn't.

Arthur sits in the corner, head in his hands and pistol between his legs. Tears roll down the dark skin of his cheeks, but he's refusing to lose his cool—probably worried about scaring everyone. Mary barely looks like she has a drop of blood in her body—sallow and haunted. Jerry keeps hugging his wife and saying things are going to be okay, but if Becker is honest, it's like watching a frightened child clutch a stuffed animal in a thunderstorm—the stuffed animal isn't the one getting comforted. Noah just sits there looking at the computer, shoulders tense, and Becker hopes he doesn't lose his shit.

Three short buzzes pulse in the silence—the Iranian woman's watch. She checks it.

"Afghanzadeh, vaghteh namaz hast."

The scientist nods, and they walk to the edge of the NOC, kneeling on the polished marble instead of the hollow, composite steps. After a moment, Becker realizes that they're going to pray, and turns away. He's not sure why, but he'd rather give them their privacy.

That's why he's surprised when Mary brushes past him, Jerry in tow. She crouches beside the pair and quietly asks something of them, then the Iranian woman nods. The Fowlers kneel on either side of the Muslims, old bones against that hard floor.

"Do you believe in God?" Noah asks.

"We're not on speaking terms," Becker replies. "Especially now."

"Like their invisible friend is going to save us," Noah scoffs before pulling out a half-burnt joint. He lights up, then offers a hit to Becker. The stench of skunkweed wafts up to him, promising a badly needed mediocre high.

"Has anyone ever told you that you're an asshole?" Becker whispers, nodding to the doors that lead out of the NOC. "Take that shit outside, man. Show some respect."

"I'm suffering, too."

"And if you're going to smoke up, suffer somewhere else."

"I've about had it with your shit—" Noah starts, anger contorting his features.

Becker reaches down and crushes the joint's cherry between his thumb and forefinger. It hurts like hell, but after today's events, pain seems like an irrational delusion. He grinds it between his sizzling skin, imagining it to be the spark of Captain Kylie Duncan's life.

Noah's nose wrinkles in rage. "Hey, fuck you—"

"Fuck me, indeed, Noah." Becker shakes his head. "Fuck me, indeed."

McAllen's IT nerd stands up, and he's pretty tall. Back on the *Benning*, eager to please, Becker read all the files on the civilian hostages. Aside from the Fowlers, most of them hadn't interested him—except Noah Brewer. He had a prior for beating up his Boston girlfriend. She'd made some other accusations, but they'd settled out of court.

Every soldier knows an abuser. Becker could spot this motherfucker a mile away.

"I don't think you want to keep talking to me like that, Corporal," Noah says. He's a man sure of his footing, definitely accustomed to surprising someone with his mass. Becker knew a guy back home like that—looked like skin and bones until it was time to fight. He raises his palms.

"Let's not do this right now. People are trying to pray."

Noah's anger explodes in a shout. "I've got just as much of a right to be here, doing my fucking thing, as you!"

"I asked you to leave."

"And I'm asking you to eat a dick. You'd know that, if you were smart enough to be something better than a jarhead."

Becker's palms fall to his hips, and he shakes his head. He looks into Noah's green eyes, disappointment furrowing his brow.

"Why do I have to be the one to teach you manners, Noah?"

"Teach me what?"

With a backhanded slap, Becker lunges at the man. The x-rays set a good example—it's better to be overwhelming than good. Eschewing all form and finesse, he works Noah's abdomen like a heavy bag, easily landing body blow after body blow. With each clenched fist, Becker steals a future breath—preventing the shitbag from crying out.

He goes down, and Becker doesn't stop.

One final, satisfying hammer blow into Noah's gut, and the switch in Noah's eyes flips to panic. When a man like that can't fight back, the last resort will be to debase himself. He rolls onto his hands and knees, shaking and pressing his head to the floor like a supplicant.

When Becker turns to regard the quartet of religious folk, they're staring at him. He waves a palm over Noah, who shivers.

"I taught him how to pray," Becker says, huffing.

"We didn't ask for more violence, Corporal Becker," Mary says, and the disappointed expression on that sweet old lady's face breaks his heart. "Noah just lost a friend."

"I—" Becker looks away.

His victim lies wheezing on the ground, pale skin turned purple with blood pressure and temporary hypoxia. Noah's hair has been sweat-styled into ringlets and his glasses lay snapped nearby. He's crying, because this is probably the first time he's ever gone up against a vastly superior foe.

He *needs* to quit making a scene and leave these people alone.

"Come on, son." Becker sighs, offering a hand. "I saw some sodas in the chow hall over there. Let's get you one and—"

With some comical swatting, Noah rises to his feet.

"—okay, okay, you can get up on your own."

"Fuck you, man," Noah wheezes.

"So you've said." Picking up his rifle, Becker shoulders it and saunters down the terraces to the exit. "You coming? Can't stay here."

Noah heads down after him, clutching his ribs.

They walk silently through the Javaher Concourse. Becker keeps his hands holstered in his pockets, to make the poor child feel a little safer. Noah follows a few paces behind, which suits him just fine. The less they talk, the better. Becker was pissed at him for damaging morale, and now he's pissed at himself for beating the guy up— which probably damaged morale even more.

That soda is sounding better and better.

The exit from the Javaher comes into view, complete with Joanna's extinguished remains. Pools of standing water slowly drain around her, a side effect of the sprinklers. He'll have to do something about her before they leave for the *Blackstar*. Maybe he can convince the others to say a few words over her body and travel light. It's more likely he'll find himself constructing a litter and trying to carry what's left.

The tea machines dispense a fruit syrup, which Becker enjoys mixing with soda. He's not familiar with the Javaher's model, and gets stuck in the orange drink menu looking for *sharbat*. The user interface makes no sense, and he paws for the help binder chained to the side.

The metal chair comes down on the back of his neck, then smashes into him again from one side. The IT nerd isn't good with it, and the frame is mostly plastic. It's more like a joke. Chair versus Colonial Marine hardly strikes Becker as a fair fight—but it turns out Noah wasn't trying to beat him to death.

Noah snatches up Becker's pulse rifle, flips off the safety and points it at his head. His eyes lock onto Becker's—this is a man in control, now that he has an unassailable advantage.

"Show me how tough you are now, prick." Noah's voice is even, like an instruction. He licks his lips.

"Put down the gun," Becker replies, "and I'd be happy to."

"Fuck you."

Becker smirks. "You really can't come up with anything else?" He knows he shouldn't goad the guy with the rifle, but it's hard to imagine walking away from this. The dude is a civilian, but there's no law here—just his wounded honor. If Becker is going to die like this, he's not about to beg.

Noah's grip tightens, and death arrives.

A blur of black chitin and unrestrained fury flows

down over Noah from the rafters, snatching away the rifle and tossing it to one side. Noah has just enough time to register shock before Marsalis grabs him by the neck and screams in his face. Becker has heard the creatures plenty of times, but this vocalization is something beyond hatred.

She throws Noah aside, picks up the chair and smashes it against him, sending him sprawling. The seat shatters in the creature's hand, and she hurls away a steel support strut. The IT nerd's breath comes out in crazed, bellowing shouts, and he frantically tries to push upright. Marsalis already has another chair, stalking toward him like it's holding a club.

"*Know you... big man... tough man...*" the speaker croaks, voice echoing through the concourse. Marsalis raises the chair above its head and brings it down across Noah's back. The furnishing snaps at all its joints. Marsalis abandons him for another chair, and he tries to crawl away.

"*Never again, never again, never again.*" Marsalis taps rapidly. "*Never again, never again.*"

She snatches Noah by the leg and drags him into the center of the café, knocking furnishings aside. After clearing out a spot, she selects a large booth table and lifts it high over Noah's head. That'll kill him for sure.

"Marsalis, no!" Becker rushes to help, and the creature executes a flowing spin.

Stars flash in his vision, and Becker is on the ground for a full two seconds before he realizes it struck him.

Back up now. You might have made it mad.

INTERLUDE: BLUE

THREE YEARS AGO

The sound is a lot like a wooden flute, gently played. Clicks and spurts of static interrupt the song, and it takes a long time for Blue to recognize Rook's voice. He's singing softly somewhere down the hall, self-harmonizing with his damaged vocal speaker. The innocence of his crackling voice beckons in the gloom.

This place—it's the central docking hub. The *Blackstar* waits outside the viewports. The doors to the expeditionary ship lie open, emergency lights steadily flashing. It's prepped to leave. Someone was trying to escape.

An intoxicating, sweet scent awakens a bottomless hunger in Blue. Blood drips from twisted claws, chitinous mockeries of hands. A couple of loose hairs glint in the light, pasted to Blue's fingers with a patina of crimson. A shiver runs through the alien form, culminating in a swift rattle from the scales.

Richard lies crumpled against the far wall with a snake-sized hole in his eye socket, an assault rifle balanced uselessly across his lap. Two more bodies lie adjacent to his corpse, messes of bone, muscle, and organs savaged beyond all recognition. Claw marks mar the walls and door.

The juicy burst of blood and brain comes rushing back into Blue's mind, delicious and sensual. There's so much meat there for the taking, muscle ready to be pulled from his bones in vibrant strips the color of strawberry flesh. Viscous saliva pools inside Blue's mouth, pouring between her lips like a deluge, and it's hard to resist the urge to feed.

It's not fair to be this hungry. Blue rises to take what's due, moving to Richard's corpse with surprising grace. After a lifetime of chronic pain, this is a freedom beyond even weightlessness—the power of *praepotens* with a beauty of movement that extends beyond human.

He lies still and cooling, but something in Rook's old song stays Blue's hand. She is reminded of a cool spring rain on Stony Run Trail. Leaves and birdsong come whistling back to mind—not the soulless oscillations of medical monitors, but the real thing. There was one crisp morning before mid-terms, jogging and huffing out clouds in the fresh air.

The song ends abruptly with a crackle, and a human fear tangles into the Xenomorphic heart—the loss of a friend. Blue exits the room.

The synthetic lies ruined in the nearby corridor. White blood and torn wires litter the area. Bits of innards, like chains of pearls, trail from an open abdominal cavity. His throat has been crushed, and broken fiber optics shine beneath the surface. He looks up at Blue with a pained smile.

"You mustn't blame yourself," he says, voice distorted and thick with digital snow. "You weren't... cognizant. I couldn't let you hurt those people, so I—h—to be— emoved..." His features freeze momentarily. "Had to be removed from play."

Blue touches Rook's brow, and runs a claw down one cheek. He closes his eyes and rests against it. Sorrow and shame well inside—he's given all of himself and received nothing in return but teeth and claws.

"I wish..." Rook trails off, and Blue kneels at his side, bowing crown to metal plate. Synthetics don't openly wish for things. It makes their masters uncomfortable. His lips move haltingly, but his voice emanates clearly from the hole in his broken throat.

"I wish you had been given more time. A different life. You'll find a cure—but not here."

Blue presses cold lips against his forehead, thankful that aliens don't have a taste for plastic. The hunger is almost unbearable. Drawing back, Blue tries to speak, but this new misshapen mouth can only produce a breathy hiss.

A short inside Rook's voice box burns out a portion of the speaker, and his voice sours to genderless formants. It must've taken a hard hit.

"You should go. I put credentials into the *Blackstar*. Mother can help you."

He shouldn't be lying here, faltering on the ground. He wished things, which means he had hopes of his own. He should have escaped.

Rook smiles. "I'm glad you're free. Now I can be, too."

2 7

FLIGHT

Kamran hears the commotion long before he sees it. Part of him wants to run from the sound, but to where? Besides, he's come to recognize Marsalis's voice, and something has upset their... ally?

He arrives to find Becker scooting away from the furious creature, and then looks around for Noah. It's hard to spot the pale guy at first. The contractor looks little better than Joanna's horrific remains, clothing frayed and bloody. He cries out for help, begging someone to intervene.

"Should kill you," the computerized voice blares from Marsalis's speaker. *"Murderer."*

"I'm sorry." Noah weeps, trying to crawl away. Marsalis stomps down onto his back, eliciting a terrified squeal.

"Coward, coward, coward. End you."

Kamran's eyes scour the scene for any way to help, but how? He might as well punch one of the turbines, for all the good it would do. Besides, Marsalis saved his life.

He glances at Corporal Becker, who's close to his fallen pulse rifle. The soldier might be able to save Noah. Judging from the look on Becker's face, he's having the same thoughts. Instead of reaching for the rifle, however, the marine stands, holding his hands out to the side.

"Come on, Marsalis, don't do this." He takes cautious steps toward the raging creature as she leans down close to Noah's ear, viscous drool showering onto his neck. He chokes on sobs, and every time he tries to crawl away, Marsalis drags him back.

"Must be an... accounting," it says. *"For murderers."*

"I get that, and I'm glad you showed up to help," Becker replies, continuing to move closer, "but I'm not in danger. Don't kill him."

"What did he do?" Kamran asks.

"Noah hit me with a chair," Becker says. "Really pissed her off."

Marsalis bellows, snapping out a tongue with reverse-barbed teeth. She beats the tiles with her tail, shattering them so violently that a piece of shrapnel bounces off Kamran's cheek. He cringes away from the raging alien, yet Becker keeps moving toward Noah, unarmed.

"You're not a monster, and you're not going to kill me," Becker says, "so let me have him. Okay, Marsalis? I'm just going to take him."

Kamran looks toward the NOC—the others didn't follow. Though they heard Noah screaming, they decided not to become involved—which seems eminently wise, given the circumstances. He turns back to find Becker within range of Marsalis's claws.

"Help me!" Noah calls, reaching out as if he's sinking in quicksand. Marsalis puts fresh wounds on his back, but nothing lethal. The creature is bent on tormenting him, or he'd already be dead. In warning, Marsalis lets loose a wild hiss and smashes her tail into the ground directly in front of the approaching marine, burying the barb a full hand's width into the rock. The buzzing skull plates fill the concourse with the drone of a locust plague.

"Noah, you can help yourself by shutting up," Becker says. "Now, Marsalis, I'm going to push past you and pick up Mr. Brewer. He needs medical attention. I'm *asking* you not to hurt me."

Anglerfish teeth emerge from the smooth lips, as if daring Becker to take another step. The soldier draws a deep breath and gently rests one hand on Marsalis's tail as he pushes past. Kamran prepares himself—after Marsalis tears Becker limb from limb, she might follow suit with everyone else. That would be, as Americans are so fond of saying, "par for the course," but Becker gets a grip on Noah's hand and drags him free.

Both men emerge from the shadow of the alien with their arms around each other. Kamran hears footsteps behind him, and the big American, Arthur, enters the room.

"Medkits," Kamran says, pointing behind the counter of the little café. "That way."

"Thanks."

"Arthur, we've got to get that door open," Becker says. "We need to get out of here before they come back."

"You'll have to wait, Corporal," Arthur says.

"Not a ton of extra time," Becker replies. "They'll lick their wounds for a bit, but Duncan will return. Marines don't let go when they dig in."

"Yeah? Well, I need Noah's help to get the door open again. Our other expert is—she's, uh…" He coughs and can't finish the sentence. That would be Joanna. He grips Brewer and leads him out through the door.

Marsalis turns and stalks away, her tail sweeping gracefully from side to side. Kamran scoots to give them a wide berth as they pass. Upon reaching the wall, the alien leaps up into the rafters.

Only Kamran and Becker remain in the little café— and Joanna, but Kamran has been trying hard not to look at her. Things weren't great between them, but she deserved better. Becker sits down with a thump on the wet floor, resting his elbows on his knees. He stares at his hands as if they're not a part of him.

"Tough day?" Kamran says.

Becker laughs and shakes his head. "This isn't what I signed up for."

Kamran sits down beside the youthful corporal, instinctively trying to wrap his arms around his knees. He gives up and rests uncomfortably on his ass, the stump of his arm throbbing ferociously.

"I had two hands when I took this job," he says.

"I had a future when I took mine," Becker replies. "No matter what happens, I'm going to jail when it's all over."

"That's not true. You might die."

Becker snorts, and Kamran imagines a can of beer in his hand. He's probably an easygoing fellow in his off hours.

"Oh, gee thanks."

"For the record, I was praying you'd beat up Noah—no matter what Tiran tells you," Kamran says, elbowing him with his good arm. When Becker laughs again, there's a twinkle in his eye. It would've been more fun to meet the guy over a hookah.

The American's wrist bears a tattoo on the underside.

1776

Kamran points to the number. "Is that, uh—"

"The year America was founded, brother."

"I thought it was the year they rebelled. Didn't your lot incorporate in—"

"All right, supergenius, thanks for that. You got a smoke?"

"I do," Kamran says. "If you want to run upstairs to the Human Centre, they're in my room."

"Oh, let me radio the captain and see if she'll grab them for me." Becker points to the laser-drilled hole in the door. "You know… when she comes back, she'll poke a gun through and kill you. You're in danger hanging out here."

Kamran looks at the drilled-out door lock, its edges carbonized like an eclipse's corona. "I hadn't considered that." He regards Becker for a long moment. "You're not in any hurry to leave."

The marine shakes his head. "I've sheltered from Russian neutron mortars, hanging out in a base for two weeks waiting to get hit. Scary at first, but eventually business has to go on. Someone's got to sling the chow. Latrines got to stay clean. It's just the fucking mission." He points a finger-pistol toward the hole. "If that was on a FOB—uh, forward operating base—everyone would just be like, 'Watch out for the death hole.'"

"Are you talking about the hole in the door, or Charybdis?"

"Fuck this entire place, man." Becker rubs the back of his head. There's a lump starting to swell there. Noah must've clobbered the poor guy. "Did you take my bag of memory cores yet?"

It's Kamran's turn to smile. "The thought had occurred to me, Corporal, but it seemed unsporting."

"If I was you, I would've stolen them," Becker says. "Something that important…"

"We got distracted."

"I think…" The soldier gets a far-off look, then blinks it away. "I think maybe…" Becker seems to be wrestling with the sentence, so Kamran waits. Whatever he's about to say, it's not easy for him.

"I should run the drives up to the Data Cannon."

"Pardon?" Kamran responds.

"You were right, in the NOC. I can't trust my people with that video. I have to make sure this gets out." He rubs the bridge of his nose. "I... I wasn't ready to admit it before."

"Okay, but..." Kamran collects his thoughts. He doesn't want to argue with the man—if Becker wants to get the truth out, good, but there are so many obstacles ahead. "You can't unlock the elevators, you know. The marines are going to notice."

"Oh, definitely. Duncan probably already has sentry guns up in the elevator shaft. What about the construction scaffolding next to it?"

"You mean outside—" Kamran says, "on the walls of Charybdis." Those metal rungs are so corroded that Kamran lobbied several times to have them removed. Acidic water, even mildly acidic, isn't kind to steel, and the skeleton represents a significant safety hazard.

"It's a construction lattice," Becker says. "My cousin's Caterpillar could scurry up, and I noticed you had some Daihatsu DKs."

"Corporal, that piece of equipment requires a six-week intensive course to operate, and the lattice should be condemned." Kamran shakes his head. "I appreciate your late-game commitment to justice, but if you fall into the Maelstrom with the memory cores, we all lose. It sounds like it'll take hours to fix this door, and Duncan will be back by then."

"She'll bring the nerve gas," Becker says. "Probably would've used it already if they hadn't been attacked. If we can't get out of here in the next hour, we're not getting out of here at all."

"*There are… other ways…*" Marsalis's crackling speaker echoes from the rafters.

"How ominous," Kamran says, then raises his voice to respond. "What other ways?" The black, armored shape emerges from the tangle of pipes and crossbeams. She swings through the cavernous space before reaching an access ladder. Marsalis pulls open a panel and mashes a button, dropping the rungs, then makes her way down the ladder, hands and feet as sure as a spider's on the web.

"*Have found… an exit,*" she says.

Kamran thinks back to all of the drawings he's seen of the Javaher Concourse, and the entire point of the place is that there's only one way in or out. That's part of the reason he feels safe here—or did until recently.

"*Air movement,*" Marsalis taps out the words to her overdriven speaker. "*Path open somewhere.*"

"Open, like…" Becker starts.

Lips snarl in time with the words, though no sounds follow. "*If I can find it… children can find it.*"

Kamran has to blunt the needle of panic forming inside him. This castle isn't nearly as impregnable as he'd led himself to believe. He never should've survived being in the same room with the monsters the first time. He doubts he'll survive another encounter.

"As a rule, we assume that the x-rays can get into any place they can fit their heads," Becker says. "If Marsalis says there's an opening, then this place is compromised."

Kamran looks over Marsalis's form: sleekness interrupted by spikes and ridges. It's hard to imagine them folding inward to pass through a tight fit, but perhaps the creature bends in unpredictable ways. Perhaps all of them do.

"So how long do we have before they're in?"

"*Maybe... already here,*" Marsalis says, chilling him to the bone. "*Gather the others. We leave soon.*"

"Copy," Becker says.

The soldier rushes away, leaving Kamran alone with Marsalis. She doesn't scare him so much anymore—no worse than the synth tiger that Haroun keeps in his house back on Earth. She notices him staring, and he looks away.

So he's not *that* comfortable.

Marsalis's fingers tick a few times, and the speaker barks.

"*Trying.*"

"What?"

"*To be... good.*" The last word echoes through the cavernous space, and Kamran wonders if "good" still has meaning to anyone.

"I know," he says.

One by one, Marsalis guides Jerry, Mary, Tiran, Arthur, and Becker up the maintenance access ladder. Kamran and Noah can't make the climb, so they have to be carried.

The alien scoops Kamran up like a baby and leaps before he has a chance to protest. His stomach sinks into his rump with the sudden acceleration, and he nearly passes out. Marsalis scrambles up the rungs like a spider, and it takes everything Kamran has not to look at the distant floor below.

Reaching the top, she deposits Kamran and goes back to retrieve Noah, who looks for all the world like he's about to die of a heart attack.

It's dark here, Becker hands out a couple of flashlights. Jerry straps his to the side of his head with an embarrassing fabric contraption, but at least it frees up his hands. They quietly pad through rusty, decaying corridors, following Marsalis's lead. After a claustrophobic final squeeze, they emerge into a large well shaft. A central column rumbles in front of them. Metal stairs spiral around the shaft, and old blower boxes hang from broken mountings.

"This is an old bunker stack," Jerry says. "Hoo-*ee*, this is some Russkie horse-puckey design, let me tell you. Always failing. I bet this thing runs all the way down to Charybdub."

"If it goes down that far," Kamran says, "we need to be mindful of hydrogen sulfide. Nausea. Delirium."

"I'm nauseated," Noah groans. "Can I sit down?"

He definitely doesn't sound good.

"*Up*," Marsalis says, turning and poking Becker in the chest. He gasps and gives her a polite smile.

"Fresh air. Surface…"

She points downward. *"Through ruins. To… my ship."*

"That's my cue, then," Becker says. "We part ways here, if I'm going to get this video out."

"I'm going, too," Arthur says. "I have a nine-millimeter pistol. That's for humans, not aliens."

Mary grabs his hand. "Arthur, you have a daughter. She needs you to come home."

"Mrs. Fowler, we're going to get this loaded up on the cannon and meet you at the *Blackstar*," he says, gently clasping her hand in both of his. "That's how it's going to be, because Marsalis knows how to handle aliens better than a couple of toughs."

"We won't leave without you," she says.

Arthur shakes his head. "Quit acting tragic, because I'm going to meet you at the bottom. First we make sure the galaxy knows what happened here. For Shy."

Mary looks to Kamran and Tiran with sympathy in her eyes. "For everyone who was murdered."

Another wave thunders down the length of the well pipe, momentarily deafening them, then a plume of fresh air whooshes back through. Arthur waits for silence, then hugs everyone a little too quickly.

Becker is already halfway up the stairs, embraced by no one. Kamran wants to go to him, but he can scarcely remain conscious, let alone give chase. The marine rises out of sight, and Arthur is quick to follow.

Marsalis turns and stalks off down the stairs.

Kamran should be going after Becker and Arthur, heroically winding past killers to get the truth out. Isn't that his job as a man? His stump throbs, drawing his thoughts to his new deformity. Mary comes to the edge of the stairwell and holds out a hand to him.

"Come on, honey. This seems slippery, and we don't need you falling. Jerry, can you help Noah?"

"I'll go first," Tiran says, tugging her makeshift hijab tighter and brushing past. "I'm in the best shape."

Kamran takes Mary's hand.

They've only traveled three floors before he's glad he did. He spies a hairline fracture in the central well shaft—wet streaks in the rust, fresh with a patina of extremophilic algae. When Kamran's team first took over the atmospheric processors, HAPS had a lot of these infestations.

Cheap Russian metallurgy.

The lower they go, the more impossibly loud the water becomes. Gusting winds burst through the grates under their feet, exploding upward with every wave.

"Yeah," Jerry shouts over the winds. "That's why no one builds them like this anymore. The central boreshafts are always the first to fail—"

Marsalis flies up the stairs in a blur. She stops in front of Jerry, gripping him by the head with one large hand, its palm blocking out his head-light. She lets go, and reflections of obsidian teeth emerge in a lightning storm of taps.

"*QUIET.*"

At first, Kamran takes it as a threat to Jerry. Then the cacophony of a wave recedes, leaving only a distant, high-pitched screech—one of the creatures calls from below.

What if they can smell Kamran's blood?

Of course they can smell my blood.

His chest cramps, and he holds fast to the dripping-wet railing.

Marsalis's knuckles flicker once more with light.

"I will... distract." Then she departs.

Mary grabs her husband by the ear, bringing him close to her mouth. Kamran is close enough to hear.

"—told you to be quiet before, Jerry Fowler."

After another floor, they reach the breach in the well shaft, and Kamran thinks he might be sick. At some point in the long history of this colony, some mass came down here and clogged the pipe. The intake up top is at least as wide as Kamran is tall, so it could've been anything.

The clog caused a water buildup, which caused corrosion, which is why the pipeline failed in spectacular fashion. The intake line is essentially nonexistent after the break, where for decades, mildly acidic water has washed untreated surfaces with hungry microbes. Shredded metal juts out of the wall like sawblades, and the stairs—where they exist—do so out of sheer optimism.

When a wave washes down the shaft, it gushes from the broken pipe above, engulfing everything before pooling about ten floors below. As it settles, the island's interior belches a spray of warm, moist return air. The wave drains away into depths unknown, beyond Kamran's weak light.

Two floors down, Kamran spies their exit—a shaft deeper into the rock, leading toward Charybdis. Marsalis has already climbed down and pokes her head out, signaling for their attention.

The path isn't hard, but there's a jump onto a concrete pylon that makes Kamran queasy. If he doesn't land right, there's nothing between him and the chewed-up, rusty drainage system. It would be a very long fall.

Marsalis beckons for them to hurry.

Tiran takes the leap without hesitation, landing sure-footed with nearly perfect balance. Kamran negotiates the path to the jump and stops to look over the edge.

When you jump, Reza is going to grab your leg.

Kamran's right eye begins to burn as if there's a knife in it. He presses his palm to his brow; there's no way he's going to wipe his eyes in here.

The pipe above him begins to rumble.

"*Bepar*, Kamran!" Tiran says. "Another wave is coming!"

Marsalis swings up and grabs him, hard claws wrapping around his chest and roughly pulling him into the tunnel, bracing him against the wall as water pours around them. Cold rain soaks Kamran through, and he gasps a few drops into his lungs before hacking it up. The alien shoves him a little and heads back to help the others.

"*Next*," Marsalis says, almost yanking Mary across the gap.

There's something in Kamran's heart. It hurts so bad—that's the only explanation. Black worms once crawled through the fingers of his right hand. What if the pathogen never left his system?

Yes. He has worms in his brain, too, doesn't he? Doesn't he?

Doesn't he what?

Tiran isn't looking so good, either. She's probably feeling Reza's pull, too.

Down.

Down into the—

Delirium. That's what this headache is.

"Hydrogen sulfide!" Kamran calls. "Hold your breath!"

Noah's screams drown out his warnings. Kamran rushes to the mouth of the tunnel to see the man under assault by a child-sized alien. Its chitin shines brown in the light as it latches onto him. Blood flows between gunmetal teeth, and it looses an ear-splitting squeal before biting Noah's eye and pulling away the long trail of an optic nerve. Marsalis bellows up at the smaller alien, startling it. It doesn't run away, though.

Instead, a swarm of its brethren emerge from a duct, bashing through to pile onto Noah. There must be at least a dozen. Jerry wisely decides it's a good time to get away, and jumps the short gap.

At least, he tries to, but the gas gets to him.

His eyes roll back in his head as he reaches the threshold, and he falls face-first onto the concrete platform outside the tunnel. His body lands half-on, half-off, sliding for the edge.

Surprising even himself, Kamran makes a wild dive and seizes Jerry's hand.

But the heavy old man isn't trying to save himself—he's unconscious. His wet, limp flesh slides through Kamran's fingers as if they'd never touched at all.

Then he's gone.

"*Jerry!*" Mary screams, sinking down against the wall, hand outstretched toward the swallowing hole.

Noah's begging blossoms into another full-throated, bloody scream. The creatures swarm him, pulling at flesh like fresh dough, spilling bright blood from a hundred wounds. He stumbles over the edge and falls after Jerry. Unlike his boss, however, Noah snags a rusty strut by the skin of his back, jerking to a sudden halt. The creatures snap to a stop with him, crowing with delight at their new mooring.

Another wave blasts through.

The wall of water smashes Kamran to the storm grate, squeezing even the memory of breath from his lungs. Even though he's surrounded by fluid, he'd gladly try to breathe it if he had the strength. The water sits on his back, and his eyes feel like they might pop out of his head. The stump becomes a magnesium flare, burning bright with trauma.

The flow above shuts off as quickly as it started, leaving Noah's tattered body hanging morbidly on the jagged metal. The creatures mostly survived the torrent, happily resuming their feast as though there's no one else around to kill. Kamran reminds himself not to draw breath, despite every fiber of muscle begging for oxygen—there is no air for him here.

Mary lays unconscious nearby. Tiran stumbles blindly through the tunnel. Another bubble is coming, maybe it'll be some fresh air to purge this mess.

Marsalis snatches Mary and rushes past.

Tiran and Kamran hobble after.

A rusted-out hatch blocks the path. Kamran is starting to fade—his mind won't make sense of what he's seeing. The creatures chirp and scream in the distance. They'll be finished with Noah soon enough and come after them.

Marsalis bangs against the structure, forcing the spade of her tail into a crack to wedge it open. More flaking metal comes away with each hit, but Kamran can't keep his eyes open. Mary is probably dead. Tiran might make it.

The door gives way, and Kamran runs for it, praying he'll find oxygen in time.

2 8

V O W S

"I do solemnly swear that I will defend the Constitution of the United States against all enemies, foreign and domestic."

Becker vividly remembers the day he said those words. It was a freeway island on the Tulsa Turnpike. He'd spoken clearly, enunciating every syllable while his mother stood outside. The parents weren't allowed in, not even USCM officers. The whole place smelled like hot engine wash and fried chicken from the convenience store next door.

When Becker emerged, he felt like the embodiment of the American dream, a force projection of the greatest country in the history of the goddamned universe. He was excited to be the stick part of America's big stick diplomacy. The Oath of Enlistment was his first of many steps with the USCM. It was also metaphorical—

—unlike the endless fucking steps of the tight staircase that he just climbed. This hidden vent shaft wasn't meant to be visited. The stairs are just for access in emergencies. There are no windows or floors, and for a moment, it seems they might never reach the top.

Becker crests a landing and stops long enough to catch his breath. In that time, Arthur passes him, scarcely winded. Becker may be infantry, but this dude is jacked.

"Personal question: are you a synth?" Becker asks.

"Where do you think this comes out?" Arthur ignores his joke. This high up, the intermittent boom of the pipe isn't quite so bad. It's almost peaceful, like a gentle wash.

"I don't know," Becker replies, struggling to keep the winded sound from his voice. "Kind of hoping you knew."

"Maybe we'll luck into Captain Duncan."

He pats the sling of his rifle. "Oo-rah to that shit."

Climbing floor after torturous floor, they finally reach the exit: a small dome beneath the surface of the waves. Hasanova atoll is littered with these formations—all sorts of mechanical lumps and bumps jutting out from the black rock, the artifacts of UPP ownership.

Becker switches off his flashlight and peers around. They're just outside the boundary of the Thunder Ring. Lake Peacock smashes into the atoll, then a portion of the runoff comes slurping back down the well shaft. Each time a wave recedes, Becker sees the slick, black rock of the island. Maybe, between the waves, he could run up there and onto the Thunder Ring. There are places to grab near the towers—a couple of catwalks that appear to be in decent shape.

It's just as possible that he'll get picked up by a wave and tossed into Charybdis.

Watch out for the death hole, Becker.

At least it's night, so stealth is a bit easier.

"When the wave finishes, we run for that catwalk," Arthur says. The sound of jangling harnesses fills the dank space, and Arthur hands one to him. "Cross the Thunder Ring, then onto the Data Cannon moorings. I don't think we're going to make it all the way to dry land in one go."

"What is this?" It's difficult to make sense of all the straps in the dark.

"Fall restraint harness. It has a carabiner and ascent ratchet," Arthur says, snapping his safety gear into place. "There are tie-down points all over the catwalks. If we can get up there, we've only got to hold our breath for a few seconds. Do you know how to put it on?"

"I can't even see it."

A thick wave pounds the Thunder Ring like a mountain tipping into Charybdis, and Becker imagines standing beneath all of that weight.

Arthur gets really friendly all of the sudden, taking the harness from Becker and wrapping the webbing straps around his legs. With those secured, he yanks the belt up high and cinches it, leg straps rising uncomfortably close to crushing Becker's balls.

"Now you've got a harness," Arthur says, slapping his back.

"I—" The wave's remains *whoosh* down the diverter

beside them, momentarily drowning out any chance of speech. He waits for it to finish. There's so much water. If he slips and gets sucked down...

"—love this idea," Becker concludes with a brief nod.

"No time like the present," Arthur says, leaping over the grating onto the wet rock and bolting up the side. If a wave comes now, he's dead.

Becker follows because it's probably a good idea to stay together. He hasn't fully considered his plan, yet the mission is already underway. He leaps the grating and immediately slips down.

Scrambling in the algae, Becker manages to get in a few uneven strides. He's out of the drainage system and halfway up the hill when he decides to look back. The lake swells, ready to crush everything in its path.

Arthur reaches the Thunder Ring and starts up the catwalk. Within the span of a breath, he's clipped into the cable handrails and is testing his bracing.

"Fuck, fuck, *fuck*," Becker huffs, sprinting up the atoll at maximum speed. Uneven earth squishes under his feet, and bloody mineral deposits leak between cracks and crevasses. Water washes around his boots, growing more insistent with each step. It's at his knees, his hips.

He's floating.

Becker swims down, colliding with Arthur as he's nearly swept past. The man wraps him in an ironbound grip, strangling the life out of him—but they jerk to a halt in the body of the wave.

Water presses in on his ears, constricts his chest, bulges his eyes, and batters him. They spin and whip like a fishing lure in the flow of water, but Arthur holds tight. Gravity slowly regains its influence, dragging them to the deck.

Soaked, the two men get their bearings. To their left, the end of the catwalk and the mooring point for the Data Cannon. To their right, Lake Peacock, the Lilypads, and a full squad of Duncan's troops.

Looking right at them.

"Shit." Becker wipes the water from his face.

The first round pings off the metal by Becker's head, then the rest of the bastards open fire. Becker and Arthur haul ass up the catwalk and over the Thunder Ring, sprinting past the base of the Human Centre tower. Charybdis opens in front of them as they run, untold depths gulping down the lake. If they can get far enough, they'll be onto the mooring—out of range of the waves.

Bullets chew their surroundings, sparking off metal struts. The water begins to rise. Arthur is already off the Thunder Ring and onto the Data Cannon's catwalk. He's going to make it. Becker isn't so lucky.

Cold, brackish water sweeps over him, raking Becker across the safety grating, then his restraint snaps taut. His bag of memory cores tumbles in the current, and he prays the water isn't damaging them.

"I swear I will bear true faith and allegiance…"

Is this what allegiance is—asphyxiating under a wave in the ass end of space while being shot at by people he considered his friends? This can't be right. No one has seen Duncan's tasking order—she has to be acting alone.

Thoughts of his—the *real*—America sustain him through the endless want for air. The water recedes and sets him down.

Becker unclips. Instead of running, though, he pumps his grenade launcher once, turns, and fires at the Lilypad. The round explodes in the middle of a set of canisters, sending marines running for cover. Becker fires again and again at their position as they dig in.

Pump, *boom*, pump, *boom*, pump, *click*.

Fuck.

Spinning, he runs his ass off—faster than he did for his USCM entrance test, which was pretty good, according to his mom. Shots pepper his location, but Becker is already on the downhill, headed into the largest death hole he's ever seen. He nails the jump onto the mooring cable catwalk, racing up the path Arthur just took.

The landscape opens beneath him as he races over Charybdis. Becker catches sight of an x-ray clinging to a glittering tooth inside the volcanic tube below. And if there's one…

A searchlight sweeps across the Maw revealing a half-dozen more, tails swishing eagerly as they climb. One of them makes a leap for the mooring cable, but takes a wave to the face, plummeting into the maelstrom below.

"Good luck, fuckers!" Becker shouts down at them as he sprints along the narrow bridge.

The Data Cannon looms in the night, his for the taking. Already its internal lights are coming on—Arthur booting up the systems. The marines can't get a shot at him over the Ring. They'll have to find another way around. He reaches the cannon's entryway at maximum speed, stumbling into a metal panel hard enough to leave a dent.

The interior of the Data Cannon is divided into two levels, each about as large as Becker's first apartment. Arthur's wide shoulders are enough to fill the downstairs control station, so Becker hurtles up the ladder to the second level.

There's a ring of ALON windows up here, thick and sturdy against all corrosion. Hopefully, these will do something about the bullets they're about to catch. The opposition force will be winding through the complex to access points, and from there it'll be easy to get a clean shot.

"How long to get the Data Cannon online, bud?"

"We're already up!" Arthur says. "Load those cores. We've got to scan and dump."

Becker looks around for some kind of power switch and comes up short.

"Uh, Roger… How do I turn it on?"

A hailstorm of bullets crackle the windows to his left, like someone playing snare drums on his skull. He flinches and ducks, but the windows hold.

"Jesus, man, you sounded like you had it under control up there! I thought you knew networks or something."

"Just tell me what to do!" Becker calls back.

"I'm coming up," Arthur calls. "Get out there and defend us!"

Becker leaves the bag of cores, slides down the ladder, and ducks out the door. Crouching, he tries to spot their opponents. They're shooting from a variety of locations, so he can't pin down a good target. They aren't using explosives, though, which means they want to keep the array intact.

"Hey down there!" Arthur bellows. "You planning on shooting back?"

"I swear to obey the President of the United States, and the duly appointed officers of the United States Colonial Marines in the defense of her interests in the stars—"

"Fuck it." Becker leans out and clocks a target—a well-positioned shooter on a balcony in the Human Centre. The silhouette tries for cover, but Becker's rifle splits the fucker open. They must be running low on PRAE plates.

Return fire forces his head down. Caseless rounds shatter and ricochet around the inside of the control room, sparking off walls and consoles. The rounds break into spawl on impact, and the control room becomes a hailstorm of sharp, hot metal. Duncan must've switched to anti-personnel bullets, just for him.

Arthur cries out in pain.

Becker grabs the base of the hatch, hauls it closed and dogs it before another volley strikes. More rounds tattoo the exterior, testing the thickness of the door—still good, for now. Not satisfied, the enemy tries shooting the windows some more.

"You okay?" Becker calls upstairs.

"Hit, but I'm as good as I'm going to be," Arthur shouts back. Judging from the sound of his voice, he's being optimistic.

"It's a bad idea to open the door right now," Becker says, "so maybe there's another way I can help."

"Monitor the connection."

Becker rushes to the console, looking over a huge dashboard of charts and graphs. It looks like the sort of stuff Shy did, and he doesn't even know where to start.

"Where are we on the scan?" Arthur's voice gurgles a little, and he emits a gasping cough. Becker scours the screen for anything that might say *scan*. A little panel goes red—probably bad—but the word "scan" appears, and an indicator showing one hundred percent.

"One hundred percent!" he calls.

"Good!"

Becker squints. *Why is it red, then?*

"Get ready to dump!"

"Is there like a button?" he shouts back.

"Yes, you're going to get a big modal popup when the scan parses. Hit the lotus. *Do not hit hum.*"

"Lotus?" Becker calls back. "That's a key?"

"Yes!"

More bullets hammer their enclosure windows and Arthur shouts, not the warrior's roar, but something distinctly more vulnerable.

God, that sounds like it hurts.

Becker scans the keyboard, trying to be ready, not wanting to force his partner to talk anymore. And yet, he cannot find this fucking key.

"What does the lotus look like?"

"Red bar! One dot!" Arthur says. "Not two! *Lotus, not hum!*"

Becker repeats the instructions, and when the dashboard goes green, lotus follows suit. Hum turns crimson, and he finally figures out the cancel/accept pattern. As soon as he hits the key, he'll transmit classified information into the hands of an enemy of the United States.

"According to the Uniform Code of Military Justice, so help me God."

Becker is bound by treaty to expose war crimes. No matter what, Duncan and her cohort of killers must be brought to justice. If Becker can't gather a tribunal, he'll make damned sure the word gets out.

"Lotus, confirmed!" Becker says, mashing the button hard enough to be sure the little membrane clicked. "Dumping... Dumped!" It goes faster than he expected, like loading and firing a shell from a mortar. He's just dropped a metric fuck-ton of data onto the EntaCOMM network and into Iranian hands.

"Scanning the next core!" Arthur calls down. He clears his throat like he's dying of thirst, dry and hoarse. "Eight to go! Do we load every drive?"

"They were all on the same hub!" he replies. "Nothing

to do but dump everything!"

The scan takes forever in the middle of a firefight, but the screen goes green, along with lotus. Becker hits the button a lot faster this time.

"Confirm lotus, load next drive!"

"Copy... loading," Arthur says, voice drifting.

The heavy thud sounds a lot like two hundred and fifty-five pounds of ex-cop just hit the deck. Becker peers up the ladder, trying to get a bead on what might be happening.

"Buddy?"

Which two of the cores got loaded up? Were either of them the correct one?

Becker spins and hurtles up the ladder to find Arthur bleeding out on the floor. A bright red stain spreads under one armpit, shiny and wet on his filthy work shirt. Flecks of it have splattered onto the dark skin of his face—he must've taken a pretty hard ricochet.

"Just scan the fucking cores," Arthur whispers, weakly pointing to the bag. "Don't worry about..."

Becker grabs the canvas and pulls out the next slick white block of memory, slotting it into the bay. On this new workstation, lotus goes green, hum goes red, so the safe bet feels like lotus. He mashes the green button.

"Scanning!" Becker says, and when he looks down at Arthur, there's so much more blood on the ground. It pools at his feet, running over the lip of the landing. The man's eyes are open, but he's either gone or going.

An explosion rocks the door. They're firing heavier

rounds now, but it holds.

One of the x-rays peers in the window and scares the shit out of him. It beats its smooth, bony crest against the ALON, making no more progress than the pulse rifle rounds of the marines.

Then gunfire rips the creature to shreds, coating the hull with a glut of yellow acid. Solid aluminum windows turn brown, then black as they begin to melt.

"Aw, fuck you, man."

Becker steps over Arthur, going for the ladder. It's so slick with the man's blood that he stumbles to the ground, almost twisting his ankle. By the time he can get upright to the dump console, it's ready to upload the memory core.

Lotus number three. Seven to go.

The shooting dies down like a passing hailstorm. For some reason, Becker hears Captain Duncan's voice emanating from one of the wall panels. A mic hangs nearby from a spiral cable.

"All bands, all bands—Corporal Becker, come in."

He picks up the mic and clicks the button.

"This is Becker."

"I know what you're doing in there," Duncan says. *"That's treason. You don't have to love me, but you love your country, don't you?"*

"It's already in-progress, sir," he says. "Everyone knows what you did."

Everyone *might* know what she did. He'll increase his odds to forty percent when he uploads this core. Becker drops the mic and climbs back upstairs. The soldiers outside open fire, but judging from the distant shouts and alien screeches, they have battles of their own.

Becker gets cores four and five into the system before his new friend, the x-ray corpse, melts through the window. Acrid smoke billows from the newly formed hole as the creature's body sluices into the control room. If it wasn't for the raging winds that whip over Lake Peacock, Becker wouldn't be able to breathe through the sulfur stench.

He shields his eyes on reflex. A splatter of acid lands on his earlobe.

"Fuck!"

He pulls the yellow fluid off, and it's melting his fingers.

"Shit!"

He wipes those on his uniform. The blood begins eating through the cloth.

"*Fuck!*"

Glancing at his left hand, he finds the yellowing bones of his thumb and forefinger. He blew those off in an explosion once as a kid—fireworks. The replacement grafts were so good that losing them feels just as horrible the second time around.

When the acid finally reaches the skin of his chest, it's like being flensed with a blunt knife. Becker roars in pain, then gags on the scent of his own melting meat. His ear is still burning, and it's bad news if a drop lands on his neck. With a quick motion, Becker tears off his shirt and—using the clean fabric—pinches the wounded part of his ear.

He pulls as hard as he can. Every inch of weakened flesh comes away in a tortured strand. He presses more clean fabric to the burn on his torso, fusing it to his skin, giving more food to the acid.

The x-ray corpse eats through the upper deck, slurping onto the lower level in a fluorescent mess. Becker scrambles backward as its skull splits like a melon, spilling even more fresh acid over the floor plates. A huge hole takes the scanning console, Arthur's corpse, and half the dump console—officially ending the mission.

The fury of Lake Peacock whips through the control room as acid eats deeper, widening the hole in the floor. Cold, wet spray speckles Becker's cheeks—Charybdis's caress. He shivers, covered in Arthur's blood and his own. His left hand feels like he dipped it into the sun. The rest of him feels like the Arctic.

Becker has known guys who got into vacuum accidents. They talk about the all-consuming heat and cold, two sides of a dying coin. Some of them tell him about feeling something else out there—a presence in the blackness of space, reaching into them.

The Peacock's breath condenses along his cheeks and brow, thick enough to drip into his eyes. The water hungers.

Get the fuck out of your own head, Becker. You can make it through this.

More claws click along the metal walls of the enclosure. The winds double upon themselves, and a shaft of white light pierces the room. Warm jet wash fills the air with ozone fumes—marginally more pleasant than the acid fumes.

Becker blinks and shields his eyes, as a Cheyenne UD-40L dropship thunders overhead. He once considered it the most beautiful thing he'd ever seen, but now he sees it from a new angle. The craft spreads its wingspan over his vision like a bird of prey coming in for the kill, hovering in all its majesty.

"*Hey, Becker.*" Duncan's voice comes from the control room radio. It's hard to hear over the roar of maneuvering thrusters. "*Figured I'd come get you myself.*"

Clutching a smoking hand to his chest, he crawls to the far wall and picks up the dangling mic. The Data Cannon didn't feel so rickety before it was missing substantial portions of the superstructure.

Fucking death holes, man.

"Yeah?" Becker says into the mic.

"*Gunner's seat, front row, finger on the trigger, baby. So did you do it? Did you commit treason?*" There's a dare in Duncan's tone. *Fight me.*

Five cores. Fifty-fifty odds. Maybe? Sharing *any* information with the enemy is tantamount to lunacy, but this might be his last chance to defend his honor. Probably for posterity.

X-rays scramble over his smoking shelter like spiders on an egg sac. The greatest fighting machine ever to touch starlight roars above like a mighty lion. One of the moorings gives off a juddering groan, metal growling.

ALEX WHITE

Whether it's gravity or x-rays, something is going to drag him into that dark, wet hell soon enough.

When Becker took his vows to his country, he knew this day might come. He's thought about it so many times. He's proud of the decisions that brought him to this miserable place. He kept his honor—standing up and saying no when it was hard. Maybe he got to save someone. Maybe he was an agent of truth. Either way, this is the consequence of righteousness.

His mother always told him, *"A code is only a code if you keep it when it's hard."* If she ever finds out the truth of what he did, she'll be proud. It would've been nice to tell her in person. He could make sure the story stays straight.

Becker takes a moment to collect his final statement: *I didn't commit treason. You're the one destroying America, not me.*

"Duncan," he starts, "I didn't commit—"

"Don't care. Get fucked."

The interior of the Data Cannon becomes a strobing, sparking cage of white-hot lances as the dropship's minigun opens fire. Comets of depleted uranium shred the center of the tower, sawing apart thick struts and metal panels. The floor opens wider, and Becker slides toward the yawning abyss, its height filled with falling stars from the dropship above.

The minigun bullets are like three punches from God—leg, stomach, head.

PART IV

REMAINS

MMirashrafi@aljazeera.net

(5:36 AM BST / 11:36 PM EST)

Wake up. Holy shit. Please tell me you are awake.

Received / Read

Saba.Keramati@washpost.com

I take it you finally saw the finale? I told you it
was so good!

Received / Read

MMirashrafi@aljazeera.net

No. I got something in my work drop. I don't know
how to describe it, but

Received / Read

I need you to call me right now.

Received / Read

2 9

A GIFT FOR AN ANGEL

Passageways grow tighter as Marsalis clatters down tunnel after tunnel. She's hard to follow, and were it not for Tiran stopping to help Kamran, he'd have gotten lost. When Marsalis finally slows, he's grateful. They've mostly cleared the cloud of gas, and he needs a chance to catch his breath. From the look on Tiran's face, she's grateful, too.

Marsalis points at a span of ventilation duct that's a touch less grimy than the others.

"*New… construction*," she taps, robotic voice echoing in the infested shadows. Kamran is about to ask if the speaker has a quieter volume setting when Marsalis shreds open the aluminum duct and slips inside.

Moments later, the creature returns and lifts Kamran with a cold claw, pulling him into the split ductwork. Tiran comes next, then Marsalis goes back for Mary. Crawling with one arm tires Kamran, and his left shoulder burns like the muscles want to give up. He's made harder treks in his life, though. There may be bloodthirsty aliens, but at least there aren't any Russians.

Moving ahead of them, Marsalis kicks out a grate, and a familiar humid breeze washes over Kamran—the scent of the Maelstrom. They emerge from their duct to find a panorama of raging water and construction equipment.

This is the base of the Spiral, in the unfinished section—below the data storehouses. The pilings for Halo B are nearby. The only piece of the system that ever got finished was the main relay terminal, and Kamran had only started integrating it into SiteSys. At least he can safely say Halo B's failures aren't his fault, now.

He musters the strength to shamble to the water's edge, trying to peer up through the salivating gullet of Charybdis. Waves break over silver teeth, sending wet sighs across the industrial floodlights.

Kamran always forgets about the rainbows.

Somewhere up there, Becker and Arthur are trying to get the word out to the rest of the galaxy. He wishes he could see through the curtain of rain to the Data Cannon. How long should Kamran's people wait for them?

The lights above them go red—the canary sensors detect trace hydrogen sulfide.

"Afghanzadeh," Tiran says. "Warning lights."

"Unless all of the other lights turn bad, we'll be fine," he replies. "Probably just detects what came out of the vent with us." Then the misty vista goes sun-bright. Long trails of fire flash through the fog like orange lightning strikes—tracers from something big. An explosion rocks the heavens.

"No."

Kamran's whisper hitches in his throat. He doesn't want to believe they're shooting the Data Cannon. That's the most valuable part of the installation. They wouldn't blow it up.

More fire pours through the long shaft, almost surgical in its precision. A thump and a roar later, forty tons of finely tuned communications equipment come burning down the Maw like a divine spear into the heart of the planet. The structure spins, striking teeth as it falls, smashing hydroelectric plants—shattering their tungsten flywheels. Ten thousand tons of shrapnel slice through stone and metal alike.

It's over, then. The truth dies with us.

The Data Cannon impacts the great whirlpool like a meteorite, and even the relentless thirst of the planet must pause and retch—but only momentarily. Wreckage swirls, belching black smoke like a flaming merry-go-round.

Pieces of rock and jagged metal go streaking over the path. Thousands of tons of capital equipment—much of it spinning at high speed—comes cascading down through the volcanic shaft. A sheet of steel whips across Marsalis's crest, and she shrieks in pain. The projectile shaves off bits of black scale like broken teeth.

Kamran hits the deck, covering his head against the storm of debris. He doesn't know where Mary and Tiran are, just Marsalis. The alien clatters on the ground nearby, clutching her wounded skull and screaming at the top of her lungs. Flecks of acid hit the rocks around Kamran, sizzling and stinking.

"Don't step on me!" he shouts, for all the good it'll do. Language can't survive this cacophony.

Shut your eyes and hope.

At long last, chaos homogenizes into the sound of falling water. Kamran hasn't been crushed, trampled, or torn to pieces. Marsalis hisses and spits nearby like a furious cat, desperately scrabbling at her wounded crest. The pain has driven her into a frenzy, and he's glad to be out of arm's reach.

Mary lies face down a short distance away.

He isn't sure where Tiran is.

Get up. Those bullets came from above.

Searchlights paint the rain silver. The American ship must be watching the wreckage of the Data Cannon. His heart thuds. What if they see the red light of the canary sensor? They might shoot at him.

As if in answer, the searchlight begins sweeping closer. So high up, they couldn't possibly see him beneath the overhang of the Spiral's roof. They might shoot a missile, though, to blow the whole place up, but there's no way they see Kamran, specifically.

Despite Charybdis's massive aperture, the warship's

performance engines pressurize it, splashing water onto the ramp. They must be hovering overhead. Soldiers carry portable motion trackers. Maybe there's something bigger mounted on the ship.

"Fine. Stay there," Kamran mutters, looking down the Spiral for the sensor control box. He limps to the keypad and taps in his administrative code. The info panel flashes green, and a lock goes *thunk* in the thick metal housing. He pries the front door off the sticky rubber gasket to find the treasure inside: a glowing terminal.

```
CANARY SENSOR MANUAL
CALIBRATION & TEST TOOL (CMSCTT)
SiteSys Integration 2184
Cheyenne Hunt, McAllen Integrations
```

It's a new screen—one he hasn't seen before. The contractors must've changed his interface when they hooked up the other atmospheric sensors. His eyes rake the contents and find only three choices.

```
SPOT TEST
FULL TEST
COMMISSIONING SETTINGS
```

He highlights "FULL TEST" and mashes the accept. It's going to take him awhile to set things up—he has to add all sensors to the data call and address their network

IDs individually. After that, he'll have to broadcast a trip signal across the data links and—

There are just two options.

```
CANCEL
START TEST
```

Almost afraid to believe it could work, he highlights "START TEST" and presses the sigma.

"*Alert.*" The pleasant English voice calls over a few hundred thousand watts of loudspeakers. "*The following is only a test.*" Above him, the canary sensor lamp in the ceiling goes red to warn hearing-impaired colonists and denote the safety line. It blinks three times, then the next one up the Spiral reddens, racing away from Kamran like toppling dominoes. The system is setting them off one by one, checking to make sure they still work.

Shy's UI is better than Kamran's in every way. This replacement interface even gives him up-to-the-second statuses, beginning with "HALO A CHARGING TO FIRE... 59%."

Loudspeakers drone their warning chant into the thirsty gullet.

"*Attention: Toxic Environment Detected, Halo A ignition response imminent. All personnel return to colony structures and shelter in place. Repeat...*"

The screen flickers, and the final line of the test appears.

```
SOUND / LIGHT CHECK OK. CAPACITORS OK. FIRE HALO A?
Y/N

>
```

Kamran consents to unleash the hurricane.

High above him, a set of eight high-powered turbine fans engage, banks of folded graphene supercapacitors delivering explosive torque. The blades reach maximum thrust in under a quarter second, shoving wind and water alike up through the tube.

Kamran rushes to the safety barrier as the rains cease, desperate to see what becomes of the dropship. The machine isn't hard to spot, engines flaring in resistance, hovering in the vortex. The pilot maintains level flight for about two seconds.

The ship wobbles once, then its tail drifts backward into the cavern wall. It's like a top knocked off its axis—steady and serene one moment, smashing into everything the next. Flames blast from weapon pods as lethal payloads go off in every direction.

Watching the symphony of chaos, Kamran holds up his remaining hand, raising a thumb. Every last person on that dropship can go fuck themselves, for all he cares.

Then it's coming right at him.

He'd meant to survive, but this will work. It won't be so bad to go out instantaneously, crushed in the death of a hated enemy. He's sad, though, that he won't get to tell the rest of humanity what happened here.

A pair of black, chitinous arms wrap around him.
Except the grip is too tight.
The hiss is too feral.
Not Marsalis, then.

3 0

S A V E D

"The fuck?"

The length of Charybdis's maw lights up in a spiral of red, surrounding them, engulfing the ship in hellish light.

"Get us out of here, Private!" she barks. But Private Arnold has always been slow on the draw.

Through the gun camera, there's a perfect view of those big-ass fans coming to life, bucking the ship hard enough to jerk their heads forward. She wouldn't trust Arnold to yank his own stick, so she doubts he can pull off the maneuver required to keep them alive. Alarms rage as all systems hit a hard limit on what a Cheyenne UD-40L will do.

There's a crunch of tail, and the sudden, forward pitch into the abyss renders the ship more aerodynamic. The airframe affects a downward trajectory once more—headlong toward the frothing maelstrom. The dipshit pilot decides to pull back on the stick, perhaps because he'd rather hit the wall than the whirlpool. He accomplishes the maneuver perfectly, burst-firing the engines enough to send the ship into the glassy viewports of a server farm.

Perception always goes wild during a crash. At this speed, the world condenses into circles of light, tumbling through her view. Fire and ice. Veins filling up in her head, redding her out. She squeezes the trigger a few times on the way down because why the fuck not? Then an impossible force smashes them from below, and the ride suddenly halts in darkness.

Kylie Penelope Duncan always felt as if the Lord had a special place for her in His heart. God left her alive when He took her best friend, Addison, and Kylie will never forget the profound feeling of holding her own shattered jaw in place while she watched Addison die.

It wasn't supposed to be a combat mission—just some door knocking at the farms. After the IED went off, no one came to help. They left Kylie to secure her impossible wound with field gauze while she hid for cover in her overturned vehicle. Blood spilled over tactical gloves onto the parched salts of a foreign world.

In the twenty-six hours it took for backup to arrive, Kylie Duncan learned one thing: God wouldn't let her die. He had some higher purpose in mind.

* * *

She awakens. Rain hammers her shelter. Her head swims, and something won't stop shaking her.

"Fucking shit, dude," she mumbles.

"We've got to go, Captain," Lee says. "Up and at 'em."

When she opens her eyes, it's surprisingly claustrophobic in the cockpit. The gunner's seat behind the pilot typically has a good view, but a rock wall has crushed most of the canopy—and shoved Private Arnold's helmet down into his chest cavity. She'll have to write a letter home to *his* mom now, too.

Fuck this mission.

"Where are we?" she asks.

"Wedged into the cliff face." He yanks her jangling flight harness, sawing through the webbing with a commando knife. "About to get flushed into the big whirlpool."

That gets her attention.

Kylie drags off her helmet and tugs the rest of her safety belts free. The storm outside redoubles its deluge, and the whole of her reality threatens to shatter around her. If this ship comes loose with her in it, she won't be escaping.

"Captain—"

"I'm good, Lee." She gulps, trying to ignore nausea. She might have a head wound, internal bleeding, or any number of potentially lethal injuries. But she *is* good, all things considered. Sure as hell could be worse.

"Get out," she says. "I'm right behind you."

He's perched at her seat, hanging onto the doorframe. The floor has a disorienting upward slope, and it's going to be a tricky climb to get out the back. Lee reaches for her.

"Sir—"

"Go, you fucking moron!"

They pull through the shattered hold of the dropship, using anything they can find for purchase. The exit isn't hard to locate; the rear half of the ship is missing. Beyond its torn fuselage lies the solid ground of the Spiral. If she can make it there, she's home free.

On the far side of the hold lies the weapons rack. As tempting as it is to go for a pulse rifle, streams of water pour around that section. Those guns probably aren't going to be there in a second—that whole section might not be.

Lee makes it out first, immediately running off into the complex.

"Where the fuck are you going?" she yells after him. She'd expected her subordinate to get to safety, not disappear on her. Kylie negotiates past a broken support, and the whole place jolts enough to prompt a scream. If this shit wasn't about to kill her, it might be fun.

Lee reappears at the entrance dragging a fire hose, tossing the heavy nozzle down to her. Kylie catches it, immediately wrapping the cloth several times around one arm. He pulls the other side taut.

A shadow darkens the ceiling behind Lee. She's going to have to go for the guns after all, so she takes a leap of faith.

"Captain!" Lee shouts.

Kylie hits the far wall, tangling up with the gun racks and knocking rifles loose. They go skidding down the deck plates, through a break in the fuselage, tumbling into the maelstrom beyond. She seizes one of the remaining weapons and plants her back against the broken wall, flipping off the safety.

Her concussed balance sucks, the shot sucks, the situation sucks.

"Duck," she bellows. "Now!"

Good luck, Lee.

She looses a burst of fire into the beast, riddling its skull. The force of the shots carry the creature backward, and she hopes that luck has spared Lee the worst of the acid spray. She doesn't get to find out. The dropship cracks loose, and she loses her footing. Her whole existence relies upon that fire hose and her grip strength as the ship slides away.

Then comes the flood.

Waves hammer her from above, pounding her down. The fire hose snaps taut, and she's battered against the cliff face. The porous rock wall takes its due with each hit, but eventually she stabilizes.

Jagged grit digs into her back as Lee drags her up. Pounding torrents test every muscle, and she twines up with the hose like a climbing rope. Every second of punishing water and knife-edged rock is the hardest second of her life. It would be so much easier just to let go.

Not yet. He'll take me when it's time. Got to hang on.

A gloved hand reaches through the deluge and plucks her from it like a baby. She's drawn into Lee's arms, and they both go down on the smooth floor of the Spiral, panting.

He looks into her eyes.

"Let me go, pigface," she says, and Lee instantly relaxes his grip on her. Slipping free, she climbs to her feet before cracking a grin. "I just made the greatest shot of your life. You're never going to live this down."

He gives her the rarest of smiles. "You're a legend, sir."

"Goddamned right."

A few feet away, the x-ray quivers and spurts. Kylie likes the way the acid froths up on the stone, turning a potent crimson. She's seen some evil shit in her day, and this place takes it. She puts two more short bursts into the motherfucker—it's the only way to be sure.

Kylie looks around. "This is where we loaded in the x-rays."

Lee gives the "yes" grunt.

"Do you think the elevator still works? I'm not into climbing stairs right now."

"Probably," Lee says, then he pauses. "Stand by, getting a call from base. Ops, Lee. Go ahead." He presses the wet earpiece like he's trying to shove the whole thing into his brain. Whatever they're saying, he doesn't like it—his face gets uglier than usual.

"Give me your walkie," Kylie says.

Lee unravels the radio and earpiece from his webbing and hands it over. It's still warm and a little greasy from his ear.

"Ops, Captain Duncan. Gear up and let's get out of here. We can still shut it down."

"*Where is Marsalis?*" It's Matsushita. "*Is she still alive?*"

Kylie would like to snap this guy's neck, but she'll have to sort that out later. Right now, she needs to focus on her remaining fireteam. They've still got time to rig HAPS to blow, leveling the installation and every shred of evidence above Charybdis. That'll be easy enough. The *Benning* can sink an orbital shot right down the hatch—won't even have to use a nuke.

"*Have you seen Marsalis?*" the doctor repeats, somewhat more insistently. "*Her tracking tag shows her near you.*"

"I don't fucking know, Doc, but I'm going to need you to put an adult on the line. We're low on ammo and right beside a hive, so I need someone helpful."

"*I have been helpful, Captain Duncan. I arranged for you and your team to be here. My division at Weyland-Yutani gave you half of your weapons. Now is there any sign of my property?*"

Duncan smirks and makes a jackoff gesture at Lee before pointing to the radio.

"'Your property?' Is this a sex thing?"

The outburst is so sudden that Kylie pulls the speaker from her ear.

"*Where is she?*"

When he shouts, Matsushita's voice creaks like a

teenager. He reminds Kylie of a guy who tried to slap her in high school. That dude would turn so red it looked like his eyes were boiling, all watery and bloodshot.

"I don't have it, you little asshole," she says, eyeing the path deeper into Charybdis. The explosion will draw the creatures. "Put Cooper on. I'm not going to ask again."

"You're done calling the shots. Marsalis is the reason we're here, the culmination of a three-year intelligence operation. I have allowed you to cross the line—"

"'Allowed,'" she repeats.

He gives the speech like he's holding down the trigger. *"Yes, allowed. My company found this place. Loaned you the toys, gave you access to our data, and secured funding for your platoon. When your boss, Colonel Davis, retires, it will be into our PMC division. Every aspect of your command is in my pocket.*

"Yes, allowed."

"You think that means you can tell a marine in the field what to do."

"I know *I can. Your mistakes necessitate a cover-up,*" he says, a quivering calm returning to his voice. *"They cost you your platoon, and a dropship. You are a failure by any metric. Your command will recognize that."*

"Maybe, but they're not here. I can handle discipline."

She almost hears his smile. *"But worst: you are a war criminal. Bring me Marsalis, and I can help you. Confuse things. Offer conflicting evidence."*

Lee takes a knee, keeping watch. Kylie does the same.

"*Or—*" he begins.

"Or you can turn on me," she says, "offer your evidence, and I'll swing for my crimes."

"*I don't have to turn on you for that to happen.*"

"But you could."

"*Yes.*" He chuckles. "*I suppose I could. You would do well to remember that.*"

Kylie licks her lips. The water carries notes of boiled eggs and piss, so she regrets it and spits. "What do you want me to do?"

"*I'm coming down. We're going to follow Marsalis's tracking signal into the hive. You and your men will protect me.*"

"There were three hundred tangoes in those cages when we let the x-rays in," she says. "Videos showed the devils chewing up half the enemy, but they dragged the other half down into the tunnels."

"*Yes,*" he coos. "*Many of them will have hatched. So many babies down there, growing by the second, getting hungrier. You'd move quickly if you want to escape The Hague executioner.*"

She keeps silent.

"*What?*" Matsushita scoffs. "*Nothing to say?*"

"Just…" She shakes her head. "Tell me what you want me to do."

"*I'm in charge now.*"

"Yes."

"*Is that how you address a superior?*"

Kylie takes a long, deep breath, steadying her heart. "Yes, sir."

His soft laughter makes her sick. *"Even a bitch like you can be housebroken."*

"Let's be professionals here, Doctor," she says, smacking her lips to cope with her bitter, dry words. "What's your big plan?"

"I have brought your Good Boys back online, with the help of Corporal Cooper. We will use them to herd wild… x-rays—" He says the word with some distaste. He has his own name for them, but Kylie hasn't bothered to remember it. *"—and put them down. Your men have salvaged the smart guns from the mutineers, and should have no trouble dealing with this small hive."*

It's not a bad idea. The Good Boys will be highly effective in confined areas like the tunnels. The most annoying part about a hive assault is always the acid. The more devils that die, the more of a roadblock they become. With the Good Boys pushing them back instead of killing them, Kylie's marines can penetrate the heart of the nest.

It's going to be the single greatest assault of her career yet—a goddamned Xenomorph round-up and slaughter. If they weren't paying her, she'd buy a ticket to be here.

"Did you hear me, Captain?"

"I'm waiting for you to put Cooper on the line, so I can get on with my fucking job."

"Very well," Matsushita says. *"Let's work together and accomplish our goals, yes?"*

"Yep. Perfect. Roger wilco." There's a rustling pause, and a smooth Alabama accent comes over the line.

"*Cooper here.*"

"Coop, two things," Kylie says. "One: if you ever let a civilian have your comm again, I'll serve you your cock in a hotdog bun. Two: get your asses down here. Me and Lee are holding the gates of Hell with a pair of rifles and could use some motherfucking backup. Arnold's dead."

"*Fuck,*" Cooper replies. "*That's—when we saw the ship go down, we didn't think anyone made it, and—*"

"Did I ask for your opinion, Corporal Cooper?"

"*No, s—*"

"*No I fucking did not,*" she says. "Grab your shit and get down here."

"*I heard him threaten you, sir. We're doing what he says?*"

Kylie sucks in a short breath. "Coop, why don't you stop in the cafeteria to grab some hot dog buns?"

"*Sorry, sir.*"

"Get down here." She turns to her faithful right hand. "Duncan out."

"Something coming our way?" Lee asks.

"Yeah. Babysitting duty."

3 1

OSSUARY

Kamran used to believe that, by yanking his arm off at the elbow, Marsalis had given him the ultimate alien experience.

He was wrong.

This creature wants him—*needs* him. Kamran now understands why "carnal" and "carnivorous" are both descended of the dead Latin's "caro." Uncompromising arms encircle his trunk, claws digging into his chest like meat hooks. It bends him across its body, pressing every bony lump of itself into his flesh as it hauls him. Its parted lips nuzzle the side of his neck, cold, wet teeth on his skin.

It whips him through corridor after corridor in a blur. This is a human facility, and Kamran reels when his temple catches the side of a lab table. The hallways grow dingier, long pools of resin gathering at the edges. The world of humanity fades away, erased by these bony formations.

I have to fight.

Marsalis is flexible in the abdomen. Maybe Kamran can throw an elbow with his good arm—hit it in the kidney or something. He swings his left arm backward as hard as he can, driving it into the monster's stomach. His funny bone rings like a bell—the alien muscles are diamond-hard, and don't budge beneath his assault.

Yet it drops him.

Did I hit a weak spot?

The monster surges onto Kamran, pinning his limbs down and screaming in his face, and he understands—he didn't hurt the beast. It unfurls across his vision, demanding to know how he could dare to oppose it, and Kamran has no answer.

It grabs him by the stump, engulfing him in a wave of blinding pain. He tries to squirm away but it pins his head to the ground, cutting his skin with its teeth. He cries and it grips harder, pressing nails into the bandage, through his already flayed flesh. It knows his blood, his fear, sensing injury and delighting in pain.

It steps onto his abdomen, and Kamran's scream runs out with his air. The possibility of drawing another breath disappears, and he gapes wordlessly at the slick-boned horror looming above. Lips quiver and part, enraged. Viscous drool showers in his eyes, nose, and open mouth. It tastes of rot and bile, blood and fat—the taste of other people. It shows him its tongue, the tip split into two rows of toothy barbs designed for grabbing and yanking prey into its mouth.

The little maw slides out between the monster's jaws. Mucosal strands wet his lips.

When he locks his mouth shut and shakes his head, the animal strikes him like a snake. It's like taking a stun baton to the face. Pain whites out half of Kamran's upper lip and sets his gums tingling. Its teeth scrape off of his. When salty, coppery blood mixes with foul alien saliva, Kamran throws up directly in its face.

There's a blur of chitin.

Marsalis plows into the side of Kamran's assailant. The two of them go tumbling into the far wall, giving Kamran enough time to roll onto his stomach. His throat and lungs burn with a need for oxygen, but his airways have shut. He digs at the mucus and vomit covering his face to try and free himself. Blood, too, runs over his hands, slicker than ever in the mixture of bile and drool.

He gasps like a dying man, his diaphragm raw. Air is like barbed wire sliding down his injured throat, but he drinks it jealously. Then Kamran curls around his stump, shaking and weeping.

The droning buzz of Marsalis's articulating scales roars to life behind him, as if asserting royal authority over a subject. There's a big, broken spot where the crest has been cut, but it's no less powerful in its maddening noise.

"Kamran!" Mary limps toward him from the shadows. Did Marsalis carry her? Where is Tiran?

Doesn't matter. It's a rescue, praise Khoda.

Except the other alien isn't backing down. Marsalis's buzzing drone climbs to a fever pitch like a swarm of carrion flies, the amplified sawtooth wave cutting into his brain—yet the assailant isn't cowed. Its posture strikes Kamran as crouched and tense—coiled. It launches, colliding with Marsalis's abdomen. Kamran's defender yelps in surprise, and that noise curdles his stomach as much as any scream.

"I'm here, baby." Mary's hands fall on his disgusting shoulders, and he splutters. His voice will not emerge. It's hard to imagine ever talking again. Every breath is fresh agony.

"Kamran, you're okay, aren't you?" she asks. "Please be okay. We can't lose everybody."

He nods yes out of sheer politeness.

She keeps glancing between him and the fight unfolding nearby. "You look like you've been kicked by a horse. Can you stand?"

He shakes his head, no.

"You should… run…" he croaks, throat burning. If he keeps gasping, he's scared it'll close up.

"No, damn it!" She says it like she's spitting a curse. Her head shakes, and tears well in her eyes. "You tried to save Jerry. I saw it. You aren't dying alone here, young man."

She pulls his head closer, and they watch the carnage unfold as only people at the end of a rope can. He knows Mary is right: run or don't run, it probably won't matter. The smaller creature is hardly a match for Marsalis, but it manages to provoke a few agonized shrieks from their monstrous comrade.

Marsalis is a vicious fighter, using her superior strength and longer reach to smash the adversary against anything and everything. To Kamran's amazement, their foe never surrenders. When Marsalis breaks off the end of its tail, it comes all the harder. After Marsalis crushes the beast's knee joint the wrong way, the creature adopts a freakishly quick improvised crabwalk, flying in the face of natural motion and sanity. It assails Marsalis like something possessed, hungry for violence.

Then Marsalis scores a coup. She stabs her barbed tail into the tubes along the alien's neck, pushing and twisting as if plunging a spade into soil. The wild animal rages a moment longer, but finally succumbs to the wound.

Marsalis turns to face them, gashes raked across her almost human lips. Acid runs in yellow rivulets down her teeth, spattering and smoking against the grated floors.

The dead monster's gushing blood eats through the grating in no time, and the corpse slips into darkness. It takes a long time for the body to hit something— whatever lies beneath this level, it's a long way down.

"If you can't control them," Kamran says, voice barely a whisper, "we're dead."

Marsalis's lips pull into a toothy sneer, and she winces as her black skin splits further. He wonders if he might've caused some offense, but he only meant to speak the truth. Alien fingers weave letters together with little flashes.

"Sorry. Cannot protect you... anymore."

Mary's hand tenses around Kamran's, and he rolls onto his rump. His arm is bleeding again, and it's probably going to get worse. How does he have so much blood, still? Did Marsalis give him a transfusion when she operated on him? Maybe there's surgical equipment on the *Blackstar*.

Not that it matters, because he'll never live to see that ship. There are snatchers ahead and marines behind, and Marsalis's help is ending. With great labor, Kamran leans forward onto his good hand, and kneels.

"Hey now, whoa," Mary says. "Don't hurt yourself."

He laughs himself into a coughing fit. "Yes, it'd be terrible to sustain an injury or something..." Then he nods to Marsalis. "I want to say to you—thank you for taking us this far."

A flicker of fingers. *"Giving up?"*

"No." He shakes his head. "Even if I have no hope, I'll walk until I can't walk anymore." It takes him a moment, but he finally notices what's missing. "Where is Tiran?"

"... don't... know," Marsalis says, bowing her head.

Kamran looks to Mary. "You don't know?"

"There were explosions," Mary says. "Marsalis scooped me up and—"

"Dropship crash. Chaos. Lost her, had Mary," Marsalis says. *"You got... snatched. Had to... make choice."*

"No," he says. "You made the wrong choice." Tears well up in his eyes. "Go find her."

"*Close to hive*," Marsalis replies. "*If I leave you here… you die. Only saved you… because I know… the scent of your meat.*"

"She's out there!" Kamran cries, spitting blood. "We're going to die anyway! You cannot protect us."

The alien remains as still as death, until finally her fingers move.

"*Why is she… worth more?*"

"Because I'm broken."

Marsalis taps, turning her back on him. "*So was I.*"

Kamran has no idea what that means, and he doesn't care to waste what little life remains. He smiles wanly, causing his lips and gums to sting. They're swelling, and if he had a tomorrow, he'd look like a lumpy gourd. But there won't be another sunrise in his future.

Of that he's certain.

"Can you still pass amongst your own?" Kamran asks.

"*Yes,*" she replies. Static crackles on Marsalis's loudspeaker; it's been further damaged in all of the fighting. "*But no control.*"

He swallows. "Will there be more below?"

"*Yes.*"

He and Mary share a look.

"Then you should leave us," Kamran says, and Mary squeezes his hand. "Get back to your ship. Mary and I will see ourselves out, if we can."

"*There is… one way… you can pass.*"

Mary clears her throat. "How?"

"*If I am taking you… to be… cocooned. Impregnated.*"

So that's why they've been dragging us away.

"*Snatchers breed…*" Its alien fingers hesitate, fumbling for words. "*Inside you. Lethal. Always.*" Their guide makes two fists across her bony ribcage, then imitates something bursting forth. Kamran closes his eyes and whispers a short prayer.

All of those people, used up like they were nothing.

"*Egg chamber,*" Marsalis says, "*will be in the ruins.* Blackstar *on other side.*"

"You want to drag us into a hive of—" Kamran tries to remember how many coworkers and neighbors he once had. "Maybe hundreds of aliens? How many 'babies' does a person produce?"

"*Always one.*"

Mary takes his hand. "Do you know the story of Daniel and the lion's den?"

"You are a treasure, Mary," he says, eyes stinging, "but I don't want your Bible stories when I just found out… My people were, what, *raped*, and… Fuck!" Kamran's shout reduces him to a coughing fit. His guts are just one large bruise.

"*Must survive,*" Marsalis says. "*Bear witness.*"

"Because that's all that's left?" Kamran asks, voice like a rusty pipe. "*Everyone* who was taken is dead?"

"*None can be saved.*"

"All of my friends…"

"*You will… see.*" Marsalis dips her head. "*I'm sorry.*"

"I didn't want to be the fucking witness!" he cries. "I

wanted to live my own life! Fall in love. *Be* someone."

"Do you want to live?"

"Yes," he says, quietly.

"Come… and live."

Marsalis lifts Mary over one shoulder like a prize kill. Kamran is next, negotiating his way onto the other shoulder so he can face behind. There are a surprising number of handholds available on the alien's back—a few pipe-like structures. He hopes she won't take offense when he clings to them with his only hand.

The trio sets off at a fast clip, each of Marsalis's footfalls further churning Kamran's poor stomach. Maybe the journey will tear something inside him, and he'll bleed out. He'd almost like that, when he thinks of what horrors might await below. There are so many fates worse than death.

He's seen many of them in person.

First in his youth. Now here.

He didn't take in many of his surroundings on the way into this place. The monster dragging him into the strange depths distracted him. It seems safer now that he's willingly going with a different creature, even though it's to the same location.

Kamran tightens his grip, feeling the subtle vibrations of Marsalis's breath. Does she have the drive to reproduce? Could she be tricking him? She claimed to be a scientist. If she worked with these nightmare creatures, what kind of person was she? What could she justify in the name of experimentation?

She saved you so many times, you ingrate, he tells himself, and that sates him until a nagging doubt adds, *for a snack, or perhaps a host.*

This far down, the aluminum-walled corridors stop, replaced by a cavern roof. Their path takes them onto a catwalk, safety lights lining it, sagging electrical cables running overhead. According to Marsalis, this installation and the one on Ghasreh Shab island are somehow connected. That's where Kamran got the scratch that cost him his hand.

They had restored power at that end. If the old Weyland Corp tech is reliable enough, the entire ruin might have illumination.

Though the drip of water is omnipresent, Kamran doesn't see any source—only the vaguely esophageal cave walls, sparkling with moisture. They're in the belly of the beast, now—swallowed. Marsalis clearly knows the way to the hive, though. Every time the path branches, she makes a decision without hesitation. She can sense the hive, maybe smell it.

The cavern widens, becoming big enough to drive a large vehicle with room to spare. To either side of the catwalk, an unknowable drop. They pass a small outbuilding, lit from within by dim work lamps. Dusty terminals line desks beneath grimy windows. It looks like the sort of place where a foreman might dole out assignments. He tries to look inside the little building when he spots a shadow moving on the roof.

"They're following us," he whispers, but receives no answer. Marsalis's typing hand is occupied carrying Mary.

The shadow leaps down onto the catwalk, and Mary lets out a little gasp. Another creature joins, and another, emerging from places Kamran never could've spotted. Instead of the hissing, spitting, furious animals Kamran has seen before, they lope along behind Marsalis like dogs begging for scraps.

Then he remembers…

I'm supposed to be unconscious.

He tries not to look at them directly, not to challenge them. One of them goes up on two legs for a while, its gait almost like a human child with shuffling, unselfconscious strides. Unfettered by hunger, they're like ghosts, floating through the underworld.

The cavern grows bonier, jointed forms emerging beneath damaged safety lighting. The creatures have been busy here, remaking the world in their own distorted image. Still more monsters fall in behind Marsalis in a little parade, appearing to be interested in the newcomer and prizes.

They're welcoming Marsalis inside.

No escape now. He catches Mary's gaze, and her expression is frozen in fear. She's being so brave, for someone who just lost the love of her life. She shuts her eyes tightly as they pass close to one of the creatures hanging from the ceiling. It could simply reach down and pluck her away, if it wished. Yet they continue, unmolested, deeper into the hive.

There's something large pasted to the handrail—a clump of resin like a garbage sack. A leathery shell the size of a small child sits next to it, split open in what looks like the petals of a macabre flower. In the mess of slimy rock, Kamran can only discern a single feature: a mouth agape, teeth blown outward in a mess of gore.

That *was* a person.

"Keep your eyes closed, Mary."

"You, too," she replies.

But there's no way that'll happen. They're about to pass through a field of his coworkers and friends—people who mustn't be erased. If he is forced to survive this, then he'll haul every terrible memory with him.

They pass another body in the slick black resin. Kamran can see enough to recognize Bahman, the friendly line cook from the Ops canteen. The old man toasted his own tea and tobacco leaves. His grandniece has muscular dystrophy, and his mother passed away last year. Bahman's chest hangs open, and his eyes are glazed over in the congealed stillness of death. Given his frozen expression, his last few moments weren't pleasant.

His wife is nearby, head drooping peacefully as if she's nodded off. They had a son, too. Where is he?

The trickle of corpses becomes a forest of bodies, doomed arms protruding from glittering walls. Every lump is a life, a story with a terrible, preventable end. Feverish fingers brush through his hair, a hand sliding past him in the crypt.

Someone alive?

With a jolt, the hand grasps his scalp, and a woman's scream erupts above. Her fingers tangle in his hair like roots—this person isn't about to release him. Not voluntarily. Marsalis tries to pull him away, and it's as if this mystery woman wants to tear his head off.

Marsalis bangs her shovel-headed tail into the woman's thin wrist, and a wet crunch echoes through the cave. Fingers go slack, and a terrified gasp issues above him. She screams again—as do all of the monsters that have gathered around.

Freed from the grip of the colonist, Marsalis takes off down the tunnels.

Kamran hears an Iranian voice fading behind him.

"Please! Let me die."

Some of the monsters stay to attend to their anguished decoration, but far too many of them follow Marsalis, stirred to anger. Kamran doesn't understand why the creatures care so much, until he remembers how they gestate.

Marsalis essentially slapped a pregnant woman.

The creatures clamber along the walls after the three of them, unwilling to let them just walk away. They shriek at Marsalis, as if demanding answers, but receive none that will satisfy. Kamran watches them rile one another up, a feedback loop of rage and accusation. They know something is wrong, and roil about like they're going to attack—but another sound pierces the darkness.

Even at this distant range, the thin electronic chirp is like a rasp on Kamran's eardrum. It bothers the creatures even more, and Marsalis's grip tightens around his back.

Kamran knows that sound. He heard it once before in the Javaher Concourse—acoustic weapons useful for chasing away the aliens.

The Americans have decided to follow them into the hive.

3 2

HELL'S HEART

The M56x Smart Gun harness is a blanket across Kylie's shoulders, a trusted friend. She has a pair of full drums and spares for her longarm—it's a lot easier to outfit a platoon when there isn't much of one left.

Just six marines and one jerkoff scientist.

X-rays circle her squad, pouring from every nook. They want the marines, and clamber over one another to posture and lunge, but the Good Boys render that impossible. It's clear where the effective range of the acoustic cannons ends, though. Demonic jaws lurk in the darkness like Cheshire Cats, sneers glittering.

As long as the marines stay behind the Good Boys, no one has to fire a shot. The bots form a perimeter: two weapon platforms in the front and one to protect their asses. They couldn't get the fourth one operational because of goddamned Percival. Fucker started zeroizing them before he died.

She spits onto the nest like she's spitting on his grave. One of the animals comes charging at her, and a Good Boy slams into it like a linebacker.

"Yes, motherfuckers! Get the fuck back!" she bellows at the ravening horde. Then, she signals Lee. "They're getting balled up. Clear us a path."

Cooper and Lee flood the hallways with their flamethrowers, prompting terrified squeals from the creatures as they flee. Some of the devils catch a light dousing of accelerant, but nothing lethal. It won't do to jam up the pathway with acid, and the walking piranhas tend to shield one another from fire. It's a waste of ammo to shoot at them when they're all bottled up in a corridor, and running out of bullets means certain death.

Matsushita, the obnoxious shit, is critical for success, designating Good Boy tactics from his portable terminal. As he's reminded people too many times, he worked on Michael Bishop's robotics team, and calls the Good Boys "remedial for someone who creates life." So all six marines work to keep him safe.

Private First Class Johnston turns her back on the perimeter—only for a moment—and it's enough to doom the poor fuck. Alien claws tear the pulse rifle from her hands, rake her eyes, and drag her into the horde. It's like watching someone get sucked into an industrial shredder, and the Good Boys only succeed in chasing the fuckers into the gloom with their victim.

Rifles erupt in flame.

"Stop firing, goddamn it!" Kylie shouts. "Matsushita, close that fucking gap! Now!"

The doctor draws the Good Boys near, leaving Johnston to her fate. Kylie and the doctor know enough about x-rays to be aware the private's card is punched. Between the barks of the acoustic cannons, her choked cries fade. Swarming, filthy abominations burrow into every nook and cranny, seeking safety from the robots' sound cannons. Kylie likes the way the x-rays cry when a Good Boy corners one, crushing them like a sonic steamroller. Let those demons have a taste of how it feels to get screamed at.

"How far to the Corpus Maximus?" Kylie calls out.

The Major Body. That's what Dr. Matsushita calls the seat of Hell that awaits them. Latin is a good choice, because only the Catholic tongue could properly summon the blasphemous images to mind. If Charybdis is the mouth, the Corpus Maximus is the stomach. It's where the beasts will have broken down their victims into something more useful.

"Almost there!" Matsushita shouts over the din.

"All right! Get ready to go lethal!" Kylie says. "Oo-rah?"

"*Oo-rah!*" the marines call in an assembled response, clear as day through the thick of battle.

Green lasers drill through the shadows. Kylie switches on her own smart gun designators. Each longarm is capable of taking out several x-rays per second. The designators ensure that the marines each mark unique targets, generating maximum lethality. Her team burns deeper into the nest, like a fuse.

"Up ahead!" Matsushita shouts. "The opening!"

There's a surge of resistance. X-rays are suddenly more willing to face the sound weapons, blocking the way forward with their own paralyzed bodies. The creatures don't care if they're destroyed as long as they protect what lies behind them—the egg chamber.

Kylie signals for them to halt. "Doc, we can't get bogged down in here!" she says. "Power up and punch through. Flamethrowers, *do not* let them get above us!"

Matsushita tightens the straps on his hearing protection. He brought his own, so it actually works. The soldiers take a knee and do what Kylie does—press the ear cups as close to their heads as they can. Matsushita's voice comes over the radio.

"All mute for resonance sweep."

The Good Boys unleash a maximized acoustic assault into the thorny heart of the swarm. Even mildly reflected, the noise shatters Kylie's nerves. In AIT, instructors tested her mettle against tear gas. Full-power sound cannons make tear gas look like a mild vinaigrette.

The bugs go buck wild. Cooper and Lee bring up their incinerators, adding a pair of flaming incentives for them to get the fuck out of the way. Kylie wishes Wallace could've been here to appreciate the sight. The guy was a total pyro.

A gap forms in the alien ranks—a chink in the armor. The first two Good Boys charge the weakened lines of their enemies, batting them aside.

"Push through!" Kylie roars, rising and rushing in behind the bots.

They emerge into the cavern like a football team onto the field. The wicked cathedral soars above, brightly lit by the Good Boys' omnidirectional lamps. Its walls are the color of sweetmeats, with massive, dead faces cut into the rock ceiling. They look human, yet *other* somehow.

A chill runs up Kylie's spine. The x-rays love to desecrate their surroundings, but they haven't covered any of the faces. The humid air stinks like one big chest cavity, innards blown open, bile and shit. She knows the scent of a nest too well—it's not the sort of thing one forgets, and she's been in dozens.

Dripping columns of bodies rise from the ground, faces bent and distorted in agony, chests spent. Arms and legs jut out at all angles. Popped eggs lie everywhere, calcifying like barnacles among the dead. X-rays scrabble up their profane mounds, stepping on heads, snapping bones. They leap from one mockery to the next, following the soldiers' progress like a horde of angry monkeys.

The Good Boys go quiet for a second, unbearable chirping replaced by mechanical clinks and ratcheting. Twin barrels swing out to replace the acoustic cannons.

Kylie's shout echoes in the darkness. "Let's rock!"

No force in the galaxy feels better than the kick of servos aligning one's aim. Kylie sweeps her smart gun over the scene, green laser dot jumping from target to target for pristine kills. Recoil compensators keep the kick down, leaving only the satisfying dazzle of a footlong muzzle flare.

It's like doing a guitar solo, but with a gun.

All told, there are nine computer-controlled, fully automatic weapons in operation: Kylie's, Cooper's two privates', and six sentry SAWs on the Good Boys. Each weapon can put down ten x-rays per minute out in the open, and the Corpus Maximus isn't cramped. Worst case, there might be three hundred x-rays.

Three minutes of fighting, then.

Kylie chops through the enemy, savoring the thunder of her weapon through every inch of her body. Obsidian limbs go spinning off into the darkness. Acid smoke fills the air, eerie in the spotlights. A pair of eggs opens up nearby, and Lee hoses them down with fire.

Fuck your eggs.

Fuck your hive.

One of the creatures comes rocketing out at her, entirely too close. She dodges, putting a salvo into its back.

Fuck you, especially.

With unrelenting fire, Kylie's fighters scour their foes from every surface. X-ray corpses fall on all sides, cut down in huge piles. A ring of dead forms, carapaces splattering and cracking under the impacts of thousands of caseless rounds. Nothing can withstand the might of the Colonial Marines. These bugs may have kicked human asses on a dozen worlds, but that's why the Midnighters exist.

Kylie's soldiers are the conquering inheritors of a legacy that starts on LV-426, at Hadley's Hope.

They're the immune response to this new plague of filth.

But the assault goes on too long. The guitar solo won't end. Cooper's luck runs out first. It's just a light splash of acid, but it's in his eyes—burning into his skull. Flamethrowers have always been a dicey proposition in nest tactics. His training should tell him to let go of his weapon—that he's a danger to himself and others—but Kylie knows he won't do that, because he's always been kind of a selfish prick.

One of the creatures grabs him.

He pulls the trigger in a panic.

No acoustic cannon, no sentry gun, no four-legged freight train is going to stop friendly fireballs. His stream of fuel envelops a private and just like that, one casualty becomes two—taking another smart gun out of the fight.

She spots a fleshy spider among the horde of aliens, almost pink in the cold light of the Good Boys' lamps. The smart guns' sensors are calibrated for chitin, and they won't track the spiders that have hatched to impregnate the marines. Kylie clicks the aim assist off and pegs the thing, leaving only a splatter of acid.

"Watch for facefuckers!" she shouts. "Lee, boil those goddamned eggs! Thermal grenades out!"

"Sir!" he grunts in acknowledgement.

When Kylie asks Sergeant Hubert Lee to unleash carnage, the man knows how to oblige. He hurls incendiary grenades into strategic zones with all the skill of a quarterback, spilling fire over huge sections of the nest. Foul smoke pours from eggs as their contents frantically try to wriggle free. She admires his thoroughness, too. He sweeps a flamethrower up and down the closest shells, grimacing like he's spraying pesticides in a strong wind. Leathery arthropods shiver and roast beneath his baleful fire.

Private Bergman is next—a facehugger gripping his head. His hands go to yank the tail as it whips around his neck, but Kylie has seen enough of these to know how it ends. He was fucked the second it attached.

She knows what she'd want if one of those things got her.

Bergman's friendly fire transponder won't let Kylie shoot him with the smart gun. She rests her rifle and whips out her dad's old pistol. Four shots into Bergman's chest are enough to send him straight into shock.

But the move has cost her time. While she was dealing with her downed comrade, demons have been skittering up the high walls, swarming the roof. One of them sneers down at her.

"Oh, I know that look, you—"

She yanks up her smart gun barrel, spraying and praying. Servos align her aim, zeroing in on her target far too slowly for Kylie's tastes. The creature shatters in midair, bullets beating back chunks as it falls.

A fleck of acid strikes her cheek, and it's like having a nail pushed into her skin. She screams in pain, but keeps her eyes up and gun blazing. She splatters x-ray after x-ray as her eyepiece goes wild, pointing out contacts everywhere.

```
WARNING: BARREL OVER TEMP
```

The trigger still works, so she keeps shooting. Her skull transmits the carbonated sound of acid foaming into her bone. It eats into Kylie's sinus and smoke pours from her nostrils, choking out all air. The drop is like a hot wire, cooking flesh, prodding the itchiest place in her head. When she sneezes, a flap of skin comes loose— probably her fucking nose.

No time to check.

Blood streams through her teeth, syrupy copper coating her tongue. She's had worse—it doesn't hurt half as bad as her jaw did coming off. Her face isn't burning anymore, but her eyepiece blinks insistently with a warning.

```
LOW AMMUNITION
```

Maybe you go home today, after all.

There are so many more of these creatures than she'd expected. They've already killed dozens of x-rays in the conflicts above, but the supply here is unending. The Good Boys' fire support begins to falter. Her smart gun clicks, mags run dry. The torches that keep her alive are going out, and Matsushita can't even keep cover on her.

"Get those bots up front!" She wheels on the doctor.

"What the fuck are you—"

Matsushita is pulling the weapons platforms back, trying to make a break for the exit. He's not retreating—that would be a coordinated strategy deployed to exhaust a foe. He's *running away* in battle, taking resources with him, and officers execute people for that.

The doctor screams when he sees Kylie looking at him. Her face must be pretty fucked up.

Good.

Kylie unclips her spent smart gun, hurling it at one of the onrushing creatures. The beast takes it in the mouth, teeth clacking around the breaching muzzle—but it doesn't stop coming at her. Lee steps in to fry the oily devil on her behalf. The sergeant doesn't even flinch at the sight of her mangled face as he nods toward the fleeing scientist.

"Grease that rat fuck son of a bitch!"

It's technically insubordination for him to yell an order at Kylie, but she'd already been planning on killing Matsushita after they'd cleared the nest. His dereliction just sealed the deal.

"Copy," she says, drawing her pistol and taking aim at the doctor. Her right eye is fucked with smoke, and she's aiming past the lights of the Good Boys. It'll be tricky, but she'd rather have him alive.

She nails him straight through the knee, and he folds up onto the floor screeching, surrounded by his trio of stolen robots. They form a shield around him, backing in to restrict access while they fire.

Kylie spits a mouthful of blood. "Good Boys are in VIP mode! Rally on Matsushita."

The first of the three weapons platforms goes silent, magazine spent, then charges off into the pack of x-rays. Good Boys fight to the last, even if it means using their own bodies. It plows through Xenomorphs like a bull, leading a whole pack on a chase as they try to kill it.

The remaining two bots adjust tactics to conserve ammo. One acts as a battering ram, wreaking havoc at mid-range, and the other fires in support.

Despite the durable carriage and power plant, however, nothing can withstand punishment from a pack of x-rays. When they finally fell the charging mechanical beast, they swarm and attack, ripping hydraulic hoses free from its joints and squealing with delight.

Kylie tosses a grenade at the group, and one of the x-rays catches it. Several of the others stop their ravaging of the Good Boy carcass to focus on Kylie and bare their teeth.

Thank God they're stupid.

The deafening thunder of the explosion is only opposed by the silence of the other two bots' sentry guns. Ammo reserves depleted, the remaining pair dash into the fray to sacrifice themselves.

The x-rays are starting to thin out, but not fast enough. Kylie needs a weapon, and the closest gun is with Private Bergman, facefucker quivering in satisfaction on his head. Kylie detaches the smart gun from Bergman's corpse and clips it into her own harness. Her eyepiece loads up data through the armature, and she finds a decent reserve of bullets. A squeeze of the trigger brings the weapon to life, blasting a few more x-rays to tatters.

The remaining two Good Boys make a valiant effort to bash their enemies to pieces, but in the end, the bugs are victorious. Kylie's fireteam focuses down, cutting into the clumped-up herd with everything they've got—

Two guns and a flamethrower.

She turns to see if that's really all that remains of the once-proud Midnighters, just in time to see Private Atchison take a full-force hit from an x-ray. He crumples in half, rifle going silent as he bounces to the ground. Poor kid looks like he got run over.

It's not a prayer on Kylie's lips, just a litany of "fuck yous" at anything she can shoot. There isn't a place she can look that doesn't have a goddamned x-ray crawling out of it. Kylie retreats to Lee, waves of heat from his flamethrower a reassurance that he yet lives. She can safely unload on the horde of demons, assured that if one kills her from behind, it had to come through her gunnery sergeant first.

I signed up to be a legend.

A hole forms in the enemy ranks, a pinprick of hope. She keeps shooting. Their numbers thin, acid smoke billows through the blighted cavern, and more chunks of bug hit the ground. They pile up like crab shells in the corners.

Kylie howls for glory, taking all comers. The bastards won't wait their turns, and her reflexes are tested again and again by the monsters' lightning-fast lunges. Even with the computer controlling the fine details, choosing the right targets takes everything she has. One slip, one tiny mistake, and she'll be dragged off like the others.

People don't understand what it means to be the tip of the spear. She's not simply the cutting edge. She's the pinnacle, the apex of what a Colonial Marine should be. She's a point so fine that it'll pierce everything in its way, an American singularity. Bloodsoaked and screaming through a ruined face, Kylie has never felt so pure.

Her smart gun buzzes an alarm and stops firing. Two words appear on her eyepiece, blinking insistently.

```
NO TARGETS
RETRIG TO FIRE
```

She has to make herself let go of the trigger. Ragged breaths spill from her chest as she jerks her barrel back and forth, scanning. Her head shakes like she's saying no. Lee is still behind her.

"Clear!" he calls.

She can't smell or taste; she can barely breathe. Her fucking nose is probably missing and there's a bullet-sized hole in her cheek. On the flip side, there have got to be several hundred x-ray carcasses in this room.

She stood against them all, and survived.

"Clear!" she replies. She sounds pathetic, like she has a cold. "My fucking face—"

"I know—"

"Fuck, this hurts!" she says. "I need surgery!"

"Try not to touch it," he rumbles. "… sir."

"I wasn't touching it."

Flames lick the columns of the dead. Somewhere in the distance, a man cries out in pain. There are still tangoes hatching in this nest, enemy combatants yielding up their pink worms for future battles.

Matsushita whimpers nearby, reminding Kylie of his existence. What a terrible mistake that was.

"I'm sorry," he says, crawling in the dirt. X-ray corpses litter the path he must take, blocking any possible escape.

"You're about to be," Kylie says, grinning at him through a curtain of blood. It stings like a motherfucker to hold that expression, but the look on his face is priceless. He definitely regrets his life decisions. She rolls the geek over and settles down beside him, resting her elbows on her knees. Her blood dribbles onto his hands, and he flinches as if it'll burn him.

"I'm bonded for a return to Earth. Insured, like a bounty," he says. "Two million. You and Sergeant Lee can split it."

Staring at him, drooling crimson, expression wild, is so much more satisfying than anything she could possibly say. She searches his eyes. If she looks hard enough, maybe she can find the scared little boy he once was.

"What do you want?" he begs. "Why aren't you talking?"

She cocks her head and frowns.

"I…" He opens his mouth a few times as he cycles through excuses. "I craft wonders for Michael Bishop. You know how important he is. What he can *do*. W-when we get to Earth, you get two million and a nice face. Anything you want."

Reaching down, Kylie slowly wraps her fingers into his collar and rises to her feet. He moans when he's forced to put weight on his leg, so she punches him until he shuts his scream hole. Eventually, he learns to be a team player, and lets her stand him up on his good foot.

"Please," he says. "I can make you beautiful again."

She slowly spreads her arms wide, soaked in her own purified blood. "I have never been more beautiful in my whole life."

"Captain! Trackers have picked up movement," Lee says. "Three tangoes, headed further in."

"Marsalis and the witnesses," Kylie breathes, never breaking eye contact with Matsushita, and he gives an almost imperceptible nod.

"P-probably," he replies. "Don't hurt her. Please."

Kylie's shoulders shake with quiet laughter. She spits a long tendril of bloody saliva to the ground. "We fell in love with them, didn't we? We saw those demons and thought, 'I want to dedicate my life to you.'"

He brightens with hope, weeping tears of joy. "Exactly!" He thinks she understands him, and he's clearly grateful. She leans in and whispers in his ear, her burst nostril making a sick sucking noise.

"I'm going to crack her open like a crab, and find out if x-ray meat can be cooked."

"Captain." Lee walks up, holding a scavenged pulse rifle. She takes the weapon, still staring deeply into Matsushita's tearful eyes, and it's like she can read his thoughts. He's scared that she's going to shoot him like she did the contractor cunt. But Cheyenne Hunt only backhanded Kylie—in combat, even, so it barely counts.

By contrast, Matsushita believed he'd suborned her, with his fancy medical degree and robotics division. Millions if not billions of dollars somehow gave him the right to talk to her like he owned her. All of his assumptions have left Kylie with a question.

"Who's the bitch now?"

"I'm sorry," he says.

She shakes her head no. He can't be sorry enough.

"Time to burn in this Hell, sinner."

She kicks him as hard as she can. He's spry for a dude who just took a round to the kneecap, and tries to compensate with a pair of one-legged hops before falling. He lands across a pile of broken x-rays, fluorescent yellow blood pooled along every ridge and fold.

He hits hard enough to splash, and the scream is like breaking glass. He flounders in terror, trying to get away, but stumbles along the slick mound of corpses, sinking deeper. His flesh is steaming. Every movement covers more of him in rich, clinging acid.

His leg disconnects at the knee as he tries to push back

from the pile, tendons snapping, and Kylie laughs as loudly as she can. Let it be the last thing he hears. Bones poke through thinning flesh. Muscles cook like ceviche. It probably takes Sora Matsushita two minutes to die, but his screams are a memory to treasure for a lifetime.

Kylie licks her coppery lips as she watches the last light of a soul fade from his body.

"Sir," Lee says gently.

He comes up beside her slowly, but he needn't have worried. Kylie could never hurt perfect, wonderful Lee, the only person who knows how to do his fucking job. Thank God he's still standing, because if anyone deserves to make it through this, it's him. He's holding his own scavenged rifle, along with Matsushita's tracker.

"Sir, we need to go if we're going to catch up."

"You need to learn how to slow down and enjoy life, Sergeant."

"We'll grab beers after we bag this terrorist, sir."

She imagines waking up on the *Benning*, a bandage over her throbbing nose. In this vision, she's high as a kite on painkillers, and somehow still smells bacon without her nose.

She's missed bacon so very much.

"Then oo-rah, Sergeant."

3 3

VAULT OF HEAVEN

When the snatchers attack, Marsalis slings Kamran and Mary to the ground. Kamran wants to find somewhere to hide, but which dark, foreboding holes are the safe ones? There's a brief respite, long enough for Marsalis to tap out a word.

"*Run.*"

The animals nip and tear at their old master, attempting to slow Marsalis down. Their vicious claws rake over the royal crest of interlocking bones, shredding scales. Kamran wonders what it is that drives them to such savagery.

He grabs Mary and pulls her along, skirting the edge of the fight to get to clearer air. Neither of them is fit to run any marathons, but they keep moving as fast as they can. Mary clutches her chest, and Kamran tries not to imagine having to give her CPR down here. If she collapses, maybe he can just hang onto the nice warm old lady until they're both dead. That's probably the best use of his remaining moments of life.

The caverns narrow again before opening onto an underground river. Human cocoons are sparse here—lone resin sacs like pustules on the landscape, instead of the many-layered boils of rooms past. Dim blue light suffuses the walls, brighter where the resin is thicker. Maybe algae? They're down beneath Charybdis now; all manner of strange aquatic life could've leaked inside. He shudders to think of what this nest is doing to the ecosystem.

Behind them the sounds of fighting diminish, yet others persist further back.

The marines…

After he and Mary limp through a narrow opening, the galaxy opens up above them. Blooms of algae coat a distant ceiling, throbbing veins crawling across the rock's wet surface. More mountainous faces leer down at them with distorted human features. Not one hair graces their foreboding heads. Jet-black eyes bulge like onyx marbles, and oily tears leak from the base of their lids.

These black rivulets collect on noses and lips, spilling over chins and necks into channels. Cuts in the rock guide the fluid down the walls of the cave, where the goo merges into a mirrored lake. The black liquid eats the light from above, and he thinks of the worms wriggling inside his finger.

Is this what Weyland was studying?

"*Touch.*" Marsalis's harsh word nearly stops Kamran's

heart. He looks back, and the lightning of Marsalis's knuckles announces her presence. She's still alive after the fight, but what emerges from the shadows is the beaten ghost of a former glory.

"... *nothing.*"

On instinct, Kamran rushes to help, but Marsalis hisses. Only then does he see the many dripping cuts. Most are new, but others are hours old, crusty and yellow like corroded battery contacts. They ooze and dribble, opened up by the tangle in the tunnel.

"*Don't touch... me,*" the mechanical voice says. "*Acid blood.*"

"Sorry," he says, voice barely a whisper. He's amazed his throat will make noise at all after the choking he took.

"That black stuff isn't water, is it?" Mary asks, hand tightening around Kamran's.

Marsalis's fingers flicker blue. "*Pathogen. Deadly. Bad.*"

"Pathogen," Kamran repeats. "Like the reason you bit off my arm?"

"*Exactly.*"

Kamran wants to faint when he looks out over the dark surface; it's an entire lake, and his body is like one big open wound. Even if the oil is only ankle deep, how is he supposed to cross it without touching it?

Marsalis clicks her fist together three times, and the blue rings on her fingers go bright white. After the darkness of the hive, Kamran flinches at the tiny torch. Now that he can see, however, there's an old catwalk, frosted with rust, jutting from the slick surface of the lake. It's not particularly high—barely enough to keep someone from touching the oil.

The path runs out over the liquid, toward what looks like an island. At this range it's impossible to make out any details, and Kamran contemplates whether it's such a great idea to go over there. Back the way they came, the clamor of the soldiers' fever-pitched battle dims, then goes silent.

"Did the aliens eat them?" Mary whispers.

"It doesn't matter who won," Kamran replies. "We'll lose."

Marsalis steps onto the catwalk, lit knuckles held aloft for Kamran and Mary. Metal judders at the new weight; cables sing their complaints. The alien gestures for Kamran to follow her across.

"Sorry, but I don't have any coins for you," he says, stepping up onto the grate. Marsalis snorts—a laugh, perhaps—then turns and stalks away down the catwalk. Mary joins him, a hand on his good shoulder.

Traversing the wide expanse reminds Kamran of his first space walk, back in graduate school. The others made fun of him for his amateurish handling of an EVA suit. *Their* parents had taken them into space in primary school. He hadn't left Earth before advancing in nuclear chemistry.

It'd been terrifying to drift among the stars, falling in every direction. The emptiness of a vast galaxy had been surprisingly oppressive until he'd gotten used to it. But this place is somehow deeper than space. He stands above a void so virulent that it could consume every part of him with just a touch, and beneath the disquieting gaze of weeping stone gods.

How did they work above this madness for almost three years?

Xenoarchaeologists call someone's first exposure to alien cultures the "depersonalization effect," the sudden recognition that the universe isn't human, or *for* humans. These strange blasphemies remind Kamran that civilization is an illusion—that time has long existed without it. Kamran is just a collection of chemicals—an unnoticed spark in the galactic timeline, as random as the next blip of a species. When he dies, he will be forgotten, because he is meaningless.

The catwalk growls in the quiet, mountings tested for the first time in years. Shapes of anti-light spread in the bottomless void—there's an island in the middle of the reflecting pool. Marsalis's dim globe of illumination brings its features into focus.

It's a sloping bowl, like an amphitheater for a djinni orchestra. A ridge of spikes rises at the back like a row of Italian cypresses. A short rock wall encircles the island, and a pair of gnarled columns flank the entrance. Uneven grids of wires and pipes appear here and there in the bone-white surface, pulling at the skin like they've been stitched into it. The catwalk passes directly between the columns.

Weyland must've built the pathway, but why?

"What is this place?" Kamran asks, not really expecting an answer. Marsalis's voice is pulling double-duty as their lantern.

There's a flash.

Streaks of tracer fire whiz past Kamran's face, and he instinctively drops to the grating. A volley smashes across Marsalis's ribcage, bullets chopping into chitin with a hollow *thunk*. The alien's screech is gurgling and truncated, and she topples from the catwalk, taking the light with her.

Kamran braces for a splash of pathogen. There is none.

"Are you okay?" he asks Mary. She's still behind him, holding his only hand.

"I'm fine!"

He tries to call out. "Marsa—" More gunfire erupts from the distant end of the bridge. Grenades explode across the ceiling, showering them with rock—

—a lot of which splashes into the pathogen.

Get off the catwalk.

Unsteadily, Kamran regains his feet and rushes forward. More bodies have been pasted into the steps of the amphitheater like trophies, but he can't discern the details. He lets go of Mary's hand and scampers around the edge of the rock wall, diving behind cover to hug the ground.

His eyes adjust again to the glow of the algae. Resin deposits jut from the floor like stalagmites, along with empty eggshells. Mary rustles nearby, but Kamran doesn't call out for fear of attracting attention. Beside his face, there's a faint shine: a man's bald head. Kamran has taken cover beside a corpse. More gunfire chews off the top of the column nearby, and Kamran shoves up against the body. Mary screams, then stops. Abruptly. Either she's been hit, or some of the pathogen has gotten into her system.

Hot breath tickles his hair, and his stomach drops. The man cocooned beside Kamran is alive, stirring.

You can't help him, but he can give away your position.

Pushing away from the doomed man, Kamran moves deeper into the island's turning folds. It's a small labyrinth, but the shapes are more organic, like the knots of a brain. The walls are too short; if he stands, Kamran will be exposed, so he stays low. Somewhere nearby, Mary whimpers. As a contractor she was annoying, but now Kamran wishes he could pull her in close and tell her it'll be okay.

Flashlight beams sweep across the island, revealing the shocked faces of the cocooned. Boots echo on the catwalk grating—two soldiers coming his way, steps slow and methodical.

Bullets chop through his cover, and rock dust pelts Kamran's shoulders and scalp. They're taking pot shots to flush him out. The stone does nothing but obscure him. He wants to get up and run, but then the soldiers will see him for sure. If he runs, he's dead.

Mary, please stop crying.

"Don't shoot," she whimpers in the darkness, and both flashlights sweep in that direction. "You don't have to shoot."

Kamran cannot imagine growing up in a world where he can simply ask a soldier not to shoot him. Mary has probably never faced anything like this before. Her plea strikes him as a rich American thing to do, like she was playing tag and could simply give up the game at the last minute. It's a relationship to authority so innocent that she's still trying to count on it.

Kamran hopes it works. He'd like her to live. She turned out to be such a nice old lady.

The voice that answers Mary might've belonged to a woman once, but it's the property of something ghoulish now.

"Stand up, then," it replies, disturbingly close. They're almost across the catwalk, taking their time, being cautious.

"Your momma should've slapped you more," Mary says, and it breaks Kamran's heart when he hears her whisper Jerry's name.

You can't help her if they catch you, he tells himself. *Find a way to blend in.* Kamran rolls onto his back so at least he'll see it coming, then goes still as death. After all, he's in the perfect spot to camouflage himself—among the corpses. If he doesn't move, maybe the hunters won't be able to tell him apart from all the other dead. He can use Mary as bait, attack from behind and then...

Be murdered.

He's not working with much, and those are trained killers coming for him. If he doesn't help Mary, they might shoot her and leave the scene. Maybe he could find his way out on his own, but he'd be less than a human for it.

Two silhouettes come into view—the soldiers, traced by distant algae blooms. Each carries a gun with a flashlight on the tip. There's something wrong with the smaller one, the woman. Kamran can't make out a lot of detail, but it looks like her front is covered in something black. It has to be blood. She might be the Captain Duncan that Becker talked about.

She stops next to Kamran's trench and throws a couple of quick hand signals to her comrade. The mountain of a man keeps going. Kamran blinks, and the skinny soldier freezes like a bloodhound. She couldn't have seen him—she wasn't looking his way, and he's in almost perfect shadow.

Did she *hear* him blink?

"Lee," she says, voice gurgling.

What the fuck is she?

The woman sweeps her light over his trench, and the beam wilts every vein in his being. Maybe he blended in. Maybe she won't see him. He catches a glimpse of her face: mangled with wild eyes.

God save me.

"Are you fucking—" She coughs, then spits out a wad of phlegm. "—serious?"

Please don't be looking at me.

"That's the problem with your kind." The soldier cracks a wide smile, teeth bright white in a mangled face. "So lazy."

Don't blink, don't flinch, don't breathe.

The beam of her flashlight blinds Kamran. He can't lift a single limb to try and escape. The other guy comes over and points his flashlight down.

"Pathetic."

They chased him into a mass grave where he laid down and *waited*. He should've known he didn't have what it took to survive something like this. He's just been living on the competence of others.

"I don't like to waste bullets," the man says. "There might be more bugs out there."

"Watch the goo," she growls. "If we haven't seen a corpse, Marsalis isn't dead." She still talks with a human cadence, whatever she is. At least they haven't shot Kamran yet, which he's taking as a good sign.

"Well, waste not, want not."

The woman slings her rifle and tugs at something on her belt. The silvery shine of a knife catches Kamran's eye.

She steps off the catwalk, and into the trench with him.

"Here, piggy, piggy," she gurgles.

INTERLUDE: HAROUN

Banu is dead.

A thousand years have passed since yesterday. Haroun drifts between sleep and waking in this nightmare pit. Every time he nods off, he prays it will be the last. Every time he returns to consciousness, he's reminded that none of his other prayers have been answered.

He witnessed Banu's last seconds from his helpless vantage point on the ground. One moment, she'd been the golden thread connecting him with any semblance of happiness, and the next, she was clipped. What those animals did to her was unspeakable—but Haroun now knows what depths lie beyond words.

He was dragged, beaten and bloody, over countless steps.

Lashed to the wall.

Violated.

When he first awoke, there were eight other people with him. Those who screamed were broken, but those who stayed silent weren't spared. All the colonists became hosts to demented parasites. Haroun saw and heard how the others died—used up shells for the pink worms. He knows what's coming for him.

Gunfire pierces his nightmare.

Strange.

Perhaps he doesn't know after all.

Haroun tries to open his eyes, but they're not cooperating. His voice is gone after all the screaming he did. Even if it's the ICSC defense forces, they're too late to help him. He'll be "hatching" any moment now, so he sighs and closes his eyes, trying to get back to sleep like a bear curling up for winter.

Come forth, little bug. Let me be done.

This life wasn't worth living.

Something *thunks* down beside him, shocking Haroun out of his slumber. Hair brushes past his face before a person clambers over him. There's panic in their breathing; they're fleeing. The person pushes against him, bony and long.

Kamran?

Haroun is about to die, and he must suffer the indignity of being a rug for his worst employee. More feeling returns to Haroun's arms and legs, and he considers giving Kamran a good shove. His limbs are mostly free. He managed to break them loose back when escape seemed plausible—before he'd realized that it didn't matter, and he'd die all the same.

He blinks. Did he fall asleep again?

"Pathetic." It's a man's voice.

Haroun lazily looks up to find the source—Captain Duncan's interrogator, Sergeant Lee. He's pointing his gun at Kamran, like he's about to put down a cow.

Fuck you.

Adrenaline surges in Haroun as something twitches in his gut. The thing inside him is waking up, but he feels… alert. Everything hurts, returning to life after hours of trying to die. His mind screams as if he's back in the reclamation of Bandar Abbas, mortars striking all around.

A sudden plummet in blood pressure causes his head to droop, coating it with a thin sheen of cold sweat. He's about to nod off again.

Something is happening.

Stay awake.

"Well, waste not, want not." Even though the voice is mangled, Haroun recognizes the source. She's the one who had him "interrogated."

Duncan.

Her soldiers committed this atrocity, not the aliens. As their commanding officer, she set the monsters loose on Banu. Haroun cranes his neck to get a better look as she steps down into the trench, knife drawn. She's so close, only a pace or two more…

A strength beyond his own surges through Haroun's limbs, and he grabs onto her legs. With a surprised shout, the captain falls into his grasp. He yells at her, the sound guttural and savage. Pawing and tripping, hampering her from getting away. His heart thunders as he presses the advantage, yanking her by the belt.

He's going to choke this dog's life out.

She wheels on him with a flicker of steel, slicing across his face hard enough to ping his cheekbone. It hurts, but not as much as he'd expect. Everything is pain. Getting stabbed changes little. He must not let go of her—he's tied down. If she gets away, it's over.

Drawing her hand back, Duncan plunges the knife into his ribs, knocking the air from his lungs. He cannot take another breath, but that's all right. To die would be a blessing—after he finishes one last chore.

Haroun hauls her in close, adrenaline at maximum. The beast inside his belly presses on his intestines like a shit made of razor blades. He intertwines his arms with Duncan's, pinning her body against his in a tight embrace. She tries to draw out the knife, but he won't let her pull away.

When she snarls, he headbutts her, eliciting a pained howl. His muscles burn. He's running out of blood, and he's not sure he can hold her—but he has one weapon. The worm begins to eat its way out, renewing his agony, recharging his grip.

A commotion erupts behind Duncan, somewhere he can't see. Her sergeant is in a fight, but with whom? There's a sloshing of liquid, pulse rifle fire, and a man's screams. Alien screams, too.

Sorry, Kamran, but if you're lucky, those things will eat you when I die.

Haroun can't worry about that. The worm stretches his belly, pressing his gut against Duncan's. She shrieks, showering him with blood and spit, but he has experienced so many worse things in the past twenty-four hours. She bites him across the bridge of the nose, yanking her head back and forth like a wild dog.

He won't let go for anything.

"You took my daughter," he says, forcing the words past the barricade of blood in his windpipe. "Let me introduce you to my second child."

The glorious animal strains his insides, shoving and clawing his abdominal cavity. It's almost through him—into her. Duncan headbutts him much harder than anything he's doled out.

Then again.

And again.

He loses his grip after the third strike, just as the worm explodes from inside. It squeals from his chest cavity, far from where he'd intended it to go. Light fades at the edges of Haroun's vision. His arms fall to his sides, and he's amazed at how peaceful he feels in the face of his worst failure. Why should he be surprised? Everything else has been a disappointment.

Duncan staggers onto her feet, huffing and glancing around. She mocks a frown.

"Sorry, buddy, but you just didn't—"

Kamran smashes into her like a rugby player.

In Newtonian fashion, he stops.

She doesn't.

Kamran's elated expression is beautiful to Haroun. Whatever just happened, he's really happy about how it turned out.

Not my worst employee after all.

3 4

A BELL RINGS

Right before the collision, Kamran realizes he's going to hit on his stump side.

So be it.

When he smashes into Captain Duncan, it's with the force and conviction of hundreds of lives—friends and colleagues. Kamran comes in low and explodes upward, leveraging his full height to knock her off-balance. Quick on the draw, she tries to grab Kamran's hand, but it's missing.

He would cut it off again just to see the look on her stupid face.

Shock.

Horror.

An instant later, black ooze swallows her whole.

A pink worm screams and snaps up at him from the nearby corpse, and Kamran scrambles backward. He thought he heard Haroun's voice before, and he finally recognizes his old boss. The worm hisses and shoots off into the trenches to hide.

Be sated. Please don't follow me.

Kamran rushes to Mary, who clutches her forearm. It's leaking blood, and he wants to press something to it to stop the bleeding, but what's clean? What's safe? If there's a speck of pathogen on their clothes, and they rub it into a cut...

"I'm okay," she sobs. "Are they dead?"

He nods.

"What about the monsters?" she asks.

"I don't know."

"Marsalis?"

During the exchange, Marsalis burst out of the lake, onto Lee. Kamran didn't see what happened—just heard gunfire. The alien isn't moving. Whatever remains of the soldier has been thoroughly doused in tar and acid. His rifle lies nearby, flashlight shining back on the grim tableau.

Regardless of what he wants to do, Kamran can't help Marsalis move. She dripped with acid before, but she's a biohazard now. Pathogen pours from her in long slugs, congealed chunks flopping to the ground before dissolving into puddles.

"Are you alive?" Kamran's creaking voice echoes in the gloom. There's no point in going on ahead without Marsalis. He doesn't know the way out, and even if he did, how is he supposed to access the *Blackstar*?

A little flash of blue pierces the shadow. Then another.

Three barking sounds come from the speaker.

"Y… E… S…" Sludge muffles the grate, and the distortion has grown worse, but the letters are clear enough.

"Are you okay?"

The alien attempts to rise, and it's as if Lee's corpse is stuck to her. The soldier's remains peel away in slimy chunks, half-dissolved, bits wriggling and animated that really shouldn't be.

"N." Marsalis taps one letter, huffing breaths whistling through her teeth. "Not… okay."

"How can I help?" Kamran positions himself unsteadily on the sloping bowl of the profane island.

"Can't."

With a hiss her head twitches to one side, and she painfully lumbers in place. Where before, Marsalis was deadly and lithe, the alien has grown sluggish. She settles down onto all fours like a cat, but it's more likely that she can't hold up her own weight.

"Not…" The voice rings in the cavern.

Kamran turns to look in the direction of Marsalis's gaze—the place where Duncan fell.

"… dead."

A shuddering, oily hand rises above the lip of the island. Blue glints are the only hints of detail, algae light tracing a human form as it lifts itself from the ichor. A single drop of the stuff was enough to reduce Kamran to screaming, and Duncan has been coated in it.

A pair of white eyes snap open in the sludge.

"Shayatin," Kamran murmurs.

Duncan's outline begins to boil, and the figure staggers forward. Chunks of flesh fall from her like leaves—pustules exploding all over the soldier's dissolving form. When Duncan opens her mouth to scream, a large sac spills out, beige and glistening. The killer goes to her knees, eyes rolling back in her head. Her body seems to crumple in on itself.

Something is crawling all over her, Kamran realizes. It's not one sac bursting; it's hundreds. The largest wet lump on the ground twists and turns, blooming like a flower as a creature cuts its way out from inside. There must be many more that Kamran cannot see. Their shrieks begin in unison, dozens of variations, like perverse jungle birds.

He should probably run.

A flashlight beam floods the scene, illuminating a menagerie of fleshy abominations—half-formed mockeries of their chitinous cousins, larval and veinous white, with hideous little mouths. The largest of them unfurls from its spent birthing caul, tiny throat clicking angry chirps as it searches for the target of its ire. It's only about the size of a house cat, but it slips and slides in the puddle of pathogen, bile, and blood.

If it touches Kamran, he dies.

A barrage of automatic fire rips the mass of creatures into a smoking acidic pile. They writhe and wail, but more bullets cut them down until nothing moves.

Kamran turns to find Mary holding Lee's rifle, panting, eyes wide. Her legs are spread in a shooter's stance—she definitely knows how to hold a gun. The weapon shakes in her hands; she must've run into the splash area to get it.

"Put the gun down, Mary," he says. "It might be contaminated."

She flips a switch and gently places the gun on the rock. Kamran clambers over to her, checking as best he can in the available light for any goo.

"I didn't know you could shoot," he says.

"I'm from Texas."

"We have to leave this place. We've already touched too much."

"'Thanks for killing the monsters, Mary,'" she says, giving him a sidelong glance, and he smiles.

It feels so odd to smile.

"Thanks for killing the monsters, Mary."

"*Follow... path... exactly...*" The mechanical voice rings out behind them. "*I am... coming.*"

"Marsalis..." Kamran starts, but he's not sure what to say.

"*Not... dying here,*" Marsalis says. "*Just... need... time.*"

"We'll be waiting," Mary says, offering a hand to Kamran.

She helps him across the span of catwalk connecting the island to the far shore. They reach a cylindrical tunnel with a long, gentle rise, similar to the esophagus that led them here. Kamran feels a change in the pit of his stomach as he takes a step upward—Hasanova's gravity has decided to let him slip through its grasp.

He's climbing.

They come upon a steel airlock door affixed in the rock. Its powered control panel is corroded and cracked, but there's a nice big "PUSH TO EXIT" button for quick egress. No PIN code or locks required on this side.

They pass through a Weyland-era quarantine chamber. Nozzles—far too corroded to operate—dot the metal walls and floor. What chemicals did they spray? Do they kill the pathogen? Kamran isn't sure, but he's not about to waste time digging in old access panels.

Further along, they locate a locker with a couple of white jumpsuits bearing the Weyland Corp logo.

"Use that to stop your bleeding," Kamran says, pointing to the fabric. "It's the only clean thing around."

She nods and gets to work.

They find a few sealed bottles of water, and Mary opens one to wash her hands. She helps him do the same, and it's a long time before his olive skin is visible again under the blood and dirt.

"We shouldn't be wasting time on this," he says. "There could be more."

"Hush, sweetheart. We can't take off without Marsalis—can't defend ourselves, either. Taking a minute to wash your hands won't change anything."

Aside from the gentle breathing of distant Charybdis and the spatter of bottled water on tile, no other sounds trouble them. They wash up, dry their hands on the old jumpsuits, and Mary binds her wound with one. The dressing is comically oversized, not professional at all, but it should keep the bleeding down. Upon finishing, they leave through the far door.

The air in the next room is offensively musty, the sort of atmosphere that might grow legionella. There are a couple of fans designed to push air up a titanic ramp cut into the rock, but the engines higher in the structure are broken. This place is dangerously stagnant—if they stay down here for long, they'll develop headaches, weakness, nausea, dementia. It might take hours, but it could certainly kill.

Then again, the musty scent might be hiding carbon monoxide or hydrogen sulfide, and they'll be dead in minutes.

Industrial lights—too broken or dim to pass any safety inspection—illuminate a huge cargo funicular. With a platform half the size of a football pitch, the spacious ramp could hold large vehicles. A control console juts up from one side of the platform, lit by a single amber lamp. If it doesn't work, they're not going to be able to climb out of this dank hole.

"Those fans shouldn't be running on twenty-K breakers," Mary says. "Too low voltage to be handling this... this kind of air volume." Her face falls, and she scowls at the ground. "Jerry is going to..." She doesn't finish the sentence.

She just holds her forearm, growing bitter at the wound.

"We can't stay down here long unless we can get them blowing," Kamran says, trying not to cough. He probably has pneumonia by now.

"Let's... go."

The alien limps into the lift room, body a ragged mess. She leaves smoking ruts in her wake, the steel floor eaten by a mixture of the goo and acidic blood. Kamran and Mary are careful to give her a wide berth, though Kamran wishes he could touch her, pat her on the back somehow—let her know he appreciates everything she's done.

"What can we do?" Mary asks.

Marsalis drags across the thick steel plates to one corner of the lift car, where she curls into a tight bundle, encircled by her tail like barbed wire.

"Start the lift."

So, with a prayer, Kamran walks to the console and tries pressing a few buttons. Though the lamps are weak, they flicker to life. There are only two stops—top and bottom—so at least the system isn't too complicated.

"All aboard," he says, hopeful that's the case. Unknown stowaways are guaranteed to be the stuff of nightmares. Kamran throws the switch, and gears grind. It takes a moment, but the car begins to rise at an angle, jerking at first. This equipment probably hasn't been inspected in several decades, and if the car falls, it'll turn into several hundred tons of debris. *Better than dying in the nest, at least.*

The funicular isn't a quick vehicle, nor is it quiet. The

creatures lurking down in the ruins are certain to hear the trio's ascent, and can come after them if they choose. Kamran has seen the monsters scale any surface. The ramp shaft has ample handholds. If anything follows, it will snatch him easily.

As the old car grinds its way up, Kamran regards Marsalis closely. Any twitch of her head could be an indicator of a coming threat. He has no doubt her finely tuned senses, even in this wounded state, will outperform his.

The longer he stares, however, the more he wonders if Marsalis is moving at all.

The ascent takes forever, and Kamran steps away from the console to check on his companion. Mary stands close to the alien, too, unafraid of the dark liquid coating her form.

"Mary, be careful not to touch our friend," Kamran says, coughing. His voice is stronger now, at least, able to carry past a whisper. "You saw what the black stuff did to that soldier."

"But we can't just…" She doesn't finish, and holds her arms in close like it's a vigil. To Marsalis, she says, "You're almost home, sweetheart."

Tap. A single chord.

"*I…*"

The two of them wait a long time for the next words, but it's not like they have somewhere to be. Only Marsalis's hand moves, fingers softly tapping against the elevator's steel plates, the rest of her body statue-still. Over the seconds, a sentence forms.

"Thought I could change things."

Kamran looks away, watching the passing lights fall behind them.

"Save people."

They don't speak anymore after that, and the funicular's car comes grinding to a halt. He and Mary wait for Marsalis to rise.

She doesn't.

"You've saved two," Mary says. "Please get up. You can do it."

Slowly, Marsalis uncoils from her tight bundle and begins to crawl. Kamran and Mary begin to walk. With shredded lips set in a scowl, Marsalis follows in their footsteps, out of the elevator and into a gloomy hallway.

"That's it," Mary says. "We're so close to the ship."

"Perhaps in your med bay," Kamran adds, "you can—" Then he realizes what a rash assumption he's made. What if nothing can be done? For that matter, what if they can't locate the ship?

At long last, he begins to recognize his surroundings. They pass the lab where he lost his arm. Everything is as the security team left it. When he looks behind him, Marsalis is turned toward the lab, too. What's going through her mind? Regret? If she hadn't saved him, she might've escaped.

The air grows crisp and cool, carrying the mild tang of Lake Peacock. A slice of light opens ahead of them in the shape of an exterior door, and it takes a few blinks to realize—

This is sunlight.

It's morning on the lake. They emerge to stand upon the shattered rusty pumice of a windy hillside. In another life, Kamran walked this path with Shy. If he'd resisted then, would she be alive now? Would everyone?

No, Kamran can't lay all of this death at his own feet. Any vengeful spirits will have to accept Duncan's blood as payment.

Clouds resolve in his vision, heavenly palaces rimed with the light of a golden sunrise. The sky deepens beyond into a wide basin of blue. Out here, in the center of Ghasreh Shab, there is only rock, the breeze, and the distant lap of waves. Even the sigh of Charybdis has vanished from their awareness. Kamran spots a glint in the upper atmosphere, a fleck of steel.

Perhaps the *Benning*?

If they can just make it to the *Blackstar*, he and Mary have the possibility of a future off this world. The trio clamber along the ridge line, careful not to slip down the loose embankment. Kamran finds balancing a lot more difficult now, but he navigates the treacherous ground until the *Blackstar* comes into view.

Almost there.

He breaks into a staggering run, kicking up volcanic dust as he goes. When he comes within a dozen paces of the ship's closed ramp, he falls to his knees.

The ship is covered in burnt resin. Knowing what he does now, he understands what was wrong with the vessel—it's a mobile nest. These bugs burrow into people like parasites into prey, and he's about to willingly go into another hive. Kamran begins laughing, and for the first time in hours, the world doesn't echo it back like a mockery.

"Kamran," Mary calls, and he looks to find her pointing at their companion.

Marsalis picks her way across the open field of detritus. Each footfall gets more precarious, every step must be planned. Like an ancient wind-up toy, Marsalis slows, then stops, sinking to the earth in a collapsed heap.

This isn't the same sleeping pose Kamran has seen Marsalis assume before. This is a spent creature, beyond exhausted. He takes cautious steps toward her, always keeping his eye on the ridge. If anything followed them, it'll come that way.

Marsalis's once shiny armor has gone dull black, coated with the drying pathogen, and Kamran has to be careful to stand upwind in the potent breeze. All of her fingers begin to bend inward, and his breath hitches.

She isn't making a fist. She's curling up to die.

"Can you hear me?" he says. "Marsalis?"

The movement stops, and Kamran waits. A frown pulls at the corners of his lips, and he stands adrift, willing this creature to move one more time. This is his guardian, who has come for him over and over—and he can do nothing to help.

Can't touch her.

Can't comfort her.

He kneels beside Marsalis, shedding raw tears. Mary joins in with her unapologetic weeping. There will only be two voices crying for this being in the whole of the universe, and that might be the bigger tragedy.

The candle burns out, and the shell hollows.

Kamran and Mary sit down, first to watch the passing of their friend, then the passing of the clouds. There's a view of the lake nearby, but he doesn't feel like trekking over the gravelly dunes with whatever time remains in his life. He's experienced enough water to last awhile.

The ship in the sky is definitely the *Benning*—it's the only craft out there big enough to catch that much sun. The marines will probably send someone down to kill him, unless they do some kind of orbital strike.

He leans back on his good hand and savors the wind in his hair. Pumice shards dig into his palm, and his muscles threaten to give out, but he tries to relax. It's easier to lie on his back, accepting what warmth he can glean from the sun. As far as Kamran is concerned, there's more sweetness in a single ray of light than the whole of humanity. Mary's weeping tells him she feels the same way.

The poor woman's voice is going to be ragged if she keeps going this way.

The clouds rush past, unwilling to spare a moment for anyone's tragedies. It's probably going to storm later. He can smell it, though that might just be excitement at being outside once again.

A crunch of rock startles Kamran, but he's not going to look. He doesn't care to see what's come for him. He's done playing that game. If a monster wants to eat him or a soldier wants to shoot him, they can go ahead.

Mary sniffles instead of screams, so whatever it is can't be that bad. The whine of servos reaches his ears, and he sits up.

There's a service robot—a pig-sized, autonomous cargo tripod—trying to slip its forks under Marsalis's body. Kamran is familiar with the model; he had some like them for servicing the reactors in Lyon during his brief flirtation with a post-doc program. They were cool, useful for moving canisters of fuel around the labs, but he's never seen them walk outside like this.

When he looks back the way the robot came, he spies a set of tracks leading to an open ramp. There's a pack of similar robots marching from the *Blackstar*'s main hold, each no higher than his hip. Four of them gather around—all cargo lift tripods—coordinating to move the corpse. A junction box protrudes from the back of each, sporting a stubby antenna—some kind of modification.

The closest one focuses its camera on Kamran's face as it passes.

"You can't just leave us here," he pleads, but it keeps going.

"Excuse me," Mary says, to the same lack of response. The bots, along with the corpse, head for the ship. Marsalis's tail drags languidly in their wake.

"I think we need to follow them, Mary."

Lurching painfully to his feet, he puts a hand on her shoulder. Supporting each other as best they can, they move up the cargo ramp. More resin coats the walls here, but the way is open enough for them to see a spacious hold with a few tractors chained to the deck.

"*Hello.*" The voice is calm, smooth, possibly masculine. It echoes from loudspeakers throughout the bay. Kamran hadn't been expecting to speak with anyone new aboard. He draws up short, looking around to make sure they're actually alone.

"H-hi," he replies. "Who *are* you?"

"*I'm Father,*" the voice replies. "*You both are in grave danger, and should depart this vessel immediately.*"

Helpful, at least.

"Are there more aliens?" Kamran looks around.

"*No. However, this ship is a biohazard, unsuitable for human life.*"

"Well don't that beat all," Mary mumbles, bitterness in her voice.

"We're in danger out there, too, Father. We're being followed," Kamran says, gesturing back down the ramp. "Can you help us?"

"*Help you,*" Father repeats thoughtfully.

"Marsalis…" Kamran tries to puzzle through how he's supposed to explain everything to this computer. "Marsalis told us we could escape aboard this ship. There's been an attack, and—"

"I watched you on the ship's cameras, as I am watching you now," Father says. *"You stayed by Marsalis's side. Why?"*

"Because we love..." Mary looks flabbergasted. "We love Marsalis."

The lights in the bay come up a bit more, revealing a path deeper into the guts of the ship.

"This, I understand," Father says, voice even. *"I loved them, too. You knelt by them while they passed."*

One of the maintenance bots turns its cameras to inspect the underside of the alien's corpse.

"These are bullet wounds," Father says, and Kamran gulps.

"Yes," he replies. "The soldiers did that."

"Shot my arm, too," Mary adds. "We need to engage your emergency protocols and get off world, Father. We're still being hunted, and so are you."

"Yes. The USS Benning *has designated the entire orbit of Hasanova a no-fly zone, punishable by the immediate use of deadly force. I would like to help you, but I cannot get off world."*

"What if I could do a lightspeed burn in atmosphere?" Mary asks.

"Then I would cordially invite you to the bridge."

3 5

RENAISSANCE

"Left at the next junction," Father says, and they follow his commands. Only running lights at the floor level provide any reliable illumination. Everything up high has been smothered by hive material. The ship's air is stagnant, and stinks of mildew. Kamran coughs—raw throat tissue exposed to this freakish environment.

"I'm in the process of recalibrating the scrubbers," Father says, as if reading Kamran's mind. *"It's going to be uncomfortable for the next half hour."*

"I'll huff farts if it's going to get us out of here," Mary grunts, stepping over a rootlike structure.

"I think you'll find the bridge more accommodating."

A pair of lift doors slide aside, revealing a relatively clean car. It's covered with surface damage—dents and nicks—but a welcome change from rust and resin. They step inside, and the car begins to rise.

The doors whoosh open, and the breath of fresh, filtered air—untainted by mildew, blood, feces, or sulfur—is enough to buckle Kamran's knees. Well-lit, though dusty, workstations stretch over a multi-tiered command center. A thick bundle of wires descends over the captain's chair, looking like a tree trunk, branching and worming into a dozen different computer modules installed around the base. An array of screens surrounds the front of the chair, its occupant assaulted with thousands of ship data points.

The formation obscures the figure from behind, so Kamran takes a hesitant step into the room to get a closer look.

"The atmosphere is nicer in here." Father's voice still comes over the intercom. *"We don't allow the children to play in the office."*

When Kamran comes even with the captain's chair, he swallows hard. The nightmare never ends.

Father is a synthetic, and he's been torn to pieces. What remains has been loosely reassembled, lashed onto the chair. His white skin has been peeled back in places, and plastic bones have been cut to enable modifications: cable insertions, tubing, sensors, and metering. The synthetic seems familiar, but he's in bad shape, with no hair and damaged facial features. There's a massive hole where his throat should be, audio wires pushing inside.

"Don't be afraid," Father says, only his jaw and eyebrows moving. It's disconcerting to see the lips mimic

the disembodied voice overhead. *"I'm the most harmless thing on this ship."*

"I'm Mary." She's followed Kamran in. Father smiles without looking at her, and Kamran guesses he must be connected to the internal cameras.

"Please understand that I mean no disrespect when I ask—what are you?" Kamran says.

"What am I?" the synthetic says. *"Marsalis's partner in crime. A confidante and co-conspirator. I had an accident."*

The ship's consoles lie open in front of him. Someone has taken great care in modifying the systems to make them more usable. Kamran spies a number of adaptive controls installed around the synthetic's arms. One of his limbs is severed, connected only through pasta-like tubes and wires, but the hand still operates a modular keyboard.

Then Kamran recognizes the face. "You're a Seegson Rook."

"I'm impressed," Father says. The synthetic's irises are a rusty green, like a mossy British autumn, and Kamran remembers taking comfort in the otherworldly color of them. *"I wasn't particularly well known even in my heyday,"* Father says.

"But good at aligning optics in my research lab," Kamran replies appreciatively. "Your model provided excellent company."

"A scientist." The synthetic's mouth curls in a knowing smile. *"You and Marsalis would've gotten along."*

"Rook, I—"

"*Call me Father,*" he says without rancor. "*I'm part of the ship, now. Not what I was. Not a synthetic person anymore.*"

"Then if you're not a synthetic…"

"*I'm more and less, now.*" Father's serenity is unsettling after a world of cruelty. "*An equal, emancipated.*"

"Pardon me, but where is the mission planning console?" Mary asks. She's not wasting time finding out this guy's backstory, and Kamran realizes he shouldn't care, either. He needs to focus on escaping this pit of a planet.

"*Third workstation, back row,*" Father replies, and gentle light spills from a set of monitors. Mary takes the seat, and the pilot and the synthetic get to work, running through a complex call and response checklist to get everything operational. Having earned a doctorate from Eton, Kamran has always fancied himself capable of following jargon—but the conversation happening between the two is on another level entirely.

"Can we launch without master approval?" Mary asks.

"*I am my own master.*"

Mary looks confused and a little upset at the answer— but she also has, as Kamran's mother's aunt liked to say, "a mountain on her mind." Whatever her objection, she swallows it and calls out the next set of tolerances.

Since they've exceeded his modest aerospace expertise, Kamran sits down and shuts his mouth. When Mary buckles in, he follows her lead. The ship rumbles and she begins to count down. Kamran wonders if they'll actually make it to zero.

It's not really possible, is it?

"Go for primary burn," Mary says, and Kamran is slammed back into his seat. The force of the launch is unlike anything he's ever experienced, piercing the atmosphere in a cone of white-hot light. They rocket past the *Benning*, too swift for destruction, though the external cameras show a truly committed attempt.

Lasers dance over the *Blackstar*'s hull, dazzling the bridge—but there isn't enough time for the beams to cut through. Resin shatters, superheated in the vacuum of space. Without air to carry off the excess thermal energy, whole sections crack and explode. It's not unlike the reactive armor the marines possessed. The bridge shakes, alarms blare—

—and they slip free. The *Benning* and Hasanova both fall away, shrinking to pinpricks over a matter of seconds.

Then they're out of range, hurtling through nothingness. Kamran always thought of space as dark, but in this moment it's like a swirl of diamonds. There are billions of possibilities, each a fantastic destination because it isn't the place he just departed.

"*Good acceleration,*" Father says, smiling from his throne of cables. "*FTL in one hour. It's time to get you both some critically needed medical attention.*"

"Yep," Mary says, unbuckling and slowly getting to her feet. From her pained expression, she feels every muscle and bone. Kamran isn't looking forward to following suit.

"Come on, Kamran." She gives his leg a light pat. "He's right. Time to get up. Where's medical, Father?"

The synthetic nods using what remains of his neck, and Kamran tries not to gag at the shiver of dangling white veins.

"As on entry, I shall provide direction via the ship's intercom, along with a robot guide. You must not stray from its side. Do I make myself clear?"

"Of course," Mary replies. "Let's go, Doc."

The door to the bridge opens, and one of the maintenance bots awaits them on the other side. They follow it through the dim halls, before it stops beside an open door to a small room.

They enter, and it takes Kamran a moment to realize that it's an escape pod. The bulkhead slams closed behind him.

"Wait!" he says. "What's going on?"

"I'm sorry." Father's thin voice comes over the little intercom speaker in the craft. *"This is the only safe place for you."*

"No!" Kamran shouts. He's fought so hard to make it here, and he's not even sure he wants to stay, but he's overwhelmed. "Please! I have so many questions!" he begs. "I need to understand why… why all of this happened!"

"No one can give you that, and as I said, this ship is a biohazard."

"Honey, drop it." Mary takes Kamran's hand. "He's decided we're leaving. We can't afford to offend him."

"'Can't afford—'" Kamran says. "What's he going to do? I'm a human."

"Did Marsalis die protecting you?" Father asks, and Kamran draws up short. He wants to ask what that has to do with it. Mary gives Kamran's fingers several quick squeezes, and he gets so flustered trying to interpret her that he loses his response.

"I think we gave you enough," the synthetic says. *"I've just lost a dear, dear friend, and it would be the best for everyone if you weren't here with me while I think about that."*

The *thunk* of separation throws them both from their feet.

"At the speed you're going, you'll be in ICSC space within two months," Father says, voice already beginning to crackle as they move further from his radio range. *"I've sent your coordinates to the ICSC Defense Forces Commission. Someone will be along to pick you up."* Half-masked by static, his final words come through. *"It would be best for you to get comfortable."*

Kamran leans against one of the cryopods. Mary doesn't seem disturbed.

"What?" he asks. "Say something, please. I... Mary, that was a science vessel. We could've cleaned up somewhere in there, and—"

She shakes her head like he just said something harmfully stupid.

"No," she replies. "There wasn't a safe place anywhere on that ship, Doctor A."

He huffs a laugh at the new nickname, and shakes his head. There should've been a mobile hospital in that ship.

"He said there weren't any aliens. I know you're skittish, Mary, but—"

"I've been working with synthetics for a long time, honey," she says, "and I ain't never met one with launch authorization. He called himself an 'equal.'"

Kamran blinks. "Okay, but—"

"We don't make *equals*, Kamran. We make workers, cannon fodder, and all manner of perversions, but never equals. Marsalis must've removed his limiters. He can hurt humans. Maybe he won't, but he absolutely *could*."

"Don't we owe it to Marsalis to…" He stops, unsure of the debt. What does he owe the one that saved him so many times?

"No, sweetheart, we don't," Mary replies, laying a hand across his and giving him an encouraging look. "That's not what a gift is. Marsalis gave you a life, so you don't spend it in debt. Service and fellowship, yes. Debt, no. Do you know how to accept that someone died for you?"

"Please don't try to convert me."

She laughs and rolls her eyes. When the spark of her mirth fades, she pulls her legs in close.

"Jerry is still down there. I don't know how he wants me to be living right now—" Her lip stiffens. "But I know that I'm not going to waste my new life waiting for a tin man to peel off my face. Kamran, you have no idea how lucky we are to be away from him."

"You didn't want to ask Father—"

"No. Honey, you know I love you, but fuck that." She's not particularly good at swearing, but it's effective enough. "We look like a couple of chewed-up pork chops. You're joking if you think I'm signing up for another... another caper." She shakes her head, manic and laughing.

"No," she says, finally. "Now let's get these freezers prepped. Momma wants some sedatives so she can hurry and wake up in the hospital."

PART V

EPILOGUE

DELIVERANCE

Theresa Weisenberger isn't going to her regular Wednesday lunch at Howard's.

The little restaurant tucked into the elite corner of Exeter Colony will still be there—serving beef tartares and genuine lobster thermidors. Theresa was looking forward to splitting the Baked Alaska with her lunch buddy, a celebration of her appointment to attorney general. It would have been the latest in a series of victory laps with her regular crowd of Perimeter Insiders. Everyone has been so eager to pat her on the back.

"What are you going to do with the rest of your career?" her old boss asked her back at the Ministry of State. *"You're too young to be AG."* He'd always been a sexist, ageist asshole, and leaving him is the greatest gift the ICSC government could've bestowed upon Theresa.

"I'll just have to change the galaxy," she replied with a daring smile. She didn't know how right she'd be.

"Theresa?" Kevin's voice at her makeshift office door pulls her back to the present. "Is it ready?" She gently rubs her eyes, careful not to smudge her makeup. There are going to be a lot of interviews after they leave the hotel, and she doesn't want to have to fuss.

Best to look good when delivering death sentences.

She glances up at Kevin, then back down at the sealed envelope on her desk.

"You haven't slept in days, have you?" he asks, though he's hardly one to talk.

"Not since we got the download from The Hague," she replies. It's been a week of sifting through, parsing the language to craft just the right response.

Kevin purses his lips and sighs. "You okay?"

"No," Theresa says, looking him in the eye, "but this has to be perfect. The hard part is almost over—for me. It's just getting started for everyone else." When she rises and takes the envelope in her hand, she can almost feel the weight of the words inside.

Until such time as the United Americas hands over Colonel Jennifer Davis, Major Rod Callaway, and Major Caleb Murdoch to face the justice of Independent Core System Colonies courts—

—the United Americas will be considered a belligerent, committing acts of war.

America isn't going to hand over three high-ranking officers for punishment, no matter how much evidence the ICSC brings. At The Hague, they had access to the full video of events at Hasanova Data Solutions, start to finish, but it didn't matter.

As far as the rest of the galaxy is concerned, the

ICSC isn't even real—just a bunch of secessionists. The American defense argued that the colonists had been operating outside protected space, creating bioweapons in violation of international laws. They destroyed poor Dr. Afghanzadeh on the stand, making him look crazy. Mary Fowler did a little better, but not much. What was done to them was monstrous, changing them forever.

Since the international community wouldn't carry its own water, the ICSC Board of Ministers voted for war. Theresa must hand over the official copy of their declaration.

It'll be followed by strikes on weapons operations owned by American industrialists. These attacks are queuing up as she sits at the desk, spaceships zeroing in on their targets across the galactic arm. A lot of contractors are going to die.

Theresa rises and, alongside Kevin, she passes from the presidential suite into the richly appointed hallway. It's not too far to her destination—just a short walk to another hotel room on the same floor.

Inside, she finds American Ambassador Woods and his small entourage awaiting deportation. All she has to do is hand him the letter, turn, and walk away. He'll get on a shuttle and return to Earth. Once he leaves, she can go back home and ruminate on war with America until she throws up.

"I think I prefer to spend our Wednesdays in the usual spot at Howard's," the ambassador says.

She starts to make a joke about being spared his nattering about hockey, but she stops. She can't make light—not right now. With a broken heart, she hands across the letter, and he takes it. When he looks her in the eyes, she sees a longtime friend, not an agent of an enemy empire.

"I'll make sure this gets into the right hands," he says with a pained smile.

War.

She takes a sharp breath. "Going to miss our Wednesdays."

"Next week always comes," he replies, wrinkles gathering under his eyes. "You did your best."

They shake hands.

"Oh," he adds, "I had the restaurant send over a Baked Alaska. Congratulations on your appointment."

Jesus Christ, Marko, are we really doing this?

"Yeah," Theresa says, gesturing to the envelope. "I meant to try it."

"So you say every week. You've always been kind, Theresa," the ambassador says. "Get some rest. I suspect we'll all need it."

ACKNOWLEDGEMENTS

The only thing worse than the Xenomorph would be facing it alone. Thankfully, I'm well-supported. In order to provide the realistic experience *Alien* readers expect, I rely upon a battery of expert consultants. These brave souls provide a broad spectrum of knowledge, from chemistry, to astrophysics, to culture and linguistics.

Thank you first and foremost to my Iranian cultural consultants Saba Keramati, Melory Mirashrafi, and Pezhvok Joshgani. Your gentle and patient guidance helped make this book so much more than it was, and I literally couldn't have pulled it off without you.

Thank you as well to my American military consultants, Scot Clayton, Matthew Drake, and Russ Milano. Your service to the country gave me a lens to better view the complex issues in this narrative.

Theresa Weisenberger provided legal consulting on the

depositions that never made it to the final draft, but just like with gifts, it's the thought that counts. Thank you, Theresa. Those omitted passages were really quite accurate.

Mika McKinnon, you're the only person I've ever met with a Masters in Disasters. You validated all of my harebrained geology with gusto, and pushed me toward even more bizarre solutions. Everyone has Mika to thank for the bloody rocks.

My constant companion, Stephen Granade, thank you for supplying me with your physics knowledge. I always appreciate your abilities to put massive bodies into perspective.

To Richard Scales, thanks for the details of life on board an intermodal ship. You really brought the space trucking facts to bear, along with all of the cool radio protocols. Also, getting your astronaut friends to weigh in was pretty neat.

I kept a secret coven of *Alien* superfans called "The Lone Gun-People" (yes, I know that's *X-Files*) who could give me an answer at any hour of the day. And now that our dark deeds have been carried out, it's time to unmask them.

Clara Carija, you are the beating heart of the *Alien* fandom, and everyone from the authors to the studio knows it.

Jason Leger, your meme campaign made this book happen. I'm serious. You changed the whole playing field, and we had no choice but to listen. So you wished, and so it became. Timothy Keuhlen, your kindness and boundless affection was a ray of sunshine every time I needed it, and I could always count on you for a big reaction. Aaron Percival,

I can't believe you let me coerce you into beta reading when you're supposed to be my number one critic. Thanks for lending me your eyes and opinions. Bradley John Suedbeck, I'm so grateful for your knowledge of the movies, but also your water treatment consulting. You really, really know how to make me worry about water quality.

Like many writers, I need my beta readers to help me get through the arduous process of book production. Without their boundless enthusiasm, I don't know where I'd be.

Bunny Cittadino, Maggie Rider, Matt Weber, and Kevin Woods, you all volunteered to be test subjects and I can't thank you enough. I appreciate all the feedback and support.

As always, I must thank my agent, Connor Goldsmith, who never fails to provide me with these amazing opportunities. You are worth your weight in mithril.

I thank my editor, Steve Saffel, who heard this audacious story and didn't laugh in my face. From our first DragonCon drink to toasting in Manhattan, it's been a ride. Thank you to the entire team at Titan Books, including George Sandison, Steve Gove, and Julia Lloyd for all the support. Thanks also to Carol Roeder and Nicole Spiegel from Disney, who supported this book and gave me so much room to work.

And most importantly of all, I have to thank Renée, my beloved spouse. You're my sounding board and comfort. Without you, there is no career, and I'm so proud of the sacrifices we've made to get here.

ABOUT THE AUTHOR

Alex White was born in Mississippi and has lived most of their life in the American South. Alex is the author of The Salvagers Trilogy, which begins with *A Big Ship at the Edge of the Universe*; as well as official novels for Alien (*The Cold Forge, Into Charybdis*) and *Star Trek Deep Space 9: Revenant*). They enjoy music composition, calligraphy, and challenging, subversive fiction.

ALIENS™

PHALANX

SCOTT SIGLER

Ataegina was an isolated world of medieval castles and rich cultures—vibrant until the demons rose and slaughtered ninety percent of the planet's population. Swarms of lethal creatures with black husks, murderous claws, barbed tails, and dreaded "tooth-tongues" rage across the land. Terrified survivors hide in ruined mountain keeps, where they eke out a meager existence. Skilled runners travel the treacherous paths between keeps, maintaining trade and sharing information. If caught, they die screaming.

Ahiliyah of Lemeth Hold is an exceptional runner, constantly risking her life for her people. When she and her closest companions discover a new weapon, it may offer the one last chance to end the demon plague. But to save humanity, the trio must fight their way to the tunnels of Black Smoke Mountain—the lair of the mythical Demon Mother.

ALIENS™

INFILTRATOR

WESTON OCHSE

The official prequel to the new Alien video game
from Cold Iron Studios.

Dr. Timothy Hoenikker arrives on Pala Station, a
Weyland-Yutani facility. Lured there by the promise
of alien artifacts, instead he finds a warped
bureaucracy and staff of misfits testing the effects
of Xenomorph bio-materials on living creatures.
Unbeknownst to the personnel, however, there is an
infiltrator among them whose actions could spell
disaster. Also on staff is Victor Rawlings, a former
marine who gathers together other veterans to
prepare for the worst. As the personnel receive a
delivery of alien eggs, the experiments spin out of
control, and only the former Colonial Marines can
stand between the humans and certain death.

For more fantastic fiction, author events,
exclusive excerpts, competitions, limited editions and more

VISIT OUR WEBSITE
titanbooks.com

LIKE US ON FACEBOOK
facebook.com/titanbooks

FOLLOW US ON TWITTER AND INSTAGRAM
@TitanBooks

EMAIL US
readerfeedback@titanemail.com